And Grace Will Lead Me Home

And Grace Will Lead Me Home

Jane Mitchell

Writers Club Press
San Jose New York Lincoln Shanghai

And Grace Will Lead Me Home

All Rights Reserved © 2001 by Jane Mitchell

No part of this book may be reproduced or transmitted in any form or by any means, graphic, electronic, or mechanical, including photocopying, recording, taping, or by any information storage retrieval system, without the permission in writing from the publisher.

Writers Club Press
an imprint of iUniverse.com, Inc.

For information address:
iUniverse.com, Inc.
5220 S 16th, Ste. 200
Lincoln, NE 68512
www.iuniverse.com

"Aragon Mill" Words and Music by Si Kahn. Copyright Joe Hill Music (ASCAP).
All rights reserved. Used by permission.

ISBN: 0-595-18763-3

Printed in the United States of America

To my daughters, Mimi and Sally.

Acknowledgements

Many thanks to my friends Carolyn Coley and Pam Horn for all their help and encouragement.

Chapter One

I am not a woman men call baby. Years of wanting them to do that have not made it happen. Females that males attach that appellation to are generally of three types: small, but voluptuously put together; tiny and slender with little bones and classic features; or tall, elegant and fashionably thin—i.e. "Long Cool Woman in a Black Dress" with "legs that go on and on," (that's what that lyric always sounded like to me). Ellott Hailey Seers—that would be me—is none of the above. At this stage in my mid-life, I am best described as round—an apple, not a pear. In the suburban library/civic center where I work, there is an area that is referred to as the rotunda where staff meetings and other official functions are held. One of our library pages—who helps out with the p.a. system and was in a snit with me for an assignment I had given her—took great pleasure in announcing for all the world to hear, "Rotunda to the Rotunda," prior to our last staff meeting. I pretended to be madder than I actually was and received a sincere apology. There is, however, a certain point in time when the truth is a welcome visitor. I am—to use politically correct terms—bulk impaired, massiveness challenged, or perhaps short for my weight. Not fat, but fluffy. And that's okay. It's certainly better than any number of alternatives.

Enough about my physique. I might be accused of lookism, inverse vanity, or just plain old paranoia. In addition to being Reference and Adult Services Librarian Extraordinaire at the Athena Villa Public

Library,—located in an elite suburb south of Birmingham, Alabama, or the Magic City, if you will—I am also longstanding good friend to two women whom men can never stop calling baby: Rosie—who along with her three daughters now shares my apartment and my life—and Grace Ann, who has come back into our lives after a few years' absence.

Rosie is small and not quite as thin as when we were all sweet sixteen in the Summer of Love. She is a lovely, dark haired woman who does not appear to have born three children by and spent twenty years with Sherman Lee Jackson, her high school sweetheart and now ex-husband. Grace Ann is a willowy blonde, long-legged and fair of face. She, too, took the off-ramp on the matrimonial highway. Bud Reese, her ex and soon to be ex-con, married Grace Ann Hardaman, his love since 11th grade after nearly ten years of trying. They have teen-aged twins, a boy and a girl, who live with Grace Ann's daddy, Fred, for the time being. When we were all teenagers, Grace Ann accepted as her aim in life that commercial slogan, "blondes have more fun." And if a situation ceases to be enjoyable, Grace Ann starts looking for a loophole.

Rosie and I have been together again for some months now and next weekend, we'll reunite with Grace Ann. She's living in a trailer on some land Fred owns out in Caloosa county. We have talked on the phone, but I haven't seen her yet. From the things she did not say and the few she did, I get the idea Grace Ann is in as big a state of flux as Rosie in her fortieth year toward heaven. On given days, when my mid-life gets too preoccupied with my spreading midriff, I ponder on our shared past. Five children and twenty something years later, I find it hard to put a finger on just what made it turn out like it did.

Those days at Samantha Jane Seers High School were an unchained melody of conversation and companionship, interrupted only slightly by the white noise of academics. We cruised and danced and loved away the years of the soulful '60s as well as anyone could in Milltown, Alabama, a small North Alabama burg, which is a part of the larger city of Good River in Caloosa County, some seventy miles north of Birmingham.

Milltown centered on two industries—White Cotton Mill, long since closed, and Grosset Steel Mill, still in operation. A majority of Milltown men were employed by the mills. Houses built for cotton mill workers around the turn of the century comprise the residential hub of our town, Milltown Village, where Rosie, Grace Ann and I grew up. Rosie lived with Miss Vancene, her aunt, at end of my street. Grace Ann's house was behind mine. From 7th grade on when Rosie first came to stay with Miss Vancene, we were always together—me, Rosie, Grace Ann and their boyfriends du jour.

In the summer when we were fifteen, Rosie and I walked the sultry streets to Broadway, Milltown's shopping district, adjacent to White Cotton Mill. Although it is mostly deserted now with only a few struggling businesses among the empty buildings, Broadway was certainly the Mecca of our youth. Its beginnings date to the turn of the century. My father managed the only dime store in the four-block area, V.J. Elmore's. Fred Hardaman, owner of multiple business concerns, made his headquarters at The Smart Shoppe—one of his many clothing stores—just down the street. Our destination that day was the icy cold RexAll Drugstore, where we were to meet Grace Ann for a mid-afternoon french fry and milkshake feast while we lolled over the newest issues of Tiger Beat and Teen.

I met Rosie at the end of our street, Western Avenue and as we moved up 30th we heard an uncommon commotion coming from Milltown Road. We hurried on to the main thoroughfare through Milltown that led to Broadway and on to Good River. Two dozen jeeps were stopped at the first light. Soldiers from Ft. McClellan, the Army base in Anniston, were returning from maneuvers.

Whistling and blowing their horns, they began to shout to Rosie in her white short-shorts, "Hey, baby, we'll give you a ride."

Rosie refused to turn and look at them, but acknowledged their attention with a delicate swaying of her slender hips as we continued toward the drug store. That only made them holler louder.

"Come on over here, babe, and let me show you my gun."

Wearing glasses that covered my freckles and loose fitting cutoffs and a baggy shirt that concealed my plump body, I began to sulk and study the fronts of the all too familiar houses that lined the sidewalks. I knew they weren't talking to me. They never let up and three blocks later their noise followed us into the drug store, where Grace Ann sat at the cosmetics counter, trying on lipstick.

"How rude," she remarked when Rosie told her what happened. But the two of them walked over to stand just inside the glass double doors of the RexAll. They watched until the last jeep pulled away when the light changed. I sat down before the mirror and rearranged my shoulder length brown curls. Continuing to pout, I began to apply several layers of Passion Pink to my mouth.

Later on that evening, Rosie and I met Sherman at the movies in downtown Good River where "Thunderball," was playing. Rosie did this every Friday at Sherman's bidding and I went along because Miss Vancene didn't want her alone in that dark balcony with Sherman Lee Jackson. When Rosie whispered the day's events to him during the previews, he frowned at the whole idea. "Them Army boys've got bullets where their brains ought to be," he remarked. The Marine Corps was his planned military destination. He later served sixteen months in 'Nam with them in the early '70s.

"If that ever happens again, then ya'll better find you another way to Broadway. But," he continued as he slid a possessive arm around Rosie and began fiddling with her long hair. "I guess they do know a pretty woman when they see one." He hummed a little Roy Orbison and winked.

Eyes on the screen, I dug my hand further into the popcorn as Sean Connery began to flash those bedroom eyes. I slowly licked the butter from my fingers while Bond, James Bond and his lady-love made the beast with two backs.

"Always the bridesmaid, never the bride," was my usual role in our little drama. With a tendency toward plumpness and an affinity for books, I never seemed to move beyond friendship with boys, a condition that plagues me to this day. I had infrequent dates, usually not more than one with the same boy. My mother, Alice Howell Seers, perhaps comforted me too often with hot cocoa and cookies when social disappointments reared their ugly heads. Only child of a widowed Methodist minister, my mother was a quiet, middle-class gentle-woman who lived the entirety of her tranquil life in Milltown. Church musician at Milltown Methodist from the time she was 20 until she died, she also worked as my father's part-time bookkeeper. Peace and harmony in her family and among her close friends was what she valued most. Discord was not to be tolerated. That quality in her might explain why I've spent half my life patching up squabbles in my various inner circles of friends. I'm the one they run to to put things right. As Rodney King so succinctly put it: "Why can't we all just get along?"

Rosie's steady from the 9th grade on and now ex-husband, the afore mentioned Sherman Lee Jackson, is some piece of work. The youngest child of the widowed Minnie Beth Jackson, owner of Minnie Beth's House of Beauty, our neighborhood's only beauty shop, Sherman was and still is his momma's darling. He was spoiled to the point of reeking by the time he met up with Rosie. He ordered her around so in high school that I began referring to him as "Woolly Bully." A tendency toward overbearing dominance remains with him to this day.

Hailing from the sure enough sticks in the rural part of our county, Rosie and her family often didn't have two nickels to call their own. Rosie's daddy, Miller Culp, was a reluctant farmer, sometime sawmill worker, and avid fiddle player for any hillbilly band that would let him join in. He took Rosie's given name, Dixie Rosalee, straight from the lyrics of "The Yellow Rose of Texas,"—"You can talk about your Clementine and your Dixie Rosalee, but the Yellow Rose of Texas is the only girl for me." In the summertime, Rosie traveled with her daddy and

Uncle Sam who played with various string and Bluegrass bands across the Southeast. She performed with them when given the opportunity, singing and playing her guitar. Miller died this past winter, not long after Rosie came to live with me.

Her momma, Millie—Mildred Mae Frazier Culp—is a grim, resigned woman who always does what she feels like she's got to. She grew up in Milltown in the house her daughter later shared with Millie's sister, Vancene. Working at White Cotton Mill from the time she was 14 until she married Miller Culp., she then moved with him to the family farm. She bore Miller's four children and his occupational instability by drawing her mouth into a thin line and getting on with it. When Rosie reached puberty, Millie determined that her middle child and only girl would not fall victim to family history and sent her to Milltown to live with her sister Vancene, our town librarian, so she could attend city schools.

When we were four years old, Grace Ann Hardaman and I began to share an adjoining back yard. Our lives soon became as interlinked as our property. Fred and Ma 'Ree Hardaman, Grace Ann's folks, and mine, Lloyd and Alice Seers, were business colleagues as well as friends and neighbors. Our fathers managed their stores on Broadway and our mothers kept the books.

Dad and Fred spent many morning hours drinking coffee and discussing business at The Confederate Cove Cafe, which is still standing. The Cove—by late afternoon and evening a teenage hangout—served the Broadway business community through breakfast and lunchtime hours. Ma 'Ree, Grace Ann's mother, got sick when we began fifth grade and by late summer, she was gone. Lupus was a mysterious illness in those days and effective treatments were rare.

The fallout from Ma 'Ree's death was more than Grace Ann or Fred expected. Fred began to drink and drive aimlessly, leaving Grace Ann for days at a time with various live-in housekeepers. She would usually sneak over to my house to sleep after Miss Whoever turned out the lights for the evening.

Grace Ann is not a crier, so her mourning didn't include sobbing into pillows and "why did this have to happen to me?" Instead, she talked, far into the nights and early mornings that we spent in my room with the white walls and twin beds.

"When I was just three years old my momma took me…" she would begin. I rarely had to say anything except a monosyllable every now and then to let Grace Ann know I was still awake. She would leave early in the morning so that the housekeeper wouldn't notice her absence. I would be exhausted all day, but too loyal to say anything to my mother about Grace Ann's midnight monologues. She wanted to say everything she could think of about her mother, as if all memory of her might vanish if she didn't. I learned a great deal more then about Grace Ann than about Ma 'Ree. Perhaps it was that experience that transformed me into the Dear Abby figure of my class in later years.

Fred eventually slowed his drinking to one or two nights a month, returning home well before bedtime most days. He and Grace Ann continued to struggle over the live-in housekeeper issue. Finally at 14, she convinced him she no longer needed a substitute mom, having gone through twelve different housekeepers in the three years since Ma 'Ree's death. Probably it would have been for the best if Grace Ann had not won this particular battle. In the early years of her adolescence she became an accomplished liar, inclined to manipulate the truth with anyone male, especially Fred. By the time we were fifteen, Grace Ann had practically anyone of the opposite sex marching quite happily to her tune. And Bud Reese eventually took his place in the procession.

Grace Ann turned sweet sixteen in the Summer of Love. Since few flower children resided in Milltown, we celebrated the Zeitgeist with as much aplomb as possible in a small, fundamentalist town whose response to the mandate: "tune in, turn on, drop out," was "say that again real slow, now. I don't think I heard you right." Acid came in batteries.

Grass was what you raked into a pile in the yard when your daddy got through mowing. Flower power emanated from the rose bushes that surrounded the parsonage where the Methodist preacher lived. But "make love, not war," began to have some meaning when the older brothers of many of our classmates got their greetings from Uncle Sam. Patriotic editorials in the Good River newspaper praised our government's military intervention in Southeast Asia and excoriated "those misguided youth who question the United States' fight against Godless communism." Rosie's oldest brother left at the beginning of that summer, heading for 'Nam.

Fred allowed Grace Ann to host a party for her coming of age, followed by a sleep-over for the girls. Most of the soon-to-be juniors of Samantha Jane Seers were invited. On that night, Bud Reese came into our lives. Although we really didn't know him, Harley John "Bud" Reese seemed to us the quintessential hood with a little bit of imagination. Driving a souped-up '55 Chevy, he wore a black leather jacket over a white dress shirt, jeans, and loafers with no socks. His long, black hair invaded his eyes, sideburns reaching close to his chin. I saw him often at school, standing behind the bandroom, smoking one last cigarette before the bell rang. Elvis was his idol—to him the epitome of the "Good Old Boy Made Good." While the British Invasion and Motown greatly affected the rest of us, Bud was convinced that musical evolution reached its apex with "Jailhouse Rock," and that's all there was to say about it. Because he was enrolled in D.O.—diversified occupation—and left school in the early afternoon to work in a nearby garage, Bud was hardly ever present at any of our extracurricular functions.

Sherman was the catalyst in getting him to Grace Ann's party. It was obvious to all of us what he had in mind. And it was not improving the social life of one Bud Reese. In our callous eyes, the Reese family was pure and simple W.T., White Trash—the kind who slept four to a bed and ate mayonnaise sandwiches. They lived in "The Hollow," a wooded area beyond Milltown Village, where run-down houses stand far apart on weedy lots. Mrs. Reese, a staunch Baptist, tried to keep the four girls and as many of the boys as possible occupied at the little mission church that served The Hollow community. Mr. Reese, an itinerant mechanic, and his five boys ran an unofficial auto repair shop in their side yard. There was always somebody's rusted-out car of indeterminate age jacked up with the legs and feet of a Reese boy visible underneath. Their lack of proximity to the rest of Milltown also allowed them to engage in the somewhat more profitable production and sale of home-made liquor—a sought after commodity in our dry county. This well-know fact was Sherman's real reason for requesting Bud's presence at the party, hoping he would bring along a little something to add to the sherbet punch. Minnie Beth would have hung him out to dry if she had ever known this.

Fred invited my parents and Rosie's Aunt Vancene to his house for a little adult soiree on the night of "the" party, which was held in the former Hardaman garage, long since converted to a nicely paneled, carpeted, and air conditioned clubhouse for Grace Ann and company. Fred, Miss Vancene and my parents sat sipping Gin and Tom Collins mix on the screened in porch that overlooked the garage. Whenever Grace Ann wanted to slow dance hug style with anyone, she would move away to the windowless area at the back of the garage where the grownups could not observe.

Minis and micro-minis were not much in evidence in small town Alabama at that time. Girls donned Bermuda shorts sets and boys wore their customary jeans or cutoffs. Bud arrived late, wearing a simple black t-shirt and jeans. Since tie-dyeing also had not caught on in Milltown, he wasn't dressed any differently than the rest of the boys. What distinguished him was the way he worked the room, nodding a polite "hey," to each girl and extending his hand to each of the boys until he greeted every person there. Most of us just slunk in and stood awkwardly in our own little groups, not venturing into unknown territory.

Bud saved Grace Ann for last, holding her hand at length as he thanked her for inviting him. He coerced her into putting "Can't Help Falling in Love with You," on her stereo and led her to the back of the garage to slow dance. He held her in the classic two-step position, not the arms-around-the-necks-can't-get-a-toothpick-between-'em style most of the other couples used.

I watched them from my haven behind the refreshment table. When the music started to play, I immediately volunteered to serve so as not to stand pointedly in a corner, hoping for a dance invitation I was convinced would not come. The punch remained disappointingly unspiked. Bud never mentioned it and after a few minutes of obvious hinting, Sherman gave up in disgust and ushered Rosie to the dance floor. When the King finished his song, someone put on the Fab Four's "Twist and Shout," and Bud walked over to the refreshment table.

"Hey there. I know who you are," he said with a slow and deliberate smile. "My big sister Mary Joyce works at Elmore's for your daddy. She has the candy and nut counter. She really does think a lot of your daddy."

We talked a few minutes about the dime store and our other favorite places to go on Broadway. Watching the dancers who were now into the Frug or perhaps the Chicken Scratch, he said, "I can't do that stuff. My sisters taught me to two-step, but that's as far as it goes."

"I can't either," I said, although in actuality I could—alone in front of my bedroom mirror or acting crazy with Rosie and Grace Ann. I was just unable to bring myself to do it in the company of boys.

"Want to go outside?" He asked me.

Astonished, I merely nodded and stepped with him out the side door near the fence and out of the line of vision of the screen porch. It was cool for early June and the full moon illuminated Bud's white teeth as he smiled at me.

"It's not like I'm not glad to be here and all that," he said. "But I don't go to many parties and if I stay in there much longer with all them people I don't know too good, I'll probably say something stupid. Do you ever feel like you ought to say something, but you don't really know what?"

"All the time," I told him and accepted the piece of sour orange chewing gum he pulled from his jeans pocket and held out to me. We stood quietly for a few minutes, looking at the car lights on the road in front of Grace Ann's.

"That Grace Ann's some girl. She dances with you like you're the best thing that ever happened to her," he said. "At least I had the good taste to put The King on to play. You still listen to Elvis, don't you?"

"Oh, absolutely," I said and I did, beginning that night. Until then I really hadn't given him much thought since about 1962, but I wanted to get closer to Bud. "Grace Ann really likes him, too."

"No lie?" he said. "I guess you and her are good friends. Do you think she would ever go someplace with somebody like me?"

"I can't see why not," I told him, politely. Personally, I thought Fred Hardaman would stroke out and turn blue in the face if he heard Bud say that. Trying to ensure his daughter's future as a pampered princess, Fred often arranged dates for her with the sons of his wealthy business friends. The son of a bootlegging auto mechanic was probably not who he had in mind as Grace Ann's escort.

"Well, I think you're just being nice," he said, smiling. "I think there's not a snowball's chance in hell myself. My momma taught me manners and how to act, but I know what everybody says about my daddy. A lot of it's true, too. People brought up nice don't always want to be around me and my brothers and sisters." He didn't seem to expect a reply to this and we stood a few more minutes in the comfortable silence of the cool night.

It occurred to me later that for very different reasons, Bud and I both were the odd-ones-out in the little group that came to form. He, mostly because of economics and upbringing, and I because of exaggerated feelings about my size and appearance and my preoccupation with books that led me toward shyness with boys when I felt romance might be a factor. Bonded by our inability to fit in, we always experienced a special communion when we were together in a crowd, beginning with that night. Just before we went back inside, Bud kissed me lightly on the forehead. Without comment, we walked back into the party where a limbo line was forming.

Later on, following the inevitable "Sixteen Candles," and the opening of gifts, we played the also inevitable Post Office, involving trips for the selected couples to the large storage closet at the rear of the garage. After an extended stay, Rosie came out sporting a hickey and Sherman a foolish smile. Bud and Grace Ann were the last to go and had just emerged at 11:00, when Fred came in to suggest that the boys should begin to head for home. Bud thanked him for his hospitality. Fred was polite enough, but before we retired to our pajama party he called Grace Ann aside to let her know in specific terms why she should not have invited Bud Reese.

He kept her in the hallway nearly fifteen minutes while the rest of us slipped into our nighties and made ourselves at home in Grace Ann's spacious bedroom, painted hot pink with fluffy throw rugs scattered on top of the already carpeted floor. A ruffled spread with pink and white flounces topped the double bed. Nestled into her headboard was a light pink princess phone that rarely stopped ringing. Someone turned her little black and white tv set to an old Lucy rerun as we awaited the birthday girl's arrival.

"My Lord, you'd think Bud was one them hippies Daddy's always ranting and raving about that you see on the news," Grace Ann said as she came into her room and began to change to pink babydoll pajamas. "I thought he was very nice."

Unable to resist forging ahead with anything Fred opposed, she added, "I just might see if he wants to take me to the drive-in next weekend." Of course he did and that was the beginning of a sad and never ending romance. If Fred had only managed to keep his opinion to himself, things might not have happened as they did.

In the fall of that year as the love feast of '67 wound down and before the blood bath of '68 began, Rosie, Grace Ann and I spent late October and November in anticipation of Grace Ann's participation in the Miss Merry Christmas contest in downtown Good River. As she moved through her charmed adolescence, beauty contests became a way of life for Grace Ann Hardaman, majorette and honor student..

In those years predating bra burning and Ms. Magazine, none of us even knew we had a feminist consciousness, much less the fact that it might need raising. Beauty contests were not the anathema they later became. So, Rosie and I did all we could to help Grace Ann win. We watched her baton/dance routine in the garage at least twice a day—timing it and pointing out mistakes. We made up questions that the judges might ask and posed them to her. If she lost, it wouldn't be for lack of preparation. The contest was held in the first week of December. The winner, Miss Merry Christmas, led the annual downtown Good River Christmas parade held every year on the second Monday of December.

Some few days before the contest began, it began to snow. The first flakes fell in sixth period on a Friday afternoon. By the time school dismissed, the streets were slippery and the dead landscape pristine and pure.

The three of us went immediately to Grace Ann's. "Momma," I said breathlessly into the mouthpiece of Grace Ann's Pink Princess. "Grace Ann said me and Rosie can spend the night so we can watch the snow together." She agreed as did Miss Vancene when Rosie called her.

The power began to fail throughout Milltown around 6:00 p.m. Fred built a fire in the living room fireplace and lit candles. Most Milltown houses were heated by gas, so no one froze. The Hardamans even had a gas stove, so dinner too was saved.

Fred sat in paternalistic serenity, sipping bourbon and reading by candlelight in his den.

We made grilled cheese sandwiches for dinner and toasted marshmallows over the open fire.

"Don't you want any, Daddy?" Grace Ann asked him as she proffered the blackened, gooey mess to Fred from the end of a coat hanger. Smiling, he shook his head no.

Later on Grace Ann practiced her routine in their living room, but without benefit of her baton, which Fred refused to allow in the house. When we tired of that, we began to sing. Grace Ann had years of piano lessons and Rosie sang, "gooder than airy angel," as Snuffy said to Loweezy. I sang moderately well. We serenaded Fred with everything from "The Old Rugged Cross," to "Louie, Louie." He finally went to bed around 1:00 a.m., but we sang on as the snow fell over Milltown.

On Saturday in nine inches of snow, we walked to Broadway. All the businesses were closed and hardly anyone was outdoors. Sherman and later Bud joined us in a snowball fight on the town square in the front of White Cotton Mill, which stood empty, having closed the previous spring due to a union/management conflict. The epic battle grew and grew, eventually including most of the junior class of Samantha Jane Seers High.

The day extended to slip-sliding on the frozen pond that stood beside the vacant mill and culminated in the construction of a snow woman closely resembling Samantha Jane Seers for whom our beloved school is named. Her family's grave plot sits on a fenced grassy knoll—with historical marker in tact—in the middle of the street that runs behind the school. Teenaged Civil War heroine and distant relation of my father's, Samantha Jane showed a Confederate general across Red Creek in 1862, thereby saving all from the Yankees. Red Creek, a tributary of the Caloosa River, which runs through Good River, flows beside the high school.

A statue of Samantha Jane with her finger pointed, frozen in her bit of episodic glory, sits at the foot of the Caloosa River bridge in downtown Good River. From the time the statue was erected, all of Milltown felt it should be on the banks of Red Creek rather than uptown. Nonetheless, it was and still is visited with great frequency. Every child in Milltown commits it to memory from the time he can talk.

When we finished our snow woman that day, we sprayed it with water and packed it firmly so it would last. "We finally got us our own statue," Sherman said and everybody cheered.

Now, decades later after middle age and reality have taken their toll, we are no longer as close as we all were on that enchanted snowy Saturday. A handful of my classmates linger in Caloosa County, but most of us have moved on. Of those who stayed, most settled in the outer reaches of the county where new suburbs have emerged. Milltown's population has dwindled since White Cotton Mill ceased operation nearly twenty-five years ago. Many of the shops on Broadway and the mill itself stand vacant and boarded over.

Sherman and Rosie married in '70 just before he left for Viet Nam. When he returned, they resided in Milltown, where Sherman continues to live. He works as owner/operator of a garage/service station/Circle K store in Caloosa County. After a series of miscarriages, Rosie bore him two daughters, Cassie and Molly, and finally, in her fortieth year, a third, Caitlin. She left Sherman near Christmas time last year and she and her three girls now live with me in my apartment on the Southside in the Magic City, where she works as assistant manager of a dry cleaning establishment. Sherman takes the girls to Milltown every other weekend for his allotted visits.

Grace Ann married Bud in the middle '70s when he got back from Southeast Asia. A decorated war hero, Bud did several tours of duty in that most ambivalent of all military conflicts, returning home only when President Nixon declared an end to it. They remained in Milltown. Fred eventually reconciled to their union, heaping financial support on the couple, especially after the twins, little Ma 'Ree, shortened to 'Ree, and Harley Junior were born.

Bud worked several years with Sherman in the garage that Minnie Beth bought for Sherman and Rosie as a belated wedding gift. But a few years back, Bud experienced post-traumatic stress from his war experiences and trouble began. Chronically short of money, mostly due to Grace Ann's spending habits, Bud eventually became desperate and forged several checks from Sherman's garage. Sherman discovered this and after an angry confrontation, he agreed to allow Bud to make restitution. A business owner who received one of the checks felt otherwise, however, and had Bud arrested. After the trial and sentencing, Bud was sent away to Atmore for three years.

At Fred's unrelenting urging, Grace Ann filed for divorce and began to roam the countryside in her Explorer, leaving the twins with her daddy. Since she returned a few weeks ago, her children have continued to reside with Fred. Bud is due to be released from Atmore sometime next month, so things should get lively. From the gossip Rosie hears from her momma, Bud is still as obsessed with Grace Ann as Fred is. He wrote her constantly from Atmore and I'm sure he's wild to see his kids.

Following undergraduate and graduate studies at The University—of Alabama in Tuscaloosa—where I majored in English and library service, I am now librarian to the wealthy in Athena Villa, a suburb southwest of Birmingham. Like the farmer's cheese, I stand alone. Old maid librarian and still my only child, I have lived out my personal life thus far "like a one-eyed cat peepin' in the seafood store," as Bill Haley once sang.

Bir-Min-Ham, Alabam, more specifically the Southside, is where I lay my head since Emmeleine Riley first hired me fresh out of library school. At that time rental costs in Athena Villa were beyond my budget. But even my moderate salary elevations through the years have not inspired me to consider moving. The south side of our fair state's largest city is a residential blend of Victorian dwellings, inexpensive apartment units, housing projects and all things between. At its center is the University of Alabama at Birmingham, which also incorporates a med school and research facilities that employ many thousands. Though the area's population density raises the roof, I am somehow comforted by the anonymity it provides. Since my mother's death from pancreatic cancer three years ago, followed six months later by my father's, my visits to Milltown have all but stopped. I don't have a home there anymore.

In rare, quiet moments at my desk in Athena Villa Public Library, I gaze out onto the tennis courts and sports playing fields that run behind the building and ruminate some more on how we all ended up. If, as they say, life is what happens when you're making other plans, then maybe all of us should have slowed down and paid more attention to the business at hand, "t.c.b.,"—"take care of business"—as the King would say. I overhear Rosie sometimes on the telephone to her momma, talking about something one of her children did, saying that she must have done something wrong early in their lives that made them behave so badly. Millie, however, tells her not to look at it like that; that if she did it over again, it might turn out worse. Nothing about any of us is settled yet, that's for certain. For now, I'll just heed the advice in that old country song, "take an old cold 'tater and wait."

Chapter Two

Months after her daddy died from t.b. and an absence of fiddle music, Rosie drives home. Her '72 Beetle misfires and dies at the four-way stop at the end of the two-lane highway. Her baby sleeps in the infant seat beside her. In the back seat, her older girls fight over a hand-held computer game. She has not been there since the funeral three months ago. She notices that the fence that runs along the dirt road leading to her family's farm has been fixed. In the years she has traveled the roads in her part of the county, known to most as Squirrel Hollow, those pieces of curled barbed wire over uprooted fence posts have always signaled the end of the highway. Her Granny Culp would have called its unexplained repair a sign.

She pumps the accelerator and turns the ignition. The car jolts onto the dirt road. Her girls face the rear window to watch dust and road signs disappear. The baby, Caitlin, does not awaken. Her face is wet and open mouthed against the padded infant seat.

Once, when Molly, her middle girl, was a baby, Sherman took the family to a drive-in to see "The Omen." Cassie, who was six then, climbed from the front seat to the back for the duration of the film. Molly woke and cried whenever Cassie moved. Rosie nursed the baby and scolded Cassie until Sherman got out of the car. He sat on the hood like a sulking cat until the movie ended. When they were back home, she asked him what the movie was about. He said, "You should have took them kids to my momma's like I told you to and you'd know yourself," and left the house for the rest of the night. Rosie watched the car's tail lights until they were out of view from the front window. Later she thought of that night as one more sign of their misalliance.

"Are you practicing being seen and not heard?" She teases the girls, who have hardly spoken for the last half-hour. She and Ell and the girls sat up last night, making up silly rules like that one for the visit to her mother's. "Go to bed with the chickens," was another one. Molly said she didn't think she could sleep in the hen house.

"Cassie bet I couldn't stay quiet until we get to Grandmom's," Molly tells her.

"You just lost, too," Cassie says.

"So what happens now?" Rosie asks.

"She has to get the eggs from those old hens and I get to play with the Game Boy for awhile," Cassie says. "It's my game anyway. Sherman said he'd get her something next month."

"Lord, don't let Grandmom hear you call your daddy Sherman," Rosie tells them. "Who told you to do that, anyway?"

"Peggy Ann's little boy does it," Molly says. "He said it when we spent the night at our old house last time. Daddy bought him a bunch of Hot Wheels and he was playing with them on the bed in Daddy and Peggy Ann's room."

Rosie licks her finger and rubs a spot from the baby's face. "Don't say a word about your daddy and Peggy Ann. Things will be hard enough at Grandmom's."

Sherman's rule for fatherhood was to be heard and not seen. He would leave detailed instructions to Rosie and the girls and head off for work or any other place away from them.

The whole time she carried Caitlin, their baby, who is nearly five months old, Sherman was hardly ever around. Staying gone for days at a time and returning with no explanation, he refused to pay the necessary bills, telling Rosie she would have to work it out herself.

Months before when she told him she was pregnant—at 39 and despite long, previously successful use of a diaphragm—Sherman told her he thought it was deliberate. He was finally at a point where he could expand his garage to include a service station/convenience store, and here she was, giving him somebody else to feed.

Three weeks after Caitlin was born, the gas company turned off the heat. Three days before Christmas, Rosie left with the girls in tow, leaving Sherman a note on the refrigerator. Selling her wedding rings and Sherman's deer rifles, she filled the Beetle with gas and drove to Ell's place on the Southside in Birmingham. Ell had told her for months that she and the girls were welcome whenever she decided enough was enough.

Two months later, Peggy Ann Prewitt and her son by her first husband moved into Sherman and Rosie's house in Milltown. Peggy Ann, twice married and divorced, is fifteen years younger than she and Sherman. Rosie has told none of this to her mother, who had always been convinced that Sherman Lee Jackson hung the moon.

She has not seen her mother since her daddy died.. When they talk on the phone, she finds reasons not to make the trip home. On the telephone she can say what needs to be said without looking Millie in the eye. As she eases the car up the rutted dirt road, Rosie recalls that Sunday before Christmas when she sat on Ell's couch and cried into the telephone that she and the girls had left Sherman.

"I'm in the middle of cutting up chickens, Rosalee," Millie said, following her long explanation. "I've got to get this done while your daddy's asleep. Can't it wait until tomorrow? There's mess all over my hands."

"Didn't you hear me, Momma?" Rosie said, louder this time. "The girls and I are here at Ell's. We're not going back to Sherman. He's been gone since Thursday night and they cut the gas off. He's not paid any bills in three months. I'm tired of him not ever coming home and then pitching temper fits when he does. We can't stay in that house with no heat with Caitlin just three weeks old."

"I reckon not," Millie said then. "Do you need me to send you any money?"

"No, I sold my wedding rings and Sherman's guns," Rosie told her. "I'll let you go, Momma. Let me know how Daddy is. Call me here at Ell's if you need me." She cried again then because her father was dying, her marriage was over, and here Millie was asking her about money.

Even when she was heavy pregnant with Caitlin, she loaded the girls into the car and drove to the farm to sit beside her daddy where he lay in the back bedroom. A stubborn strain of t.b. compounded his emphysema those last months. Even when he used the liquid oxygen, Miller's breathing rattled his chest. But most days, he knew who she was. Rosie sat for hours, holding his hand and singing "The Wabash Cannonball," or whatever it was he wanted to hear.

"Watch after them young'uns, Rosalee," Millie told her that day before they hung up. "They're liable to start running wild without their daddy."

Rosie stops the car now in her mother's front yard. She takes her guitar from the trunk, carries it to the front steps, and sets it down. Her family home, wood frame with porches running the length of the front and back sides, seems as though it belongs to someone she has not met before. The outer walls glisten with a fresh coat of white paint and the porch railing no longer sags at the edges. She and Molly hurry up to the door. Cassie, who is twelve and against coming for the weekend to begin with, moves more slowly, carrying the baby.

"The door's locked," Molly, her six year old, says as she rattles the door knob. "Reckon Grandmom's not at home?"

Millie Culp comes to an open front window and pushes her face against the screen. "You all come around to the back. I just got through waxing in here."

"We've not been to your house in a while, Grandmom," Cassie says later as they all sit eating stewed apples at Millie's kitchen table. "Your new storm door's just like the one at our old house."

"Sam put that up for me before he got so bad off last time," Millie tells them as she stacks their bowls on the cabinet top—recently finished in white pine—beside a new kitchen sink that is stainless steel and double-wide. "He done the sink and my cabinet tops too, before he took to coughing too bad and had to give it up."

Rosie puts the baby on a blanket on the newly laid vinyl flooring that resembles the cabinet tops. The old rotting linoleum is gone from the kitchen and dining areas. "You didn't tell me anything about Uncle Sam being sick, Momma. Are they still planning on the music festival? My guitar's out on the porch."

"You know Sam," Millie says. "Him nor Miller'd miss their fiddlin' get together unless they was dead and gone. Miller is, but Sam's not quite. He was down for a week or two, but he's back at hisself again. Him and Clettus's been down there in the woods, hammering and cussing since Wednesday. If you're wanting to go down there with them, the girls can stay here with me."

"No, Momma, I'll wait awhile. We can talk some," Rosie tells her as she walks through the house, finding other changes. All of the dark, hardwood flooring has been stripped and restained. The bedroom where her daddy lay the three months before he died is closed off. The other rooms are light and open and seem much larger. Her mother replaced window shades with sheers and blinds and the walls are newly painted white. Groups of three and four still-life prints decorate the walls where faded portraits of dead family members hung. Rosie thinks it looks like the Day's Inn where she and Sherman stayed the night once.

"It looks real nice, Momma. You're not getting it fixed up to sell, are you?" Rosie asks as she picks up the baby, heading toward the front door. Millie follows close behind her. Molly and Cassie head out the back door for the tire swing that still hangs from the oak tree.

"No, ma'am," Millie says to her as they choose rockers on the porch. "I always contended a body could fix up a place and live decent if there was money enough and time. A little of both's come to me with Miller's passing. I waited on him and Sam close to fifty years and I reckon this is my pay." She takes the baby from Rosie and nuzzles her neck.

"Daddy loved you, Momma," Rosie says, swallowing quick and deep so that she won't cry. Even after her father's death and her own marital break-up, any mention of her parent's chronic domestic difficulties makes her sad.

"And me him," Millie acknowledges. "But that don't always fix everything. I believe you could speak on that subject your own self after these last few months. All you girls a-quittin' on your husbands. First Grace Ann and now you."

Rosie rocks quietly and squints her eyes out toward the woods and her uncle's cabin. She expects her mother to continue about the divorce, but instead Millie changes the subject.

"Run on down yonder where Sam and Clettus are at and find out how many of them fried pies they're going to be wanting for tomorrow night. I been doing for these to-do's so long I don't reckon I can quit on 'em now."

Her uncle's cabin stands on the other side of the woods to the rear of the farmhouse. In the clearing between the woods and her uncle's property, Sam polishes a rectangle of varnished planks. A finished platform sits behind it. Ashes from his Marlboro trail him as he works. Behind him, Clettus, his boy, runs a power saw through a pine log and tokes a joint.

"What happened to last year's benches and platform?" Rosie asks them as she reaches the wood's edge. They pause their work to look at her. "I thought they'd hold out three or four years or more."

"Some of them fools down the road run through here with one of them all-terrain vehicles last New Year's Eve," Clettus tells her as he pinches the smoldering end of his joint and puts it in his pocket. "Tore everything to hell and back. I reckon if it ain't the weather that messes us up, then it's some idiot. How you been, Rosalee? I didn't expect to see you here. I figured you'd be too busy with your job and your young'uns to make it."

"I don't work on the weekends," Rosie tells him. "And I have one Friday a month off. Uncle Sam, that's some slick looking dance floor. Are you expecting that clogging group from Fort Payne again?"

"No, ma'am, I don't expect we'll be seeing them again," Sam says, grunting as he takes off his gray hunting hat and fans his face "They wanted four hundred dollars to come back here. I had it more in mind to feed 'em and give 'em gas money. Looks like string band music's uptown business here lately."

"It wasn't ever for you and Daddy, though, was it, Uncle Sam?" Rosie asks him.

"God-a-mighty, no," Sam says. "If it had of been, I wouldn't have worked at the cotton mill nor at that saw mill all them years. Me and Miller had us a good time, though. We played to the backsides of more big timers than you can shake a stick at. But I don't have to tell you that, Rosie girl. You was with us for part of that time."

"You remember that time when I was about twelve and you talked Momma into letting me go with ya'll and you ended up playing somewhere with the Stanleys when a couple of their band members were sick? I though I'd died and gone to heaven just being there to watch," Rosie tells her uncle.

"Old Miller'd be proud you come on down here even with all that's happened in your family," Sam says, sitting down on an unfinished pine log bench to rest. "He told me more than once he hoped you'd do something with your singing and picking besides just fooling around with us."

"I am playing some at this place in Birmingham," Rosie tells him. "There's a country music bar over close to Bessemer called the Wells Fargo that has a Bluegrass and Old Time Night on the weekends. Ell and I go sometimes when there's somebody to watch the kids. A couple of men that own a fretted instrument store have a band that plays there. I've played with them two or three times. They're trying to get me to join up with them. I got to say, I'm tempted. Ell's said she'll see after the girls and the baby, if I decide to."

Sam smiles encouragingly as he stands back up, motioning for Clettus to bring him the hammer. "I say go after it," he tells her. "Now that you've not got Sherman breathin' down your neck every move you make. Truth be told, Rosalee, you're well rid of that'un. I know it's hard on you and all, but you look happier than I've seen you for some time."

"Lord, don't say that around Momma, Uncle Sam," she laughs as she gives Clettus a hand with another pine log. "That'll get her wound up for sure. I've been expecting her to give me down the country about leaving Sherman, but all she's done so far is mention it in passing."

"You and Sherman calling it quits and Miller a-dyin' has hit her hard," Sam tells her. "But she's done lived long enough to know that things don't dance along to a special tune just because you're humming it. She's not give up, though."

"That's for certain," Rosie says. "All that fixing up the house and everything. The next thing we know, she'll be taking a ceramics class at the community school in Caloosa City. By the way, she sent me down here to find out how many fried pies ya'll want for tomorrow night. She feels like you're counting on her to do 'em again."

"Millie's always going to do what she feels like she's supposed to," Sam says. "I finally learned that about her. Me and her done a Mexican stand-off the first twenty years that her and your daddy was married. But we finally decided to take each other for what we are and we come out all right."

"All them months of waiting on your daddy wore her to a frazzle," Clettus comments. "Me and Daddy tried to help her much as we could, but she wouldn't let us much. She's got right active these last few weeks though. Puts me and Daddy to work whenever she can."

"I hear you've been under the weather some, Uncle Sam," Rosie says to her uncle, who sits down on a pine log bench again, coughing and wheezing and fanning his face. "You've not got what my daddy did, do you, Uncle Sam?"

"It's just old smoker's cough," he tells her as his breathing begins to quiet itself. "You tell Millie we'll take as many of them pies as she'll fry up. That bunch'll be hungry for sure. You come on back down here after while and me and you and Clettus and Jimmy and Junior'll make us a little music. We got to get ready for tomorrow night."

In the kitchen the next morning, Millie rolls thin dough and frets over a berry stain on her new counter top. "Rosalee, tell the girls to stay away from that empty chicken house. There's still a mess of filth in there. I'm of a mind to burn it down."

Rosie stirs bubbling blueberries on the stove-top and raises her eyebrows at her mother. "I thought you loved those chickens, Momma. You always talked about how much money they saved us."

"When there was eight or nine of us to feed, they did," Millie tells her. "But I never did like foolin' with 'em. There's plenty of things you do when you've got to, but it's not usually what you like doing."

Millie shapes the pastries, filling each one with warm berries. Her hands are the texture of the wooden spoon she dips into the fruit. The cluster ring of minute diamond chips that always cut into her finger is gone from her left hand. Rosie does not ask her about it. They work until dozens of pies line the counter top. Millie covers them with dishcloths.

"I hear Caitlin a-crying," Millie says, washing her hands. "Where did you come up with a name like that? It sounds like somethin' you'd call a kitty-cat."

"I got it out of a book I checked out of the library one time," Rosie says. "It was about this poet from Wales—that's close to England—who died quite a while ago. His wife was named Caitlin. She put up with more from him than I did from Sherman. I decided she needed a namesake." Rosie goes into the bedroom for the baby and takes her to the front porch. They settle into a rocker and Rosie lifts her blouse, putting the baby to her breast. Both smile at their union.

"I'm glad to see you still nursing her," Millie comments as she sits down in the porch swing. "I didn't know if you could keep it up with you working."

"We do it at night and in the mornings," Rosie tells her, tracing the grooves in the arm of the rocker with her free hand. "You know something, Momma? There aren't any front porches where Ell and I live. Only decks. People put plants on them."

"Your Granny Culp wouldn't've lasted two days living like that," Millie says.

Rosie nods, remembering her daddy's mother, her head bent over her sewing as she sat in this very chair, rocking day into night. "She didn't have to find that out, though, did she? Granny spent her whole life and died right here on this land."

"She never even left the state, except once to go to a funeral in Georgia," Millie tells her. "The Culp family was never ones for going places or seeing different things. Me and Miller lived our whole lives standing still."

"Was there a special place you wanted to go, Momma?" Rosie asks her. She never thinks of her mother away from the farmhouse or the fields. She tries to imagine her mother in the apartment she and the girls share with Ell. She would be like a butter churn at McDonald's.

"Any place and no place, Rosalee," Millie tells her. "When there's no place you've been, then you don't know where it is you would go if you got the chance. I worked in White Cotton Mill from the time I was 14 until I married Miller Culp. I thought I was getting me a pardon after all them years of picking lint off of me. But I believe instead I was sentenced to forty something more years in another type of jail."

Millie's face is squenched as though she is eating sauerkraut. Rosie cannot remember her mother ever speaking so frankly. "I didn't know you felt like that about living here, Momma."

"I didn't always," Millie tells her. "It's just that I never did know what it was your daddy was after."

Millie rises and begins to pace the porch, pounding a fist in her open palm. "Him and Sam would work at that sawmill all the day long and then come home with a bunch of them old men for me to feed," she continues. "Then they'd sit up half the night, drinking and playing them old guitars and fiddles until I was half crazy. I had to put all you kids to bed in the back room so you could sleep."

"We could hear them anyway," Rosie tells her. "Me and Matt and John Luke would try to pick out who was playing just by listening. Mark slept with a pillow over his head most of the time. That was when he was in that stage where he hated anything country—which is pretty funny, considering how they're all living now."

"You couldn't get much further in the country than them three," Millie agrees. Her sons own a successful farming co-op in east Tennessee, traveling home only a few times a year. Although she is silently proud of their prosperity, she often laments that none of them have married thus far or seem likely to in the near future.

"They figured out early what it was they wanted and went after it. Miller and Sam spent most of their lives chasing rainbows. When that sawmill shut down every winter, they'd take off for the Lord knows where to fill in with this or that old hillbilly band, a-trying to get to play back-up at the Opry. And me left here with the four of you all and Clettus and a yard full of chickens." Millie begins her nervous pacing again, back and forth across the newly mended porch.

"Was Granny not much help?" Rosie asks her. She thinks her mother looks like Ernest Angley, the way she is ranting and carrying on. Or maybe it was Jimmy Swaggert. Rosie hasn't felt the need to watch television evangelists since she left her husband.

"Your Granny Culp liked to supervise," Millie says. "That's about all she ever did here from her chair on the porch, except keep you kids in line with a willow switch."

"At least you had some idea of what it was Daddy was supposed to be doing," Rosie tells her. "Sherman tried to make me think he was putting in overtime at the garage when he didn't come home at night. But I drove by there with the kids in the car one night and the whole place was dark. We rode around two solid hours until we found his car in a back alley. I never did learn what he was up to."

"I knew what your daddy was doing," Millie tells her. "But I never could figure out how come. Seemed like to me with us living here with a leaking roof and an old coal stove for heat, he could've found something more lucrative than that old whining music to make us some extra money. My people might've been millworkers, but we wanted a better life. Your daddy never did."

"We did live a pretty lean life," Rosie says. "Maybe his fiddling helped him not to dwell on it so much."

"If he'd a-put more energy into earnin' a livin' and less into that hillbilly mess, it might not have been so lean," Millie says. "People around here acted like it was the Lord himself that decreed your daddy to play a fiddle. Anybody with half a ear knows that kind of music ain't nothing but old tacky mess—just a bunch of people dressed up and playing their fiddles and their guitars and banjos, singing about wallowing in the misery they helped create in the first place."

"It's not all like that," Rosie says. "Lots of the music Daddy and Uncle Sam played was happy music. Daddy said you even used to go hear him and Uncle Sam sometimes."

"That I did," Millie admits. "When you and the boys was little and your granny would agree to keep you all. Let me tell you what I seen one time, though. I went with your daddy and Sam over somewhere in Tennessee. Everybody was a-playing outside. It was in the springtime and it started to rain. One young girl was watching while one of them pretty boy bands was up on the stage. And she was a-holdin' a crying baby. Well, the rain was just a-pouring and that little baby lost its breath and started gasping for air from the rainwater running down its throat. One of the pickers noticed it and motioned to the girl or I reckon she'd have let that baby strangle to death. That silly girl got so caught up in the music, she mighty near let her baby choke itself. That's when I got me a bait of country music. I can still remember that girl's face and it's been more than thirty years ago. She looked just like Grace Ann Reese, or Hardaman as I hear she's calling herself again. I guess you know she's finally come back."

"She's called Ell and me several times," Rosie says. "She said she's coming here tonight to see us. You know Ell's coming this afternoon. She had to work at the library this morning. Grace Ann always did come to hear me and Daddy and Uncle Sam and Clettus when she and Bud were still married."

"It certainly remains a mystery to me what people see in country music," Millie says. "What do you think it was that brought Grace Ann back here after gallavantin' around the West Coast for three years? I bet Fred cut her money supply off."

"Grace Ann never did like to stay still, even when she was married to Bud," Rosie says. "When Bud was working with Sherman at the garage, he was always telling Sherman about some place Grace Ann was after him to take her and the kids."

"Must of had her a case of the chronic runarounds," Millie says. "Like Miller and Sam did. Take all that chasing around after Big Jim that they done. I'll never understand nothing about that until the day I die."

"Didn't they help Governor Folsom get in office that first time?" Rosie asks her mother.

"Lord, yes," Millie says. "They played in that old hillbilly band he carried around with him on the campaign trail, what was their name, The Strawberry Pickers? They even got wrote up in the newspapers. Made me so ashamed I could hardly go to church."

Rosie shifts Caitlin to her shoulder and watches her mother peering out through the trees toward Sam's cabin. "The whole county knew Daddy was a fiddler in his spare time, Momma. What bothered you about it?"

"It's time for us to get them pies fried," Millie says to her. "That crowd'll be here before you know it."

She moves into the house, heading for the kitchen. Rosie takes the baby and follows her. Cassie and Molly sit in Millie's front room, watching cartoons and eating cereal dry from the box.

"Girls, I got some biscuits left from mine and your momma's breakfast if you want them," Millie says to them as she passes. "And I'll be glad to fix some eggs and bacon to go with them."

"They're fine, Momma," Rosie says. She lays Caitlin down in the playpen. "They don't usually want much to eat on Saturday until lunchtime. Are you going to answer my question about Daddy and Uncle Sam and Governor Folsom?"

"The answer to that one is that it was just more of your daddy acting a fool and not tending to the business of earning a living for his family. That's what bothered me about it," Millie says flatly, as she melts Crisco in a black iron skillet.

"And, come to think of it, I guess I know why it was he cottoned to Big Jim so. There's a line in one them old songs your daddy and Sam used to sing, about not getting above your raising. He must've took that to heart and saw the same thing in old Big Jim. Big Jim earned him some money and got famous, but he stayed what he was."

"We've got a lot of pies to finish," Rosie says as Millie lays the first few into the pan. She is uncertain whether she wants to hear Millie out on her daddy's lack of ambition. "I'll stay here and help you awhile, but then I've got to practice a little more with Uncle Sam and them for tonight."

"I know you're anxious to get down there with the rest of them," Millie says, shaking her head disapprovingly. "You're letting Cassie and Molly go, too, I reckon. I ought not never let you go with your daddy and Sam and the boys to all them fiddling and picking get-togethers when you was little. You might not be mixed up in all that mess now."

"I just want to have a good time with it," Rosie tells her. "It's not like it's a life's calling. I know I've got to earn a living."

"Let me tell you one more thing about Mr. Big Jim," Millie says. "You know what he done one time when he was still the governor and he was up in New York with a whole bunch of other politicians and such? They were at this big hotel they got up there, the Waldorf Astoria. Well, Mr. Big Jim was about four sheets in the wind and he up and danced barefooted in front of all them people. And they took a picture of it and put it in Life Magazine for all the world to see what a bunch of backwoods hillbillies come out of the state of Alabama."

They fry pies in silence. The dough sizzling in the hot oil sounds like applause. Grease splatters the stove and countertops as they remove the pies from the skillet

Chapter Three

Twin bonfires light either side of the platform where Rosie sits tuning her guitar that evening. As it nears 7:00, men in jeans and overalls carrying their instrument cases step around endless lines of extension cords that disappear into the dark. The annual one-night festival, a favorite musical venue for amateur Old Time and Bluegrass locals, draws slightly larger crowds as each year passes. Sam and Clettus direct people to the pine log benches and the food laden tables beyond them. The late April night is chilly and moonless and two men argue whether it will rain before midnight.

"Friends and neighbors," Clettus says as he steps to the microphone. "We are more than proud to welcome you all to the Fifteenth Annual Squirrel Hollow Bluegrass and Old Time Music Festival." He pauses as the audience, some 170 strong and mostly from the area, claps and cheers. Old men in their overalls and workpants, accompanied by their wives, children and grandchildren line the benches Clettus and Sam put together.

Ell sits four benches back from the platform beside Cassie and Molly. Rosie left Caitlin with Millie at the farmhouse. Two rows over, Grace Ann Hardaman, blonde hair on top of her head in makeshift bun and decked out in L.L. Bean attire, holds hands with a balding man wearing a ponytail.

"But we are lonesome tonight," Clettus continues and his voice is somber. "For an important member of this affair is not here with us anymore. You all know that my uncle Miller Culp died this past winter from t.b. Him and my Daddy Sam begun this thang with fourteen people and a half gallon of Jim Beam fifteen years ago. Miller loved his music and I know tonight he'd be honored that from here on out, we'll be calling this get-together the Miller Culp Memorial String Band Festival." He stops again for the crowd's response. They stand, clapping long and hard. A small boy's whistle is heard above the noise.

"Joining us again this evening, though her daddy can't be here, is my cousin, Rosalee Culp Jackson," Clettus introduces Rosie and the rest of the band as they stand and mount the platform to gather near the microphone. "She'll be playing the guitar and singing with me. Daddy here's on the five string and Junior's playing bass. His brother Jimmy's on the fiddle and I'm on the mandolin. We're the New Squirrel Hollow Puddle Jumpers and we'll lead off with 'Molly and Tenbrooks.'"

The crowd is full of food and expectation. Clettus' tenor rises in a respectful imitation of Bill Monroe. Rosie's eyes close, her fingers tense on the frets. Their brief practice and Millie's words about the hopelessness of it all thrum in her head. Sam and Junior smile to her and the crowd. Their playing blends smooth and drifts into the pines. Rosie watches a solemn little girl clap time to Molly's demise. When the song is over, people on the benches begin to shout the names and words of other songs and the Squirrel Hollow Puddle Jumpers play on.

Later when they stop to let Hot Rizin', an all-male fiddle, banjo and guitar trio, take the stage, Rosie walks over to Grace Ann, who is standing by the food tables talking to Ell, Molly and Cassie.

"Hey, girlfriend," Grace Ann says easily, as though the three of them had last been together just a week ago instead of three years prior. She grasps Rosie in a bear hug. Her blonde hair, straying from its bun, shows no sign of gray.

"I want you all to meet somebody," she says to Rosie and Ell as she points to the man with the ponytail who is deep in conversation with Sam and Clettus over by the wood's edge. They are examining a guitar the man has pulled from its case. Rosie and Ell follow her to where they are standing.

"This is the real star of the show," Grace Ann says to the man as she slips her arm into his and turns him away from Sam and Clettus. "This is my best friend, Rosie Jackson and my other best friend, Ell Seers. Girls, this is Tanner Hope. We met out in Colorado and he's come down to visit with me."

Tanner shakes hands with Ell first and then takes Rosie's hand, holding it. "You've got about the prettiest voice I've heard anywhere, Rosie," he says with a glad-to-meet-you grin. "I play some myself. I've been talking to your uncle and cousin here and they say you might let me back you up on a number or two. How about it?" His sun weathered face lights expectantly. He is a short, slightly built man, perhaps ten years older than Grace Ann.

"That would sure be all right by me," Rosie says, looking to Grace Ann, who nods her approval. When Hot Rizin' finishes up, the two of them mount the platform. Tanner sits down on a low stool to play. After some discussion and a brief warm-up, they settle on "Wildwood Flower."

"He taught me to love him and called me his flower," Rosie sings as Tanner plays, softly and flawlessly.

That song was the only one of the many she sang to Molly and Cassie that Sherman ever claimed to like. He would never allow her to play for company. His attitude toward the hillbilly and Bluegrass music Rosie was weaned on was dismissive at best. He once told her he knew for a fact that Hank Williams paid somebody else to write "I'm So Lonesome I Could Cry," and that he stole most of his music from an old black blues singer. "Hillbilly Shakespeare, my ass," he said and Rosie refused to talk to him for two whole days. Hank was safe inside the gates of Country Music Heaven as far as Rosie was concerned, right up there with Uncle Dave Macon and the Carter Family and all the other pickers and grinners that Miller and Sam taught her to love. Once though after she sang "Wildwood Flower," for the girls just before she put them to bed, Sherman said that maybe it wasn't so bad and even had her sing it again for him after the girls were asleep. Then he took the guitar from her hands when she finished and made love to her on the sofa.

"...he'll regret the dark hour, he's gone and neglected his pale wildwood flower," Rosie finishes and the crowd begs for another one. She and Tanner go into a rollicking "Sally Ann," and much of the crowd gets up to dance as Ell and Grace Ann carry full plates to a spot beyond the food tables to talk. They spread a blanket and sit down. Molly and Cassie fill their plates with fried chicken and potatoes and some of Millie's pies and return to the benches to watch their mother.

"Lordy me, it's good to be back in Alabama," Grace Ann says as she takes a bite of corn bread. "If I had to listen to one more aging pothead who's still stuck in the '60s tell me how it never got any better than Woodstock, I think I'd have lost my mind. Believe you me, there's a million of them out West—California, Montana, Colorado. And I really put on my Southern redneck best when they started in on that. I said we never even heard about Woodstock in Alabama until sometime in the late '70s. We were too busy burning crosses and making moonshine. That usually shut them up."

"What brought you back?" Ell asks her, sipping iced tea.

Grace Ann's willowy body has not succumbed to middle age spread. Only the lines about her eyes and forehead reveal her years. She fixes that same flattering smile on her old friend. "Well, I missed you all like crazy," she says. "And of course I had to get back to the kids. It took me awhile to get my head on straight after the divorce and Bud getting sent off to Atmore and all. I thought for awhile I'd just send for the kids and stay out West. But Daddy's been pestering me ever since he found out when Bud was getting out of Atmore to come on back home. He felt like Bud would try to get full custody if I wasn't around."

"Have you heard from Bud lately?" Ell asks.

"Oh Lord, yes," Grace Ann sighs. "Two letters a week for the whole three years he was in prison. I moved around a lot, but somehow the letters always got to me, one way or another. You know, he's due home in two weeks. He's still begging me to go back to him."

"And are you?" Ell can't seem to stop herself from inquiring.

"I still love Bud," Grace Ann admits, starting in on a side of mashed potatoes. "But there's not any going back. We'll always have some kind of relationship because of the twins, but I can't see it being marriage again. So, tell me about you and Rosie. How is life together in the Big City?"

"Great," Ell told her. "We're making it fine. Can you believe she finally had it up to her eyebrows with old Sherman Lee?" Ell asks her. "She and the kids have been at my house since just before Christmas. She's got a job now and everything. Did you know she has a new baby?"

"It happens to the best of us," Grace Ann says, setting her plate down beside her. "Truth be told, I'm three months on the road to motherhood again my own self. That's the reason Tanner Hope followed me back here. I was idiot enough to tell him about it before I drove back to Alabama."

"Oh, ye gods and little fishes, as Miss Vancene used to say," Ell remarks. "Have you told Bud yet? What about Fred and Ree and Harley Junior?"

"No indeed, and definitely not Daddy. It'll be goodnight Gracie sure enough when he finds out," Grace Ann admits. "He's met Tanner and he likes him about as well as he ever did Bud, which is to say, not in the slightest. I doubt he'd like Jesus himself if he was dating me. The kids were with me at the trailer until Tanner came and when Daddy found out he was there, he came and carted them back to his house. Makes me sorry I ever came home."

"Are you glad about the baby at all?" Ell asks. Grace Ann had tap danced through motherhood most of her life, leaving the twins with Fred or Bud's parents whenever she needed a break.

"It's hard to say," Grace Ann says. "Pregnant and nearly 40 is not exactly the mid-life crisis I had in mind. And Tanner's pushing me to marry him. I don't know yet how it's all going to come down."

On stage, Rosie and Tanner continue their picking and singing. The rest of the Puddle Jumpers join them as the audience makes more requests. Ell and Grace Ann go back to the spectator benches to sit near Molly and Cassie.

"Are Ree and Harley coming?" Cassie asks Grace Ann.

"I think so, honey," Grace Ann says. "My Daddy promised he'd bring them awhile."

As it grows later and the crowd gets livelier, Rosie and Tanner and the boys go into "Rockingham Cindy," an upbeat version of the Appalachian Cindy of old. Tanner joins Rosie at the microphone to sing harmony and those so inclined rise to buck dance across the polished plank floor. The mood is so light that no one notices Fred Hardaman weaving his way through the crowd. He moves loutishly past the dance floor, in front of the stage where Rosie and Tanner sing, and on to the bench where Grace Ann is seated.

Bending low over Grace Ann, he mumbles in her ear. Ell tries, but cannot hear him over the music and the crowd. Grace Ann shakes her head at him as he continues his muttering. His gestures are angry and emphatic. Finally, he shrugs and with a disgusted gesture walks back through the crowd. He stops once in front of the stage to look Tanner full in the face. Tanner nods a silent greeting, but Fred does not acknowledge him as he moves away, back toward the woods to his car.

When Rosie and Tanner and the Puddle Jumpers finish up and step down, Grace Ann is close to crying. A gospel quartet is warming up at the microphone as Tanner sits down beside her, taking her hand in his. "Now,

now. My girl's not going to cry, is she?" He says soothingly. "What did Fred say to you? I thought he was bringing the twins to hear the music."

"Damn that old man," Grace Ann says, trying to compose herself. "He can still yank my chain and me turning 40 in less than two months. Here he was drunk as Cooter Brown and he's telling me that Ree and Harley are so ashamed of the way I'm behaving with you living up there at the trailer with me that they didn't want to come here tonight to be with us. He's even saying he's going to let Bud know and that maybe he'll want to keep the kids with him and his momma. Daddy would use anything to get me to do what he wants. He's always hated Bud's guts and now he's claiming the kids need their daddy. I agree with that. But I can't see what that's got to do with you and me."

"I wouldn't pay him any mind, Sugar Bear," Tanner tells her firmly. "I think you and me need to get ourselves a good lawyer and get those kids out of his house. He only had temporary custody while you were away and Bud was in jail. It's time they were back with their momma."

He continues to talk softly to her and they walk off together as he places a protective arm about her shoulders.

"That Tanner talks like he's got some sense," Clettus remarks. "It really ain't none of Fred's business, what Grace Ann and him are doing. He's just going to have to get over it."

"He'll get over it about the same time the Pope conducts services at Milltown Methodist," Ell remarks to Rosie, who nods agreement.

"What did she say about Bud?" Rosie asks her as they listen to a medley of old time hymns. "Isn't he coming home pretty soon?"

"Week after next," Ell tells her. "Grace Ann says he wrote her twice a week the whole time he was at Atmore. She said he ended every letter with 'I love you more than you will ever know.' Some welcome home this'll turn out to be."

"I doubt Grace Ann and Tanner'll be tying a yellow ribbon 'round the old oak tree to greet him," Clettus says, laconically.

He points his thumb at the platform where the gospel group is finishing up. "They're wanting us to do one more set, Rosalee," he says. "Let me go round up Daddy and the other two and we'll get back up there."

As he moves off, Rosie says, "What else did Grace Ann have to say? Tanner nearly talked my ears off about her when we weren't singing. Says she's the best thing to come into his life since his wife and boy got killed in a car wreck ten years ago. He's helping the builders with that house Fred is having built for Grace Ann. Tanner's a carpenter when he's not fooling around with his guitar."

"Apparently that's not all he fools around with," Ell tells her. "He's the daddy of the baby Grace Ann's going to have in another six months or so."

"Jesus save us all," Rosie says. "Who do you reckon's going to take it harder, Fred or Bud?"

"Neither one of them is going to let go of her," Ell predicts. "Not in this lifetime."

The New Squirrel Hollow Puddle Jumpers play until the night is cold and the suggestions slow to only one or two after each number. Rosie thinks about her momma at the farmhouse with Caitlin, singing and rocking her to sleep in the same chair she used with her own babies. It was listening to Millie at bedtime when she sang hymns to Mark, her younger brother, that nourished Rosie's love for singing. She and Miller stood outside the bedroom door in early evening time while Millie sang verse after verse of "In the Garden," or "Whispering Hope." "A whole choir of angels couldn't do it better," he said. Millie never sang for her husband.

Not one time has her momma said to her what a mistake she made by leaving Sherman Jackson. Twenty-four years ago when Rosie first brought Sherman to the farm to meet her, Millie said to her what a fine boy he was. He had called her "Miss Mildred" and treated her like a lady.

That Sunday last December, Millie set her mouth and bore the inevitable when Rosie gave her the news. She sends Rosie envelopes of money and gives her advice about the children only when she is asked for it.

To finish out the evening, Rosie and the boys do a rousing "Ya'll Come."

"Getting late," she says to her uncle. "But you know what, I think I still see a light on up there," she points through the trees to her mother's house.

Sam nods agreement. A few stragglers linger on the back benches, hollering out for one last song. "Let's do that'n we did last year when Miller was still here with us," he suggests.

Rosie nods and they go into "The Fate of Ellen Smith." As she sings on this one, her voice is plaintive and low as it mourns a woman shot through the heart and the man who pays for the deed.

Chapter Four

In the '60s, we looked for truth in the words of rock and roll song lyrics. But today as the Big 4-0 descends on one and all, if any of us still believe that truth can be found, we seek it in the words of the hymns we sang every week in the churches of our youth. "(Can't Get No) Satisfaction" has metamorphosed to "Amazing Grace" as the soundtrack to our lives. Such lyrics as "no sad farewells, no tear-dimmed eyes…where the soul of man never dies," or "when peace like a river descendeth my way," are now a bit more relevant than "hey, hey, you, you, get off my cloud," or even "speaking words of wisdom, let it be." Perhaps we have replaced the here-and-now overtones of the rock and roll that ruled us with the eternal nature of those hymns.

Once Rosie, Grace Ann and I, attired in various seasonal robes, sang, "Early in the morning, our songs shall rise to Thee," in the Youth Choir at Milltown Methodist on each and every Lord's Day. The light penetrating the stained glass rendering of the Angel's Appearance to Mary shone directly onto Grace Ann's blonde, perfectly coifed hair, giving her the illumined look of those blessed by the Almighty. A goodly portion of the solo renditions featured Rosie's lilting soprano. And I could certainly follow the notes and carry a tune in any number of buckets due to my mother's patient instruction from the time I was five. As our church musician, she always said that if any one girl ever possessed Rosie's angelic voice, Grace Ann's beatific appearance and my unfailing sense of timing, she would undeniably waltz straight through heaven's gates and into the arms of St. Peter. Rosie's Aunt Vancene was choir director. She and my mother saw us twenty-four tempestuous teenagers "through many dangers, toils and snares," in our years together in the Youth Choir.

Our best moment—possibly their worst—occurred in our senior year during the performance of the Easter cantata. Roxana Srimpsher, daughter of our high school's secretary, returned from a weekend runaway episode just in time to join the rest of us in the choir loft. We wore our freshly dry-cleaned purple robes for the performance. Roxanna, who had gone with her boyfriend, aged 20, to a concert in Atlanta, didn't quite make it to the dry-cleaner's. She came to the performance solely because she was slotted for a solo of "Were You There When They Crucified My Lord," and didn't want to disappoint Miss Vancene. The only robe they could locate for her was red. Miss Vancene and my mother fretted over this until Rusty, Roxana's younger brother, proposed the following: since the church lights would be dimmed throughout the service, when Roxana sang, instead of spotlighting her, use the color wheel from the aluminum Christmas tree and set it on blue so she would match the rest of us. Reluctantly, Miss Vancene agreed to try and placed Roxana near the back so her unseasonal robe would not be visible through most of the cantata.

Placing the color wheel atop the baby grande and locking it on the blue component, Miss Vancene nodded to Roxanna when her time came. Initially the intensity of the blue light transformed Roxanna to "Deep Purple," in the flesh. Then the wheel, slipping from its locked position, began to turn, flashing various colors as Roxanna became the girl in the kaleidoscope robe. Most of the congregation—with the exception of Roxanna's mother—was rolling in the aisles as the unfortunate soloist sang her last notes. Mrs. Srimpsher then marched to the choir loft and jerked Roxanna down from the last row and out the side door.

It is perhaps the memory of my mother patiently accompanying four generations of hymn singers through "The Old Rugged Cross," that keeps me going back to church Sunday after Sunday. I never really "lost my faith," as many of my generation claim, though there have been times when I thought I had misplaced it. In recent years, I have been a frequent church goer—to churches of my own Methodist persuasion and a myriad of others. About once a month, I attend Mass with Mrs. Emmeleine Riley, director of Athena Villa Public Library and one of my dearest friends. Emmeleine, a feisty red-head, has been my boss for sixteen years. Having successfully reared two equally spirited daughters, Emmeleine spends a great deal of her off time at the Church of Our Blessed Mother, a large and prominent parish just south of the Magic City. I enjoy going with her, chiefly for the reverent atmosphere and the beauty of the liturgy. Them Catholics—whom we were so often warned against as small town Protestant children—can really put on the dog when it comes to religion.

On this last Sunday of August, Rosie and I are just leaving the noon service at Southside Methodist with a horde of girl children in their summer-white Sunday best. She buckles Caitlin into the back seat of my Cherokee and the other young ladies climb aboard. Immediately, Meaghan, Cassie's friend, and Cassie herself switch on their Discmans and attach the headphones and begin to twitch their nubile bodies to whatever auditory horrors emanate from I-91, the station of choice for want-to-be-cool-almost-teenagers. Molly and her friend Helen make fun of them from the rear. Helen, who is deaf, has inspired Molly to learn sign language and the two of them gesture away as they point and giggle at the older girls. Molly so enjoys little Helen's company that she has even begun going with her to community wide church services for the hearing impaired.

"Maybe we could see about joining the choir," Rosie suggests as she turns around to slip a pacifier into Caitlin's fretting mouth. "I reckon I'm just about ready to sing in church again."

"Let the woman start singing with some old string band and you can't get her to shut up to save your life," I tease her. Rosie has found her musical voice again and is rather beside herself with pleasure. She recently became vocalist and guitar player for a local Old Time Music ensemble that calls itself Wildwood Flower. One of its founders shares a bit more with Miss Rosie than a love for fiddle band music.

"Why don't we stop and get some chicken and stuff to take with us to the park?" Rosie suggests. "Michael and Gabriel are coming at 2:00 and we won't have much time to fix anything."

While not the archangels of Biblical renown, Michael and Gabriel Pace have rather graced our lives in many ways these past few months. The brothers, who by day own and operate a fretted instruments store on the Southside, are the founding members of Wildwood Flower. They became acquainted with Rosie at the Wells Fargo, our favorite weekend culinary and musical haunt, when she sang a few times with them on amateur nights. Tall and slender with shoulder length brown hair, Michael is late-twenty/early-thirty-something and plays the fiddle. Gabriel, Gabe, a giant, husky fellow six or so years older with sandy blonde curly hair and sky blue eyes—resembling a slightly better looking Hoss Cartwright—can work a five string so expertly that you'd swear somebody cloned Earl Scruggs. Another set of brothers, who play the mandolin and bass, began playing with them around the same time and Wildwood Flower was born. Michael and Rosie's association as fellow band members segued into romance and they are now together on a daily basis.

Rosie's children received Michael warily at first, but he slowly won them over with his good-natured kindness. For a never-married man, he exhibits a rare ability with children. He is patient enough to interact with them for long periods of time without projecting heavy authority. He even changes Caitlin's diapers, which enrolls him on the short list for sainthood in my book. He and Gabe are frequent visitors to the little six-room flat we call home. The first time we had them over for dinner,

Gabe told me quietly that he is gay. And it is this very lack of availability that allows a friendship—that might otherwise come to naught–to flourish between us.

Our planned afternoon outing is to Oak Mountain, a nearby state park. With the girls' two buddies joining us, the nine of us will just fit in my Cherokee. A divorced woman of 40, her late-twenty/early-thirty-something lover, her spinster librarian housemate, his gay brother and five children. Not exactly the stuff on which great romance thrives, but maybe more typical than not in this decade of extended families.

Later, as the children and hungry men crowd our living quarters, Rosie and I throw bags of chips and cookies into an old picnic basket to supplement the Colonel's fare. Molly is reading **Green Eggs and Ham** to Michael, who gives her his complete attention. Gabe softly sings "Itsy Bitsy Spider" to Caitlin, walking his fingers up her chubby arms and chucking her multiple chins as she giggles. Cassie and Meaghan dance the twist to my old '45 of Joey Dee's "Peppermint Twist," which they have playing on my old stereo. Screaming with laughter, Cassie swings her arms and twists to the floor as Meaghan follows her lead.

The phone is ringing and I answer, "Ell and Rosie's Day Care and Disco."

"Aunt Ell?" asks a voice I don't immediately recognize.

"It's Ree. I can't find Momma. I've been calling and calling the trailer and nobody's there to answer. Granddad's not here and Harley's getting real worried."

I sense anxiety in the generally calm and collected Ma 'Ree Reese, Bud and Grace Ann's fifteen-year-old daughter. "She's not down there with you, is she?"

"No, no she's not, Ree," I say, motioning to the girls to dim the stereo volume. "Who's there with you and Harley?"

"Just Mrs. Johnson, the housekeeper. She won't take us to the trailer without Granddad's okay. Momma was supposed to come and get us two hours ago. We were going swimming with her and Tanner. Granddad said we could go."

We talk for several more minutes. I hold the cordless phone to my ear with my shoulder as I move about the kitchen. Rosie brings a tablecloth and paper napkins to top off the picnic basket. She looks inquiringly at me as I mouth "Ree," to her.

"Honey, we're going out for awhile, but I want you to call me when you find out where Grace Ann is. If we're not here, you can leave a message on the answering machine," I say to her. She promises that she will and we hang up.

"Ree can't find Grace Ann," I tell Rosie. "She sounds worried to death and that's not a bit like her. That girl's learned how to keep her head through almost anything. I guess it comes with the territory when you live with Grace Ann and Bud."

"It would probably be a bad idea for her to call Bud and ask him where Grace Ann might be," Rosie says, closing the lids to the picnic basket and ice chest. Her long, dark hair is braided and wound around her small head. Since our teen years, her glossy, sable locks have flowed past her shoulders to the middle of her back. After she began seeing Michael, she's started spending a lot of time experimenting with her mane—braiding it, curling it, sweeping it on top of her head. When I tease her about the affects of mid-life romance, she smiles much like the Mona Lisa, as though she possesses some secret just too personal to tell.

"The way I hear it, Bud's having a hard time keeping one foot in front of the other," I say. "The last time I talked to Grace Ann, she told me that he's living with some New Age group in that old run-down house across the street from the high school. She said he moved out of his folks' place right after he found out about her and Tanner and the baby. The New Agers let him live there with them and he keeps their cars running and the plumbing fixed. I think they even pay him a little something. He spends a lot of his time riding around on that old motorcycle he had back when they were married. She's not seen him lately, but she said he sees Ree and Harley nearly every day. Fred lets him come to his house anytime Bud wants to."

"Lordy me, I wonder how this is going to end up," Rosie says as she goes into the living room to take Caitlin from Gabe's lap.

"Come here Little Miss," she says to the laughing baby. "Let's get you cleaned up so we can go bye-bye."

"Da," Caitlin says, waving her arms as Rosie picks her up.

"Don't take my baby away," Gabe complains. "She's the only one who loves me."

I pat Gabe on the shoulder as I follow Rosie into the bedroom. She wipes Caitlin's face and hands with a fresh wipe and I give her a clean diaper and playsuit.

"Let her wear that little dress I bought her with the sunbeams," Gabe calls out. "She'll be the envy of all the other fashion minded infants at the park."

We laugh and I find the little white cotton dress covered in yellow sunbeams. Rosie pulls it over the baby's head.

"You would have made the ideal daddy," I tell Gabe as we take Caitlin back into the living room for viewing.

"Or momma for that matter," Gabe says with a grin. "Our Mother used to tell all the ladies in her bridge club, 'Now girls, if you'll just find your daughters somebody like my Gabe to marry, they'll never have a minute's worry about what to wear. He knows everything there is about fashion.'"

"Bless her heart," Michael says. "She thinks Gabe is just too nice and shy for most women. Every time we go home, she tells him the right girl's just around the corner."

Later when we round up food and children and begin to load them into my Jeep, I ask Gabe, "What in all of creation got you into Old Time Music?"

He climbs into the back seat with Molly and Caitlin. I am driving with Rosie beside me and Michael riding shotgun. The two older girls ride in the rear seat with little Helen who is teaching them the names of their favorite Rap artists in sign language.

"Are you saying my gender preferences and my musical preferences are a bit incongruous?" Gabe asks, good-naturedly. "Blame it on Michael. He got us into it when he was still in college. Our mother made us take piano lessons from the time we were school aged. And later, both of us majored in music at Emory. We lived together after I finished up and was working at a bank in the day time and playing piano in whatever restaurant around Atlanta I could find work in at night. One of his professors was this old dude who was real into the folk revival thing in the late '50s and early '60s. He took Michael and me to Bean Blossom one time." He looks at me to confirm that I know he is referring to an annual Bluegrass gathering hosted by the Daddy of the genre himself, Bill Monroe. "That was all it took. Both of us started going to any Bluegrass or fiddling convention we could find. I taught myself the five string. I don't exactly go around announcing that this gentleman prefers men to our customers at Picker's Palace or when we're playing somewhere either, for that matter. I've never had the least bit of trouble."

"But what do you reckon Roy Clark or Earl Scruggs would have to say?" I continue badgering him. "Do they allow gay boys into the banjo picker's union?" Gabe has such an extraordinary sense of humor that I can't resist baiting him.

"Why I think if Lester came back to life and reunited with Earl that they'd write a song about it. They could call it, 'Ballad of the Banjo Pickin' Queen,'" Gabe says. "Some of those early banjo pickers and fiddlers were wilder men than I'll ever be. The stuff they tell on Uncle Dave Macon makes me look pretty tame. He used to have fits of depression and some of his family got so worried about him that his brother-in-law drove him to the state mental hospital without telling him where they were going. Uncle Dave figured it out though, and when they got there, he jumped out by himself and ran inside and told the nurse at the desk there was a crazy man in the car out front and then high-tailed it out the back door."

We all laugh and ride a few minutes in silence as I move the car up the I-65 ramp to head for Oak Mountain.

Rosie snuggles into the curve of Michael's arm and says, "I hope to goodness Ree finds Grace Ann. But you know, with Bud and Fred on her case about Tanner and the baby, they might have taken off."

"I just feel like she'd take the kids with them," I say. "From what I can gather, she and Tanner have talked seriously about heading back out West. She's not going to put up with Bud and Fred acting so goofy. Bud's moaning like a lost puppy dog over her and Tanner whenever he's with the kids from what Grace Ann says Ree tells her. And Fred's back on Bud's side now that Grace Ann's found somebody new."

"Momma heard that Fred's hooked up with Brother Anson Gallworthy from the Temple of the Almighty," Rosie says. "Remember, we used to know him back in high school, a long time before he ever became a Holy Roller preacher. According to Momma, Fred got him to talk to Grace Ann and Tanner about their living in sin and what did they plan to do about the baby. Tanner just laughed and Grace Ann showed him the door."

"Lord help us all," I say. "Fred used to be a right sensible Methodist. What's got into him in his old age, aligning himself with the likes of Anson Gallworthy?"

James Anson Gallworthy—a former Seers High classmate, who in our junior year moved out into the county and finished up at Caloosa County High—established the Temple of the Almighty some years back following a "Road to Damascus" conversion. On a return trip from delivering Amway products one rainy night, he hit a pothole and blew out a tire, sending his automobile plummeting into the Caloosa River. As he was struggling to emerge from the submerged vehicle, he vowed to God that if his life was spared, he would turn it over to Him. God kept His part of the bargain, but it's hard to say about Brother Anson.

He immediately began referring to himself as Brother Anson—we all knew him as Jimmy—and purchased an old closed up Baptist mission to hold services. His services are said to be Pentecostal in nature—involving a lot of shouting, and speaking in tongues, and spirited singing and preaching. Some say he had it in his blood all along, since his daddy was a preacher who also worked a full week at White Cotton Mill. Others feel he might have profited from a little more growth in the Spirit before he took to the pulpit. Brother Anson, they say, has fairly substantial knowledge of the scriptures, but his theological erudition is slim to none, perhaps due to his lack of formal religious schooling.

His first congregants were mostly white working class families from the area around his church. As his flashy and fervent preaching style developed, however, he began to attract more educated worshipers. The last I heard, The Temple—as Caloosa Countians refer to it—has a current membership of around four hundred and is looking toward building a new church in a better part of the county. Once a week, Brother Anson broadcasts his "Hour of Redemption" from the tv station at the community college in Good River. All this evangelical activity calls for big bucks, so I'm certain Brother Anson is tickled to have Fred Hardaman at his particular Sunday-Go-To-Meeting. And somewhere in the misty waters of my memory, I seem to recall some prior connection between Fred and Brother Anson that occurred long before he heard the Good Lord a-knocking.

"You know how Fred always was about getting Grace Ann to do the right thing," Rosie says.. "I guess he thought she might mind a preacher quicker than she would him."

"You two have been promising for weeks to tell Michael and me about these friends of yours in Milltown," Gabe complains. We exit the interstate and head up the narrow road to Oak Mountain.

"Soon as we unpack and eat lunch and get the kids settled," I say to him, as I locate a parking spot. "We'll unfold the unfolding saga of Fred and Grace Ann Hardaman and Bud Reese."

We set up camp on a hillside near the playground area. Following our Kentucky Fried lunch, Michael joins Cassie and Meaghan in a frisbee toss while Rosie nurses Caitlin. Molly and little Helen head for the swings at the playground

"My little brother's not got nearly the strong streak of curious that I do," Gabe says, patting his full stomach as he and I seat ourselves on a blanket on the ground. "So, do tell, Miss Ellott, and start at the beginning."

"Once there was, and still is today, a Daddy's Darling named Grace Ann," I begin. "And Daddy Fred loves her to distraction. But Grace Ann is only as good as she wants to be most of the time and this does not sit well with Daddy Fred. He is constantly pulling her in one direction and she's pulling just as hard in the other. She broke his heart by marrying the youngest son of the town bootlegger many long years ago. But Fred came to terms with it and even helped the young couple out with many generous donations from his overflowing coffers. In time, they produced two children, twins named Harley Junior—for Bud—and Ma 'Ree after Grace Ann's late mother. Said offspring are now teenagers and currently reside with Fred due to Grace Ann and Bud's divorce some three years ago. The divorce having resulted from Bud's conviction and ensuing incarceration in Atmore for forgery. Following the incarceration, Grace Ann took off in her RV for the Wild, Wild West where she remained until a few months ago. She is now home and living in a trailer on a plot of land in unincorporated Caloosa County where Fred is having a house built for her. This same trailer is also occupied by one Tanner Hope, a guitar picking carpenter from the great state of Colorado, who has lost his heart to our Grace Ann, who is carrying his baby. Baby is due in late November. Ex-husband, Bud, was released from Atmore in May. When he found that his beloved former spouse is with child by Another, he up and joined some New Agers who have infiltrated Milltown, spreading their heathen ways and flashing their crystals among all the good Baptists and Methodists."

As I pause for breath, Gabe comments, "Now, if that's not prime material for a country song, then I don't know what is."

"That's not even all of it," I say. "Those are just the highlights."

Michael, Rosie and Caitlin soon join us on the blanket. As Gabe recounts the Hardaman-Reese chronicles, Michael pulls a harmonica from his back pocket and plays softly. He finishes with a flourish when Gabe ends his recital.

"You're right, Big Brother, this may have more of the elements of the perfect country song than that Steve Goodman thing," Michael says. "What was it, something like 'She Never Even Called Me by My Name'?"

"Something like that," Gabe says. "Let's see, we could put it in words to accompany your music and call it, 'Bud's Breakdown,' or how about 'Daddy Tried'?"

"What about 'Fated Love?'" Rosie asks, seriously. "I've always felt like Bud and Grace Ann were meant to be together, but they never would be very happy."

The heat of the afternoon fades somewhat and the girls beg us to walk the trail to Peavine Falls. Michael gallantly puts Caitlin in a backpack seat for the steep walk down the slope to the water. Soon we are wading and splashing and thoughts of Bud and the missing Grace Ann diminish. It is nearing 6:00 when we troop back to the car to drive home. All five girls nap on the drive back. We wake Meaghan and little Helen as we stop at their houses to let them out. Still merry from our afternoon of frolic, we invite the boys in for a pot-luck supper and I open the door to a ringing telephone.

"Ell and Rosie's Bed and Breakfast," I answer as the crowd comes in behind me. Rosie takes a sleeping Caitlin to her crib. Gabe, Michael and the older girls settle on the living sofa to play video games. As this pleasant day culminates into complacent domesticity, I am ready for rest.

"Ellott, put Rosalee on the other telephone," Millie says from the other end. "I got some real bad news for you all and you need to hear it together."

"I'm on the line, Momma," Rosie says from the phone in her bedroom. Everything is quiet in the apartment now. The only sound is the faint blipping of the Nintendo game from the living room.

"They found Grace Ann and her friend Tanner, too," Millie says and pauses to clear her throat. "Both of them are dead. Shot to death in that trailer sometime earlier today. They found them around 3:00 this afternoon. Grace Ann's baby died, too. They didn't get to it in time. It was a boy."

Neither of us can speak immediately. I hear a sharp intake of breath on my other phone. Rosie is crying. "Where is Bud?" I am finally able to ask.

"Can't nobody find him. They're saying it's him that done it. Somebody driving by seen him on that motorcycle out there early this morning."

Millie and I talk a little longer. She says that Brother Anson Gallworthy is with Fred and the twins. Millie and Minnie Beth, Sherman's momma, are already calling people to bring food to them all this coming week. Because the Caloosa County coroner's office generally holds bodies in deaths from unnatural causes for several days, the funeral will probably not be held until the end of the week. She promises to call when the time is set. We hang up the phones. Rosie is still crying as she comes to me in the kitchen. We both cry and hold each other for several minutes before we go into the living room.

When we tell Michael and Gabe and the girls what Millie said to us, Molly climbs into Rosie's lap. Even Cassie, who is often irritated these days by physical contact, sits next to me with her head against my arm. Gabe makes herbal tea and brings it into us. We drink it as the miasma of death permeates us.

Chapter Five

When the coroner released the bodies late on Wednesday, Fred arranged graveside services for Grace Ann and the baby for Friday afternoon. The Caloosa County Sheriff had previously contacted Tanner's elderly mother, who asked that his body be flown back to Colorado when possible. Fred is still under heavy sedation and there will be no visitation. The caskets will remain closed at all times.

On Thursday evening Sherman calls to ask Rosie to bring the children to Minnie Beth's Friday morning. Saralee, one of his sisters, will keep them there with her while we attend the funeral services. He wants them to stay for the Labor Day weekend with him there at Minnie Beth's. Old Sherman Lee no longer shacks up with Peggy Ann Prewitt. Last month, he came home early from work to find her still in bed at 3:00 PM and indulging in a marijuana cigarette. Her little boy was playing with his cars on the floor beside her. A lifetime beer drinker, Sherman Jackson does not sanction the use of controlled substances, especially when he is paying the rent. He ordered her out. About a week later, he put his and Rosie's house up for sale and moved in with Minnie Beth. His older twin sisters, whose children are grown and gone, live close enough to help out when he has his children over for the weekend. He calls Rosie often now and wants to talk more to Molly and Cassie.

Early Friday morning, we pack my car and make seating arrangements for the trip home. We discuss where we will lay our heads for the duration of this long and tragic weekend. Since my parents died, I have spent few nights in my home town. I sold our white house on Western Avenue and really have no place to call home in Milltown.

Finally we decide that I can stay with Rosie and the baby at Millie's farmhouse since the older girls will be at Minnie Beth's. Michael and Gabe, who insist on coming with us, will bunk with Sam and Clettus in their cabin. Rosie has not disclosed the full nature of her relationship with Michael to her mother. We plan to introduce the brothers as friends and fellow band members, who came along for moral support and to talk string band music with Sam and Clettus.

"Well, at least Grace Ann didn't die in her majorette uniform," I say, as we move down the interstate into St. Clair county. "Remember how Fred's biggest worry used to be that the band bus would have a wreck and she'd have to go to the hospital in that little short costume."

"Fred never could make up his mind," Rosie says. "One minute he was dragging Grace Ann off to have her picture made in a bathing suit and the next he was telling her to cover herself up, that decent girls didn't show off their bodies like that. I reckon that won't be his worry any more. I feel so sorry for him. No matter how upset he got with her, he thought the sun rose and set in Grace Ann. This is going to make him act crazier than he ever has to date."

Rosie has had no true regard for Fred since an incident, which occurred once after a football game. One of Samantha Jane Seer's own faithful cheerleaders for our junior and senior years, Rosie usually rode with Grace Ann on the band bus to football games. One particular Friday when Grace Ann was grounded for slipping out to see Bud, she was not allowed to ride the band bus and had to go to and from the game with Fred. Out of loyalty, we rode with her. It was mid-October and unusually cold. Fred had a flask of Jim Beam with him and began to really feel it by the time the game ended. He reeled a bit as we walked to where his car was parked. When he opened the car door for us, he pinched Rosie on the butt, reaching up under her cheerleader skirt. She was too shocked at the time to say anything. Of course, she told me about it shortly afterwards. Fred, most likely, did not remember it. It never happened again and no mention was made of it. Rosie, however, is slow to forgive and has politely kept her distance since that night.

As I stop the car at Minnie Beth Jackson's residence and House of Beauty, Molly jumps out and runs inside. Cassie follows a little more slowly. Now in her early seventies, Minnie Beth does not keep a full work week schedule of hair appointments. She still tends to her regulars, women who have come there once a week since the late '50's. She only works now when she wants to. There is a large "CLOSED" sign on the storm door of the House of Beauty. I take Caitlin from her car seat and go inside behind Rosie, Michael and Gabe. We find Minnie Beth in the kitchen making potato salad. Cassie begins to help her cut up boiled eggs and Molly adds mayonaisse.

"Hello, honey lamb," Minnie Beth says to Rosie, giving her a big hug and smiling a hello at me. She holds no grudges over the divorce. Sherman may still be the apple of her eye, but that does not mean she is blind to the rotten spots. Over the years, she came to love Rosie as much as her own daughters. "Isn't this awwwwful," she says, drawing out the word mournfully. "And Fred Hardaman is one pitiful sight. He can't say two words without busting out crying."

"Minnie Beth, this is my friend, Michael Pace," Rosie says as Michael gives her his hand. "And his brother, Gabriel," she indicates Gabe, who is standing beside me and Caitlin. He extends his hand as well. "I play and sing in a string band with them and they were with us when we got the news about Grace Ann, so they offered to come with me and Ell and the girls."

"According to Ellott and Rosie, you are the Vidal Sassoon of Milltown," Gabe ventures, turning on casual but courtly charm. "They say people come from miles around just to have your fingers in their hair."

"Now, I don't know about that," Minnie Beth says, blushing a little. "I do right well with some of the older styles, but it's hard to keep up with everything changing so quick. One day they're wanting corn rows like the black folks and the next it's buzz cuts, even for the women. I've never seen the like."

I try, unsuccessfully, to hide a grin as Gabe talks cosmetology with Minnie Beth for a few minutes to try to prevent her questioning his and, particularly, Michael's presence. Minnie Beth is as gracious as always and probably not really fooled by Gabe's gabbing. It is unfortunate that her son didn't learn manners from his momma. Sherman comes in from outside and, after grasping his older girls in a big hug and giving Rosie and me a brief squeeze on the shoulders, nods curtly at Michael and Gabe. He reaches for Caitlin, who reluctantly leaves my arms. He has met Michael and Gabe once before. Rosie has said nothing to Sherman about her and Michael's relationship. However, Sherman being the control freak that he is, I can sense the antennae of suspicion emerging.

He cuts his eyes to me, and I say, brightly, "I heard the Confederate Cove is open for business again. Why don't we go there for lunch before we go out to the cemetery?"

"That's a fine idea," Sherman says, as he awkwardly pats Caitlin's back when she begins to fuss. "We can show your friends a little of Milltown's culture. Tell you what though, let's go by Miss Samantha before we go eat. Can't leave Caloosa County without paying your respects to Miss Samantha."

A few moments later, as we follow Sherman's old blue pick-up into Good River, we explain the socio-economics of Caloosa County to Michael and Gabe. A small body of water—Red Creek—rather than the requisite railroad tracks, divides Milltown from the more affluent Good River. In our growing-up years, the "good" residential part of the city was actually the tail end of the Appalachians, an area reverently referred to as "The Mountain." It is not that way now. The county's population is moving southward toward the Caloosa River and away from the city of Good River. Both Milltown and Good River itself have been strangled by economic downturn in recent years, dying in that languid way that Southern towns do.

In the '60s—when all our world was young and things seemed more hopeful—we burned the roads of the main thoroughfare between Milltown and Good River to get downtown. Now, as we reach Good River Avenue, smack in the middle of town, we point out the courthouse and accompanying jail, and many of our favorite shops from earlier years. The street ends at the foot of the Caloosa River bridge where the statue of Samantha Jane Seers stands. Michael and Gabe have been thoroughly versed in the lore of Samantha Jane's heroic double back ride behind Confederate General Bilson Beauregarde Woods in 1863. The "Sun Bonnet Heroine," for whom our alma mater was named, stands noble and proud in all of her granite glory. We get out of the car and stand with Sherman on the grass below the statue.

"Old Bud climbed up there one night and kissed Miss Samantha right on the lips," Sherman says. "Me and him'd been riding around drinking beer before he done it. Liked to broke his fool neck. Bud's a good old boy. I just can't believe it's him that did that to Grace Ann and her friend."

Gabe and Michael stand respectfully back as Sherman, Rosie and I stare wordlessly at Miss Samantha for several more minutes and then at each other. None of us can think of what to say. Everything about the last week makes our past seem as unreal and unnatural as a painting by Norman Rockwell. Perhaps, we are thinking that if we just blink our eyes a few times, we'll be back in high school. Our biggest desire back then was a future without parental constraint. Before we leave, Sherman puts his hand over his heart and softly sings our alma mater.

The front wall of the Confederate Cove is solid with video games—flashes of light and noise replacing the old juke box. Piped in music from the local Oldies' station fills the room. Sitting on the corner of Seers Avenue and Broadway, some five blocks from the high school, our little culinary spot of paradise has been restored to some of its former splendor. New red leather pads the u-shaped benches of the booths in back. A new shiny chrome soda fountain has replaced the old one. Its '50s diner decor suits well, giving the mostly vacant block a little life. For many decades, Seers High football victories led to snake dances up and down these streets and ended in love feasts of burgers and fries at The Cove. Olive Ann, the thin-faced, sharp-tongued waitress who pulled duty behind its counters for over thirty years, now owns the place along with her husband, Buck.

"Sherman, do you remember the afternoon Olive Ann chased you with a spatula down Seers Avenue?" Rosie asks him as the five of us stand just inside the door, looking for a place to light. "What was that all about, anyway?"

"Seems like to me that I bad-mouthed her cooking," Sherman tells her with a sharp look. "You know a lot of women just can't take negative talk from a man."

"And some of us pay no attention to it at all," Rosie says, refusing to start a fight. Sherman has hovered over her like a dog around marked territory all morning, making ambiguous remarks and trying to start something. Rosie isn't having it.

"How about a round of Mortal Kombat?" Sherman challenges Michael.

"Sounds good to me," Michael says, quietly, as they go to the front of the room.

Old Sherman Lee may be biting off more than he can masticate. Although he often lets Molly and Cassie win, I've seen Michael wipe Gabe out more times than not in this particular video game. I consider these new additions to the refurbished haunt of our halcyon days. Local high school boys can no longer romance their dates with rock-and-roll love songs emitted from jukeboxes. They can't feed their quarters into the slots and select, say, "Cherish," by The Association, or "Baby, I Need your Loving," by Johnny Rivers, or even some smarmy, seductive single by Gary Puckett and the Union Gap and then stare some girl into submission. Video screens don't seem to inspire such intimacies.

Rosie and I slide into our old booth in the rear and Gabe sits beside us. Some of our old friends are here, many with unfamiliar spouses. Grace Ann's murder being region wide news, perhaps they are here for the services. Former brunettes with tiny waists are now bottle blondes in size-18's. Many of us from the last class of the Soulful Sixties, however, have only added a few pounds and some gray hairs, embellished with a hardening of facial features no longer softened by youth and illusion.

Many of the chaotic forces of the 1960s that so rocked the rest of the country were slow to reach North Alabama. Political and social changes crept in at a turtle-like pace. Popular music, however, was an exception. The Beatles, the Stones, et al were very much present and attending in all of our lives except for Bud Reese's. To this day, Elvis is the Once and Future King. He once sweet-talked the former owner of Confederate Cove into keeping fifty of the two hundred jukebox slots filled with Elvis songs. Grace Ann, who by that time was very into dating Bud because of Fred's ill-concealed dislike of him, pronounced that very act the coolest thing she had ever encountered. The rest of us endured it because of Grace Ann. One Friday night after a lost football game, Bud played "Hound Dog," for what seemed hours. Every time some hapless Seers High player wandered into The Cove, Bud shouted, "They said you was high class, but that was just a lie," referring, I suppose, to their ineptness on the field. We were all a bit high on defeat and Rebel Yell and thought it all too funny until the quarterback pulled his pocket-knife on Bud. Olive Ann showed us the door around midnight. I almost loved Bud that night as we all stood on the sidewalk, trying to decide who was sober enough to drive home. And he winked at me as he and Grace Ann climbed into the back seat of Sherman's car.

The newspaper accounts of the murders are filled with speculation about the absence of Bud Reese, but they have been unusually kind and sparing of feelings in their assessments of Grace Ann's last few years. The actual details of the murders are gruesome, according to Minnie Beth. Neither Rosie nor I have read all of the accounts.

I am whispering comments about the classmates that I recognize to Gabe when someone calls out, "Ellott Hailey Seers and Rosalee Culp Jackson." An enormous woman in a black tent-like dress that extends to her mid-calves is making her way toward us through the crowd. Past the layers of fat, I see that she is one of Bud's older sisters, Mary Joyce.

"Well, hey, Mary Joyce," I say to her as she stops in front of our booth. "How are your Momma and Daddy?"

"They're holding up all right, I reckon," she says as she sits down heavily beside Gabe, who nods his head at her. "Cain't a-one of us believe that Bud done this thing. If it was him, though, I personally feel that it was them New Agers must of got into that boy's mind. Ain't nothing else could make him do something as awful as that."

"I've never heard of New Agers being into violence," Gabe comments. "Most of them are just recycled hippies with a new name tag. Peace and love and all that."

"Well, all I know is that he moved in with that bunch from California that wears the crystals that's a-livin' across from the high school. They've done messed up what's left of my baby brother's brain. What with them flashbacks from being in Viet Nam and then getting sent off to Atmore, he ain't been cooking on all four burners most of the time anyway. There's not no telling what kind of mess them people's brainwashed him with. They've done took his soul," Mary Joyce says, trembling righteously.

"I am truly sorry," I say to her, for lack of anything better, and pat her dimpled hand.

"I can tell you for a fact that all in the world he wanted when he got out of Atmore was to get right with Grace Ann and them children.

When he found out she'd hooked up with somebody else, he went off the deep end. Maybe he thought them people and their crystals could help him get Grace Ann back. All that craziness they teach has done took the place of the Lord Jesus in his heart. I reckon he's just come undone." Rising with difficulty, she waddles away.

"Lawsy, Miss Scarlett," Gabe says in his best Butterfly McQueen imitation as soon as she is out of hearing range. "I don't know nothing about them heathens with the evil crystals."

Before I can come up with a witty retort, Michael and Sherman join us at our booth. Michael sits down beside Gabe. Sherman pulls Rosie to her feet and they go over to a couple from our graduating class who married and endured. I search the crowd for the faces of the few boys who once hugged me tight after winning football games. I cannot find a single one.

Sherman's belly jiggles as he walks. Michael's slimness is that of a dancer's. Neither man has been able to move his eyes from Rosie with her dark hair floating freely over her shoulders. At a recent Bluegrass festival, I watched Michael buck-dance to another fiddler's "Cripple Creek,"—his long legs graceful and rhythmic in that most pedestrian of dances. On that day I truly accepted Rosie loving him. But, past and present sins aside, old Sherman Lee is still a vital part of that fondly remembered camaraderie we share from our years at Samantha Jane Seers High School.

It certainly is old home week here today. The majority of our graduating class within driving distance made the trip for Grace Ann's last rites. In this very room, the women come and go and talk about cellulite and growing children. Everyone speaks to Rosie. And today she is not the free and independent working mother with the too young lover. Instead, she plays dutiful ex-wife and friend as she slips her arm into Sherman's.

Sherman is sailing, soaring in this company of familiar strangers. His head bobs like the ones on those insipid toy bulldogs that are often mounted in the back windows of mufflerless Chevys as he talks up his newly expanded garage/service station/Circle K store.

"Fresh doughnuts delivered every morning," he tells them of his convenience store and pats his pudgy middle. No one sees that it is loneliness, like so much dead air, that has inflated him as of late.

"Rosie's going to have to come back to me so I can put her to working the cash register," he punches her lightly on the arm as she looks over at Michael and smiles.

"Maybe if old Bud ain't sent off to the Big Yellow Mama, he can come back to work for you," someone I don't immediately recognize comments.

"Say what you will about him," Sherman says. "But remember one thing: Bud Reese is a grade-A mechanic. He just went nuts a few years back when Grace Ann started wanting all them things he couldn't afford. He started spending money that wasn't his. Poor old boy never was bad, just not real smart about women."

"I call blowing Grace Ann's face off pretty bad," a woman says. "It ruined her so they couldn't even open the casket."

"I heard Bud got real agitated when he learned Grace Ann was pregnant," someone else says. "But I don't ever recall his being violent before."

"It's not been proved that he had anything to do with it," Sherman says. "But Bud come up with a pretty rough bunch over there in the Hollow. Even a good man can go nuts when the woman he loves takes up with somebody else." He looks pointedly at Rosie, who quickly leaves his side to talk to another classmate.

It seemed to us that all of those years ago we let Bud into our lives because of Grace Ann and eventually grew to care for him. Later, we forgot him when anxiety got the best of him and he turned to petty crime. It could be that he did pull the trigger. Grace Ann tried to leave him, but Bud did not want to turn loose. Maybe Grace Ann got to feeling that she married neither wisely nor well and later paid for it with her life. While a good man may be hard to find, a bad one's even harder to lose.

Lawson Funeral Home's dark green canopy is stretched above the folding chairs that face a lectern standing beside the newly dug graves. Standing near their mother's casket, Ree and Harley, Jr., hold hands. A smaller casket sits beside it. Both are closed and covered in sprays of white roses. Rows of cars line the path leading to the community church that sits in the middle of Cedarwood Cemetery, located in De Kalb County. It lies in a small valley, a two-lane highway topping the hills above it. My parents and my father's people are buried here. Years ago when they first moved to Milltown, Fred and Ma 'Ree visited this little country graveyard with my parents. They loved it at first sight and chose it then as their eternal resting-place.

The murders have attracted an embarrassingly large crowd. The cemetery's parking area is full to overflowing. Cars line the graveled drive leading to it and extend to the edges of the road beyond. Men and women in their Sunday best mill about the churchyard. A photographer snaps pictures as more people arrive, making their way up the graveled drive lined with oaks and hickories. The cemetery dates to the early nineteenth century. It is filled with hardwoods and lasting memories. Magnolia trees and cedars shade its many rows of graves. After searching unsuccessfully for a spot in the cemetery's lot, I end up parking the Cherokee down the road in front of a cotton field and the four of us make our way through the crowd to the funeral site.

"It's only the Good Lord's mercy that them kids was at Fred's when Bud come a-blastin' in," a red-faced woman in a brightly colored dress says to us. "I got no doubt but that they'd be as dead as them others."

Rosie and I answer her, proclaiming Bud's innocence until more of the facts are in, but we stop talking when Fred comes slowly up the path. Leaning heavily on Brother Anson's arm, he moves like an invalid. Dark glasses shade his eyes. He acknowledges no one as Brother Anson leads him to his seat on the front row. He sits in silence, staring at the open graves.

It is some thirty minutes before the service is to begin. Rosie goes over to speak to Ree and Harley, Jr., taking them both in her arms. Michael and Gabe stand beside me as I point out various classmates of ours who married and stayed that way. There are five or six couples. If the words from that old Motown classic—"the purpose of a woman is to love a man"—are true, then I've somehow missed the boat. Except for an undisclosed two month period during my college days, I have spent my life alone.

Michael leaves us to join Rosie. Impulsively, I turn to Gabe, "I want to show you something," I say and lead him to the top of the hill.

There is a grove of cedars in a fenced family plot belonging to an earlier generation of the Seers family. A rusted iron fence encloses four graves with eroding tombstones. At the far end, a crumbling granite lamb sits atop the marker on a child's grave. The epitaph, barely visible, reads "Sweet Jesus called his Little Lamb home. Jesse John Seers, June 28, 1879-December 20, 1880."

"Don't you find that touching in a maudlin sort of way?" I ask him, indicating the little lamb. "I adore this place. I used to play here a lot as a kid, on Decoration Day and when my parents came to tend to the graves."

"I like cemeteries myself," Gabe admits, bending his large frame and squatting to examine the moss covered gravestone. "Think that makes us fellow ghouls or something? I heard that people who frequent grave yards have a secret death wish."

"You're the second person to say that to me," I tell him. "The first one is dead."

"And just who was he?" Gabe asks in a gruff voice, smiling as he stands up. Over the past couple of months, we have developed a great affection for each other, indelibly Platonic as the day is long, but there nonetheless. He jokingly plays the jealous suitor.

"For about two months in the early '70s, he was my wedded spouse," I tell him, surprising myself. No one other than my deceased parents ever knew of my short-lived marriage. "We had a picnic here once at this very spot."

"Ellott Hailey Seers, last of the vestal virgins, was married?" Gabe is surprised now and walks around me, mouth open in disbelief. "I've got to hear about this before I believe it."

"Cross my heart," I say, and doing so, briefly related the tale of Bryan and Ell.

We were twenty and twenty-one, I and my husband, and our two-month, furtive marriage was still unreal and exciting. I was a sophomore at The University and an English major and Brian was a junior majoring in art. We met during the fall quarter at an all night film festival held outdoors on Woods' Quad. And later, as the leaves tumbled around us, we fell in love. He was my first real boyfriend. Christmas break was a time of yearning and sighs and anxiously awaited telephone calls. A few weeks into spring semester, we eloped, spending a quick weekend honeymoon in Yazoo, City, Mississippi, before returning to classes on Monday morning. Our hasty plan was to tell our parents at the end of the semester. I continued to live in my dormitory room and he in his apartment, where I would go to stay long hours into the early mornings of most days.

One Sunday in April, we drove to this very cemetery to spend a long afternoon. Following food and wine, we talked, my young husband and I, of Viet Nam and his draft number, seven. Bryan often stayed in his apartment and painted instead of attending classes. With an average somewhat below the C range in most subjects other than art, he had little hope of academic success or avoidance of military service. He wouldn't, he told me, stay around and let those Army Nazis come to take him. He would go on up to Canada and send for me from there.

My clearest memory of him is an evasiveness in his eyes as we drove from the cemetery that afternoon. Bryan Best died three days later in a head-on collision one hundred miles from the Canadian border. I will never know whether he ran from the rumor of war or the actuality of life with me. I often imagine him in this cemetery, but his body lies over in Rome, Georgia, where his folks live.

I took my final exams early that year and went home to tell my parents of my marriage and of Brian's death. Several weeks after the accident, I met Bryan's mother and father in a restaurant on the outskirts of Rome. Just before he died, he wrote home about his new bride. My father drove me to Rome to meet the Bests. I talked with his parents that day of Bryan and his talent as an artist. Before I left, his mother gave me a small painting of Bryan's of an unclouded sky above a lake. There are human figures on the shore, but you cannot distinguish their features. It hangs in my bedroom in the apartment. The next fall, I returned to Tuscaloosa where I remained to complete my undergraduate degree and later enroll in graduate school, where I double majored in English and Library Service.

I tell all this to Gabe rather matter-of-factly, in a steady unemotional voice. When I finish, he removes his sun-glasses and dabs at his blue eyes.

"Christ, honey," he says to me. "It's no damn wonder you're shy of men." He links my arm in his and we go down the hill to Grace Ann's funeral.

Chapter Six

The canvas-topped chapel is full to capacity. People stand beneath magnolias and in the cedar grove nearby. The Confederettes, the all-girl choir from Samantha Jane Seers High School, is warming up. Gabe and I slip into the seats Michael and Rosie saved for us near the front. I nod at Sherman and Minnie Beth, who are seated across from us. Rosie's momma, Millie, and her Uncle Sam sit to the rear of us. The Confederettes open with "In the Sweet Bye-and-Bye," as Brother Anson bends over Fred, Ree, and Harley, Jr., talking to them in a low, gentle voice. He continues talking as the Confederettes go into "When the Roll is Called Up Yonder." I recall being somewhat discomforted by that song and its classroom references as a child. I was an inveterate daydreamer, prone to not answering when my name was announced. I worried that I might be denied entrance to the Pearly Gates for not paying close attention. As the choir finishes, Brother Anson steps up to the lectern. Clean shaven and graying at the temples, Brother Anson is portly but dignified in his Sears and Roebuck blue suit and striped tie.

"Beloved people of God," he says into a portable microphone that resounds clearly across the graveyard. "We are together here today to pay our loving respects to Grace Ann Hardaman and her unborn baby boy. Cut down like the corn in the fields before it ripens, they have gone to be with the Father and the Son. Grace Ann was a loved and loving woman. Her children, Harley, Jr., and Ma 'Ree, will remember her as she brightened their lives and gave of herself to them. To her Daddy, Fred Hardaman, she will always be his little girl, the bright and shining star of his life after his wife, Ma 'Ree, went to her rest."

Fred sits immobile, one arm around each of Grace Ann's children. Harley, Jr., is crying, but Ree is as stone-faced as her grandfather.

Brother Anson continues, "We cannot dwell on these last few years of Grace Ann's life when she drifted away from her loved ones after her marriage broke apart. Divorce is an evil thing. Many good people go wrong during this difficult time. It does not reflect her whole life. As a young girl, she attended church whenever the doors were open at Milltown Methodist. She sang in the choir each and every Sunday. I believe that in the last moments of her life she got right with her God."

Women touch handkerchiefs to their eyes and the men beside them pat them absently. I glance through the crowd to see if Bud's people are here and spot them standing respectfully to the side of the tented area.

"Jesus forgives and Jesus saves," Brother Anson says. "Jesus will even forgive the murderer of Grace Ann Hardaman, her friend, Tanner Hope, and their unborn baby. We do not know who committed this heinous sacrilege. In our hearts, we may harbor some suspicions, but until it is proved in a court of law, we cannot know for certain."

"The fate of the murderer of these good people is in God's hands," Brother Anson goes on. "As David said in the Psalms, 'Do not worry about the wicked. Do not envy those who do wrong. Quick as the grass they wither, fading like green in the fields.' Let us go now to the Lord in prayer."

The crowd listens with closed eyes and bowed heads to Brother Anson's words. "Lord Jesus, make us worthy to enter into your kingdom some day. Free us from the clutches of sin and the shame it brings us and our loved ones. Cleanse our hearts and fix our minds on your saving grace. Amen."

"Amen," the crowd responds.

Brother Anson then says, "If any one of you here does not know Jesus as your personal Lord and Savior, today is the day to meet Him. It's as simple as a prayer. Ask for His forgiveness and surrender yourself to his loving embrace. Then, as He promised, you will receive riches untold. Now let us join hands together as we close with the Lord's prayer. Our Father…"

Much of the crowd joins hands for the recitation.

As the last "amen" sounds, a tall, blonde Confederette sings two verses of "Amazing Grace," and the funeral is ended. Brother Anson leads Fred to his car. Ree and Harley, Jr., look about uncertainly until Mary and John Reese, Bud's parents, and some of his sisters come over to them. They all leave the gravesite together. As their cars trail dust and gravel in their wake, the Reeses and Fred Hardaman leave so that the attendants from Lawson Funeral Home can put Grace Ann and her baby into the ground.

Minnie Beth offers to feed out-of-towners or anyone else hungry back at her house in Milltown. As some of the other mourners move from the graveyard, Sherman comes over to me. Rosie and Michael are sitting in my car. Gabe stops to introduce himself to Rosie's Uncle Sam.

Sherman loosens his tie. "I'm glad we're not at an age where we're called on to go to too many of these things. I am wore out. You all planning to come back to Momma's for a bite to eat?" He looks over toward my car where Michael is tickling Rosie's face with a frond from one of the mimosa trees. "I reckon you can bring the odd couple if you've got to."

"Are you referring to Rosie and Michael or Michael and Gabe?" I ask him. Sherman Lee Jackson can be the least tactful person on God's green earth when he sets his mind to it.

"I mean that long-haired baby hippie that's hanging all over my wife," Sherman says. "And that homo brother of his. How much longer do you think that boy's going to keep going after Rosie?"

"Until Rosie asks him to stop," I tell him. "They're both nice men, Sherman. And Rosie's not your wife any more."

He opens his mouth to argue, but decides to bide his time as Michael, Rosie and Gabe come over to us. "I was just asking Ell whether ya'll are coming to Momma's house to help eat up some that grub," he says as pleasantly as his nature will allow him. "She's fixed enough food to satisfy most of the county."

The four of us confer briefly and agree to do it, only to forestall trouble. Sherman climbs into the restored '65 Mustang he drove to the funeral. Minnie Beth waves him on, indicating she will ride back with neighbors who remain in the graveyard, waiting to pay last respects after the graves are prepared. The late summer sunshine belies the tragedy of the day. We get into my Cherokee, silent and weary from the strain. Rosie lays her head in the crook of Michael's arm. Gabe reaches over to rub my shoulders as I turn the car onto the last of the dirt roads leading to the main highway. As we round a curve, a black motorcycle buzzes past us like a big fly. Bud Reese swerves the Honda to the side of the road and motions us over. I pull the car up behind him and we get out. Sherman stops up ahead of us.

Bud dismounts his motorcycle unsteadily and stands beside it. His prison pallor is darkened by a few weeks in the sun, but he is still rather unearthly in a '50s style pink sports coat, dark slacks with a stripe up the side, a lacy shirt and saddle shoes. His dark hair is combed to a pompadour and his sideburns extend to his earlobes.

"Thank you all for coming," he mumbles. "Thank you very much."

"Bud, are you all right?" I ask him. "I am so very sorry about Grace Ann." I go to his side and hug him briefly. His clothes are grimy and he is sweaty from riding. He must have been on his motorcycle for days.

"Somebody's done killed her. She's done gone on to the other side," he says, still in a mumble, twisting his hands despairingly. "But that's all right. We're going to be together again, her and me. Somehow, some way."

I look to Sherman and Rosie for help. Sherman goes to Bud's other side and grips his arm. "Hey, buddy. Is there something we can do for you? You want us to take you to your momma and daddy's?"

"Cain't go there," Bud says. "Cain't get there from here. Been so long on lonely street I'll never get back."

"How can we help you?" Rosie asks him. Michael and Gabe stay near the car as we continue talking in low, soothing tones to this stranger dressed like Elvis circa 1956, who is currently occupying Bud's body.

"Help me get to Grace Ann," he says, urgently. "They said her and me's got other chances in other lives. We might be happy the next go-around."

"Who said that to you?" I ask him as he begins to pace and wave his arms.

"Them folks that I been living with that's taught me about crystals and channeling," he says, impatiently, as though we should know this. "They showed me how to reach the King's spirit. Me and Elvis are one now. And something else, too: they said me and Grace Ann's done had our time together in this lifetime, but that we might could get together in the next, if we get evolved enough. That's what I went to the trailer last Sunday to tell her."

"And how did you tell her?" I ask, softly.

"That's just it, I didn't tell her. She was laying there dead and that man that took up with her, he was dead, too. This old life's done treated me mean and cruel. Broke my heart, tore it all apart. I been on my bike and I been riding for days. My insides is shaking like a leaf on a tree. I got to find where Grace Ann's gone to. Got to find her." He is sweating as though he has been running, not riding, for days. He gets back on the Honda and rides away before any of us can stop him. Dirt and gravel fly as his motorcycle churns the North Alabama hills.

"Jesus in heaven," Sherman says. "We got to call the cops, don't we?"

"Yes," I say. "Even if it's like he says and he didn't really do it, he needs some help. Where is it he thinks he's going?"

"To the next life," Gabe says. "But I'm not sure he's too clear on where that is, cosmically speaking. His grasp of reincarnation theory is a little 'ass-backwards,' to say the least."

New Age philosophy does have its limits with redneck sensibilities. Bud has understood just enough to confuse himself. Sherman, Rosie and I try to decide where the closest phone might be as two police cars tear past us, heading for the highway. Sherman has a police scanner in his Mustang and listens for a few minutes to hear them say that they lost Bud when he veered off the interstate and into the woods.

On the way back to Minnie Beth's we stop by Sherman's Circle K/Service Station/Garage to see the latest changes. He has replaced the old service counter and put in a snack area. He has plans for more improvements. Something about the meeting with Bud seems to have hit home with him. He is friendly to me and Rosie, ceasing his accusations, and is even polite to Michael and Gabe. He offers us coffee and doughnuts and invites Michael and Gabe to see the rest of his little commercial kingdom. They go with him to the garage while we wait inside.

Rosie and I stand near the cash register, beside where the week's newspapers are displayed. Sherman saved all the news of the murders. The tobacco-chewing clerk behind the register passes papers to each of us. A six-column photo of attendants carrying the bodies away dominates last Monday's Good River Journal. "Double Murder in a Double Wide: Daughter of Local Businessman and Friend Slain," the headline reads. The article spares no details in describing the bullet-ridden bodies. Every article makes a reference to the missing Bud Reese and his possible implication.

"Poor Bud," Rosie says when she finishes reading. "He can't let go of it, can he? He can't come out of the past. That's where his life is and that's where he wants to stay."

I agree with her. We are all haunted by what went on before. William Faulkner once said that in the South, the past is never dead; it isn't even past. A remark I've always considered right on target, even coming from an old alcoholic white man. On the drive to Minnie Beth's, I can think of nothing but Grace Ann and her baby on the hillside, down in the cold, cold ground.

Sated beyond satisfaction on Millie's apple cobbler, Gabe and I rock away Saturday evening from the confines of the Culp front porch. With two more days of the Labor Day weekend before us, Gabe and I are content to recap the past several days since the murders. Michael and Rosie are out sparking in the woods that surround the farm. The baby is inside, asleep under Millie's watchful care. Molly and Cassie are spending the remainder of the holiday with Sherman at Minnie Beth's.

Gabe sighs with palatal contentment. "Rosie's momma is nearly as good a cook as mine is. For all her occasional Savannah blue blood pretensions, Amelia Gayle Pace can spread a fine country table when she wants to."

"Is your mother from one of those 'fine old Southern families' we all know and love?" I ask him, teasingly. Gabe and I share similar views on lineage—that it matters little if you turn out well but seems to account for a great deal if you don't.

"Blood rich and cash poor," Gabe says. "That's our daddy's favorite line whenever they get into a tiff. Speaking of family genes, is there anything in your friend Bud's background that would account for his performance Friday afternoon? To quote him and his mentor, 'I'm all shook up.' Between meeting up with him yesterday and the murders and the funerals, I haven't had this much emotional turmoil in my life since Michael and I ended up in jail when we were still living over in Georgia."

"Do tell," I say, moving my chair closer to his.

"It started out one fine summer evening when this cop pulled us over for speeding," Gabe says, tilting his rocker and propping his size 12 Nikes on the porch railing. "Normally that would have been of little consequence, but Lady Luck gave us the middle finger that time. My dumb-butt brother was smoking a joint just before the cop stopped us. He put it out quick enough but the good officer was blessed with excellent olfactory senses and knew that it was not burning leaves emanating from our automobile. We went to 'a party at the county jail' that night for sure."

"How did you get out of it?"

"Our daddy has been one of Savannah's finest boys in blue for nearly forty years and he used his connections to get us a suspended sentence, right after he got through screaming at Michael for 30 minutes. Needless to say, we have not partaken of the killer weed while inside a moving vehicle since that time."

"Bud will be 'dancing to the jailhouse rock' his own self unless the local law enforcement folks can find another suspect. After yesterday, I can't say I really think that it's him."

"Something's got him spooked though," Gabe says. "And I don't think it's just the ghost of Elvis. Was he one of those that claimed the King never died?"

"Yes, indeed. Thought so for years. Apparently he's changed his mind though if he thinks he's communing with the King's spirit. For a long time though, Bud bought every National Inquirer that had Elvis sightings on the cover. That was back in the days when he and Sherman were working together. Sherman egged him on for all it was worth. He got friends of theirs to call Bud at work and say they'd just seen Elvis at a truck stop in Oneonta or someplace. And Bud would drop whatever he was doing to high-tail it over there."

"I can picture Sherman getting a certain pleasure out of that," Gabe says. "He can probably be a mean one if he sets his mind to it."

"Indeed he can," I tell him. "He hasn't totally gotten the picture about Rosie and Michael yet, but when he does, Michael had better look out."

"My little brother can put that grease monkey away any day, any time," Gabe says, firmly. "For that matter, so could I."

I look at him in surprise. "I don't really see you as a fighter. You don't seem…"

"You mean, my muscles must be flabby and my wrist limp because I like men?" Gabe smiles. "Ellie, for such a smart woman, you have some disappointing attitudes."

"I didn't mean it that way," I defend myself. "I mean that you just don't seem violent."

"If you're gay in certain parts of the South, you learn how to take care of yourself," he says. "Situations come up where my winning smile and these baby blues no longer do the trick." He bats his long-lashed blue eyes at me. "More elementary measures are sometimes needed."

"You do have beautiful eyes," I tell him.

'Why, ma'am, if it wasn't for these baby blues, I'd still be a virgin today," he says with a wink. "What about you? What won the heart of young Bryan Best and why wouldn't it work today?"

"It might, if I wanted it to," I say, anxious to change the subject. "You've heard about as much of my story of heartbreak and desire as I'm willing to share. I am not by nature romantically inclined. Sex is easily expendable in my book."

"So, no more 'gettin' down' for Ellott Hailey Seers?"

"Just give me my Eric Clapton records and some chocolate and I'm perfectly content," I say.

"Say what?" Gabe is laughing. "You're into chocolate?"

"Oh, definitely," I tell a disbelieving Gabe. "Godiva is best, naturally, but Russell Stover or even a Whitman's Sampler will work."

When he stops laughing, he tells me what doing chocolate means in gay and bisexual vernacular. I am, to say, speechless, and try to decide how to better phrase my substitution of eating chocolate for engaging in sexual intercourse. Some married friends of mine and I share this particular practice. We even formed a club, calling ourselves Chaste and Monogamous Chocoholics Anonymous, wherein we are able to maintain fidelity and/or purity by indulging in a chocolate binge whenever we get the hots for someone to whom we are not wed. We jointly decided that it beats the hell out of phone sex and is not nearly as distasteful as pornography.

Michael and Rosie emerge from their wooded bliss and join us, sitting side by side in the swing. Together, we critique each other's theories about the murders. Gabe contends that if Bud did do it, he was not cognizant of it at the time. I say that Bud may not have been involved at all, since newspaper accounts indicated that several things were missing from the trailer. Robbery may have been a motive. Rosie feels it could be some long lost suitor of Grace Ann's from our high school days. Male jealousy, she says, often knows no bounds.

"It's probably the New Agers," Michael says, as dead-pan as possible. "You know how those secular humanists are. Not a moral scruple among them."

This causes all of us to smile a bit. Those not of the Christian persuasion are often the object of ridiculous rumors in this heartland of fundamentalism. Whoever the perpetrator is, Fred Hardaman will find him or have him found as soon as he is able to manipulate without medication. Knowing old Fred, he'll have anybody remotely connected with law enforcement hot on the trail of Grace Ann's killers.

On Sunday morning, Gabe and Michael join Sam and Clettus in a little backwoods jam, filling the fields and farmyard with wild banjo picking and mournful fiddle tunes. Rosie joins in and before long I sing along with them. When we all but shout the chorus of "I'll Fly Away," Millie herself comes over and pats her foot to the good Gospel hymn.

Some good will must have been generated by our spiritual sing-along for on Monday when we are packing the car to leave, Millie, Sam and Clettus sincerely invite the boys back anytime they want to come. They wave until we are out of sight down the dirt road. Michael winks at Rosie and chalks one up in the air.

Back at work on Tuesday, I spend my lunch hour walking the trail below the library/civic center. Down at the highway intersection beyond the jogging trails, there is a black Honda motorcycle waiting for the light. I stop a moment to look closer to see if it is Bud.

As traffic starts to move, the rider weaves through Volvo's and BMW's. Brakes squeal as he zips through and collides with a tractor-trailer rig coming through the intersection. I begin to run toward the accident. I have not seen the driver's face. Passersby leave their automobiles to aid the biker lying in the road. Within minutes, paramedics and police cars surround the accident scene.

"Please let me see him," I say to a police officer controlling the crowd. "I think it may be somebody I know."

A large, black paramedic leaning over the prostrate biker says, "Sorry, baby. This one's dead. Dead and gone."

He and another man lift a stranger's body onto the stretcher and get him inside the ambulance. The body is a small, blonde man's and the license plate on the bike is from Mississippi. The crowd breaks up and heads for their cars. The truck driver, supporting himself with one hand against the cab of his truck, stares open-jawed at the wreckage. Moving through the shards of glass and metal, I go to his side and take his other hand in mine.

Chapter Seven

Tuesday morning at Paradise Dry Cleaning and Laundry, Mabel June Long wants to be Ethel Mertz. At home yesterday, sick with allergies and apathy, she watched a Lucython on one of the cable channels. She decides that she could do that: be chunky sidekick to crazy Lucy with fractious Fred to pay the bills, live in a nice apartment and not have to work. It's a thought worth pondering as she rips the sales sheet from the pad and copies Monday's sales into the ledger. The day's cleaning hangs on racks to be bagged. She opens a box of powdered sugar doughnuts and eats.

"Is my favorite dry cleaning lady here this morning?"

Mabel June looks up to see Mickey Mann standing at the door with dirty mechanic's jumpsuits in his hands.

"She's ba-ack," Mabel June drawls. "Did you miss me? Come look here at my new sign."

A small wooden plaque that reads, "I've got what it takes but it breaks my heart to give it away," rests on the edge of the front counter by the ticket spike. Mabel June purses her lips at him and winks, jokingly, as she twitches her bulky body.

"Well all right then," Mickey laughs as he hands her two pair of coveralls, oil splotched and pungent. "Rosie was so busy in here yesterday when I come by that I didn't get a chance to ask her where you was. Did you have a mental health day, or what?"

"Or what, I reckon," Mabel June tells him. "I got over it though."

"Not much option about that, is there?" He asks.

"Now that's the truth if I ever heard it," Mabel June says as she writes the ticket for his clothes. "You want these back tomorrow?"

"Fine," he says and shakes his head as she offers him the ticket stub. "No reason to give me that. I'd just lose it."

"See you then," Mabel June says as he goes out the door. She lights a cigarette and drops into the swivel roller chair. In high school, Mickey was her friend. She was her thinnest self then—188 pounds stark naked in the early morning before breakfast. All the men who come into the cleaners now that she knew as high school boys joke with her and are generally pleasant as they exchange soiled clothes for a ticket and a promise of service. She briefly imagines marriage to each of them. She knows all of their children's names, but not their wives'. Later today she will see Fletcher, her new florist friend from the Fleur de Lis down the street, who is due to pick up his gardener's smock, crisp with a little starch.

Later when Rosie comes in to work, the two of them remove mounds of clothes from the dry cleaning machine and set them aside to be pressed. As the presser, a thin black man who rarely speaks, finishes, they place each piece on a wire hanger and bag it. As Rosie attaches the tickets, Mabel June hangs each piece of clothing on a revolving rack. They work quickly, endlessly it seems to Mabel June, until they finish just before noon. Soon the lunch crowd will be in. Mabel June runs her fingers through her damp red hair and wipes her sweaty face with her sleeve before she sits down.

"I am ready for this day to be over and done with," she tells Rosie. "I don't know how I stood it here without you, Rosie-Posie. I hate it that that sorry butt from the home office didn't send you anybody to fill in for me yesterday. That's their general m.o. over there though—work the crap out of you, give you little if any help and if you mess up, it's still your fault. If I didn't have fifteen years of retirement built up and some stock in the company, I'd quit tomorrow."

"I'm just glad to have a job," Rosie says. "I've told you before, it's the first time since before I married Sherman that I've worked for pay. It pleases me to have my own money."

"If you've got to work, I'm glad it's here with me," Mabel June tells her as she reaches for another doughnut. "Did I tell you that Fletcher come by again when you were gone to lunch on Friday? He left me a jade plant this time. Makes me wonder what it is he's up to."

"It would seem to me that he likes you," Rosie says. "This is the second time he's brought you something from the Fleur de Lis. Did you say he's the new owner?"

"So he tells me," Mabel June answers her. "Says he owns a number of businesses and likes to visit them all every so often, just to keep his hand in. Said he bought this flower shop back in August and he's just now got around to visiting it. He says he'll be coming around every two weeks or so to help Horace, the manager, out. That's why he brings his smock and doesn't pick it up again for awhile."

"Wonder where he lives?" Rosie asks her. "Must not be around here."

"He's not ever said, exactly," Mabel June says. "But I think it must be close to where you and Ell come from. He talks about spending a lot of time driving on I-59 between here and Chattanooga."

"Find out his last name," Rosie says. "If I don't know him, Ell probably does. What does he look like?"

Before Mabel June can answer her, four secretaries from UAB come in to pick up their cleaning. Rosie waits on them while Mabel June finishes up in back. Mabel June collects the powdered sugar residue from the doughnut carton on her fingers, licks them, and throws the carton in the trash. The morning's sugar intake and the fumes from the dry cleaning fluid leave her dizzy and light-headed. She sits down among the newly bagged clothes and drops her head down, trying her best to get it between her knees.

At 5:00 p.m. as she heads down the sidewalk toward her car, she sees Fletcher in the window of the Fleur de Lis. His dark head is bent over an arrangement of roses and baby's breath and he does not notice her at first. Remembering that he has not been by to pick up his smock, she hurries back to the cleaner's and retrieves it from the rack. Returning to the flower shop, she taps on the glass and Fletcher looks up and waves to her to come inside. He wipes his hands on the soiled smock he is wearing and holds the door as she enters.

"I'm so glad to see you," Fletcher tells her. There are crescents of dirt under his fingernails. He smells of roses and fertilizer. "If you hadn't come by, I wouldn't get to see you again until week after next when I come back."

"Well now, we couldn't have that, could we?" Mabel June says, smiling and winking a little. "I'm glad to see you, too. That plant you give me the first time is not doing too good. What do you reckon can be done about it?"

"You mean the pot of bluets?" Fletcher asks her. He takes the clean garment from her and goes to the back of the store to put it on.

As he returns, he repeats his question. When she affirms that it is, he says, "Maybe I ought to come by your place and have a look-see. Plants and flowers are a lot like people. They've got to have special attention to thrive."

"I bet you know just how to make them do that," Mabel June says.

Moving closer to him, she notices how his lined face contrasts with his shiny dark brown hair. She thought before that he might wear a hairpiece, but decides she really doesn't care. No one has paid her this much attention since Bobby Joe Sutton, Mickey Mann's best friend, in the 11th grade. He took her to the movies and sometimes she met him in the boy's locker room after school. Bobby Joe had a cast in his left eye that made if difficult for her to tell whether he was focusing on her when they made love. When he died in a car wreck five years ago, Mabel

June went to the funeral and sat in the back pew so she could cry without his wife and little boy seeing her.

"I've got the cure for all that ails it," Fletcher tells her, winking smugly.

They settle on a time for him to come by later in the evening and she gives him directions to the house her momma left her when she died two years ago. She leaves the flower shop, but stops to watch Fletcher in the window as he bustles about, fussing with flowers and plants. His gardener's smock billows about him like a clergyman's cassock.

At 7:45, Mabel June stands in front of the bathroom mirror, carefully applying another layer of Maybelline to her pale red lashes. Cascades of gold bracelets dangle from both wrists. The telephone shrills and she stops to answer it.

"M.J.," Rosie says on the other end. She always addresses Mabel June this way since she told her that the love of her life, Bobby Joe Sutton, called her that. "I'm on the committee at the girls' school for the Halloween carnival this weekend and we're in a pickle. One of the mothers canceled out on us. We need somebody to give out grab bags. Can you help us? It's this Friday night."

"Shoot, honey, I can do you one better," Mabel June tells her as she sprays a mist of Chanel No. 5 into the air around her. "I'll get my old Pick-a-Pocket Lady costume out. I used it all the time for things like this a few years back. It's this great big tent-like thing covered in pockets. I put prizes in all the pockets and the kids get to choose which one they want. They love it. I walk up and down the hallways and they can stop me any time."

"Wonderful," Rosie says. "I can't tell you how much I appreciate it. The girls will be glad to see you again, too."

"Likewise," Mabel June says. "And don't go leaving that baby at home. She's the cutest little young'un I've seen in a long time. I got to go now. My plant doctor's coming by soon."

"I want to hear all about it tomorrow," Rosie tells her as they finish their conversation.

Mabel June slips large gold hoops into her earlobes and studies herself again in the mirror.

"Ready or not, here I come," she says and goes into the living room. She flips through her CD collection until she locates *Sinatra's Greatest Hits*. Somehow, Fletcher just seems to her like the Sinatra type. Bobby Joe was partial to Bruce Springsteen.

Old Blue Eyes is crooning "All the Way," as she shows Fletcher into her living room shortly after 8:00.

"I brought you something from the shop," he tells her. "These are real special roses, Fusiliers. They were left over from a wedding. Got to get them in water quick. I brought some Prolong with me and if you put that in the water, they'll last nearly two weeks." He hands her the flowers and the packet of Prolong. Mabel June goes into the dining room and returns with a lead crystal vase. She places the flame colored bouquet in it and sets it on the coffee table in front of Fletcher.

"That certainly is fine music," he says, listening for a minute. "What might you have in the way of something to drink?"

"How about a little Jim Beam?" She asks and Fletcher nods his approval. Frank is singing "Strangers in the Night," as she goes to the kitchen for the bottle and a glass.

"I bet you take it neat, too," she calls out to him.

"You got it," he says and smacks his lips as she brings him his drink.

He sips silently for a few moments until he finishes and then lights a cigar he pulls from his jacket pocket. He takes a few puffs and then says, "Let's take a look at that plant of yours. Maybe we can fix it up." He stubs the cigar out in an ashtray as she leads the way.

They walk to a glassed-in room in back, where Mabel June keeps her plants. The pot of withered bluets is in a darkened corner. Fletcher flicks his cigarette lighter to get a better view. "Looks like these have done dried up," he says. "I'm afraid we'll have to dispose of them." He touches her arm. "Let's take them outside and I'll show you what we need to do."

Cicadas serenade like distant ambulances as Mabel June shows Fletcher into the back yard. It is a humid night and Fletcher leaves his jacket inside. They kneel together under a full moon to bury the dead plants beneath a pile of leaves.

"Later on you can chop all this up with your mower and make a nice mulch for your grass," he tells her. He takes her hand and pushes it into the damp mixture. "See how nice that feels. You can even add the petals from the roses when they die."

Pulling Mabel June against him, Fletcher presses her hand against his crotch. She moans and tosses her head. He blinks as though he can't quite see her face. The dead leaves and flowers are wet against her back as Fletcher softly eases Mabel June onto the ground.

Some time ago Mabel June became certain Friday mornings at Paradise Dry Cleaning and Laundry were God's little payback for her multitude of sins. From 7:00 until noon, every blue collar worker she knows brings in bag after bag of dirty work clothes and piles them in front of her on the counter. Tickets cover the spike, their stubs scattered like used condoms on the floor. Her only respite is that the home office actually agreed to send in a substitute so she can leave at lunchtime to help Rosie prepare for the Cahaba River School's Halloween carnival that night. She looks up from the cluttered counter to see Mickey coming in the door.

"M.J.," he greets her and throws his dirty coveralls to her. "How's my buddy today?"

"Like Old Minnie Pearl always said, 'I'm just so proud to be here,'" Mabel June answers him. "But only because I'm out of here in thirty minutes. What's the weekend got in store for you?"

"I'm going with my wife and kids to the Cahaba River School's carnival," he says. "I'm supposed to man the spook house."

"Rosie's got me lined up for a job at that thing, too," she tells him. "I'm not going to tell you what it is. You'll just have to be surprised when you get there. But you can bet it ain't the kissing booth."

They both laugh as she writes out his ticket. Rosie hurries in the door, carrying Caitlin on her right hip. A witch costume is draped over her left arm.

"Hey, there," she waves to Mickey as he leaves the shop. She turns to Mabel June. "I need a little bit of cleaning fluid to get a stain off the skirt of this costume. Can't have a messy witch now, can we?"

She looks at the counter piled with clothes and tickets. "I thought they were sending you a substitute for this afternoon. What happened?" She hands Caitlin to Mabel June as she walks to the back of the store for a bottle of cleaning fluid.

"She'll be here in a few minutes, I hope," Mabel June says, shifting the baby to her other hip and wincing when she turns the wrong way. Rolling on the ground with Fletcher the other night put her mind and body all out of sorts. Caitlin is feeling her face. Her soft little fingers feel like air on Mabel June's skin, not rough like Fletcher's when he dug into her.

"By the way," she says to Rosie. "I want you to meet somebody since you're here. I'm going to surprise Fletcher with some lunch in a little while. I reckon he came back to town for something today, because I saw his car in back of the Fleur de Lis when I was parking this morning. Maybe you could go with me, just to say, 'hey.'"

"For a minute, maybe," Rosie tells her as she dabs at the grease spot on her costume. "I've got four billion things to do before that carnival even starts."

The substitute worker arrives. She helped Mabel June out a few times before Rosie was hired, so only minimal instructions are needed. Mabel June hands the baby back to Rosie and goes into the small bathroom in back to pat her hair into place before she leaves the store.

"Come on down to the Fleur de Lis in a few minutes," she tells Rosie as she stands in the doorway. "I got to run over to the Golden Temple for the sandwiches, but that won't take long. I really do want you to meet him. That Fletcher's something else."

Walking carefully back from the Golden Temple a few minutes later, she carries a bag of sandwiches and two cups of herbal tea. She hopes Fletcher will approve her choice—veggie pitas with various cheeses. An ecumenical partaker of good food—low fat or fat laden, Mabel June usually visits the Golden Temple every Friday. She hopes to impress Fletcher with her health conscious eating.

As she approaches the Fleur de Lis, she spots him inside with his back to the window.

He is holding the hand of a thin woman in blue jeans. Mabel June trundles closer to the window. The smiling woman holds a plant in her free hand. One lone Fusilier rose is draped carelessly over her ear.

Moving back into the shade of the tall plants and potted trees that line the front of the store, Mabel June waits while the woman leaves. Fletcher does not see her as he stands in the open doorway. Cleaning his hands on his soiled smock, he calls the woman's name as she climbs into her sports car. She waves and drives away and Fletcher goes back inside.

For just a few minutes, Mabel June has some trouble breathing. She is uncertain whether her arms and legs will function well enough for her to leave her hiding place without having to ask for someone's help. After taking several deep breaths, she moves cautiously from the sidewalk jungle and lays the sack of sandwiches and cups of tea down in front of the store and ambles slowly to her car. She does not hear Rosie calling her name from down the street.

Unable to catch Mabel June, Rosie and the baby pause briefly in front of the Fleur de Lis. Framed in the front window, Fred Hardaman, wearing an ill-fitting toupee and gardener's smock, is hard at work with a large arrangement of cut flowers. Rosie and the baby hurry away before Fred can lift his eyes to see them.

Ghosts, goblins and ghouls throng the hallways of Cahaba River School. Mabel June's head feels all light and electric as she passes them, looking for Rosie. Many of her customers from Paradise Cleaners touch her arm in recognition, but she pays them no mind. Walking slowly and deliberately, she holds a sack of goodies in her right hand and her costume is folded over her left arm. She considered not coming at all tonight following the afternoon's revelation of Fletcher's true nature. But then she thought of Rosie and her children and came any way.

She babysat the girls a few times when Ell had to work on weekends that Rosie's band was playing somewhere. Once she french-braided Cassie's hair and then did Molly's when she begged her to. She rocked little Caitlin outside on the balcony in the warm night air until she almost fell asleep herself. Later that evening when the girls were in bed, she took clothes from all the closets in the apartment. She even found a man's shirt and jeans she supposed belonged to Michael. She arranged the sets of clothes side by side on the living room sofa and placed one of Caitlin's rompers on the baby swing. Then she stood back to admire her handiwork: a disembodied family at home for an evening of relaxation in front of the television set. Her little family.

Inside a classroom lit with lanterns, a woman in gypsy garb holds a small boy's hand and strokes his palm. One Fusilier rose is wound into the woman's bandana. She points wordlessly down the hallway when Mabel June asks which room holds the country store.

"We're back here, M.J.," Rosie calls to her as she sticks her head out of the classroom on the far end of the east hallway. "Come on down."

Rosie, Ell, and several other women supervise the tables in the well-lit room that contains baked goods, homemade crafts, clothing, toys and other treasures. Michael and Gabe man a special table of folk-crafted instruments near Rosie and Ell. Rosie offers Mabel June a fudge sample from their table. She eats it quickly as Rosie explains the layout of the school. When she finishes talking, Rosie asks her to model her costume. Mabel June shakes the wrinkles from the orange and green tent-like garment and pulls it over her head. Then she ties a green bonnet over her red curls. She twirls on her toes for them, arms extended. Michael, Rosie, Gabe and Ell give her a standing ovation and begin to take goodies from the bag to fill the pockets.

"Kind of like a choir robe, huh?" Mabel June asks, closing her eyes as she feels their touch against her body. When the pockets, seventy-two in all, have something inside them, she straightens the garment from the top, preparing for her journey.

"I've had this thing for ages. My Momma made it a long time ago so I could wear it to things like this back when I was living at home with her. It's been awhile since I've done it, but I think I can get back into it with no problem. I was pretty good at it, to tell the truth. Little kids just love getting to reach in the pockets and pick what they want without having to pay for it."

"You may be mobbed," Ell tells her. "You know kids can't resist anything that's free."

"Them nor anybody else," Mabel June says. "At least not until they figure out that you get what you pay for." She waves goodbye to them and as she moves down the hallway, she notices that the cloak lies flat. It does not puff up like Fletcher's gardening smock.

"Come back by here after you go around once," Rosie calls to her. "I'll put on my witch costume and go with you next time."

"When are you going to tell her who her boyfriend is?" Ell asks Rosie as she straightens a table of rag dolls dressed in antebellum clothing.

"Not now," Rosie says as she puts more fudge on the candy table. "She seems a little rocky to me tonight. I think something must have happened between her and Fred. She didn't stay long at the Fleur de Lis, if she went in at all, and she wouldn't turn around when I called to her."

"It probably wasn't anything good," Ell says. "Fred's gone around the bend this time for sure. Why do you think he told her his name is Fletcher Smith?"

"God only knows. Isn't his full name Frederick Smith Hardaman? Ell, you should have seen him in that awful toupee. He was a lot scarier sight than anybody you'll see here tonight. Be interesting to know what he's up to."

A distraught Molly, in fairy princess attire, comes into the room just then, carrying a broken tiara. Rosie takes her hand, saying, "Here, honey. Let's look in Miss Hamilton's cabinet and find some glue. We can fix it." Together, they go to the back of the room and look in the supply cabinets.

"Fred probably hurt Mabel June's feelings," Gabe says. "She sure is quiet tonight and that's unusual for her. Most of the time, she's so busy trying to top my one liners that nobody else has a chance to talk."

"If Fred's anything like Rosie says he is, he's probably just going to use her and lose her," Michael says. "Those charmer types usually operate like that."

"Will one of ya'll take this baby for awhile?" Cassie asks as she comes in, carrying Caitlin. She wears a granny dress and sports granny glasses. Her long brown hair, flowing freely down her back, is laced with flowers. A "Make Love, not War," sign trails behind her on one side and Caitlin is balanced on the other. "Meaghan's here and we want to go see the Fortune Teller."

Michael reaches out to a pumpkin-suited Caitlin, who jumps into his arms. Her little mouth is ringed with a red sticky substance and she grins happily from the center of it. "Found the cotton candy, did we?" He comments.

"I just gave her a little," Cassie says. "You know what's the coolest thing here?" She does not wait for their answer. "Mabel June in that pocket suit. She's like this gigantic kangaroo on steroids or something. Everybody wants to find out what's in those little pouches." She takes a piece of divinity from the candy table, hands the attendant a quarter and takes her leave.

Children's hands and faces looking up follow Mabel June through the winding hallways. She stops every few feet for another child to reach a hand into one of the pockets and slowly withdrawing it, either smiling or frowning at what came out. If a child looks too disappointed, Mabel June tells him to put the prize back and try again. Got to make them happy. Relaxing a little, she strolls regally through the building. Hosts of costumed children call out to her and like a celebrity accommodating her fans, she graciously stops to allow them to choose a treasure. Tonight, they're her children. When she is alone again, she locates the packets of flower seeds in the inside pocket of her cloak. She decides to put them in the outer pockets for the children.

That afternoon, Fletcher knocked for several minutes at her front door and then pressed the doorbell. Mabel June sat silently in the house, listening to the ringing bell. After a time, he went away, leaving a box of flowerpots, soil, and seed packets. Mabel June considered throwing the whole lot into the trash, but at the last minute slipped the seed packets into the inner pocket of the Pick-A-Pocket Lady costume to bring to the carnival. Some little boy or girl would want them. Bluets and other unusual flowers and plants will bloom in their gardens when spring comes again.

It takes Mabel June several tries to open the security door at Paradise Cleaner's on Monday morning. Over the weekend, the home office installed heavy metal barred security doors in response to a rash of burglaries in the twenty-chain store. She leans hard against it and when the tumblers finally click, she lunges inside, almost falling on her face. To Mabel June, this management action is just another prime example of penny-wise, pound-foolish spending. What they need are security systems for each of the stores—with motion detectors keyed to a command pad. Without security bars on the windows, the doors will do little to stop determined robbers. But then again, nobody asked her.

Intensely focused on the door situation, she almost misses the envelope stuck on the ticket spike on the front counter. Addressed "Miss Mabel June Long," it is pink and rose scented. The letter inside is four sentences long and Mabel June commits it to memory before Rosie arrives and then puts it in the trash.

"Goodness," Rosie says as she comes in and hangs her sweater on a hook in the back room and locks her purse into the desk drawer. "I believe the weekend crew actually did some work here on Saturday for a change. And I see they got the doors up. This place isn't in as big a mess as it usually is on Monday morning."

"Miracles do happen," Mabel June says and places a new sales sheet on the clipboard. "I had me one good time on Friday night at the carnival. That Cahaba River School's something else now, isn't it? I bet there's not another one like it in the whole country."

Rosie considers the Cahaba River School, a privately funded educational institution for K-8, a gift from God. It was opened in the late '70s with a trust fund from Janson B. Northfleet, a retired Army colonel. Miss Northfleet, who returned to Birmingham to spend her twilight years, was a devout believer in quality education for all. Feeling that she was undereducated and consequently chose the military for her life's work, she vowed to make a better choice available for others with limited income. By endowing a family inheritance and her own life savings to the establishment of the school, she provided a way for Birmingham children with modest family incomes to be as well-educated as their wealthy suburban peers south of town. Naming the school for the county's largest river, she limited its enrollment to two hundred.

The school carefully interviews and investigates each applicant's family. A generous sliding scale fee system is used to determine tuition payments and tuition is often waved entirely for families whose income warrants it. Emmeleine Riley, director of Ell's library, is a long-standing board member and used her influence to gain admission for Molly and Cassie.

"That school's sure made my life less hectic," Rosie says. "I don't have to worry about them there. And all of the mothers were real pleased with your Pick-A-Pocket Lady. They asked me to make sure you'll come back next year."

"Of course," Mabel June tells her. "But have I got to wait a whole year? Is there some other way I could help the school out?"

Rosie says, "We'd be glad to have you anytime. They need volunteers to read to the kindergartners and to make cookies for special days. I'll be glad to give the volunteer coordinator your name."

"Do that," Mabel June tells her. "I need to get focused on something. Maybe I won't be idiot enough to get involved with somebody else like that Fletcher. He turned out to be a ringtailed tooter if there ever was one. He left me a letter, too. I reckon he did it on Saturday when he knew I wouldn't be here. It's exactly four lines long, and I quote, 'Mabel June, I treasure our night together. You will always occupy a part of my heart. My business will take me away from home and prevent me from returning to Birmingham for some months. When I can come back, I will give you a call. Regards, Fletcher Smith.' How's that for a 'Dear Jane'?"

"I need to tell you something about him, M.J.," Rosie says as she begins to staple tickets to laundry bags. "His name's not Fletcher Smith. It's Fred Hardaman. He's the father of that friend of mine who got killed the weekend before Labor Day. You remember the one whose funeral we went to that weekend?"

Her jaw slack with astonishment, Mabel June finds it hard to speak for a few minutes. She gets up from the desk chair to help Rosie with bagging and stapling. In a few minutes she says, "'Katie bar the door!' as my grandma used to say. You mean that Fletcher, or Fred, is the daddy of that girl that got her head blown off in that trailer? The one with the teenaged twins and the Colorado boyfriend and the baby on the way? God almighty, that must make that man 60 to 65."

"More like 70 or better," Rosie says. "Didn't he look a little old in the face to you, in spite of that ridiculous wig?"

"Well, as they say, love is blind," Mabel June says, shaking her head ruefully. "Mine wasn't just blind, it was deaf and dumb to boot. I haven't made this big a fool of myself over a man since high school. When did you figure out who he is?"

"On Friday when you asked me to meet you at the Fleur de Lis," Rosie says. They finish bagging and stapling and she goes to the front door to open up for the day. "I saw him in the window after you had already gone down the street. I knew something must have happened between you two then or I'd have told you right away who he is. I've known Fred since I was little, back when I first met Grace Ann. He's always been kind of an odd-ball, but since Grace Ann died, he's really whacko. Sherman's momma, Minnie Beth, told me he's stopped most of his drinking and is taking Prozac. Everybody knows how crazy that can make somebody. That's what that Lorena Bobbit was taking when she whacked off her husband's privates. You're lucky Fred didn't do you more damage than he did, whatever it was he did do."

They are interrupted as a very small woman with a baby on one hip enters the store. A little boy holds on to her jeans leg. She deposits two bags full of soiled clothes on the floor in front of the counter.

"Would I be able to pick these up by Wednesday?" She asks politely as she gives Mabel June her name and address for the ticket. "Mickey's got clean jumpsuits to last until then. He's working over at the Bessemer Jiffy Lube this week or he'd be in here himself. He says you're always so good to ask about the boys. This here's Moses," she points to the little boy beside her. "The baby's Amos. Jeremiah's in the second grade at Cahaba River School and he's doing real good. I forgot to say, I'm Judith Ann."

"Well, hey, Judith Ann," Mabel June says with a smile. "I'm glad to finally meet you. I guess Mickey told you him and me finished high school together. You've got a nice husband." She gives her the ticket stub.

"You'll have to come in more often. Maybe we could go to lunch or something."

"That would be good," Judith Ann says. "My sister keeps the boys for me sometimes. I could ask her next week. I'll give you a call." She waves cheerily as she leaves with her sons.

"She seems sweet," Rosie says as she and Mabel June sort the clothes for the laundry pick up. The store only does dry cleaning at the branch. Laundry is taken to a central facility over in North Birmingham.

"Yeah, she does," Mabel June agrees. "But isn't it strange how women never seem to be jealous when their husbands are friends with a fat woman? I guess they must think we're no threat. Not of course that I'd be interested in Mickey Mann. He was Bobby Joe's best buddy and me and him have stayed friends since high school. It'd be like having a crush on your brother. Not that I've got any brothers. Just two sisters, both as big as me. Both of them's married though and got bunches of kids. One of them's husband's a pretty good man, but the other one's a slug demon from hell itself. He beats up on Jenny Sue and the kids. And she'll leave him and then he'll cry and she'll go back to him. That's happened more times than I can count. Maybe I am better off single. I know I couldn't put up with that."

"Sherman never did that, but he did things that were almost as bad," Rosie tells her. "Any woman that wants to bad enough can get married. Finding somebody that you can live with without wanting to murder him in his sleep is something else all together. Getting back to Fred though, what did he tell you about himself?"

"All he ever said was that his wife died a long time ago and he has a grown up daughter," Mabel June says as she opens another bag of clothes. "He certainly never mentioned grandkids. He talked mostly about his businesses. The flower shop was something he got into recently and was still trying to learn about. He said his best friend is his preacher and that the two of them spend a lot of time riding around in his Cadillac. Doing what, he didn't say."

"I can tell you what," Rosie says as she takes a load of freshly cleaned clothes from the machine to the presser. "The preacher is Brother Anson Gallworthy who heads up the Temple of the Almighty in Caloosa County. Fred and Brother Anson are hunting for Bud Reese, Grace Ann's ex-husband. They think he's responsible for the murders. I get the idea that Fred's plan is for Brother Anson to save Bud's soul real quick and then Fred's going to kill him."

"Is that the truth?" Mabel June says, horrified. "Lord above, I'm going to forget I ever knew that man."

"I'm exaggerating a little," Rosie says. "But if they do find him, Fred'll drag him to jail personally. He's not at all adverse to carrying a gun. I don't know about Brother Anson."

"I believe it best that I turn my attention to being a help to little children like you suggested," Mabel June says. "They're usually real grateful and they don't lie like a dog to you at the first opportunity."

Chapter Eight

The day is here. The much debated *New Age Gardening in the New South* seminar will begin in an hour. In early to facilitate the setting up process, Ell directs two maintenance men lining up chairs and tables in Meeting Room Number 4 in the Rotunda of Athena Villa Library/Civic Center. The conference, which is the baby of the mayor's new wife, has been subject to endless speculation among Athena Villans since it was announced two months ago. Perri-Young Snowden, the thirty-something wife of fifty-something Mayor Handy Snowden, is determined that the event will be well attended.

Hanford "Handy" Snowden,—longtime mayor of Athena Villa—wed Perri last spring in an outdoor service held in the rose garden on civic center grounds amid a flock of doves with a Unitarian minister conducting the services. Concealing distaste because of affection for Handy, nearly six hundred Athena Villans attended the ceremony. Having been a widower for nearly ten years, Handy was eager to do anything to please his bride-to-be. A real estate agent most of her adult life, Perri-Young decided when she sold Handy his spacious new house that she would very much like to live there with him and things developed from there.

A devotee of aromatherapy, channeling and holistic health practices, Perri-Young quit real estate altogether shortly after she said, "I do," to seek further enlightenment. She then set about to usher Athena Villans into the Age of Aquarius with subtle attempts at injecting New Ageism and Political Correctness into its midst. This seminar is her first big coup. Sensing in Ell an open and intelligent mind, she enlisted her early on to help bring the gardening seminar to fruition. Perri and several of her peers are due to arrive momentarily to oversee the morning session.

A tall, full bodied woman wearing a dashiki and Birkenstocks with knee socks enters the meeting room. Flanked by a teenaged boy carrying several boxes, she holds an armload of notebooks and gardening manuals balanced against her chest. After showing the boy where to put the boxes, she gives him her car keys and tells him to get the other things from the trunk. Arranging her notebooks and manuals on the speaker's table at the front of the room, she looks up and smiles a greeting at Ell, but then looks more closely at her.

"Didn't I meet you somewhere recently?" She asks Ell.

"Perhaps in another lifetime?" Ell considers, but does not actually ask. Then she recalls where she saw the woman, and says, "Two months ago at a funeral in DeKalb County?"

"Of course. Bud Reese's ex-wife and her baby," the woman says. "Bud told us so much about them and he was so devastated by it that I felt like I had to go, even though I no longer conform to Judeo-Christian customs regarding the migration of souls." She speaks the last part of this sentence as though she has rehearsed it.

Towering inches above her, the full-hipped woman with healthy, flowing hair and no make-up appears about five or so years older than Ell. The woman straightens the crystal she wears around her neck and extends her hand. "I am Zaia-Danda of New Age Gardening, Inc. I live in the house where Bud's been staying in Milltown. You must be Ellott Seers. Bud told me you work at a library in Birmingham, but I had no idea it was this one."

"Is Zaia-Danda really your name?" Ell has to ask her.

"My birth name is Mary Jean Jones," Zaia-Danda says with a self-contained smile. "I use my evolved name because it is more suited to my new self. Bud told me quite a lot about you and your friends Rosie and Sherman. And of course all about Grace Ann and Ree and Harley, Jr. He's not been around much since the murders, of course, with the police so hot on his trail."

"Have you seen him at all since the funeral?" Ell asks her as Zaia-Danda begins directing the teenager in setting up gardening tools, pots of soil, charts and other materials for the session.

"Twice," Zaia-Danda tells her. "He called once in the middle of the night and asked me to bring some clean clothes to a spot in the woods he told me how to find. The police have been watching the house every second. I'm certain they've got the phones bugged, but I've got a cell phone I keep in my purse and that's how he called me. He was in such a rush we didn't get to say much to each other. Frankly, I just haven't told the police about it. I don't really think Bud did it."

"Neither do I," Ell says. A few people are beginning to wander in. Perri-Young and three of her expensively dressed friends wave to Ell and Zaia-Danda from the doorway. "Can we talk more about this?" Ell asks her. "I'd like to hear any kind of news about Bud."

"We break for an hour and a half at 12:30," Zaia-Danda whispers to her. "I'd really like to get away for lunch. Since I'm not being paid for it, I don't intend to spend it answering questions. My car is the white Honda CRX in the back parking lot. Meet me there at 12:35 or so, if you can get away."

Zaia-Danda greets Perri-Young and her friends enthusiastically. Ell smiles and nods, edging away as they women tighten a circle around Zaia-Danda.

"...just the beginning," Perri-Young is saying. "We started with plants because they're harmless and Zaia's so knowledgeable, she'll draw them in like flies. After this one, we can move on to aromatherapy or meditation. Then maybe we can try channeling later on, since that's what seems to scare all the Christians so much."

Ell stands in the hallway a few more minutes as Zaia-Danda goes over the itinerary with her admirers. "This morning's session is 'Holistic Horticulture.' It's really an overview of everything that New Age Gardening incorporates, with some specifics on chemical free pesticides and how to show respect for each form of plant life in its various stages of process so that it achieves its maximum potential. This afternoon, I do 'Cultivation Through Channeling.'"

The group breaks up as Zaia-Danda moves to the registration table. She and the boy accept each $50 fee, log it carefully beside the registrant's name into a ledger, and place the money in a strong box on the floor beneath them. The room is nearly full as the boy closes the meeting room doors and the session begins.

Beneath the trees at the edge of the parking lot behind Athena Villa Library/Civic Center, Ell removes her sweater. Many of the leaves have dropped from the trees, but Indian Summer has arrived, leaving it quite warm for early November. In a few minutes, Zaia-Danda exits quickly from the rear door. She waves to Ell, motioning her over.

"Is there somewhere we could go that the others from the seminar might not be?" She asks. "They're really quite motivated, but I have to have a little quiet time so I can conserve my energy for the rest of the afternoon."

"How about the park at the end of the playing fields?" Ell suggests, holding up a bag of sandwiches, chips and two bottles of water. "I got these from a sandwich shop up the highway by Food World that makes wonderful pitas. Is that okay?"

"Perfect," Zaia-Danda tells her, clutching her arm in gratitude. "Lead the way."

She and Ell walk the winding jogger's trail that leads to the park. They spread their fare on a table under red and golden maple trees. Zaia-Danda eats her pita quickly and starts on the chips before Ell hardly begins.

"All that talking and moving around starves me to death," Zaia-Danda tells her. "But now I can tell you about Bud while you eat."

"Before you start, you have to answer one question," Ell says. "What in all of creation is 'Cultivation through Channeling'? I'm not trying to insult your beliefs, but surely you don't expect the good garden club members of Athena Villa to communicate with the spirits of flowers to make them grow better?"

Zaia-Danda laughs. "That's just an attention grabbing title. Channeling refers to the irrigation system, not to extrasensory activity. I like to generate a little controversy just to keep things interesting."

"That's good to hear," Ell says. "New Age practices are subject to great misunderstanding and misinterpretation, even in affluent places like Athena Villa. How did Bud Reese ever get connected to your group? The last I knew, his mother and most of his family still goes to the Baptist mission church in The Hollow. Do you think he understands much about what your group believes?"

"Certainly not all of it," Zaia-Danda admits. "My brother, Joe, who also lives with us, met Bud at an auto supply place last summer. Joe was trying to fix one of our cars and had to go get some parts. Mechanics is really not Joe's thing. He's an excellent computer programmer, but the inside of an automobile leaves him mystified. When Bud tried to give him some advice, Joe just brought Bud home with him to fix the car. They ended up making a trade-off. Bud could have a place to sleep and something to eat if he kept the cars running and the plumbing and what-not fixed inside the house. It worked out great for everybody."

"Rosie and I saw him right after the funeral," Ell says and tells Zaia-Danda of Bud's fixation on the spirit of Elvis and his seeking of Grace Ann in the great beyond.

"Bless his poor misguided soul," Zaia-Danda says when Ell finishes. "I knew about some of this already. I actually told him some of those things myself, but not quite in the way he understood it. I had the feeling he wasn't totally grasping he concepts of karma and reincarnation, but I had no idea he had it that muddled."

"You have to keep in mind that he's a high school graduate who served several years of active duty in Viet Nam and who has spent the majority of his working life with his head under an automobile hood," Ell says. "Eastern religious philosophy would go right past him unless he can connect it to something concrete, like being taken over by Elvis's spirit and trying to locate Grace Ann somewhere tangible."

"Actually, I sort of encouraged the Elvis angle," Zaia-Danda admits. "He seemed so traumatized by losing Grace Ann and her having somebody else's baby on the way, that I thought if he could become like his idol then he might take on that Elvis ego and win her back. He had the distinct impression that she wanted to go back to him, but couldn't because of Tanner and the baby. He also said Fred encouraged him to try and get her back. He found that real odd, because Fred apparently never liked him much before. Bud said that when Fred found out about the baby, he nearly went nuts. He was even saying Grace Ann ought to have an abortion. He told Bud that if he would just act like he used to—all sure of himself and everything—that Grace Ann would come back to him."

"Grace Ann always did like that about him," Ell says, finishing her sandwich. "Over the years, he sort of lost his confidence when he couldn't seem to earn the kind of money Grace Ann needed."

"From everything he said about Fred, Bud didn't really have to make a lot of money. Sounded like Fred gave them everything they needed and more," Zaia-Danda says. "And apparently his always being around and poking into their lives caused lots of problems for Bud and Grace Ann. Bud felt like he could never do anything good enough. Whatever he did, Fred did something a little better."

"Fred has focused the total of his energy on Grace Ann and his businesses since Ma 'Ree died when Grace Ann was 11," Ell says. "He can't even stop now that Grace Ann's dead. I'm sure he's pestering the

Caloosa County Sheriff's Department on an hourly basis for updates on the investigation."

"You don't know the half of it," Zaia-Danda tells her. "He's even put up a website."

"Lord above," Ell says. "I didn't know Fred was computer literate. How did that come about, do you know?"

"My brother Joe set it up for him," Zaia-Danda says. "I know that sounds crazy, but it's really kind of a good thing. Joe and I met Fred when we sold him the Fleur de Lis. Joe and I owned three flower shops until a few months ago when we decided to do New Age Gardening full time. So, we advertized the floral shops in the paper in Good River and here in Birmingham, which is where they are. Fred responded to one of the ads. This was shortly before Grace Ann's death. When we met Fred to sign the legal papers, we got to talking about business and the Internet and so forth. Joe told him that he does Internet sales and website development. So, after Grace Ann and her boyfriend got killed, Fred called Joe up and asked him to design a website to help find Grace Ann's killer. Joe and I talked it over and decided that even though Fred thinks it can't be anybody but Bud, the police aren't that convinced of it. So, the more information that's made available, the likelier they are to catch who really did do it. Joe agreed to do it only if Fred gave the police full access to the site, and he said he would."

"Have you told Fred about seeing Bud those two times?" Ell asks her. "And when was it you saw him again? We haven't got to that and it's time for me to go back to work."

"I didn't tell Fred or the police about seeing Bud either time," Zaia-Danda says. They dispose of the trash from their lunch and walk the trail leading back to the Civic Center. "The second time was just three weeks ago in a nightclub in Atlanta."

"What was Bud doing in a nightclub in Atlanta?"

"An Elvis act, what else?" Zaia-Danda says with a laugh. "He wrote me a postcard about a week before that and signed it 'The King,' asking me to meet him in this nightclub on the far side of Atlanta. I do a lot of gardening seminars there and he knows that. It was late one afternoon and I had to get back home, so I couldn't stay to see his performance. He didn't have a great deal to say and what he did get said didn't make much sense. I took him some more of his things. God, he even looks like Elvis. He's dropped so much weight that he's the spitting image of him in his pre-Army days. I don't know how his singing is, but I'll bet he has those old sisters that were teeny boppers in the '50's squealing in their seats."

"I'm sure that's amusing to you," Ell says, a bit disappointed that Zaia-Danda would look down her nose at middle class pop culture.

"Oh, now, don't get your panties in a wad," Zaia-Danda says. "As we all used to say before our consciousnesses were raised. I'm not sneering. I screamed with the best of them for John, Paul, George and What's-His-Name when I was Mary Jean Jones, college coed in 1964. I still get wet eyed when I hear 'Hey, Jude,' or 'Yesterday,' don't you?"

"You'd better believe it," Ell tells her. "Whatever brought you to Milltown? My hometown is not exactly a hotbed of New Age activity."

"Honey, I grew up in St. Clair County," Zaia-Danda says with a smile. "Many light years ago as Mary Jean Jones, daughter of George, the hardware salesman. After I dropped out of college from Bama in 1965, I went out to the West Coast and did that scene for a long time. Got married, had kids, got divorced, got married again, had more kids and got divorced again. You remember that song, 'All my Exes Live in Texas'? Well, all mine live in California and my kids too, except for Shane, the youngest one who's here with me today. He's just 19 and he's as clueless as I was about things when I was that age. Anyway, I moved back to Alabama about five years ago and bought into my brother Joe's flower business. Both of us got into the New Age movement two years ago. The gardening thing's grown out of our readings about New Age philosophy and knowledge of horticulture. Joe sells gardening supplies and plants and things over the Internet and sets up my seminars for me. I do the dog and pony show. We set up camp in Milltown because the rent's cheaper than here. We need low overhead while we get the business going."

They are back at the library/civic center now and the crowd is reconvening for the afternoon session. Zaia-Danda holds out her hand. "I am very glad to have met you, Ell. Can I call you at the library when I hear from Bud again? I don't want to call your house. The police probably know you and your housemate are friends of Bud's. So far, they don't suspect Joe or me of anything, especially since Joe set up the website. Bud's a good guy, even if he is a little nuts right now. He's not the one that killed his ex-wife and her boyfriend and their baby. But Fred's pretty intent on having it pinned on Bud."

Before she goes back into the building, Zaia-Danda gives her the web address for Timeofgrace.

"Call me here any time," Ell tells her and walks back around the complex to the library to finish her afternoon.

A crowd of early birds from the high school are awaiting her help with the online indexes. She assists them until they leave at 5:00 to go home. When the last student is out the door, Ell logs on to Fred's website. A golden scales of justice looms large against the black background of the Time of Grace home page. One column of the page features news accounts from the Good River Journal in the week following the murders. It also lists the e-mail address to report information on the slayings as murderx2@userv.com. Parallel to the news story are five interactive buttons labeled: Other News of the Murders, Police Report, About Grace Ann and Tanner, Suspects, and Information from Browsers.

Ell clicks on the Suspects button, which opens to a detailed biographical account of Bud Reese, the only suspect included. She looks at the other pages included in the site, which she considers modest, taking into account Fred's usual penchant for showiness. The Other News page mentions the condition of the trailer and the missing items. Browser information includes accounts from people claiming to have heard gunfire and yelling on that final Sunday morning of August and a few Bud Reese sightings, but none of them in an Atlanta nightclub. The police report ends with a series of photographs from the crime scene. And after viewing them, for the first time since the day of the funeral, Ell weeps openly and clicks away quickly from the bloody ruin of Grace Ann Hardaman's lovely face.

Chapter Nine

Rosie loops the extension cord into a small noose as she argues long distance with her ex-husband. She pictures Sherman dangling from it, twisting slowly in the wind. Sherman Lee Jackson, who claims descent from Stonewall, was named by both grandmothers. His momma's momma felt Lee was a proper given name for any Southern boy. His daddy's mother contended that William Tecumseh Sherman was the MacArthur of his era and that anyone named Lee Jackson would grow up a loser. Throughout their marriage, Sherman starred as all three generals. Once following a fight over money and children, he told her that the original Sherman said, "War is cruelty and you cannot refine it." Rosie decided then that was his abiding philosophy. She is certain of it now as she listens to him lay plans to ruin her weekend.

"Old South Days are Saturday and Sunday, Sherman," she says. "I told you that three times already. Our band doesn't play until Saturday. There's no need for you to come down on Friday," Rosie carries the phone to the balcony. Below her on the back lawn of the apartment building, Ell, Michael and Gabe play volleyball with a group of eight.

It is a warm night for November. Rosie's dress is damp from heat and frustration. They are beginning their second half-hour of conversation. His call interrupted supper. Her Suddenly Salad sits half-eaten on the table.

"Yes, Sherman, I am very aware that they are your kids, too. And that you pay your child support on the first day of every month, hallelujah and amen." Rosie says, watching her daughters among the volleyball players. Cassie holds Caitlin, raising her chubby arms in cheerleading motions to boost Ell and Michael's team. Molly practices tumbling routines behind the other court.

"It certainly is your weekend for custody," Rosie agrees. "And I am grateful to you for offering to stay here at the apartment with them so you can take the girls to Fall Fest at the church, since Molly wants to go so badly," she stops to listen to him for a few minutes. "I know, I know, you could just take them back to your mother's. Okay, then. I'll see you Friday afternoon. I'll be at work. You can pick the girls up at Aftercare at the school. They can show you where Caitlin's daycare is. Bye." Rosie hangs up the telephone and changes her clothes to go and join the others.

Even since the formal ending of their long and unsatisfactory marriage, Rosie still finds contact with Sherman to be and endless dance of bullying and concession. When the two of them were in high school, Sherman controlled her by sulking or storming and stomping until he got his way. The same pattern continued throughout their twenty-four years together.

On the back lawn, Rosie takes the baby from Cassie and spreads a blanket on the ground opposite Michael and Ell's court. She sits down, opening her blouse to nurse Caitlin. None of the men notice her except Michael, who winks and waves. Between games, he comes over to sit beside her and stroke the baby's head, his hand brushing Rosie's bare breast.

"Sherman's coming a day early," she tells him. "I never could really find out why. He says it's so he can see the baby before we take her off for the weekend. And get this, he's staying at the apartment with Ell and the girls instead of taking the kids back to Milltown. He says it's so Molly can go to Fall Fest at the church while we're gone."

"That's okay, then," Michael says. "Molly told me how much she wants to go. Maybe old Sherman's just trying to be a better daddy."

"It means we can't have Friday night together," Rosie says with a little pout. The baby's hard and hungry suckling stimulates her. She turns her face to Michael and kisses him.

"That's not really a problem," he says and caresses her hair. "We still have Saturday and he'll be gone by Sunday night. Don't worry about it."

"Sherman's on a tear, though," she says to him. "I can feel it just like Momma used to be able to when Daddy wasn't going to come home for a week or two. He kept going on about Cassie and Molly's sense of connectedness being broken since the divorce—just like he knows what that means. He must be watching Oprah on that little tv he keeps at the Circle K. I have no idea what it is he wants. I just hope it's not me."

"Like the man said, 'you can't always get what you want,'" Michael says with a smile.

"All this time I thought you only knew Old Time Music," Rosie says as she shifts Caitlin to her shoulder. "And here you go, quoting Mick Jagger."

"It's still rock and roll to me," he says. He plays his air guitar and kisses her ear.

The cadence of Caitlin's sucking and Michael's closeness soothe and relax Rosie. She feels she can almost sleep. The other team volleys the ball toward her and the baby. Before she can move, Michael blocks the ball with his body and rejoins the game. His back to her and Caitlin, he moves adeptly around the court to keep the ball from disturbing them. Rosie places Caitlin on the blanket beside her and pats her to sleep. Sometimes she thinks Michael feels Caitlin is his. The baby was only four months old when they met in the spring. More like a big brother to Cassie and Molly, he alternately teases and protects them. He often takes them to the corner convenience store for cokes and snacks. When Rosie grows weary from rocking and nursing Caitlin, he takes the baby and walks with her. Bouncing her at his shoulder, he sings, "Paddy, Won't

You Drink Some Good Old Cider," or some other quirky song. He calls her Queen Cait and treats her royally.

The volleyball players—some, fellow band members and others, residents of the apartment complex—end the game and crowd around Caitlin. Most are single and childless and want a temporary object of affection. They touch the baby's downy head and insert fingers into her small, curled fists. Caitlin sleeps on. Her mouth sucks in the night air.

Michael lifts the baby. Rosie, Ell, and the girls say goodnight to the others. Gabe follows them all up the stairs to the apartment. Ell starts bath water for Molly. Cassie stands before the bathroom mirror rolling her hair. Michael lays Caitlin in her crib and joins Rosie and Gabe in the living room for the late news. As soon as she herds Molly to the tub and makes sure Cassie is at least thinking about getting ready for bed, Ell comes in to sit beside Gabe. Michael and Rosie are entwined at the far end of the couch.

"My, how cozy," Gabe observes. "Kind of like the Ricardos and the Mertzes settled down for an evening of leisure."

"If that makes me Ethel, I'm not sure I mind that," Ell says. "This is the week before first drafts are due for the 11th graders' term papers. Athena Villa's going to be the library from hell until Monday and I've got to work this weekend. Give me Fred or Lucy to contend with any day before I have to listen to another kid ask me to find images of male oppression in 'Daisy Miller.' They should not force Henry James on teenagers. It's like feeding caviare to possums."

"I don't recall much about Henry James except that I felt like I'd been on a merry-go-round for several hours when I finished one of his stories," Michael says. "Ricky Ricardo had a pretty good life, though. His band always had work. No second job for him."

"I should have it as good as Lucy," Rosie says, leaning forward to talk. "Only one kid, no job and Mrs. Trumble down the hall for emergencies."

"You never saw Fred do much work," Gabe says. "He collected rent and griped a lot about spending money. Speaking of money, Little

Brother, did you tell Rosie what Bubba Smith said Old South Days is going to pay us for two days' work?"

"I forgot," Michael slaps his forehead and pulls Rosie closer to him in a squeeze. "It's high cotton time, babe. Two thousand to split among the five of us. Not bad for a bunch of would-be hillbilly upstarts."

"Four hundred dollars for two days' work," Rosie marvels. "Lord, for that much money I might even work up some enthusiasm for all that Civil War/Old South crapola."

"I wouldn't be thinking of quitting my day job just yet," Gabe advises and then points to the television screen. "Look, there's something about our upcoming event on the news."

Samm and Dean, a local late-night news anchor team, are chuckling over some footage of a practice session for the battle reenactment that is to be the central focus of Old South Days. An unexpected downpour drenched the ravine where the original skirmish occurred in 1864, located forty-five minutes from Birmingham in what is now a state owned park. The eager warriors slip and slide down the grassless landside, climaxing in a muddy pile-up of made-to-period blue and gray uniforms. Rosie thinks it good enough for them. Certain that her ancestors never owned large amounts of land, much less slaves, she does not feel the same nostalgia for the Lost War and its culture that her former husband does. Sherman displayed a Stars and Bars on their front porch on every holiday. He practically genuflected at the mention of Robert E. Lee or Jefferson Davis. With little prompting, he could reel off exact dates, commanding officers, and the number of dead and wounded for every significant battle or skirmish on Southern soil. Rosie still does not see the point.

The girls come in to tell them goodnight. An arm around each daughter, Rosie goes with Molly and Cassie to their room while Michael slips discreetly to Rosie's room and closes the door. He will spend most of the night with Rosie, leaving before the girls get up to dress for school. Gabe grins at Ell as he channel surfs for a good sit-com rerun.

"That boy is smooth, isn't he though? I don't feel like I'm telling tales out of school to say that, all told, he really hasn't had that much practice in clandestine romance. At least not of the 'stay all night, stay a little longer' variety. I think the idea of confronting Cassie and Molly at the breakfast table is more than our Baptist upbringing will allow him to deal with. It doesn't take a great deal to get him red all over, given the right circumstances."

"You, on the other hand, probably haven't blushed since you started shaving," Ell says teasingly.

"Almost," Gabe says, settling for Channel 9's M*A*S*H* rerun. "I may get the chance to find out if I still can this very weekend. An old buddy of mine that I shared some real adventures with a few years back is playing with a group out of Huntsville that'll be performing at Old South Days. They call themselves Grafton Street. I've not seen Ian McDaid in six years or more. It will be interesting to see how a couple of gay boys can manipulate some quality time smack in the middle of the biggest white bread gathering since Reconstruction." He watches Ell, waiting for her reaction. He considered not telling her, but now that he has, he wants to know how she feels.

Fixing her gaze on the screen where Klinger is fastening his bra, Ell merely comments, "Enjoy then, and think about me being held prisoner by a crowd of term paper crazed sixteen-year-olds."

"You've got it, honey," Gabe tells her, lightly touching her arm. "And like the Old Soldier said, 'I shall return.'"

As she lay naked in her bed, curled into Michael's body, her breasts and belly warm against his bare backside, Rosie smiles in the dark. From the time she married at 19 and began to accommodate herself to Sherman's matter-of-fact lovemaking, she always put her gown back on before going to sleep. Sherman slept in his underwear and on his stomach, never wanting her against him in the night. Extremely respectful of her in front of others, Michael delights in her body when they are alone. He tells her that clothes are a necessary daytime evil and are unhealthy to sleep in. In the summer, when they first began to make love, Rosie was still nursing Caitlin several times a day. Her breasts often leaked milk into Michael's face. He laughed and licked it from his mouth, saying it didn't have much taste. As she lies awake, stroking Michael's back, she wonders briefly what it was Sherman had been trying to tell her on the phone.

On Friday afternoon, customers line up at the counter as Rosie broods over Sherman's impending arrival. Paradise Dry Cleaning and Laundry is filled to capacity with UAB students, faculty and local business workers eager for the weekend. She and Mabel June work busily at the counter and in the back, trying to get everyone served by 5:00. As she hands bagged clothing and change to an impatient Lebanese man, she calls to the presser to bring in the rest of the clothes so they can finish bagging them and staple the tickets to them.

Booker, the almost totally silent presser, pushes a rack of aromatic clothing to the front. When she first began working at Paradise, Booker's taciturnity made Rosie quite uneasy. She was certain that he somehow found her distasteful. She found herself talking too much to fill the quiet. One morning after they had worked alone for several hours and she had gabbed at him nonstop for almost the entire time, he looked at her for a few minutes and said, "You don't have to keep running your mouth like that, Rosie. I like you good enough. I'm not shut mouthed because I don't like you. I live with my mama, who can't hardly hear it thunder and she talks like that Joan Rivers lady on the tv and about that fast. I have to nearly holler to get her to hear me when I answer her. And there ain't no not answering my mama. I don't say much at work because my voice's nearly wore out from dealing with her."

When Rosie asked him why she didn't just get a hearing aid, Booker explained that she had owned several, but kept losing them and the insurance would only pay for so many in a given period. So Rosie developed a system of nods and gestures to communicate with Booker. When she finally admitted all this to Mabel June, her supervisor laughed and congratulated her. Booker, she said, had preceded Rosie by only a few weeks and all this time, Mabel June thought it was that he didn't like white people that made him so quiet.

Shortly after 4:00, Rosie looks up from the counter to see Sherman on the sidewalk in front of the store. On either side of him, Molly and Cassie are eating ice cream cones and rolling their eyes at some corny joke he is probably telling them, just as he had when they all lived together. Sherman holds Caitlin on one arm and a cone of soft ice cream in the other hand, allowing the baby small licks from the top of it. When he notices Rosie watching, he hands the cone to Cassie and raises Caitlin's hand to wave at Rosie. They walk toward the door.

"This is real nice, Rosie," he says to her as they come into the store. "You never told me it was in this nice of a place."

"Yes, Sherman, I did," she says as she continues working. "But you probably weren't listening to me."

Sherman chooses not to respond to that and asks instead, "So, is your boss here? Uh...Mabel June, isn't that right? I want to meet her."

"M.J." Rosie calls to the back of the store. "Can you come up here a minute?"

Mabel June is wiping sweat from her face as she walks slowly to the front counter. She smiles the briefest of smiles at Sherman. On seeing her, Caitlin grins and holds out her arms in Mabel June's direction.

"Looks like you got a big fan here," Sherman says as he allows Mabel June to take the baby. "You ought to be flattered. This one won't go to just anybody."

Mabel June, after babysitting Caitlin several times, knows the little girl to be the friendliest of babies, due in part to her early placement in daycare. She is about to argue when she catches Rosie's eye and decides to let it pass. "Oh, I think Miss Caity here knows a pushover when she meets one," she says. "She knows Aunty Mabel will do anything she wants as long as it don't hurt her."

"She sure is a good baby," Sherman says. "I really do miss all my girls. Once every other week's just not enough for me."

"Daddy's got something for you in the car," Cassie says to her mother before she can respond to Sherman's words. "But we told him you wouldn't want him to bring it in."

"Not unless it's dirty clothes," Rosie says, looking at Sherman. "I've still got a few more minutes here. M.J. and I have to go over the books and finish up before we can go. Why don't you take the kids down the street to the Fountain for a little bit. Molly likes to draw pictures of the animals and things in it. Here, let me get her a pencil and some paper from the back." Rosie goes to the back of the store while Sherman reclaims Caitlin from Mabel June.

"Is my Rosie's work up to snuff?" Sherman asks Mabel June as he fusses with Caitlin's little dress. "You know she hasn't worked in more than twenty years. She didn't have to work when she was my wife."

"Rosie's the best I've ever had," Mabel June tells him, flatly. "She'll probably be managing her own store by this time next year. That is if her band don't take off the way they want it to. I've heard them play a time or two and let me tell you, they are hot…"

"Here, Molly," Rosie says as she comes back to the front. "You and Cassie go show your Daddy the Fountain and tell him all about the Big Bad Satanic Goat and all his evil friends who are going to bring about the destruction of Southside any day now."

The Fountain, replete with anthropomorphic characters from folklore, serves as the focal point of the Five Points area of Southside. Following its erection, some area fundamentalists said that its figures—particularly the storytelling ram—represented the occult and asked for its removal. The fountain remains and fundamentalists occasionally still protest, but no evil results have ensued.

Carrying the baby, Sherman and the girls file out. Framed in the store window, they stop for a few minutes on the sidewalk while Molly points out where they are going. During her long hours at work, Rosie often thinks of her family like that—in still shots, frozen in motion until she returns to them. Although many months have passed since their divorce, she wonders if she will ever be able to remove Sherman from that picture.

"He don't seem to be doing too bad with the older girls." Mabel June comments when Rosie's family moves on down the sidewalk. "But he don't know B from bullfoot about you or that baby. He had the nerve to ask me if I thought you was doing a good enough job. I let him know real quick just how you stand with me. I bragged about your band, too. I hope that was okay."

"Absolutely," Rosie says, locking the door so they can get to the paperwork. "Sherman's got to feel like he's in charge and that nobody can do anything without him. It's time he found out the truth."

They review the day's sales sheets and Mabel June enters the correct information on the weekly report form for the home office. Finishing shortly after 5:30, Rosie is locking the security door as Sherman and the girls come up behind her. All except Caitlin are smacking gum. Sherman is blowing oversized bubbles to entertain the Molly and Cassie.

"I bought them sugarless gum, don't worry." he tells Rosie as they walk to the car. "I'm making an effort at cutting back on my sugar intake. I give up all them doughnuts I was eating at the store and switched to them little packs of fat-free cookies. And I started drinking diet drinks most of the time. It ain't the same, but I got to have something sweet without my best Sugar around." He smiles tenderly at Rosie.

"Sugar kills," Rosie tells him as they get into his car. "A substitute's better." She wonders at his newfound capacity for metaphor. Maybe he watches some PBS along with all the talk shows on the little tv inside the Circle K.

"I hope you can come see what I got done to the store since you all seen it two months ago." Sherman tells her. "I put in a yogurt machine and some tables. And in a few months, if I can get me somebody reliable,

I'm going to put in a little sandwich shop to serve the business people around the area. What do you think of that?" Sherman is driving them to the apartment. Her own '72 Beetle is in the shop. Ell has chauffeured her and the girls for the past few days. Rosie sits beside Sherman in the leather bucket seat of the same '65 Mustang Sherman drove to Grace Ann's funeral. Caitlin is buckled in the back behind her. Cassie and Molly are on either side of her. Cassie holds a long box in her lap.

"I think you must be doing good business if you can afford all that," Rosie says while he parks the car in front of the building. "Must be time for me to ask for more child support."

"I've already seen to that," Sherman tells her as they go inside the building and up the stairs to the apartment. "Your check next month will be a good bit bigger."

Too surprised to reply, Rosie unlocks the door. Inside, she puts Caitlin down in her walker. Sherman and the girls sit down on the sofa. Cassie hands her the long box. Slipping the bow from the outside, she opens it to find a bouquet of tissue wrapped daisies.

"See, I remembered," he says proudly. "That was what I gave you for Valentine's Day our senior year because you said roses cost too much."

"They're just lovely," Rosie says, again at a loss for words. She goes to the kitchen for a vase, runs some water in it, and brings it back into the living room. Placing the flowers carefully inside, she sets the vase on a piece of absorbent stone on Ell's roll-top desk near the window.

"Wildwood Flower is the opening and closing act at Old South Days," she says, veering away from Sherman's attempt at intimacy. "And we've got a couple of sets in the middle. Michael and the boys and I even got ourselves new outfits for the finale. Want to see mine?" She does not wait for a reply and goes to the bedroom to change.

"Ah, Rosie," he says as she comes back in. "You look just like Scarlett at the barbecue." He fondles the sleeve of her gown. The dress is low cut with a scooped neck, full-length and cream colored with little green and lavender flowers. Its sleeves are puffed and the waist cinched. Rosie wears a voluminous crinoline underneath. Her dark hair lays soft on her shoulders. Sherman moves his hand to the nape of her neck and lightly caresses her.

"Actually, the music's just sort of an added attraction to Old South Days," Rosie says, moving away from his touch. "It's not the main reason folks are coming. There'll be food and lots of crafts and trades and there'll be a real blacksmith, I heard. But most everybody's coming to see the battle reenactment on Saturday. A lot of people will come in period dress to watch it. They're even opening up the old ironworks they used during the war. You'd probably love it. But you know how I hate that kind of thing. However, they're paying us $2,000.00 for the two days. You can't say no to that."

"Ya'll must be pretty good then," Sherman says and turns on the television. "Maybe I can come hear you sometime when the girls don't have something else going on." He channel surfs until he finds an old "Family Ties" rerun to watch with Molly and Cassie. His arms are around both girls who sit on either side of him on the sofa.

"We could've had us a house like that," he says, indicating the Keaton house on the screen. "If you'd just stuck it out a little longer…"

Caitlin crashes her walker into the coffee table and begins to cry. Rosie lifts her out and after quieting her, sits her in the high chair. She places some lima beans on the tray and the baby feeds herself.

"I didn't know she could do that," Sherman says. "I need to be around more."

Ell comes in the front door, laden with stacks of xeroxed sheets and periodicals. The girls get up from the couch to take some of the things from her. Ell opens the roll-top desk and puts the papers inside, showing the girls where to put the other materials. "Hell-o," she says, picking up the vase of daisies. "Has my unknown admirer finally come through or are these yours, Rosie?"

"Daddy bought them for her," Molly tells her. "Aren't they neat?"

"Well, two points for you, Sherman," Ell says as she sits down in the recliner near the sofa. "I can hardly believe you remember all the way back to high school."

"How come you do?" He asks her. "Rosie barely remembered it herself."

"Oh, we librarian types have many, many megabytes of memory," Ell tells him. "We can even put Microsoft to shame if we set our minds to it. For instance, I remember what you said to me a few days ago on the telephone when I told you I thought you were being selfish coming down here a day early just to horn in on Rosie's weekend."

"Now, Ellie May, let's not get into that right now," Sherman says, knowing full well that Ell would as soon be called Big Bad Mama as Ellie May. "I'm already here and the girls and Rosie are glad to see me, even if you're not. Just you wait and see, me and you and the girls are gonna have ourselves a good time this weekend."

"Hmm," Ell says, noncommittally. She turns to Rosie. "If you will get that tupperware dish full of spaghetti sauce out of the freezer and put it in the microwave, I'll start the noodles."

The women go to the kitchen, leaving Sherman and the girls to watch Caitlin. They work quickly and easily together in the small kitchen as they put dinner together. They talk in hushed murmurs so that Sherman and the girls won't overhear. Rosie tells Ell of Sherman's conciliatory behavior earlier. Ell reminds her of the times that Sherman behaved similarly and what the end result was. Rosie agrees, saying that her beloved ex-spouse is most likely just oozing ointment to hide the fly underneath.

They carry dinner to the dining room table that overlooks the back lawn. Located in an elevated section of Southside, the rear of the apartment building presents a twinkling night-time view of moving headlights and the illuminated city below. Now that many of the leaves are off the trees and they can see more clearly, Molly usually spends supper time pointing out familiar sights to Cassie, who mostly wants her to be quiet.

Tonight, however, with their father at the table, Cassie pays attention and even joins in. Sherman nods seriously at each sighting in the Magic City.

"Sure is good eating," he says to Rosie and Ell, lifting his water glass in a singular toast to them. "They say pasta's the food of the '90s. All them runners and joggers got it right. You need all the energy you can scrape together just to make it through this decade."

When they finish the main course, Ell brings in a fat-free cake she picked up at Food World and begins to serve slices to everyone.

"No thanks," Sherman says, holding a hand over his plate. "I'm satisfied with that fine dinner you served."

"Sherman's swearing off sugar, can you believe it?" Rosie says to Ell as she cuts a bite of cake with her fork.

"I'm doing lots of things different," Sherman says. "Even more than you know about. Say, Ell," he turns to her. "Rosie's been telling me all about this band of hers. Would you mind staying with the girls tonight for awhile and letting me go hear them practice? That is, if it's okay with Rosie and the girls." He smiles brilliantly at them as though his request would cause no conflicts.

CHAPTER TEN

Shortly after Sherman accompanies a reluctant Rosie to Wildwood Flower's pre-festival practice, Ell loads Molly, Cassie and Caitlin into the Cherokee. Since her daddy won't be there for a few hours, Cassie feels she must, must see Meaghan since they won't see each other again until Monday. As they drive the few blocks to Meaghan's mother's condominium, Cassie and Molly, in a rare moment of agreement, plan the things they will do with Sherman over the weekend.

"I'll be back at 10:00," Ell tells Cassie as they check in with the guard at the gatehouse. She drives past the meticulously manicured lawns of the condominium village to Meaghan's door.

Dr. White-Curtis, Meaghan's single parent mom, also a pediatrician, waves from the doorway as Cassie runs up the front steps. "Come on in, if you can," she calls to Ell. "I'm listening to a Prairie Home Companion tape and drinking some Chablis."

"Sounds good," Ell calls back. "But I've got the baby with us. It's nearly her bedtime." Dr. White-Curtis offers to bring Cassie back home. "That would be great," Ell tells her, waving as she drives away.

"We had the best time with Daddy today," Molly says on the drive home. "He told us knock-knock jokes and even sat there real quiet while I drew pictures of the animals in the fountain. He used to tell us lots of jokes when we lived together."

"Your daddy's a very funny man when he wants to be," Ell says as she parks the car. She lifts an already drowsy Caitlin from the car seat. With Molly close behind her, she climbs the steps to the apartment.

The little girl is asleep by the time they reach Rosie's bedroom. Ell lays her carefully in the crib, patting her back as she rouses a little before settling down. Turning off the ringer on the telephone in Rosie's bedroom, she goes into the living room, opens the desk and takes out papers she brought in earlier. Settling down in the lounge chair, she highlights sections of the xeroxed material for the 11th graders working on literary papers. Molly asks if she can look at the *Junior Worldbook* on Ell's recently purchased p.c. After giving her permission, Ell is just booting up when the telephone rings.

Deciding to let the answering machine pick up, she hears, "This is Zaia-Danda, Ell. Remember Mary Jean Jones from New Age Gardening? I wanted to let you know I've seen Bud."

Jumping up from the computer chair in her room, Ell races for the phone. "Zaia, where are you, in Milltown?" She asks.

"No, I'm right here in the Big City," Zaia-Danda tells her. "I just got through with another gardening seminar and I'm headed home. I thought you might want to hear the latest from our favorite Elvis."

"Come on over," Ell invites her, giving the woman directions to the apartment.

Molly is happily exploring the interactive section on mammals when Ell meets Zaia-Danda at the front door.

"Nice," Zaia says as she walks in, admiring the apartment. "Maybe in about another year or so the group and I can afford something along these lines. I've got to get New Age Gardening a little more solid first."

Attired in a black and white caftan, Zaia-Danda lifts her long hair off the back of her neck as she settles on Ell's sofa. She feels in her shoulder bag for a scrunchy and balls her hair into a makeshift knot. "Hot tonight. You'd think it was August instead of November. What happened to the fall, I wonder?"

"The heat'll pass," Ell says, offering her guest a glass of iced tea. "In another month or so, we'll be screaming for nights above freezing."

"Never satisfied, I know," Zaia-Danda says, sipping the tea. "Joe says that's the story of my life. You ever notice how quick men are to point out a woman's shortcomings. But just try to do the same to him. He'll jump on you quicker than one of the Kennedys on a sexy teenager. I'm about tired of dealing with them, truth be told. Brothers included."

"That old line about the good ones all being married or gay is not too far off base," Ell comments, thinking of Gabe and his plans for the weekend.

"I'd say that's the gospel if I still believed in that," Zaia-Danda replies. "Instead I'll just say its a universal truth. I saw a t-shirt slogan recently that sums up my current philosophy on men in general: "If it has tires or testicles, it's bound to cause you grief."

"Amen, sister," Ell says. "Now, how about Bud? Is he still acting 'wild as a bug'?"

"Wilder, honey. That boy is 'wild in the country', wild in the city and every other place. Two days ago, he was still at the Hunka Hunka Burning Love Lounge on the far side of Hot'Lanta, drawin' 'em in like bees to the hive. But he said he had to move on. The club manager told him a cop came around asking about him earlier that day. He was planning to head out of there after his last set that night. If he gets across the Georgia state line without somebody pulling him over, it'll only be through the grace of God."

"Is he real bad off?" Ell asks, taking a sip of tea.

"Honey, you just listen and I'll tell you about it. That man's so far into grief and denial that Heartbreak Hotel would look like Disney Land to him about now," Zaia-Danda says as she recounts her Wednesday evening adventure in Elvis World.

Old, young and middle-aged women—some in groups, some with husbands or boyfriends—packed the Hunka, Hunka Burning Love Lounge. A small night spot on Atlanta's outskirts, its doctor-owners exclusively engage Elvis imitators for its shows. At 8:00 when Bud opened with his first set, the whole room was 'itching like a man on a fuzzy tree." Twisting and gyrating onto the stage with "Hound Dog," Bud was clad in a pink sport coat, lace shirt and black pants with a stripe up the leg. He abandoned himself to a non-stop medley of pre-Army Elvis.

From a sneering, swaggering "Don't Be Cruel" to a melting "Love Me Tender," Bud got the women out of their seats and up to the edge of the stage. The very walls of the building threatened to fall like Jericho's as they stood in their chairs and on the tabletops to join him in "Jailhouse Rock." Backed up by only a bass player, another guitar player and a drummer who weren't bad and grew better as the audience yelled its approval, Bud brought the women to sweaty satisfaction by the time the Good Rockin' Tonight Elvis set ended. Zaia-Danda talked with him briefly between sets in the little room behind the stage where he sat gulping a Big Gulp and eating a moon pie.

"I got to split," he said and told her about the two policemen who had been in asking questions about him that very afternoon. Mr. Phillips, the club owner, did his best to divert them, but he told Bud he thought they'd be back.

Then Bud talked of Fred and Grace Ann. Once before the murders, Fred told him that Grace Ann was going to have an abortion. A few days later, his story changed and he told Bud that Grace Ann made her bed and now she had to lie in it. He began urging Bud to seek custody of Ree and Harley Jr. "So they won't have to live with that little bastard," he said to Bud. Bud was uncertain whether Fred was referring to Tanner or the unborn baby.

On the morning of the murders, Bud made up his mind to help Grace Ann do whatever it was she felt was best for her, their kids, and the baby she was carrying, even if it meant going back to Colorado with Tanner. He wanted to tell her that with Fred acting so crazy, he would understand if she wanted to leave Alabama. He would tell her that he still loved her and that they would have other chances in other lifetimes. But when he arrived at the trailer, Grace Ann and Tanner were lying dead in the doorway. Bud couldn't bring himself to wipe the blood from her face.

Shorter than the first, the second set "Swinging Elvis," began with "It's Now or Never," moving to "Surrender," "Feel so Bad," "Little Sister," and some lesser known R & B numbers such as "One Night with You," "Trying to Get to You," and "Baby, What You Want Me To Do." Bud wore black leather and a bad boy smile as he wailed out lyrics of love desired, love experienced and love lost. He ended with "Can't Help Falling in Love with You." The audience softly joined him on the chorus.

The intermission was a short one, but Zaia-Danda managed to ask Bud about his intended destination. Bud didn't know, but he would call or write.. "T.C.B, honey," he assured her. "Always, T.C.B." he said as she left the dressing room.

Spotlighted in the darkened nightclub for the last set, "Come Back Elvis," a sequined jumpsuit-clad Bud presented a blend of hits from the early, middle and late years of The King. Saving many of the best for last—"Are You Lonesome Tonight?" "Teddy Bear," and "Crying in the Chapel," he reached the peak of yearning and regret with "Unchained Melody" and "Always on My Mind."

In a short, rambling monologue near the end, he confused Priscilla with Grace Ann as he admonished the men in the audience to do right by their women. He ended on an up note with "Burning Love," kissed his hand to the audience, thanked them, thanked them very much, and mounting his Honda, rode off into the night.

By the time Zaia-Danda finishes, it is nearing 10:00 and Ell walks her outside to her car, calling to Molly that she will be right back. As she unlocks her door, Zaia-Danda gives Ell a slip of paper containing Fred's password to Murderx2 E-Mail.

"That old man's up to something," she says as they stand in the parking lot. "When Joe did some work on timeofgrace last week, he said that it looked like Fred was wiping out half the stuff people have sent to him.

Joe retrieved most of it from the Trashcan. Could be there's something that might help the police find the real killer. I don't want to get involved because of Bud keeping in contact with me. See what you can find out."

Ell promises that she will as Zaia-Danda drives away. She lingers in the parking lot a few minutes to see if Meaghan's mother might be bringing Cassie back. Looking up at the night sky, she can think only of Bud Reese riding on a lonesome two-lane blacktop, sequins from his jumpsuit flying in the wind.

Wildwood Flower's practice room is an old warehouse at the rear of Michael and Gabe's music store, Picker's Palace. Sherman examines the room, frowning at its contents as the band tunes their instruments. Michael puts a new string on Rosie's guitar and tightens the others. Rosie moves nervously about the room, shuffling handwritten sheets of lyrics and singing softly as she reads. Sherman's presence is heavy in the warm room.

"Have we decided yet just what all we're doing for this shindig?" Gabe asks as he moves some boxes until he finds a folding chair for Sherman. "I think we ought to put in some Civil War stuff since that's what the whole thing's about."

"Don't you think people are going to be sick of having it rammed down their throats all weekend?" Rosie asks.

"Now, you listen to him. Gabriel is right, Rosie," Sherman says to her in that all too familiar you-don't-know-what-the-hell-you're-talking-about tone she so despises. "Alabama folks know the importance of the War."

"What you mean is that they love wallowing in something that's long past and best forgotten and was never all that glorious to begin with," Rosie says to him as she steps to the microphone.

"You all said for sure that we'd do 'Lula Walls.' Let's do it," Michael says, taking his place beside Rosie. Gabe is to her left. Charlie, who plays mandolin, is on Michael's other side. Curtis, the base player, is next to Gabe. They bog down on the chorus, and since no one can agree on the words, Michael goes to the music store and comes back with a copy of *The Carter Family Song Book.*

He picks the melody as he sings the song of "that aggravatin' beauty, Lula Walls."

"I like that one, Rosie," he says as he finishes and squeezes her hand.

"If there ever was an aggravatin' beauty, then it's got to be Rosie," Sherman says as he moves his chair closer to the band. "Did she ever tell you about the time she threw all my fishing gear in a box and sent it to GoodWill because I forgot her birthday."

"He got his fishing gear back," Rosie says. "But I never did get a birthday present. I never forgot one of his, not in twenty years."

"That 'Lula Walls' was a pretty good one," Sherman tells them, trying to change the subject. "What else have you got?"

"We can't decide between 'Mary Danced with Soldiers,' and 'Willow Garden,'" Gabe says. "'Mary' is this Civil War ballad about a Yankee woman whose husband dies in the war. She goes to work in a cotton mill at night to support herself and her little boy," He plays the opening bars. "It ends with her dancing with Rebel soldiers and falling for one of them. The Yankee soldiers find out and here's what happens."

Gabe sings the murder ballad in a soft voice.

"It's got a nice tune to it," Sherman says as he finishes

"Too bad about old Mary though. I reckon that's what happens to women who step out of line." He raises his eyebrows in Rosie's direction. "'Willow Garden' is another murder ballad," Rosie says, gazing directly into Sherman's eyes. "A man and woman are walking in a grove of willow trees beside a river. He gets drunk on wine and kills her and throws her body in the river. This is the part where he's looking down from the gallows, just before they hang him."

She sounds the beginning notes on her guitar
"My race is run beneath the sun,
and hell now waits for me.
For I did murder that pretty little miss
whose name is Rose Conolee."
Rosie sings forcefully, exaggerating the ending syllables.

"You like that one, don't you, Sherman?" She asks her ex-husband bluntly, staring him down. "Good old fashioned justice on all counts."

He looks away from her, mumbling, "Is that the whole story? Why does he kill her?"

"He probably thought she had money or that she was stepping out on him," Michael says. "Or maybe he was just a mean son-of-a-bitch. Those old ballads aren't always real specific."

He puts a protective arm around Rosie and they run through several songs. Their voices rise to the ceiling of the old warehouse, the sounds becoming lost as they bounce against uninsulated walls. Rosie moves closer to Michael as they sing a duet of a song Flatt and Scruggs made famous, "Old Salty Dog Blues." Her face is hot as she hits the guitar licks. She looks only at Michael as he sings, his reedy tenor rising.

The band stops for a break and Gabe tells Sherman how they decided on the name Wildwood Flower. "We were still playing at the Wells Fargo and were backstage listening to this family Bluegrass band that was really pretty pitiful. Michael was making real loud remarks about their bad picking, so to get him to shut up, I went out to the car and came back with a joint. 'Have a little of the weed and chill,' I told him. And Charlie said, 'You mean the wildwood weed? Like from that old song in the '60s about marijuana?' And Curtis said, 'Wildwood flower,' when it was his time for a toke. Then Rosie said, 'That's our new name, Wildwood Flower.' And it stuck."

Sherman glares at Rosie as though she is one of their children. "I didn't know you smoked that stuff, Rosie. You hardly ever even used to drink."

"You did enough of that for both of us," Rosie says. "And for your information, I don't smoke that stuff. If you'll recall, I'm nursing a baby. What the boys do is their business and..."

"Come on, let's do 'Year of Jubilo,'" Michael interrupts. "It's Rosie's favorite."

The band lights into a post Civil War song hailing the end of slavery. They sound particularly fine on the chorus, wherein the slaves rejoice over locking the "Massa" in the cellar as they celebrate their newly won freedom.

"Rosie's always saying how free she feels now," Michael comments as they finish and he wipes his face on his shirt sleeve. He nods in Sherman's direction.

"She ain't quite as free as you two seem to think she is," Sherman tells them.

But they are not listening. Rosie and Michael practice the song they plan for the band's finale, a shape note spiritual titled, "The Parting Hand." The band sets instruments aside for the a capella rendition. Their harmony is close and near perfect as they reach the final lines.

Sherman declares the room too warm and opens the door, stepping into the alley. "Rosie," he calls to her. "Isn't it about time for you to get back to Caitlin. I'm betting she misses her momma."

He remains outside for the rest of the practice, coming back in only when they are packing their instruments to leave. As they are walking out of the warehouse, Sherman wedges himself between Rosie and Michael and catches hold of her guitar case to steer her to his car.

Chapter Eleven

"I come bearing supper," Sherman announces loudly as he and the girls enter Ell's apartment on Saturday evening.

Having preceded them through the door by only a few minutes, Ell is lying prone on her bed. In utter exhaustion from a day of hunting term paper sources for frantic teenagers, she is not certain she ever wants to move again.

"In a minute," she calls to them. Moving slowly to her bathroom, she washes her face and hands and walks slowly into the living room.

Setting styrofoam containers on the dining table, Sherman tells Molly, "Run into the kitchen for some silverware and napkins, baby."

Molly does as her father asks. Cassie follows her, saying, "I'll pour us all some tea, Daddy. We can put our food on the tv trays and watch the movie."

"They had more food at that place than I've ever seen in my life," Sherman says to Ell, speaking of the Fall Fest at Southside Methodist. "There were dishes from nearly every country in the world, I think, except maybe outer Mongolia. I got lasagna since I'm sure what it is. Remember how all of us used to eat my Momma's lasagna on Sunday nights after church."

"Do you recall the first time Bud Reese ever ate with us?" Ell asks him, smiling. "He kept sitting there looking at it and not eating."

"And Grace Ann said, 'What's the matter, Bud? It doesn't have teeth,' And he sort of stammered a little and said, 'Do you eat it with a fork or pick it up like pizza?'"

"Bud's cultural horizons were a little limited back then for sure," Ell comments as she sets up tv trays in front of the living room couch. The four of them take styrofoam meal containers, utensils and a glass of tea to their trays.

"Can we watch 'Willow' now, Daddy?" Molly asks him as they sit down. Their middle girl has Sherman's features and Rosie's personality. He loves her to distraction.

"Turn it on, baby," he says and then, thinking better of it, looks at Ell. "That is, if it's okay with Ell. Was there something you usually watch?"

"Go ahead, it's fine," Ell says to Molly. "I may be watching the insides of my eyelids before long. Those kids at the library sapped every ounce of energy I ever hoped to have. Thank God tomorrow's only a half day. I don't know if I could take another eight hours."

"What's the matter, Ellie May?" Sherman teases her as he lifts a forkful of lasagna. "Is the princess of the library ready to give up the rights to the throne?"

"Why of course," Ell says, trying to refrain from tossing her iced tea at him for calling her Ellie May. "I'm just certain the man of my dreams is due any moment to take me away from all that drudgery."

"It could happen tomorrow," Sherman says with a straight face. "When are they going to put you in charge down there at the library, anyway? Is Miss Emmeleine planning to stay until she's 90?"

"Quite possibly," Ell says. "We all want her to. And there's no guarantee I'll be director when she leaves. I'm happy with what I've got."

"Might as well be," Sherman advises. "If there's not nothing you can do to change it. Now take me though, I've been changing a lot of things here lately. And there's more to come. I'm not going to end up like Bud Reese just because I didn't wake up and smell the coffee."

"Daddy, we can't hear 'Willow,'" Cassie complains. "If you and Ell want to talk, can't you go in the dining room?"

"Yes, Sweet Pea, I expect we can," Sherman says with a resigned grin. His oldest daughter is the spitting image of Rosie, but a child more like himself in temperament has yet to see life. "Let's be a little more polite, though. After all, we are your elders."

Ignoring him, Cassie returns her attention to the screen to watch the little people exclaiming over the stolen baby.

"Jesus, help me," Sherman says, shaking his head. "It's just like listening to myself twenty-whatever years ago. That one," he says, pointing at Cassie as he and Ell take their coffee into the dining room. "is going to be the death of me and Rosie both. Do you know what she asked me while we were at the Fall Fest? If I thought 12 was too young to start going on dates in cars. I told her she'd have to take it up with Rosie to be sure, but I thought about 15 sounded right to me. Wait'll I tell Momma. She's going to be in hog heaven. Before Rosie and me ever had any kids, she had all her fingers and toes crossed that I'd have one just like me and get paid back for all the aggravation I caused her."

"What goes around do eventually come around, don't it?" Ell asks, taking a sip of coffee. "Remember the Milltown Mom and Pop Guilt Trip Travel Agency?"

"Oh, Lord, I'd forgot all about that one," Sherman says with a laugh. "Remind me again."

"It was when Grace Ann was grounded for taking the Skylark out in the middle of the night to meet Bud. I was grounded for telling my mother I was going to Queen's Theater in Caloosa City to see 'The Bible,' when I really went to see 'Valley of the Dolls,' at the Cosmo with Rosie. And Minnie Beth had just finished giving you forty whacks with one of those steel backed brushes she kept at the House of Beauty after she overheard you on the telephone in one of your finer conversational moments."

"Now I know," Sherman says, clapping a hand to his forehead. "She heard me talking to Big Boy after he backed into that souped up '57 Chevy I was driving then. I called him a low down, sorry…"

"Derriere orifice and fornicator of his maternal parent, so to speak," Ell says, laughing.

"Right," Sherman is chuckling now himself. "I thought she was going to break that damn brush on me before she got through."

"Bud and Rosie were the only ones who weren't in trouble," Ell says. "When we could all finally see each other again, you said something like you'd rather be hit any day than to have to listen to Minnie Beth go on and on about it."

"And we all decided that they got a kick out of sending us on guilt trips, that it was like they were in a club. And if they weren't, we'd set one up for them and call it the Milltown Mom and Pop Guilt Trip Travel Agency."

"My trip was non-stop flight," Sherman says. "Momma never let up for the whole two weeks I was grounded. She'd preach me a sermon on bad language and hand me a bar of soap so I could go scrub my mouth. I can't stand the smell of Dial soap to this day."

"Mother's little sojourn for me had many layovers," Ell says. "First she'd cry and say she knew I was really a good girl and that good girls must feel really bad when they lie to their mothers. And for a day or two, she wouldn't say anything, but the next thing I knew she'd bring me a Bible passage to contemplate. You and I got off light compared to Grace Ann though. That was one time Fred didn't let her wiggle out of it."

"Yeah, he made her hand over the keys to that new Skylark and then he put an ad in the Good River Journal and sold that sucker right out from under her, if I remember it right," Sherman says. "And she didn't get to drive again for three months."

"Funny thing," Ell says as she gets up to pour them some more coffee. "When I was looking at Fred's website last night, somebody mentioned seeing a car just like that old Skylark near Grace Ann's trailer on the day of the murders. Same year and everything."

"What all did it say?" Sherman wants to know. "I don't have me a computer yet, but one of my regular customers does and he keeps me up to date on Timeofgrace. He didn't say nothing about that, though."

"Fred didn't bother to put that little bit of information where just anybody can see it," Ell tells him. "I found it in his e-mail and put it in myself. And there were several things in his Recycle Bin that needed to be put in as well, so I did that, too. I don't know what it is he's up to. But something's not right."

"Wait now," Sherman says. "I don't claim to know much about the Internet but I didn't know just anybody could look at a person's e-mail. Isn't that private?"

"Well, yes," Ell admits. "But let me tell you a little story." She briefly fills him in on Zaia-Danda and her involvement with Bud and Fred.

"Her brother Joe, the one who did the website, is the one who figured out that Fred's trashing a lot of information that could be useful to the police. She wanted me to see it, so she gave me the password. So, I took a look at it and found plenty. Besides that stuff about the '68 Skylark, there was information about Grace Ann's mother's wedding rings and Tanner's wallet being found in the woods behind the trailer. That sort of destroys the idea of the killings being connected to a robbery'"

"Why didn't she just call the police and tell them?" Sherman asks her. "They've got a right to know this, too."

"Zaia-Danda doesn't want to get too closely involved with the police because of Bud keeping in contact with her. But at the same time, she wants them to find the person who really did kill Grace Ann and Tanner. We both agree it's not Bud."

Sherman is nodding seriously. "I'm inclined to agree. And what's stranger still is when I talked to Fred last week and he asked me if I thought there was anybody else that could have done it besides Bud. He said he's got to thinking here lately that it might not be Bud after all."

"What do you think he means by that?" Ell asks him. "We both know he's had it in for Bud since the first time he laid eyes on him at Grace Ann's Sweet Sixteen party. He's played him up, down and sideways all these years, but when you get right down to it, he still hates his guts."

"Old Fred's mercury's not moving to the top of the thermometer these days for sure," Sherman says. "I don't know if it's that Prozac he's on or what. And he looks like death on a stick. He come by Momma's one night when I had to work late and she like to never got rid of him. He put 'The Tennessee Waltz' on that old stereo of mine and started dancing her around the living room. He even invited her to dinner. Momma was flabbergasted. In the thirty-three years since my daddy died, Fred Hardaman's hardly even acknowledged my momma's alive, much less somebody he'd want to take out to dinner."

"Death can make people do crazy things," Ell says. "I've heard divorce does, too."

"You won't get no argument from me on that score," Sherman tells her.

Sitting at the dining room table, they look through the window at the lights moving on the highways and byways of the city below them. Ell fills two wine glasses from a bottle of Blue Nun on the sideboard. Sherman sips for a few minutes before he continues. "I just wish Rosie had give me some warning before she high-tailed off with the kids last Christmas. I was so damned mad at her for several months there I couldn't hardly see straight. I couldn't even bring myself to discuss things with her. But now though if I had it to do all over again. I'd do it different, real different."

"And what would you do now?" Ell asks him, softly.

"I'd light out after her," Sherman says, without hesitation. "And beg her to come back."

They drink in silence until the girls finish watching "Willow." Molly and Cassie come in and get on either side of Sherman. Both take an arm and escort him to the living room couch.

"You said you'd play the old Mario game with us, Daddy," Molly reminds him. "Like you used to."

"Come watch us, Aunt Ell," Cassie calls to her as Sherman takes the joystick. "We always beat Daddy on this one. He never wins, not even once."

It is nearing midnight when they all get to bed. Sherman sleeps in Rosie's room instead of on the couch like the night before. It does not occur to Ell until they are all in their rooms that she should have removed Michael's belongings from Rosie's bedroom. Lying in bed, she hears Sherman opening and closing dresser drawers and closet doors.

"While the band is playing Dixie, I'm humming home sweet home…"

The Backstep Sidewinders perform as Rosie and the rest of Wildwood Flower check out Old South Days. Michael, Curtis and Charlie sample funnel cakes and sweet cider. Rosie and Gabe walk among the other vendor booths. Gabe is uncharacteristically swigging from a pocket flask as he guides Rosie by the elbow through the crowd.

"And that one song just about sums up the essence of this little gathering, now doesn't it?" He asks her, referring to the string band on the performance platform. "Great God in heaven, did you ever see a whiter, straighter crowd? I don't think there've been this many sons and daughters of the True South together at one time since George Wallace was campaigning."

"Well, now, honey, what did you expect?" Rosie is more than a little amused at her lover's brother, who is usually so measured and controlled. He makes an entertaining drunk. "This is Old South Days, after all. 'Old times there are not forgotten,' 'To live and die in Dixie,' and so on. What did you expect them to be singing, 'New York, New York?'"

"No, I suppose not. It's just that they're all such straight, solid citizens," Gabe remarks as he takes a swig of Jack Daniels. "Just look at all those fine upstanding men with their wives or girlfriends. They'd string me up from that hickory tree over there if they knew I was going to spend the night camping in the woods with the lead male singer from Grafton Street."

"But they don't know it," Rosie says. "And even if they did, it's not their business. Let's get you some coffee or you're not going to be able to do the next set." They stop at the next booth and Gabe buys a large coffee.

An overnight rain dropped the temperature, banishing Indian Summer. Vendor booths and tables spread across the grounds of Bucksville Ironworks Park. A small, generally quiet state-owned recreational area forty-five minutes from Birmingham, the park thrums with activity on this early November day. A large number of festival goers will stay the night in the park's spacious campgrounds, which offers RV set-ups as well as a primitive camping area in the woods beyond. Charlie and Curtis hitched their old Airstream trailer to the back of their Explorer to accommodate Wildwood Flower. The trailer sleeps six. Gabe brought his own tent.

The performance arena, some fifty yards beyond the vendor area, is surrounded by lawn chairs and blankets filled with music lovers. Much of the crowd that is milling around the vendor area came for the Battle of Bucksville reenactment scheduled for mid-afternoon. Rosie plans a long stroll with Caitlin while the battle rages. Charlie and Curtis' sister, Maithel, came along and is helping out with Caitlin.

As they stop at a table of pine needle baskets, Rosie picks up one to admire its intricate handiwork. The basket weaver, a tiny, ancient woman with a face like walnut shells, talks about the difficulties of her craft.

"These'ns here is likely the last ones I can do," she says to them. "Hurts my fingers so bad I have to stop fer purt' near an hour after I get through with a row." She holds up hands gnarled from arthritis. "That's why I got to ask $50 for one of 'em. I hate doing it. I'd as soon give 'em away, people like 'em so good."

As Gabe and Rosie leave the woman's booth, the rest of Wildwood Flower comes toward them, carrying plates of barbeque and fixings and cups of tea. Maithel follows them, bringing Caitlin. The seven of them walk to the shade of an oak tree where Michael spreads two blankets.

Then they sit down for a dinner on the ground. Gabe leans against the foot of the tree, sipping his coffee as his plate of barbeque, corn, and baked beans cools beside him.

"That's not pig meat on that plate, man." Michael says to his brother, indicating the barbecued meat. "That's genuine Texas barbecue. Hot off the cow." He and Rosie hold Caitlin between them, feeding her small bites of baked beans.

"Smells good, but I believe I'll pass." Gabe says. "Mr. Daniels might disapprove of me adding anything to the fine effect his concoction seems to be having on me." He gets up to go a few yards beyond them and brings another large coffee, walking carefully as he cups it in his hands. He sits down closer to Rosie and Caitlin, who reaches for him.

"Is it all right?" He asks Rosie as he sets the coffee down and takes the baby. "You sure you want your little one in the arms of a tipsy queen?"

Rosie, not knowing quite how to answer him, turns to Michael, who is looking thoughtfully at his older brother. "It's like that, is it?" Michael asks him and squeezes his brother's shoulder. "You could always just not find that dude, Ian, is it? There's enough people milling around here that you could probably get away with that."

"You're right about that," Gabe says. "I could do that. I could spend the rest of the weekend with Miss Caity here. She's probably a better date at that." He smiles, ruefully, as he settles Caitlin into his lap and picks out bits of food for her from his untouched plate.

They finish eating and Rosie thanks Maithel for tending to Caitlin for the duration of the festival and takes the diaper bag from her. "I really do appreciate it," Rosie says to her. "Ell usually comes with us, but it's her weekend at the library."

Maithel, fiftyish and comfortable with it, stands and brushes leaves from her jeans skirt. Originally from Sand Mountain, located to the north and east in our fair state, she traveled to Birmingham a decade ago with her brother Charlie. Both childless and long divorced, they share a house with their younger brother, Curtis, on the South Side. "Charlie in a dress and ten years older," as Michael describes her, Maithel is head teller at a bank branch near their home. Charlie, Wildwood Flower's mellowed out mandolin player, is the band's own instrument of peace. Whenever inevitable musical squabbles erupt, Charlie says in his unmistakable Sand Mountain twang, "Now, ya'll keep your britches on a minute and let's figure this thing out." Charlie works days in a fine jewelry and watch repair shop, painstakingly tinkering with minute parts until each item is made whole again. Curtis, the band's bass player, is closer to Michael's age and works as a waiter at one of Southside's more exclusive eating establishments.

"You just let me know anytime you need me to keep Little Miss Caitlin," Maithel says to her. "She's a pleasant little lady. You say you're going to look after her while the battle's going on?"

"Yes," Rosie says to her. "Don't tell me you want to watch it?"

"Oh, Lord yes, honey," Maithel says. "One of mine and Charlie and Curtis' great-greats was in that battle. I just love anything to do with the Civil War."

"You're in the right place then," Rosie tells her as she stands up to help Curtis fold the blankets. She turns to the rest of the band. "Do ya'll want to go watch some of the others before our next set?"

Everyone heads for the performance arena where Bon Temps Rouler, a Cajun band from Ferriday, Louisiana, is warming up. Rosie takes Caitlin from Gabe as they spread their blanket near the edge of the crowd so that they can leave easily when it is time for them to play. As a teenager, Rosie traveled often with her daddy and her Uncle Sam to various country music festivals in Louisiana and Mississippi where Cajun and Creole music were the order of the day. Recollections of swarthy men, hot fiddling and spicy food fill her. To date, Wildwood Flower has not shared the bill with a Cajun band. She locates a bottle of apple juice for Caitlin and settles back for pleasurable listening.

Following a little good natured patter in English and Fractured French—Michael's term for Cajun—the band opens with an old standard, "Pauvre Hobo." After a few more numbers, couples move to the polished plank floor below the stage to render variations on the Cajun jitterbug. The crowd loves the band and the band loves them back as they fai-do-do through both a familiar and obscure repertoire. They close with "Jolie Blon," inviting the crowd to Cajun two-step. The dance area fills quickly and the crowd begins to move chairs and blankets aside to join the dance. Michael bows to Rosie, who hands Caitlin over to Gabe. Their bodies merge, stepping and swaying to the song of the beautiful blonde.

Grafton Street, a six-member Irish band from Huntsville, mounts the stage. Replete with guitar, fiddle, tin-whistle, bass, melodeon, bodrhain and bones, plus a variety of occasionally used instruments, the group is a regular feature of Old South Days. Influenced by such groups as The Chieftans and De Danaan, they perform traditional and modern with Celtic pride and flair. Only Gabe's friend, Ian McDaid, and the lead singer, Maura O'Grady are actually from the Old Country. The remainder of the band was hand picked by Ian and Maura who became friends while waiting tables in a Huntsville Restaurant. The other four members hail from Boston, Dallas, Seattle and Huntsville, respectively. All responded to an advertisement Ian placed in a Celtic Music magazine. Their performance today is speckled with rigs and reels, haunting ballads and rowdy drinking songs. Maura's clear sweet soprano moves Rosie to tears and envy with "When You and I Were Young, Maggie."

The five men and a lady, as they often introduce themselves, accept the crowd's requests for the last half of their set. "Ragland Road," someone shouts as Ian steps to the mike.and sings in a raspy baritone.

During the instrumental interlude, the long-locked, blue-eyed redhead searches the crowd for Gabe and finding him, sings the remainder of the ballad gazing in his direction. A small, wiry man a bit older than Gabe, his yellow teeth flash a killer smile.

"Now, let's do one you all know to finish this out," he says to the crowd. "We know you're anxious to get to the battle that's taking place a little later on. The Irish know a little something about rebels, too, you know," he pauses as the crowd laughs. "So to put everyone in a happy mood, won't you join us now in 'Molly Malone?" The band and most of the crowd sing along.

As they finish up, Gabe makes his way carefully through the crowd to join his friend as he steps from the stage.

Wildwood Flower's performance, several acts later, is neither brilliant nor dreadful. The crowd is somewhat restive, ready for the action to come. Gabe's picking falters on "Fox on the Run," but he compensates with a rare solo on an old Carter Family standard, "Are You Tired of Me, My Darling." Gabe sings in a soft low-register baritone, focusing his eyes on the distant trees.

Rosie and Michael close out the set with Carter and Cash's rendition of "Jackson." They sing to each other. As they finish and Rosie wipes the sweat from Michael's face, he promises not to tarry long at the Battle of Bucksville.

Except for a few women and children shopping the vendor booths, the main grounds of the park are mostly deserted for the three hours of battle reenactment. Rosie pushes Caitlin's stroller to the playground above the battlefield ravine. She takes the baby out and sits down with her in a swing. Snuggling Caitlin across her, she pumps her legs, sending the two of them high into the air. Caitlin squeals and claps her hands.

Listening to the battle cries in the distance, she considers her ex-husband's affinity for vicarious violence. His life-long love affair with the Lost War. His favorite television shows are reruns of westerns and police dramas from the '50s and '60s. Boxing, football, hockey, wrestling. Any contact sport, just name it and Sherman likes to watch it. Even played some in their high school years whenever Minnie Beth would allow it. And Michael and Gabe—two of the least violence prone men she has ever encountered—looking like two little boys off to play soldier as they go to watch the battle. She is glad, as always, that her children are girls. She is uncertain how she would handle a little boy's need for physical confrontation.

As she pushes herself and the baby higher into the cool November air, she tries to remember whether she ever observed in Bud Reese any overt attraction to violence. She cannot recall anything specific. Somehow, she thinks that someone so overly attentive to Grace Ann's every want and need could not also be her killer.

On Sunday morning while many campers sleep in, Gospel groups gather at the performance arena. A tiny crowd greets them at 8:00, but by 10:00 or so, most of the festival-goers bring out their blankets and lawn chairs. They sit, eating sausage and biscuits and sipping coffee as they attend the Church of the Open Air—as the 8-11:30 segment is billed. Maithel and Charlie remain in the camper with the sleeping Caitlin. Huddling together in an Afghan, Michael, Rosie and Curtis sit on a blanket at the edge of the crowd. The Son Lighters, an all male a capella quartet from Tennessee, warms up.

"Jesus, the Son, is the light and the way," the tallest member of the group is saying. They wear blue suits with red ties and look much alike. "Through his light we are led to the Father. And that light is what we want to share with you this morning."

Their medley traverses from "Heavenly Sunlight," to "The Light of God is Falling," to "Let the Lower Lights be Burning," and ends with "I Saw the Light." They invite all to sing.

The crowd is on its feet, clapping and shouting the chorus as Gabe and Ian emerge from the woods of the back campground. They stop at the wood's edge where each nods a brief goodbye. As they move away from each other, Ian calls Gabe's name. When he doesn't turn to acknowledge him, he shrugs and goes over to join Grafton Street in their lawn chairs near the stage. Gabe ambles over to Curtis and Michael and Rosie and sits on the blanket's edge. Rosie gets up and goes to the nearest vendor stand and brings him a large coffee.

"I thank you," Gabe says, accepting it. He takes small sips and listens reverently to the last Gospel group. Many of the performers bring out their instruments and join in "When We All Get to Heaven." Gabe is still sitting on the ground when everyone moves away and the stage hands begin to set up for the final session in the afternoon.

The men of Wildwood Flower divide a couple of six packs for the ride home. They secure the trailer hitch to the Airstream and climb in the Explorer. Rosie rides shotgun with Maithel driving. Caitlin sleeps in her car seat behind them, between Michael and Gabe. Charlie and Curtis occupy the rear.

The men are well into their Budweisers when Michael says to Gabe, "So, what about last night."

"I guess all told it beat a poke in the eye with a sharp stick, but not by much," Gabe told him.

"One night of loving don't make up for 364 alone," Charlie sings, trying a variation of an old song Willie and the Family used to sing at concerts. Curtis resounded with the rest of the tune about a cold and distant woman.

"I might have a better one," Michael joins in as he notices Gabe begin to smile. He begins a chorus of "Good Hearted Woman in Love with a Good Timing Man." By the time they pull into the parking lot at the apartment complex, they've sung every macho posturing song any of them can recall, closing out with "I've Gotta Get Drunk and I Sure Do Dread It."

Rosie gets out of the car and kisses Michael goodbye, since Sherman is still upstairs with the older girls. "Come at 8:00," she tells him as she takes Caitlin and her carseat inside the building. "Sherman's bound to be gone by then."

Chapter Twelve

Still in her long dress from the band's last performance, Rosie accepts Sherman's dinner invitation with some misgivings. He insists on taking her to Twelve Oaks, the new restaurant in an antebellum styled house several blocks away. It is featured in this weekend's *Haute Cuisine and Country Cookin'* column in the newspaper.

"The way the man in the newspaper wrote it up, why it'll be just like a dinner at the real Wilkes plantation," Sherman tells her as they drive to the restaurant. "It even has twelve columns and a winding staircase, just like at Ashley's place."

"I got us a table by the window since it's right by that park where I heard all the queers go," he says as they near the restaurant. "We can sit and sip our mint juleps and watch them mate."

He stops in front of the white columned house to let the valet park the Mustang. "Should be some sight to see when they all start swishing their tails," he remarks as they enter the foyer and wait for the hoop skirted hostess to seat them.

"Kindly watch your mouth," Rosie says to him. "There are probably any number of gay people in this very room. Besides that, you know good and well Gabe is gay. And he's our friend, mine and Ell's."

"Well, pardon my French, or is that Greek," Sherman says, dryly. "All right, I'll zip it up for now. I didn't bring you here to start a fight, Rosie. I want to hear about your weekend. How was the festival?"

"The band went over great," she tells him. "They've asked us back for next year already. You would have enjoyed it, I expect—all the crafts and food. And I heard the battle reenactment was top notch."

"Maybe I ought to get involved in something like that," Sherman says. "Momma's all-the-time telling me I need to join up with one of them play-soldier groups since I've always took such an interest in the war."

"If you do it right, like they did, it can get pretty expensive," Rosie tells him. "The uniforms and artillery and all run into big money."

"Well, I'd want to do it right," Sherman says. "I'm through doing things half-assed. From now on, it's all the way or not at all."

"Michael and Gabe and I feel that way about the band," Rosie tells him. "Michael sees to it that we practice enough and get the sound just right. There's not a thing that's half way about Michael,"

"Seems like to me he's only a fair to middling fiddle player," Sherman says. "But then I don't know much about that kind of music."

"Michael's the best." Rosie tells him, looking evenly into Sherman's green eyes. "Is there anything else you wanted to know about the festival?"

"I expect not," Sherman says as the waiter fills their water glasses. "I'm just glad you all had a good time. The girls and I had a killer weekend. The Fall Fest was great. Molly won herself some little trinkets playing Go Fish and they both did the Moonwalk three or four times."

"Tell me about the rest of it," Rosie says, hoping to move the conversation away from Michael. "What all did they have there?"

After the waiter takes their orders, Sherman goes into great detail about each event at the Southside Methodist Fall Fest. He emphasizes how many mothers who were there with their children asked after Rosie. Then he talks about the girls' school and questions Rosie's involvement there.

Rosie holds up her hand. "I worked the Halloween carnival last weekend," Rosie tells him. "And I've been to every P.T.O. meeting this year. And I fully intend to help with the Christmas programs and parties. I am not 'too busy,' if that's what you're trying to get at, Sherman." She glances out the window at the park. A young boy leans into the window of parked Mercedes. She cannot see the driver's face.

"That's certainly real good to hear," Sherman says to her. "I'm glad you are able to tear yourself away from Baby Boy long enough to see to your children's needs."

Rosie stands then, placing her napkin on the white linen tablecloth. "His name is Michael, as you are more than well aware. And I do not have to listen to your garbage, Sherman Jackson. I see to my children's needs more than you do now or ever did do, truth be told. It's only since we've been gone that you've even realized you have any kids."

"That is probably true enough," Sherman says, placing a hand on her wrist and gently pulling her back into her chair. "See, I'll even admit it, I didn't do enough with the kids before. But I'm willing to do different. I'm not trying to make you mad, Rosie. I'm just concerned."

"And just exactly what is it that's concerning you?" Rosie asks, flinging his hand from her wrist and taking a sip of water. "That I might actually be enjoying my life for a change instead of chasing my tail trying to please you and never succeeding?"

"I never wanted you to be unhappy," Sherman says quietly. "And you pleased me just fine. If I acted like you didn't, then I was just stupid. It's just that I don't want that baby hippie." He stops when he notices her expression. "All right, all right, Michael then. I do not want Michael to get the idea that he can just move right in and take my place."

"No one is taking your place, Sherman," Rosie says to him. "The girls talk about you all the time. Even Caitlin gets excited when she sees you. They know who their daddy is. It's different with them and Michael. Molly and Cassie like him. He pays attention to them and plays with them. He does actual child care for Caitlin. But Michael is my lover and it's time you accepted that."

"It's not got nothing to do with accepting anything," Sherman says to her. Their waiter, in full Confederate uniform, brings their orders to the table. Sherman stops talking until the young man pours their wine and departs. "It all comes down to this: I think you made a big mistake, running off like you did and up and divorcing me without so much as a second thought. I know I pissed you off when I disappeared them three days. But I tried more than once to explain it to you. The only reason I left was to go up to Tennessee to see Uncle Gene about some money to help me make those improvements at the garage…"

"Well, that's certainly a very convenient excuse and everything," she tells him. "But I know it to be a lie. You may have gone to see your uncle, but the real reason you took off was because you didn't want Caitlin. You made that more than clear the whole nine months I was carrying her. And you thought running off and leaving us in the house without any money and the gas company about to cut the service off would teach me a good lesson for having her."

"Where you cooked that one up, I'll never know," Sherman says. "But that's not really the point. The point is, I think we ought to give this thing some more thought. It's our kids that's suffering."

"And how exactly is it that they're suffering, Sherman? I'd like you to explain that."

"By having Michael spend the night with you with them right there in the house," Sherman tells her bluntly. "Did you think I didn't know that he's over there nearly every night?"

"I think you have nothing to say about that," Rosie says to him. She has not touched her dinner. The prime rib sauce is congealing on the plate. "And what of it anyway? Peggy Ann Prewitt and her son spent two months living with you in our old house, if I recall."

"And that was wrong," Sherman says. "But at least I didn't have the kids right there with me all the time. I don't like this, Rosie. And if I have to do something about it, I will."

"What does that mean?" She asks him.

"What it means is, you're acting like a teenager. You and your little lover boy. You haven't done nothing but got yourself another kid with that little wimp. And if you keep it up, having him spend the night with the kids right there in the house, I'll go see Judge Brown."

"And tell him what?" Rosie stands and throws her napkin down again.

"I'll let him know every bit of what I've said to you here today," Sherman says as he stands and faces her. "And then, I'm going to ask him for custody of my children. He give it to you because you was acting like a fit mother at the time of our divorce. But if you keep acting up like you are, he'd be just as quick to give it me. Yes ma'am, when he finds out that dope-smoking hippie is sleeping in the bed with you with them right there in the house, why he's gonna turn them girls over to their daddy. You can count on it." Sherman signals the waiter and pays for their uneaten meals with an American Express Gold Card and leaves the restaurant.

The evening crowd is coming in. The hoop skirted hostesses seat several more tables as Rosie makes her way to the door. When she reaches the front of the restaurant, she does not look around to see if Sherman waited for her and begins to walk the ten blocks home. A light drizzle begins to fall as she moves down the sidewalk past the men waiting in parked cars, watching the park below them.

Alone with "60 Minutes," and a microwave dinner heating in the kitchen, Ell props her legs on the ottoman to enjoy the peace. As soon as Rosie and Sherman left for the restaurant after loading Sherman's luggage in the car, Molly and Cassie begged to spend the remainder of the evening with Helen and Meaghan, promising to return by 9:00. Caitlin went to sleep in the car on the drive back from the girls' houses. She did not rouse when Ell laid her in the crib. Her long weekend of term paper crises at an end, Ell is quite content to watch Mike Wallace make minced meat of a small town funeral director who bilked some elderly people of much of their life savings. She starts when the doorbell rings and runs to answer it before it wakes the baby. Before she finishes opening the door, an arm and hand waving a white handkerchief reach around it. Smiling, she steps aside, flinging it wide to let Gabe in. They sit down at opposite ends of the couch. Neither speaks for several minutes.

"I could say a lot of things about this weekend." Gabe begins and moves closer to her. "Most of them would be true and none of them would be very pretty. I think one of the best things I could say is that it was a mistake to try and reignite the fires with Ian."

"And what might another best thing be?" Ell asks him, not moving any closer, but not moving away.

"That I spent a good part of the weekend thinking about you," Gabe tells her as he takes her hand. "I'm not at all sure how I mean that."

"It doesn't matter," Ell says. "I'm glad you said it. You look tired."

"I'm about to drop," Gabe says. "Now that I've got this said, I might go home and lay down."

"You can do that here," Ell tells him. "Nobody's here but me and Caitlin. You can use my room if you want to."

"Will you come with me?" Gabe asks her, softly, and before she can refuse him, he is leading her to the bedroom.

"Gabe, what are we doing?" She asks him as they enter her darkened bedroom. She does not switch on a light as she feels for the covers and turns them back. Climbing across her queen-sized bed, she snuggles underneath the down comforter.

Gabe gets comfortable beside her before he answers. "We are two friends, two very tired, good friends in need of some touch," he says and pulls her against him.

"Okay," she says, tentatively. "But it seems reasonable to ask whether I'm being made the surrogate here. Ian didn't work out, so I might?"

"No," Gabe says, firmly. "And if you think that, then we'll both get up right now. One of the reasons it didn't work out with Ian is that I didn't just want a quick fix. We mostly talked a lot about where we are at this time in our lives. And, it seems we're miles apart. He's still the same

Good Time O'Charley he was when we knew each other before. I want more than that. Maybe I want it with you." He begins to stroke her hair.

"Okay," Ell says again and burrows into his arm. "I can accept that, I think. But what exactly is it that I'm supposed to do here? It's been more years than I care to mention since I was in flagrante."

"We don't have to flagrante any further than you're comfortable with," Gabe tells her, tracing the lines of her face. "I'm sure as hell not going to hurt you."

"I know that," she says. "But is it safe?"

"Oh, that," Gabe says. "Well, frankly, my dear, I had the test recently and I was negative all the way."

"That's good and everything," Ell says. "But what about last night?"

"Goodness, darlin', do you want a money-back guarantee?" Gabe asks her, laughing a little. "Let me just say that my former inamorato and I did not engage in any activities that would spread the dreaded virus, if indeed he is infected with it. 'Nuff said?"

"Just enough," she says.

He kisses her forehead and then her mouth. He moves his hand inside her sweater just as Caitlin begins to cry.

"Son of a bitch," Gabe says and Ell begins to laugh as she reaches over and turns on the bedside lamp.

"'Just lost when I was saved. Just felt the world go by,'" she says softly and gets up, straightens her clothes and goes to the crying child. Caitlin sits up in bed and reaches her arms out to Ell. Pulling the baby against her chest, she sits down with her in the rocker. She sings a few verses of "Bringing in the Sheaves," as they rock. The cadences of the hymn always lull the little girl. In a few minutes, she is asleep again. Waiting an extra five minutes, Ell then lifts Caitlin's arm and when it drops back down without stiffening, she lays her back in the crib.

Gabe is watching "Murder She Wrote," and eating a slice of cold pizza when she joins him in the living room. "Too bad Jessica Fletcher's not helping out the Caloosa County fuzz," he says, between bites. "They'd find out who killed Grace Ann lickety split, just in time for the commercial break."

"Strange things are happening on that front," she says and tells him about Zaia-Danda's visit and what she revealed. Then she goes on to relate what Sherman had told her and what she discovered in Fred's e-mail.

"Seems to me Bud's doing the only thing that'll let him go on living," Gabe says, still munching on the pizza. "He's become somebody else. Somebody who can cope with being a divorced ex-con whose ex-wife was murdered along side her lover whose child she was carrying."

"What about Fred though?"

"Fred's like a big ol' lonesome tom cat that's been neutered. He can't quite quit his old habits, but they no longer have any results." Gabe stops talking and goes to the kitchen, returning with more pizza and a beer. "Brooding over Grace Ann's death made him horny, but he's mostly too old and too stressed to do a whole lot about it except maybe when he's acting like he's somebody else, like he was with Mabel June."

"I've read that the death of someone close can have that effect," Ell says. "I seem to recall that in Seventeenth Century Literature, intercourse was even referred to as 'the little death.'"

"Easy to see why," Gabe says through another mouthful of pizza. "It's so hard to come by at times that when you finally do succeed, you're close to death."

"I'm not sure that's the way it equates," Ell says, watching him chow down on the pizza. "Not hungry or anything, are you, dear?"

"Yeah, imagine that," Gabe says, taking a swig of beer. "Haven't got any chocolate, have you now?" He asks her with a grin.

"With pizza and beer?" Ell asks him, repulsed, and then notices him laughing. "Oh, that's what you mean. I don't think it has the same effect on men. It's chocolate and estrogen, dear, not chocolate and testosterone. Keep that in mind."

"A woman thing, in other words," Gabe says. "Well, then, how about a rain-check on our rudely interrupted moment of bliss? Say another place, another time?"

"I'm on tap," she tells him, holding up his empty beer bottle. "But getting back to Fred, what about all that information I found in his e-mail that he failed to put on the website? Any thoughts on that?"

"Fred knows something he's not telling about the murders," Gabe says. "Maybe…"

Following a quick knock on the door, Michael comes in carrying cartons of Chinese take-out from the Merry Mandarin down the block. He sets them on the coffee table in front of Gabe and Ell and goes to the kitchen for plates and utensils.

"I'm starving," he says. "Want some?" He holds out the cartons to them.

"More than you know," Gabe says and takes the rest of the pizza to the kitchen for disposal.

"Lay it on me."

"Me, too," Ell says as Gabe hands her a fork and plate. "Sounds like just what I need."

They feed each other bites of chicken chow mein and egg foo young, thoroughly mystifying Michael with references to food and desire for the next half-hour. All three have full mouths and quiet tongues when the deadbolt turns and Rosie comes inside. With wisps of hair working loose from her French braid and her wet dress tail in her hand, she murmers a soft, "hey" as she passes them, heading for her room where she goes inside and closes the door.

Quickly setting his plate down on the coffee table, Michael goes after her. "Rose," he says from outside her bedroom door. "Rose, do you want to talk?"

"Come in," she says. She sits on the edge of the bed, facing the window. The small lamp on the bedside table is on its lowest setting. "If I look like I've been rode hard and put up wet, that's just about how I feel."

"Did Sherman say something ugly?" Michael asks her, sitting down softly beside her without touching her rigid shoulders.

"Maybe," she says. "And maybe he was just telling the truth, or at least the truth the way he sees it. He says that I'm acting like a teenager and that I ought to be seeing after the girls."

"You see after the girls just fine," he tells her. "What else did he say? That can't be all of it."

"That he knows you stay here most nights and that he's going to try and get custody of the girls if it continues to happen." Rosie is crying now. "I don't want to put them through that, Michael. I really don't."

"Ah, babe," he says and takes her in his arms. "Don't let that fucker make you cry. He's just blowing smoke. You've told me a hundred times how he likes to jerk you around. He just wants to see how far he can make you jump."

In a low, steady voice, he continues to reassure her that this is not the unsurmountable problem that it appears. "We'll handle it," he tells her. "I'll go on home tonight, babe. We'll talk some more after work tomorrow."

After he is gone and the girls are in bed, Rosie lays down in the darkness. She thinks of Michael inside the house he shares with Gabe, sitting on the side of the bed, smoking a joint before he lays down to sleep. He says it relaxes him, helps him to forget the day's troubles even if it does mess up his short term memory. She always marvels at the ease of his manner, the calm way he assesses any problems. She considers all they discussed over the course of the evening and wonders whether Michael will remember any of the things they said by morning.

Chapter Thirteen

I have this bone to pick with Tolstoy. I don't see how he can conclude that "all happy families are like one another," From my observation, most families are never happy long enough to invite lengthy examination. In the near year since Rosie and her girls left Sherman and came to live with me, I have watched different familial alliances and loyalties form, break apart, and restructure like the lava globules in those lamps we were all so enamored of in the '60s. At six, Molly is her momma's girl. Cassie, at almost thirteen, is at that stage of adolescence when she immediately bonds with anyone who appears to be the underdog—Sherman's current depiction of himself to her. Following his confrontation of Rosie regarding her and Michael, he began a series of nightly telephone calls to Cassie, which she answers in Rosie's bedroom, closing the door and shutting us out. This week's topic of these clandestine conversations is Cassie's proposed entry in a beauty contest which is to take place later this month at the Athena Villa Library/Civic Center. Cassie spends many of her waking hours in front of the mirror, and I believe she feels this new experience will merely expand her adoring audience. Rosie thinks otherwise. Last night after a long session of arguments and threats, she and Cassie agreed on nothing except that each felt the other was dead wrong.

Never one to suffer in silence, Cassie so ardently shared her hurt and displeasure with her younger sister that Molly refused to sleep in the same room with her and made a pallet on the floor in Rosie and Caitlin's room. Caitlin, who will celebrate her first birthday this week, was much disturbed by all the discord and woke often to cry in the night. In the early hours of the morning when I heard her crying again, I went to Rosie's room to take her from her crib and hold her against me in the rocking chair where we comforted each other until it was light.

It is 7:00 now and Rosie, after oversleeping, rushes with Molly and Caitlin in tow—off to school, daycare and work. I am indulging myself by taking a personal day away from the library, so I follow them to the car with packed lunches to wave goodbye. Cahaba River middle schoolers are excused for the day due to teacher workshops and Cassie remains home with me, sleeping late. At 11:00 she wakes and asks for fried eggs with toast.

Rosie's girls often look to me now for a little tea and sympathy—or fried eggs and toast—if the occasion warrants it. Once when she was feeling particularly damaged by something Cassie said to her, Molly climbed into my lap and snuggled against my shoulder. "You sit better than Momma," she said to me. "Her bones are too hard." Rosie, who has lost equal amounts of weight and patience since the divorce, is nearly as thin as she was in adolescence. Stepping onto any scale would surely constitute an invasion of enemy territory as far as I am concerned. What I do not know for certain can happily be left to the imagination. There is a certain comfort in ignorance in such situations.

As I stand at the stove while Cassie showers, I think of that coldest of days late last December when Rosie arrived with the girls at my apartment door and announced that she had left Sherman. Having previously written to her that she and the children were welcome if ever she decided enough was enough, I opened my home and myself to them. Until that day, domestic involvement, rather like any sort of sustained romance, had eluded me in my adult life.

Placing Caitlin, still buckled into her carseat, between us, Rosie and I worked out the practical details of a living arrangement. Swaddled in receiving blankets with only her little pink face visible, Caitlin made pleasant infant sounds and did not cry. Molly and Cassie, who did not look particularly disturbed, turned the television to Nickelodeon and paid us no mind. All through that day I kept repeating to myself and to them, "You are home. You are home."

In jeans and a ragged sweatshirt with her long hair wrapped swami style in a large towel, Cassie comes into the kitchen and I slide the eggs and toast onto a plate for her. "Don't you think Momma's making too big a deal out of my wanting to enter the Junior Winter Solstice Maiden Contest?" She asks me as we go into the living room where she sits on the sofa to eat her breakfast. "It's not like I want to be Miss Beauty Queen of the Whole Universe or something."

"Your mother is probably remembering the last beauty contest she and I had anything to do with," I tell her. "We weren't in it, of course, but Grace Ann was and it turned out rather badly in a lot of ways. After that, she and I didn't want much to do with beauty contests."

"That was a hundred years ago at least," Cassie says, rolling her eyes. "And besides, it's not her that's going to be in it, or you either. This is for me."

'That's not how it will end up," I tell her. "Grace Ann thought it was just for her, too. It's always about something else. Things like that often involve more than they seem to at first."

"Daddy says he thinks I should enter it," Cassie says, flatly. "He says I shouldn't let you and Momma talk me out of it, if it's something I really want to do. He says ya'll talk things to death anyway."

"He may be right about that," I agree. "Rosie and I do look at things a lot harder than your daddy does. Will you at least let me tell you about the thing Grace Ann was involved in? If you still want to enter Junior Winter Solstice Maiden after I finish, then I'll talk to Rosie about it for you. Fair enough?"

"I guess," Cassie says with a dramatic sigh. "Is this going to take forever? I want to watch 'The Young and the Restless,' since I get to be home from school today. Me and Momma used to watch that all the time when she didn't work."

"I promise to finish in time," I tell her and begin my tale. "You remember that Grace Ann's daddy, Fred, owned The Smart Shoppe, that dress shop your Momma and I talk about all the time? It's closed now, but we spent a lot of time there when we were close to your age. Anyway, Fred always did think he was a little smarter than anyone else around. And, our junior year when Grace Ann entered the Miss Merry Christmas contest in Good River, he made up his mind she was going to win it. Fred had this photographer friend of his who worked down at the other end of Broadway to take a million pictures of Grace Ann in this pink chiffon evening gown Fred special ordered from The Smart Shoppe. Then he had some posters made with the picture on it and plastered them in every store window on Broadway and even in some Good River stores. Some of his business friends from different parts of the county were judging the contest that year and Fred played up to them for months before it got underway. He had Grace Ann up at the crack of dawn to practice her twirling routine before she went to school."

Cassie is dipping a corner of her toast into the egg yolk and not really listening, but still, I continue. Fred backslid into hard drinking that year, checking himself into the Catholic hospital to dry out some few weeks before the contest, which took place at the beginning of December, just in time for the winners to ride the lead float in downtown Good River's annual Christmas parade. Grace Ann's new association with Bud Reese and her otherwise unruly behavior were continued stress factors in Fred's otherwise tightly controlled life. He was looking for something to distract her from Bud, and that year, it was Miss Merry Christmas.

"Girls," he said to me and Rosie one afternoon in his store while Grace Ann was at band practice. "I think Grace Ann's got a real good chance of winning this thing. I'm counting on you two to help me out. I think it'll be good for my little girl, real good." He extracted a small stub of cigar from his mouth and ground it into the ashtray he kept underneath the counter below the cash register.

"If you girls will make sure Grace Ann goes to her baton lessons and practices her routine, I'll see to it that both of you get a new dress." He indicated racks of expensive clothing in junior sizes that lined the front walls of the store.

"How is this going to help Grace Ann?" Rosie wanted to know.

"It's going to help her feel good about herself," he said. "Winning's always good. Besides, the more of these things she enters and wins, the better her chances of getting some kind of scholarship money for college." He lit another cigar and smiled. He thought he had us then. He made no mention of Bud Reese.

"Me and Ell will think about it," Rosie told him. We both knew how expensive college was, even for someone as seemingly affluent as Fred Hardaman. We left his store and walked to the corner RexAll. I purchased a magazine titled *Fab Four*. Rosie and I were sharing an order of french fries and debating the desirability of John vs. Paul when Grace Ann walked in from band practice all sweaty and exhilarated.

"Ya'll won't believe it," she said, twirling her baton absently as she sauntered over to us and flopped onto a stool. "Dr. Lear is one of the judges in the contest this year. Isn't that the coolest thing you ever heard? He thinks I've got a good chance to win. And now, I think I want to win."

Rock Lear, Samantha Jane Seers' diminutive band director, was a personal friend of Fred's and Grace Ann's. Dying in strange and violent circumstances the year following our graduation, he was long noted for a tendency to hurl his director's baton at misbehaving band members. At the end of our eighth-grade year, he chose Grace Ann as the only majorette from our class out of a line-up of forty seven. Dr. Lear's musical and leadership talents were second to none. Our band won innumerable honors, state and national, during his tenure.

Grace Ann helped herself to a handful of our fries and said, "Things are getting too complicated. Tell me what to do, Ell. You can always figure things out and tell me and Rosie what to do." She smiled at me as though I was the only person who mattered to her.

"You can do it," I told her. "I know you can. Rosie and I'll go with you to Lainie Black's house on Saturday for your baton lesson. We'll help you, if this is really what you want to do."

But on that Saturday, Rosie's daddy and uncle took her with them to play Bluegrass music with The Strawberry Pickers, Big Jim's string band, at a political meeting in Arab. So, Grace Ann and I walked the hilly streets of the mill village to Lainie Black's house. A former head majorette at Seers' High, Lainie won the Miss Merry Christmas competition in her senior year. Home then for semester break in her last year at The University, Lainie was engaged to a millionaire's son she met at a fraternity party two years earlier. She knew that soon she'd never have to teach baton lessons again.

Her daddy had stopped working when the mill shut down the previous year, but their family remained in the house allotted to them when he was a mill boss. Referred to by millhands as Palace Walk, the row of management houses was set on a higher hill overlooking the many streets of millworker houses. Antebellum in design, although they were not built until the middle 1890s, the seven houses were well-kept and well-structured. Lainie met us with baton in hand in her wide back yard, which opened onto a wooded slope.

"Grace Ann, you've just turning out to be the prettiest thing, darlin'," Lainie said as we walked up to her. "I told Momma the last time I saw you at the end of the summer that you'd fill out some more. Turn around for me now." Lainie squinted her lovely brown eyes as she assessed her pupil.

"Hey, hon," she then said to me, smiling vaguely in my direction. "You're Ellott, isn't that right?" Rosie and I had accompanied Grace Ann to baton lessons for years, but Lainie could never seem to remember our names. She once told Rosie that she had lovely skin and hair, but that her legs were much too thin for her to ever consider being a majorette. She never offered even that much to me. On that day, she just sighed, shook her pretty brunette head, smiled regretfully and turned her attention back to Grace Ann.

After watching her go through her routine, Lainie said to her, "When you do the salute at the end, smile and tilt your head back just a 'smidge. Be sure and look right at Dr. Lear."

"And when you strut and do your turns, point your toes hard and make sure they notice your hips moving. Let's see you go through it again." She observed Grace Ann silently, walking round her, occasionally touching her with the tip of her baton when her movements were off center.

"Good, but it's got to be better," she said when Grace Ann finished and then proceeded to show her. Together on that hilltop in the warm late fall air, strutting side by side, their small-boned bodies moved with a feminine fluidity that I neither possessed nor understood. Looking down at my large-framed, somewhat overweight self, I felt like a species apart from Lainie and Grace Ann. They talked about aerials and blind catches and body wraps and I walked over to the porch where Mr. Black was reading the paper.

"Ellott," he nodded a greeting at me as he raised his eyes from the sports page. When I was quite young before my father went to work for V.J. Elmore's, Mr. Black was his supervisor in the spinning room of White Cotton Mill.

"Your daddy coming to the Lodge meeting tonight?" He asked me.

I don't remember how I answered him, but he talked pleasantly to me until Grace Ann and Lainie were finished. When it was time for us to go, he looked seriously into my eyes. "Don't you be one of those silly girls, now," he said, indicating his daughter and Grace Ann. "Your daddy says you're real smart. You stay like that."

Grace Ann was Miss Merry Christmas that year, but on the afternoon following the competition, a few hours before the parade, she disappeared. We—Fred, Rosie and I—searched all the stores on Broadway and a dozen other places without finding her. Bud Reese didn't know where she was either. Fred gave up and went home to drink and worry with the parade only two hours away.

Walking back to my house in the December twilight, Rosie said, "There she is," and pointed to Grace Ann sitting on the ground beneath an oak tree at the end of our street, crying.

"Hey," she said as we knelt down beside her. "I know what this is all about now, ya'll. And I'm not going to do it any more. I'm ashamed of you all for not telling me."

"What?" We said at the same time. "Your daddy just wants you to get used to being in beauty contests so you can win some scholarship money for college."

"Bull hockey," Grace Ann said, wiping her eyes. "The only thing he wants is to show me off to as many boys as he can in hopes that I'll forget about Bud. Let me tell you what went on at that contest."

A group of older men at the competition stood in the wings of the stage, talking about Grace Ann while she twirled and whirled. Their voices were loud and rude and they made obscene gestures as they pointed to her breasts and behind. From where Rosie and I sat with Sherman and Bud in the audience, we only heard catcalls and occasional wolf whistles from boys our own age. After the winners were announced, Fred quickly whisked her away.

"He must have introduced me to twenty boys before we got out of that auditorium," Grace Ann said. "And on the way home, all he could talk about was how pretty I looked and didn't I think so-and-so was cute and maybe he'd ask me out. Bud is good enough for me, and if he's not for Daddy, then I'm just sorry. How could ya'll have ever believed that this had anything to do with college? You know how Daddy hates Bud."

All of us cried then, the way adolescent girls do. We reminded her she had promised to ride in the parade and that if she backed out now, it would just embarrass everyone. Finally, she agreed and we went to her house to help her do her hair and get her dress ready. I pressed the folds of her evening gown while Rosie helped her with her makeup.

She arrived just in time to make that ride through downtown Good River. The parade featured bands and floats from all the neighboring communities and lasted for hours. One of its chief attractions was the high stepping Rhythm Girls Team from Booker T. Washington High, the only remaining all-black school in Caloosa County. Attired as brightly wrapped Christmas packages, the fourteen girls performed an elaborate routine at each stopping point.

Grace Ann's float led the entire parade and when it reached the spot where Rosie and I were standing, she waved as though she were delighted to be there. When the parade ended, we helped her sneak away to see Bud, telling Fred she was going to the late movie with us. She wore her tiara that night and lost it by hanging it out the window of Bud's car.

"I can't see how that's got anything to do with me," Cassie says as she puts her plate in the sink.

"It seems to me that any contest you win mostly because of the way you look—which is something you have no control over—is not really the best thing to pursue," I say to her. This seems a bit lame to me now; but when I said it to Rosie following our experience with Grace Ann, it seemed as right as rain.

"Says you," Cassie says. "And Momma, probably. It's not like she doesn't spend enough time primping in the mirror for Michael."

"But you like Michael, don't you?" I ask her.

"Liking him's not got anything to do with it," Cassie says, sounding much like her father. "She's too old for him. She ought to be spending her time with us when she's not at work."

"Maybe you ought to say that to her," I suggest.

"Like she'd pay me any attention," Cassie says. "Well, I still want to enter the Junior Winter Solstice Maiden Contest. Are you still gonna help me convince Momma?"

"Let me talk to her when she comes home," I tell her.

"My daddy said he'll come see me in the contest," Cassie tells me. "And if I need some new outfits or whatever, then that would be no problem."

Partly to distract Cassie from her aggravation and also because it needs doing, we spend the afternoon baking Christmas cookies. Visions of sugarplums doing the macarena fill our heads as we mix and measure. Months ago, I purchased a twenty-four piece set of Christmas cookie cutters from Dottie Dunwald, our children's librarian. I unearth them and we sally forth into confectionery land. An image of my mother, face flushed, as she bent over the oven to remove a tray of gingerbread men pops into my thoughts. We may even do a chorus of "I Enjoy Being a Girl," before it's all over.

"Me and Momma and Molly used to do this every year, three days before Christmas," Cassie informs me as she ties on one of my mother's old aprons. "We made all the different kinds. Molly likes to do wedding cookies the best. She always got powdered sugar all over her face and once Momma took her picture like that."

Molly and Cassie's church group holiday parties are this weekend, beginning a schedule of much anticipated seasonal celebrations. When they arrived at my door, three days before Christmas last year, Rosie had only a few hastily wrapped packages for the older girls and nothing for Caitlin, who was only three weeks old. After we settled the more practical details of sharing a household, I took Rosie aside and offered her the monthly check I receive from an investment my late father made some years ago.

"The girls need a really good Christmas," I told her. "Pay me back when you get a job." Rosie's tears and hugs were more than enough thanks.

On the morning of Christmas Eve, Rosie shopped, taking advantage of last minute mark-downs. We stored the packages in my room. When night fell, I gathered everyone in my Cherokee to roam the metroplex, looking for Christmas lights. One of the newspapers provided a guide to lavish holiday displays. A yard in Mountain Brook featured an entire North Pole with gargantuan Santa and Mrs. Claus, elves, reindeer and the whole gang. Two houses down "O Holy Night," played on a p.a. system as Bethlehem was reborn. An exquisitely crafted Mother and Child were lovingly overseen by Joseph, wise men, shepherds, et al. Molly wanted a closer look. Seeing her kneeling by the Baby Jesus, a little boy ran from inside his house to offer her a Christmas cookie.

Last year Rosie endowed them with a guilt-driven bounty of Christmas excess, frosted with beautiful Yuletide scenes. This Christmas with their involvement at church and school and Rosie's stabilized work situation, a more normal time of family togetherness is planned. Christmas Eve is to be spent in Birmingham with Michael and Gabe. On Christmas day, we'll travel to Millie's farmhouse in Caloosa County to feast on quail and cornbread dressing. Sherman will pick up Molly and Cassie at 3:00 and they will remain with him in Milltown until after New Year's. Cassie and I discuss this and all the impending excitement Christmas can hold when you're not quite 13.

While a batch of Christmas cookies bakes, Cassie suggests we sing carols. I unearth one of my mother's old lesson books and place it before me as I sit down at her old Spinet piano. "Let's do 'What Child is This,'" she says, finding it in the book. "We're doing that in Youth Choir the Sunday before Christmas."

I familiarize myself with it for a few minutes and as Cassie's young girl soft soprano fills the apartment, I begin to see a way to convince Rosie to allow her oldest child to enter the beauty pageant.

The jolly spirit of the afternoon so envelopes her that when Rosie, Molly and Caitlin arrive, Cassie actually runs to greet them. Proudly displaying a tray of macaroons, wedding and sugar cookies in various Christmas shapes, she insists that they try some. She feeds tiny bites to Caitlin, who says, "Mmm," with each mouthful.

Scarcely believing this to be the same sullen adolescent she left in bed that morning, Rosie looks questioningly at me. I make the "wait" sign. We leave the room, placing Caitlin in her walker and asking the girls to watch her. Molly is sampling each delectable as Cassie describes each recipe in lengthy detail. In the kitchen, I heat water for blackberry tea as we sit down at the counter.

"Who kidnaped Cassie?" Rosie wants to know. "That can't be my kid in there, acting so sweet."

"I got her mind off herself for awhile," I say. "We needed to do the cookies for their church parties and we did so many, I'll be able to freeze some for the library party. She loves doing that, Rosie. We ought to let her cook more often."

"I never knew she wanted to," Rosie says, looking sad. "Maybe Sherman is right. Maybe I ought to quit seeing Michael and just be their mother."

"I think moderation is the word here," I say. "Cassie and Molly are old enough not to need you every waking minute. Maybe you can spend time with each of them alone. I read somewhere that makes kids feel special, especially when there's been a divorce.

"I'll try that," Rosie says. "I'll try anything that'll stop those temper fits Cassie's been throwing lately. Lord above, she gets more like Sherman every day. I never pulled any of that crap on Momma. Millie Culp would've warmed my backside real quick and that would have stopped that. I always said I'd never use a belt or a hickory on any of my kids. God, I used to hate that. All I've ever done is swat them on the butt from time to time. But, I tell you, thinking back on it, being scared of what my momma would do kept me from doing a lot of things my kids do as a matter of course. Corporal punishment does that much at least."

"It's a little late for that," I say. "Besides, I've got a way to make Cassandra Lee Jackson the happiest camper around."

"Whatever it is, I'll do it," Rosie says. "Even if it's letting her enter that ridiculous beauty contest. I don't know why that still bothers me so much. All that mess with Grace Ann was a long time ago. With this thing, I think it's partly because it's Sherman's idea. He only wants her to do it because I'll hate it. It's like he's out to destroy me because I won't give up Michael. You'd think he was still in love with me." She says this as though a sudden declaration of world peace would be likelier.

"So you would think," I say, remembering what he said to me the weekend of Old South Days. "However, getting back to Cassie. We sang Christmas carols all afternoon. She has a lovely voice, Rosie. You know that. Couldn't you accompany her on the guitar and let her do some Christmas song at the Junior Winter Solstice Maiden competition? As beauty contests go, this one's not as bad as some of the things Grace Ann was in."

Even all that unpleasantness with Miss Merry Christmas didn't dim Grace Ann's competitive spirit. There were many more walks down runways and late night practice sessions of baton and dance routines. One contest she entered the next summer actually won her a four-year scholarship to Jacksonville State.

"I expect I could do that," Rosie says. "She doesn't have to show up in a string bikini or anything, does she?"

"Surely, you are not serious, darlin'," I say in my best moonlight and magnolias accent, which involves dropping consonants at the ends of words and elongating vowels. "Athena Villans do not recognize the string bikini as proper beach wear for young ladies from good families." We laugh as I continue in my normal voice. "Actually, the swim wear competition was dropped years ago. Perri-Young pressured them into changing the contest name a few months ago to Winter Solstice

Maiden. She really wanted them to discontinue it altogether, but it would've been over Eleanor's dead body."

"Where in creation did she come up with Winter Solstice Maiden?" Rosie wants to know. "Sounds like something from a mythology book."

"I've told you enough about Perri-Young for you to understand that her personal mission in life since she became the blushing bride of Mayor Handy is to bring unenlightened Athena Villans into the New Age. Political correctness is part of that package. Apparently, moving back to the rites celebrated in ancient Rome meets p.c. requirements by celebrating seasons, but not a Christian holiday. In all truthfulness though, some cities have been sued for promoting Christianity on government property. However, no one complained about Athena Villa's rather pointedly Christian Christmas displays until Perri-Young kindly brought it to the mayor and council's attention a few months back. Now, however, the Powers That Be have reluctantly mandated that there be no more manger scenes or anything with Christmas in the title that is sponsored by the city. The only way we get to put up a Christmas tree is if none of the ornaments are directly connected to the birth of Jesus. Apparently, the popular culture of Christmas is acceptable as long as it does not imply the birth of Jesus. This is just another coup for Perri in her quest to dethrone Eleanor as Athena Villa's Queen Bee."

"Lordy me, Cassie certainly picked some contest to get mixed up in," Rosie comments.

"But I guess I can stand it this once. That ought to take some of the wind out of Sherman's sails.Let's go tell Cassie. You know, she might could even wear that old blue velvet evening gown Aunt Vancene bought me for the Christmas Ball our sophomore year. It's been stored in the cedar chest at Momma's all these years. I could probably take it up and make it fit her just perfect."

We link arms and go into the living room to deliver the good news to Cassie.

CHAPTER FOURTEEN

Ma Bell and her offspring have not urged us to reach out and touch someone in many a year. That this particular commercial mandate ceased around the time beepers and pagers and cellular and cordless phones began to proliferate is hardly just coincidence. All this constant ringing, buzzing and beeping and endless, unnecessary chatter ought to qualify as noise pollution. There is literally no place to run to, no place to hide when it comes to telecommunications. Being on the telephone a large portion of my work day has made me a fervent crusader against this unfortunate trend. I refuse to own a car phone. I only bought an answering machine since Rosie and the girls moved in. The apartment contains one cordless phone and the telephone in Rosie's bedroom. E-mail is a good thing, at least it's quieter. The lost and lovely art of letter writing needs to be revived. Face to face conversation is even better.

Cassie finds this attitude as antiquated as rotary dial telephones. She spends as much time shut inside Rosie's room, gabbing happily into the mouthpiece with her father or her friends as Rosie does urging her to hurry up and get finished. Tonight is no exception. Hardly able to contain herself until we finish dinner and she can first call Meaghan, who is also entering Junior Miss Winter Solstice, and then her father, she blabs for so long that we finally send Molly in to tell her to get off so we can put Caitlin to bed. She is surprisingly amiable when she joins us in the living room.

"Daddy said to tell you he thinks you made the right decision," she tells Rosie when she comes back in from putting Caitlin down. "He says he'll buy me a whole new wardrobe for this if I need it. Just call him and let him know how much you need, and he'll send you a check."

"Let's wait and see," Rosie says. "Have you thought about what you want to sing? You'll need to start practicing this week."

A freshly bathed and ready for bed Molly comes in to the living room as Rosie and Cassie are going through old piano lesson books and sheet music. Cassie makes a few selections and takes them to her room to look them over. Molly kisses us goodnight and follows her sister.

Rosie sighs heavily and tucks her legs underneath her as she sits down on the sofa. "Look at the time, Ell," she says. "Reckon the Pace brothers have forgotten us?"

Michael and Gabe have been traveling both separately and then together since mid-November. This week, they are on a buying trip in New York and then will proceed to Music City itself for a two-week workshop for Old Time and Bluegrass musicians and teachers. The boys offer lessons to anyone who purchases any instrument at Picker's Palace. Rosie has not slept well in Michael's absence. I often hear her in the kitchen in early morning hours, microwaving water for herb tea. Sherman's threat of legal action over the locale of Rosie and Michael's cohabitation resulted in a move to Michael's place for overnight stays. This appeared to work well for the week or so they tried it before Michael left town.

Michael's out-of-town sojourn left the responsibility of the music store with Gabe until last week when he took off for the Big Apple. We've had little time to restage our interrupted tryst. He mentions it more often than I do. As I have often stated in any number of clever ways, sex is neither urgent nor even totally necessary in my quiet little life. The abstract far exceeds the actuality in my limited experience. Gabe has taken to calling me, "Miss Emily," whenever I express this particular thought. I am uncertain if he is referring to Emily Dickinson or Emily Baldwin from "The Waltons." I'm not sure I want to ask.

The brothers have been fairly faithful communicators thus far. Their evening calls tend to occur before 9:00, however, and it is nearing 10:00. I say to Rosie, "I'm certain they'll call soon. Why don't you turn off the ringer in your room so it won't bother Caitlin."

She does this and soon the cordless phone pulses. "Absence makes the heart grow fonder," I answer.

"Don't I wish," Gabe says on the other end. "Are you sure that's not abstinence? How's my favorite witty lady this evening? Do you really miss me?"

"Like the flowers miss the dew," I say. "What delights does the Pleasure Dome hold for you two this evening? Have you managed yet another day without being mugged?"

"I keep expecting it every minute," he tells me. He rattles on for a few minutes about their plans for the next few days. I remind him he promised to procure something for me from the offices of *The New Yorker* before they leave town.

"Like what, a lock of Tina Brown's hair? An original Charles Addams cartoon? What?"

Something to prove to me you made the effort," I tell him. "If you can't get anything from there, then a pack of matches from the Algonquin. Just anything literary that reeks of New York."

"Will do," he says. "Here comes the pale young lover pining to speak with the fair maid," he says, indicating Michael is asking for the telephone. "'Til the sun shines, Nellie," he tells me and gives the phone to his brother.

I pass the telephone to Rosie, who takes it into the kitchen. They're set for an hour. She is probably telling Michael of her submission to Cassie over the beauty contest. And Michael, who I firmly believe never actually saw what the fuss was all about anyway, is affirming her decision. Talk may indeed be cheap, long distance charges not withstanding, but it's usually what women want. The right kind of it anyway, coupled with the right kind of listening. Although he is probably unfamiliar with the writings of the linguist Deborah Tannen—"Men talk status, women talk connection,"—Michael has somehow learned just enough of the politics of successfully communicating with a woman to please one Rosalee Culp Jackson.

"It's a mighty sad day for Athena Villa when you can't even display the Baby Jesus without being accused of violating somebody else's rights."

Eleanor Edge Snowden is talking to Emmeleine Riley as I unlock the library's doors on Wednesday morning. The two women, friends for more than forty years, stand before the recently completed seasonal scenes in the front display windows. For more than 25 years, Eleanor Edge has spent the entire first week of December building her miniature Bethlehem in one window and Santa Land in the other. As president of the Athena Villa Arts Council and only sibling of the long term mayor, Eleanor felt immensely qualified to do this. A twenty-piece ceramic nativity scene, lovingly crafted by Eleanor and painted and glazed by Handy's much-loved late wife, Margaret, was always placed delicately in and around a tiny stable. Santa Land featured collectors' item three-inch figures of Santa, Mrs. Claus, elves and reindeer.

Until Perri-Young's revolution at the September council meeting, no one ever challenged Miss Eleanor's decorative domain. However, in this year of our Lord, Perri-Young decided that the Lord could no longer make his annual appearance in a manger scene at Athena Villa Public Library. Perri stood her ground while Eleanor howled her protests to the mayor and council. When they reluctantly ruled against her, citing legal precedent, Handy added that of course, they definitely wanted Santa Land in its rightful place. Miss Eleanor replied that the North Pole would most likely melt into the Arctic before that occurred. She then stalked from council chambers, refusing to look Handy in the eye.

The other arts council members volunteered to create the winter scenes Eleanor and Emmeleine were now assessing. Frosty the Snowman is the central figure on the left side. Set in a backdrop of fake snow and angel hair, he is surrounded by sleighs and children having snowball fights. Santa makes a return visit on the right side. Various depictions of the Jolly Old Elf—from Thomas Nast to the Coca-Cola Santa—fill the display window.

Eleanor, however, has managed to get the last word in. The tree, which stands just inside the library to the left of the front doors, is covered in over three hundred crocheted white ornaments—bells, stars, icicles, candy canes, Santas—all those secular seasonal symbols smiled on by the law of our land. Following Eleanor's encounter with the mayor and council, the Mayor himself went to his only sister to mend fences, asking that she not totally remove all of her artistry from city property. Eleanor finally agreed to decorate the tree in the library, a task generally allotted to students of the elementary school. Taking several decades worth of her very own needlework from storage, she trimmed the towering fake fir in almost politically correct splendor. However, at the very back of the tree, where Perri is unlikely to look, there is a tiny virgin and child hanging innocently among the snowflakes. Miss Eleanor nods triumphantly as I hold it up to her.

"What Ms. Perri-Young doesn't know won't hurt her one iota," she says with a smile.

"How's the beauty contest shaping up?" I ask her. Since Cassie has chosen to involve herself and us as well, I feel the need to be polite about this thirty-year tradition as dear to Miss Eleanor's heart as the Baby Jesus.

"We are proceeding on schedule. Thank you for asking, Ellott," Eleanor says. "Even Ms. Perri-Young's making us change our name to Winter Solstice Maiden—My God, have you ever heard anything more ridiculous in all your born days—has not stopped Athena Villa lovelies from having their moment in the sun."

"I'm glad to hear that," I say. "My roommate's daughter is entering the junior contest, so I need to get an application from you."

"How wonderful," Eleanor Edge claps her hands. "I'll get it for you and bring it by later this afternoon. Is she a singer, like her mother? Emmeleine has told me a great deal about your roommate's musical accomplishments."

Earlier in the fall, Emmeleine attended a charity event that Wildwood Flower performed at. She was inexplicably enchanted with their music and talked it up to all her friends.

"Yes, actually she is going to sing with Rosie accompanying her on the guitar," I tell her. "Do you know who's judging it?"

"I just received confirmation from all three judges this very morning," Eleanor says. "It should prove quite exciting. Of course, I can't tell you who, being that I'm the coordinator. But I do believe if you'll keep your ears and eyes open you might hear something that would be beneficial." Eleanor Edge smiles her wealthy spinster smile as she leaves the building. "I'll be late for my bridge luncheon, honey. I'll get the application to you this afternoon."

On Wednesday mornings, our cataloger, Joseph Paramon, and I move the trucks of newly processed books from technical services to my desk. As we push the trucks past Dottie Dunwald's—the children's librarian—office, she pokes her head out to say, "good morning," through a mouthful of Snackwells. Constantly on a diet, Dottie compensates by continually stuffing herself with low-fat foods. Joseph and I exchange a look and manipulate the new books through Circulation and over by the windows to Reference. He fusses with the trucks and their contents until they suit him and gives me a brief assessment of each book. Although he has done this once a week for several years now, I never grow tired of his patient, slightly nasal voice talking on and on about books.

Some years younger than I, Joseph lives with his parents and two sisters, long-time Athena Villans, in a large, old, rambling house a few blocks away. Joseph and his two sisters live a much-speculated about and fiercely private existence. They work their jobs and take care of their parents and bother no one. I dined with them once, several years ago. It was wonderful food, but no one spoke except to ask that some item be passed in his or her direction. When the meal was over, I thanked Mrs. Paramon profusely and she smiled without speaking. The sisters, Faith and Hope, complimented me on whatever it was I wore that night and then Joseph drove me home. I've never been asked again and neither Joseph nor I have mentioned it.

Unspoken understanding of our friendship exists during our work hours and we often go out to lunch together or eat our packed lunches during the same hour in the small kitchen. He is quietly devoted to Emmeleine Riley, who hired him so many years ago as a page. She saw to it that the city financed his library education. Generous to a fault, Joseph buys elaborate presents for me and Emmeleine at Christmas, on our birthdays, and spontaneously throughout the year. When he met Rosie's children, he immediately included them in his gift-giving cycle.

"Cassie's going to enter the Junior Winter Solstice Maiden Contest," I say to him as he rearranges the rows of reference books on the truck.

"That should be interesting," Joseph says and looks at me with a grin. "You do know Lover Man is one of the judges."

"Oh, my God," I say with a sigh. "Not R. Andrew Swayne himself? Whatever possessed Eleanor to ask him?"

"Who could be better?" Joseph asks, actually smirking a little, as much as anyone so inhibited can actually do so. "Is there another male on the planet who appreciates the female sex more than Andy Swayne?" more than An Chuckling, I shake my head without comment. "Who else is on the judges' panel, do you know?"

"Sure, Rainier Brown and Howell Rushton. Howell Rushton was tickled to death to be asked, Eleanor said."

Howell Rushton, a nondescript, balding man in his early fifties, is Athena Villa's newly hired city comptroller. His position replaces that of the treasurer, an elective post hastily laid to rest when its last occupant embezzled some $2 mil from city coffers over a four-year period. Following an internal audit and some swift decision making on Handy's part, the council advertised for a financial officer, or comptroller, and selected Howell, who was working for his father's accounting firm within the city. His family are founding citizens and lifelong bachelor Howell is considered a good catch. I would personally rather date a cadaver. The conversation would probably be livelier.

Rainier Brown, a former Miss Merry Christmas, is a drop dead gorgeous young Athena Villan embarking on her third career and second divorce. Recently trained in the real estate office that employed Perri-Young Snowden before her premature retirement, she is a very familiar face in our little 'burb. A Bryn Mawr graduate in English Literature, she came back to her hometown to stay with Mamma after Pappa passed on. She immediately enrolled at The University and obtained a degree in Library Service. She married and worked for a year or so at one of the suburban libraries until she decided magazine editing looked more stimulating. Following a divorce and remarriage she spent a few years of struggling on the meager salary that the locally published, nationally distributed magazine offered.

Earlier this year, she quit that establishment to embark on a real estate career about the time her second marriage began to fail. Her matrimonial ventures tend to collapse, seemingly, because of her close proximity to Mamma, who shares her living quarters. Husbands One and Two were so dazzled by her beauty and charm that Mamma, initially, seemed a minor inconvenience. Mamma proved otherwise in the long run, however, being a willful old woman who expects Rainier to leap when she yells, "froggie." Rainier is as well read as anyone I've even encountered and participates in my monthly reading group. She should make an interesting beauty contest judge.

My extensive acquaintance with Andy Swayne stretches through the duration of my career. He began his rise through the rank and file of the city-wide library system shortly before I came to Athena Villa, which is its own municipality. The city of Birmingham boasts a central facility and multiple branches to serve that largest city of our fair state's largest county. Several years ago, Andy accepted the position of department head for Literature and Popular Reading at the central facility. Having come into the system a few years earlier as A.B.D. (All But Dissertation) in Renaissance and Restoration Literature at The University, he soon began work on his library degree. He received it and the good favor of the former Literature Department head, wowing her with equal amounts of charm and extensive subject knowledge.

No one expected anyone but Andy to move into her place when she retired about a decade ago. What was unexpected is that Andy has thus far remained only a department head, not progressing to the upper supervisory level everyone assumed he was soaring toward. Rumors abound and I have never ascertained the exact truth, but I suspect a woman is involved. The department he so genially supervises is comprised mostly of females who have worked there many years. His staff is fiercely loyal to him and will brook no gossip or criticism.

Andy is tall, thin with dark gray-streaked curly hair and deep-set brown eyes full of self-amusement. He has yet to meet a female he didn't attempt to charm. He married late, divorcing soon after the birth of his son, and now lives the life of the merry bachelor God intended him to be. A long-time Athena Villan, he makes the daily commute with all the other morning traffic maniacs on 1-65 to the downtown facility.

Librarians are a very intertwined group of folks, especially in a county with as many libraries as Jefferson. Local and state committees, reading groups and social functions bring us all together at regular intervals. Following a long ago stint on a planning committee for a lecture/reading series sponsored by the state humanities forum, Andy and I began a literary flirtation that waxes and wanes to this day. The series, which featured local scholars in a lecture/discussion series, focused on 20th Century poets. It continued over a six month period with lecture locations rotating to various libraries within the county.

My degree in English won me a spot on the planning committee which Andy chaired. We traded witty quotations and outrageous biographical anecdotes about the various poets, amusing the rest of the planning group and nurturing our friendship. Once over a lunch following a committee meeting, we argued the merits of our favorite poets—his, Robert Herrick and mine, of course, Emily Dickinson. I share a certain suppression of the libido for which Miss E.D. is so noted. And perhaps it is the polish and charm of Master Herrick's unabashedly romantic verse that draws Andy to that Cavalier poet, also clergyman.

One of Andy's better pieces of e-mail included the following from Herrick's "To the Virgins, to Make Much of Time" Then be not coy, but use your time /And while ye may, go marry./For having lost but once your prime /You may forever tarry.

I answered him with: "Wild nights, wild nights/Were I with thee/Wild nights would be our luxury," with full knowledge that Miss E.D. did not have an earthly lover in mind when she wrote those lines.

Once, Joseph intercepted one of our steamier correspondences in which I sent Andy the "Yes, I will, Yes," monologue from Ulysses. Joseph—whose reading tastes run to spy and intrigue fiction—was quite mystified and probably disappointed. Andy's equally salty answering passage from the pages of D. H. Lawrence was probably less baffling. We've both been busy with other things for the past several months, so it will be rather entertaining to see how he handles the job of judging the quality and quintessence of all that young female flesh.

His Lothario-like reputation preceding him wherever he goes, Andy sometimes has trouble attaining the companionship of women with both brains and beauty. Our on-line correspondence and literary flirtation is merely that. Neither of us would ever consider the other romantically. There would be about as much likelihood of that pairing as there would have been, say, for a romance between Miss E.D. and Lord Byron, who is Andy's more approximate literary prototype. For awhile he shared his romantic woes with me in our frequent correspondences, but I've had no news for awhile.

Now that romantic possibilities loom ever so faintly in my own horizons, I can better understand Andy's frustrations that so amused me in years past. Gabe's absence has set me to "flashing and yearning," as the doomed poet John Berryman once expressed it. If Berryman did indeed spend much of his life in that particular state of flux, then no wonder the poor soul jumped from the river bridge. Despite an inner Greek chorus screaming, "caution," I am still quite drawn to that tall, sturdy man with the deep voice, quick wit and alternating gender preferences. It is not that I am not fully aware of the risks involved in this yet to be consummated relationship. But, no one since the ill-fated artist husband of college days has affected me quite like Gabriel Pace. The old Hispanic proverb, "where there is love, there is pain," is as right as that rain that falls on the plains of Spain. Ah, well, I suppose that "men have died and worms have eaten…" does apply to the fairer sex as well. I must finish this truckload of books and meet my public, who are coming through the doors.

A crowd of women in suits and heels are power-stomping toward my desk. Perri-Young Snowden and associates are early for our meeting. I can think of few things more intimidating than a bunch of women on a mission. Equal in zeal and dedication to Temperance Leaguers in the war on Demon Rum, Perri and the Youngettes (as Eleanor flippantly labeled them) lead the brave fight to end the oppression of the male dominated, Judeo-Christian ethic still alive and well in Athena Villa.

In addition to politically correcting our public Christmas observances and displays, Perri Young has organized yet another educational seminar for those unwashed in enlightened culture. The success of New Age Gardening inspired her to plan a three-day event to coincide with the beauty pageant. Shortly after Zaia-Danda's presentation, she approached me with the idea for a series of lectures about the way men perceive women. After deciding this to be one of Perri's better ideas, I suggested a friend of mine as presenter and a new conference was born. My former roommate at The University, Charlotte Johnston, who now teaches English literature and women's studies at a small liberal arts college in Lower Alabama, agreed immediately to put something together since the conference will take place during their semester break. Perri telephoned me at home yesterday to say that Charlotte had sent her some preliminary information and that the committee needed to meet. And here they are.

"The library couldn't look better," Perri Young says as she sets books and folders on a study table near the Reference Area. "The displays are marvelous and Eleanor's tree looks really nice. I told her I knew she could decorate a tree without propagating the Christian myth. And she has."

Far be it from me to point out the illicit madonna and babe on the back side of the tree. Instead, I say, "If you ladies will excuse me a moment. I need to locate someone to watch over Reference. I expect our meeting will take some time and the desk needs to be covered.

"Is Sha 'Neece here yet? I need her to help me out in Reference while I meet with Perri and the committee," I say to Cora Moon, the library clerk at the Circulation Desk. A permanent fixture at the library since its inception thirty-two years ago, Cora cannot abide to leave the Circulation Desk in anyone's hands but her own. So, Sha 'Neece Robinson, a student at Miles College's School of Law, who works part-time with Cora at the desk and occasionally with me in Reference, is really the only one I can ask except for Emmeleine who is at a meeting at City Hall. On occasion, Joseph is willing to emerge from the Technical Services area, but he is generally so busy I hate to ask him.

"She just came in. She's hanging up her coat in back," Cora says. "Are you going to be long? We've got to get reserves called and your list marked before this afternoon." The Circulation Desk indicates the library's holdings on the *New York Times* Bestseller List each week and posts it for patrons.

Cora considers *The New York Times Book Review* a promoter of near-pornography. Most of its recommendations are far too worldly for her preferences, which generally fall somewhere between light love and Christian fiction. To dissociate herself from all that prurient literature, she refers to it as "Ellott's list" to our patrons. Eugenia Price is her favorite writer, and the one she will unfailingly suggest if a patron asks for "something good to read."

"I'll try not to take too long," I tell her. "But we have to keep Perri happy or the Mayor won't be happy and we don't want that, do we?"

"Her mama should have spanked her good and hard when she was little," Cora says firmly.

"And she wouldn't be acting like a spoiled brat now."

Cora attends Athena Villa First Baptist with Perri-Young's parents, Robert and Dolores Overton, themselves long time residents. Over the years, Cora observed Dolores and Perri as they frequented the library. An adopted child, Perri was catered to almost as much as Grace Ann, according to Cora. In her mid-twenties, Perri decided to find her natural parents. Robert and Dolores supported her initially, but later regretted it when Perri insisted on taking the surname of Cheyenne Young, her Native American biological mother. Cheyenne gave birth to Perri in the mid-'60s while she was a part-time waitress and scholarship student at Samford University. Professor of history at that fine old Baptist establishment then and now, Robert became acquainted with Cheyenne on her appearance before the scholarship committee.

There were unsubstantiated rumors that he was Perri's true father. Robert denied it, Dolores never believed it and Cheyenne refused to say. At any rate, the unmarried and ill-advantaged Cheyenne was unable to care for the child she was to bear and allowed the Overtons to adopt her. She returned to her native North Carolina, where she lives to this day on a reservation in Eagle Rock. When Perri located her, they immediately bonded. Perri then defected from pampered, wealthy suburban princess to minority child and champion of the oppressed. Attaching Cheyenne's surname, Young, to Perri, she became Perri-Young Overton and now Young Snowden since she wed Handy. She and Cheyenne see each other several times a year and correspond frequently over the Internet.

An accounting graduate from Samford herself, Perri-Young chose to go into Real Estate because of its lucrative benefits in the over-the-mountain area. After her cultural awakening, she began contributing a large portion of her earnings to Cheyenne's tribe in North Carolina. Now that she is "retired," I am uncertain how she continues to provide her guilt money. I rather suspect Handy's coffers are frequently popped open for this funding.

So, in our little corner of paradise, what Perri wants, Perri gets. I am here but to serve. I go to the back to find Sha 'Neece downing a quick cup of coffee before she goes to the front desk.

"Hey, lady," I say to her. "How about a little R & R at the Reference Desk while I meet with Perri and the Youngettes about the conference?"

In her middle twenties, Sha 'Neece lives in Athena Villa Chateau—an apartment complex located just off the highway that runs through town—with her mama and little boy, JaMal, who is five. Mama keeps JaMal while Sha 'Neece works and goes to school. JaMal's daddy, whom Sha 'Neece refuses to talk to or about rationally, is a landscape gardener with the City. He makes occasional visits to the library to see Sha 'Neece. She usually orders him out or answers his inquiries about his son in reluctant monosyllables until he gives up and leaves.

When I asked her about this once, she said, "Huh, I don't owe a dime's worth of my time to that man. In the five years since I had JaMal, he's paid me exactly $200 in child support. He comes to see JaMal on Christmas and his birthday and that's it. I got nothing to say to him for sure."

Not having seen JaMal's daddy in several weeks has had a positive effect on Sha 'Neece, who is often quite stressed. She laughs at my reference to Perri-Young. "You better not let her hear you now, child," she says. "She'll get the P.C. police after you. She'll claim you're dissing her because she's Native American."

"Well, then I'd best hush, huh?" I say. "Let's go tell Cora that we're getting fifteen more copies of *Dogwood and Desire* and see what she says."

Sha 'Neece and I take shameful pleasure in shocking Cora Moon, who is, truth be told, the sweetest soul on earth unless you offend her moral sensibilities. My rather broad-stroked reading selections for the library often do just that. Quality and demand should take a back seat to decency in Cora's opinion. Sha 'Neece is as addicted to reading as I am—her preferences leaning toward black female authors and hard-boiled detective fiction when she has time for reading between work, school and child care. Several weeks ago, Sha 'Neece and I concocted a non-existent soon-to-be-released bodice ripper, titled *Dogwood and Desire*.

A certain contingent of older ladies, and a few younger ones as well, devour bodice rippers like crazy and are always hot for any new one. Cora blushes whenever she checks one out to a patron. For our fictitious fiction, we placed the setting in antebellum Mississippi and named our heroine Pansy Wilkes—combining Margaret Mitchell's original name for Scarlett and Ashley's surname. We told Cora that the plot centers on Pansy's undying love for a slave on her daddy's plantation. The more appalled she becomes, the more we embellish the story. As we pass the Circulation Desk, however, we find Cora engaged in her weekly chat with her pastor's wife. Sha 'Neece follows me to the Reference Area and I gird my loins to face Perri and company.

"Let me know if it gets too busy," I say to Sha 'Neece and go over to the table near the front of the library where Perri, Sherri Winetraub and Terri Cotter—two of Perri's fellow warrior women—are seated. Both have husbands with six-figure salaries and young children who attend kindergarten in the mornings at the church just up the highway. That the three have remained friends since elementary school is, I assume, partially due to the assonance of their given names.

"So, what did Charlotte send you?" I ask Perri, who is distributing materials to the rest of us from a folder.

"We have the itinerary for the three days," Perri-Young says. "It sounds marvelous. I do hope I can persuade Handy to attend the session on the way men depict women in the media."

The four of us study the agenda for the three-day conference: *Through A Glass Darkly: Men's Images of Women in Contemporary Popular Culture*. As I scan the pages, I can see that Charlotte has certainly outdone herself this time. The first day will focus on the way men picture women in advertising and the media; the second will switch to men's images of women in literature; and the last day—best of all—is titled "Ruby Tuesday or Lady Madonna : The Female Icon in Popular Music."

Never one to let a sleeping controversy lie, Charlotte makes quite a stir wherever she chooses to roam. In our undergrad days, she was one of the first to shed her bra, refuse to shave her legs and quote lines from Betty Friedan or Germaine Greer at the top of her lungs when she had too much to drink. She did not marry until her late twenties and she and her contractor husband now have two sons. Both as outspoken and courageous as their mother, they have their father's red hair and blue eyes, rather than Charlotte's raven tresses and green eyes. We exchange Christmas presents and I drive down into the wilds of Lower Alabama to see them when our schedules permit. Motherhood and many years of teaching undergraduates have not diminished her capacities.

"We could have a bigger turnout for this than we did for the gardening thing," Terri says. "And since the humanities foundation funded it, we don't have to charge any admission."

Perri wants to intensify publicity in the two weeks before the conference. "Maybe we could get something in the over-the-mountain paper," she says. "Could you write up a little something and send it to them? I'm sure they'd use it."

I agree to do this and we move on to seating arrangements, handouts for participants and the p.a. system. Sherri is saying that her husband agreed to videotape it for us when Eleanor Edge walks up to the table.

"Ellott, honey, I'm sorry to disturb you, but…"

"Then please don't, Eleanor," Perri-Young says firmly. "We're in the middle of a meeting."

"Perri-Young, I do wish you would take it upon yourself to remember the manners I am quite sure Dolores taught you when you were a child. I do believe even enlightened women like yourself can show some common courtesy," Eleanor says sweetly, sitting down at the table with us Her face as red as the skin of her forbears, Perri-Young stutters a few minutes before she speaks. "Eleanor Edge Snowden, I am sick to death of your demeaning me at every given opportunity. I am Handy's wife now. Your beloved Margaret has been dead long enough for you to come to grips with that. It's time you gave me my rightful place."

"Darling heart, if I gave you the rightful place you truly deserve, it would probably be down behind the garbage dump," Eleanor snapped, angry at Perri's reference to Margaret and forgetting her own usually impeccable etiquette.

Terri and Sherri are speechless as I move discretely away from the table to see if Emmeleine has returned from City Hall. Only she can defuse this brou ha-ha.

Chapter Fifteen

It is Friday evening and the night sky is white with snow. Four excited girls stand at the dining room window of the apartment, watching the flakes glisten in the floodlights on the back lawn. Cassie's friend, Meaghan, and little Helen, Molly's friend, are spending the night. Paper plates of pizza and chips are left half-eaten on the table behind them.

Cassie lifts Caitlin from her high chair to hold her to the window. Her eyes grow big.

"Ook," Caitlin says. It is her birthday. Rosie brings in one big cake and a smaller one.

"She said, 'ook,' again, Momma," Cassie tells her. "I think it does really mean look."

"I think so, too, honey," Rosie says to her.

They are in tune again. And our little family is made whole. The mother and child reunion was only a gesture away—that simple 'yes, yes,' to Cassie's cry to be recognized by way of a beauty contest. They have worked the entire week on "What Child is This?" with Rosie patiently guiding Cassie through, telling her when to hold a note and when to soften her voice.

Cassie has stood for long periods on a stool while Rosie pins the hem of the treasured blue velvet evening gown. It was Rose's first formal, bought for the Christmas Ball in our sophomore year at Samantha Jane Seers High School, 1966. I accompanied her and Miss Vancene to The Smart

Shoppe some two weeks before the dance to purchase it. Fred was the courtly southern gentleman personified that afternoon, personally bringing dress after dress out for Miss Vancene and Rosie's consideration.

Grace Ann and I put in our two cents worth as well, but spent most of the time snickering over the date Fred had selected for her for the ball—the rather short son of a very well-to-do downtown merchant. These were pre-Bud days and Grace Ann played the field more adeptly that Mickey Mantle ever dreamed. She acquiesced so graciously to Fred's suggestion that she allow Bucky Saks to escort her to the dance, that I had to wonder what she had in mind. It turned out later that all she really wanted was to show up in his Corvette, dance a couple of dances with him, and then work the crowd of boys clamoring to be her partner.

The previous weekend Sherman had presented Rosie with a Going Steady heart shaped ring of 10k gold with a microscopic diamond chip at its center. When Rosie came toward us in 3" heels and a blue velvet gown, with clinging bodice, three quarter sleeves and a flowing skirt, we stopped gabbing mid-sentence. Simultaneously, Grace and I did the entire chorus of Bobby Vinton's "Blue Velvet," and told her that was definitely the one, no question. Following the ball, Miss Vancene had it carefully preserved for her at a local dry cleaner's and Rosie has kept it stored at Millie's all these years. Cassie loved it on first sight.

"There's some on the ground, Aunt Ell," Molly says, interrupting my reverie. "Come look."

I set the plates for the cake down and go to the window to stand beside Molly and Helen, who is signing to Molly.

"Helen says if this keeps up, she thinks we can build a snowman in the morning," Molly says.

"Won't that be fun," I say to them. Large flakes are falling and a small amount is sticking to the ground. "Let's light the candles and sing to Caitlin. I'll bet she's ready for some birthday cake."

They reluctantly sit down and Cassie positions Caitlin in the high chair, removes the tray and scoots her up as close to the table as possible. Rosie places the little cake with one candle burning in front of Caitlin. A larger Winnie-the-Pooh cake sits to the left of it.

"Go whoosh," Molly coaches her. The baby blows a little and Cassie blows with her to extinguish the candle.

We sing a pepped up rendition of "Happy Birthday," and clap. Caitlin digs into her little cake with both hands. I cut slices of Pooh cake for Rosie and me and the girls, who have gone back to the window to monitor the snow. Bits of wrapping paper and ribbon litter the floor. Miss Caity has enough toys and clothes to make Christmas presents all but redundant. I am sampling a bit of Pooh cake when the phone begins to ring.

"Many happy returns of the day," I answer.

"I couldn't get out of the durn driveway," Sherman says on the other end of the line. "It's been snowing and sleeting hard since 4:00 when I closed the shop. We're froze in here at Momma's

"We might be in the same fix," I tell him. "Rosie said a few minutes ago that you probably wouldn't be able to get here. Do you want to talk to her?"

"I do, but put Caitlin on the phone first," Sherman says. "Maybe she'll know it's her Daddy calling."

I take the cordless to the baby, who is one big smear of chocolate and sprinkles, and hold the phone to her ear. "It's your daddy, baby. Say 'hey there' to him."

"ADAAA," Caitlin says loudly, through a mouthful of cake. "Ook."

I take the receiver back and say, "She's telling you to look at her cake, which she's mostly wearing. It certainly becomes her."

"I hope it wears well," Sherman says, laughing. "I remember Cassie's first birthday. It took us the rest of the afternoon to get the cake out of the carpet."

"Caitlin didn't waste any of hers," I say. "Here's Rosie." I give the phone to her.

She takes it into the kitchen and I sit with the baby and enjoy my cake and her dining performance. Cassie and Meaghan quickly finish their cake and ask to be excused to go and practice.

"Your Momma's on the phone right now," I tell Cassie.

"Oh, I don't need her yet. I'm just gonna sing without music right now," Cassie says. "Meahgan says she can hear me better without Momma playing. She wants to see if I'm getting all the notes right and everything."

Also a Junior Winter Solstice Maiden contender, Meaghan will play a classical piece on her flute. The girls have been critiquing each other for several days now. Molly, who is already sick of "What Child is This?" asks if she and little Helen can go to my room and play computer games. I give permission and they bounce off with Helen signing away and Molly laughing uproariously at whatever she is saying. I really do need to learn signing, little Helen could be relating off-color jokes for all I know.

"Well, that was actually pleasant," Rosie says as she comes back in. "Not a cross word between us for once. When he acts like this, I can kind of remember what it was I found to love in Sherman Lee Jackson." She sits down to finish her cake.

"What did he say about the contest fee?" I ask her. "Is $200 not too big a sacrifice for his first born?"

"Apparently not," Rosie says. "He just said, 'okay,' and that he'd get it in the mail. He mostly talked about Fred Hardaman. It seems he wants to come with Sherman and Minnie Beth to see Cassie in the contest."

"That's not too surprising," I say. "He loved going to those things when Grace Ann was in them. And it's not likely Ree is going to get involved in anything so frivolous. That's one serious kid."

"Well, she's had to be," Rosie says. "Grace Ann was flighty enough for the both of them. But Sherman did say Fred is going to bring Ree with them. I don't know about Harley, Jr. They've both been spending a lot of their time at the Reeses'. I get the idea that Fred's worried they'll want to stay there permanently."

"If they can't be with Bud, I guess they feel like being around his people is the next best thing," I say. "But I can see where Fred would take exception to that."

"Sherman says he seems to have changed his attitude a little bit toward Bud and the Reeses," Rosie says. "And he's still claiming that he thinks somebody other than Bud killed Grace Ann and Tanner Hope. He won't say who though. But Sherman says otherwise, Fred's oars are slipping further and further out of the water. Half the time when he's talking to Sherman about Ree, he calls her Grace Ann."

"In a way, I'm glad they're coming," I say. "There're some things I need to ask him about Timeofgrace. I wonder if he's still fast friends with Anson Gallworthy?"

"Sherman said Brother Anson called him the other night about Fred. He's real worried about him. He said Fred calls him at 3 or 4 in the morning to go out riding with him to hunt Grace Ann's killer. Fred keeps saying if they just ride long enough, they'll find him."

As the night grows old, the snow begins to thicken, piling on the back lawn and trees. I recount Wednesday's cultural clash at the library for Rosie's entertainment after we put Caitlin to bed and see that the girls are settled for the evening. I suggest that a therapy session with Miss Manners would benefit Eleanor and Perri-Young. Rosie says Handy needs to draw some boundaries for them if they won't do it themselves. Our discussion drifts to Joseph Paramon and his peculiar household. They bring to mind the Learys from Anne Tyler's *Accidental Tourist*—never marrying and shelving their groceries in alphabetical order. I then mention that Andy Swayne is going to help judge the Winter Solstice competition and that I have missed our correspondence since I became involved with Gabe. The Brothers Pace then receive a conversational going-over as the telephone begins to pulse.

"Lonesome Town," I answer.

"I would respond 'City of Broken Dreams,' but I think that's on the West Coast," Gabe says. "We're in the middle of a blizzard here. I saw on the news that some of the white stuff is actually falling on the Magic City."

"Falling and sticking," I tell him. "We got your presents for Caitlin in time, Gabe. She loves the talking Mickey Mouse. She laughed and laughed at him."

"Glad to hear it," Gabe says. "I do like to please my women. And how did you like your little present?"

"Did I get one?"

"Damn, Michael wins," Gabe says. "We had a bet going on whether you would think to look in the pocket of Mickey's overalls. I even hinted about it in the birthday card."

"Just a minute," I say, intrigued. I go to the couch where Caitlin left Mickey and slip my finger into the pocket of his overalls to extract a gold "Going Steady" ring that is a dead ringer for the one Sherman gave to Rosie all those years ago.

"Oh, my God," I say as I pick up the phone again. "I didn't even think you were listening that time I told you about that ring and how much I envied Rosie for having it, even if it was from Sherman Jackson."

"I always listen," Gabe says. "Read the engraving."

Inside the band is "Queen of my Heart." "I love this," I say. "And no, it's not too corny, before you even ask."

"You know me too well," he says. "So what's cooking at Chez Seers/Jackson this frosty winter's eve?"

"Mostly a house full of girls and Cait's party. I imagine we're stuck here through most of tomorrow. The snow's not supposed to stop until sometime tomorrow morning."

"I'd like to be stuck inside with you or even of you," Gabe says. "But let's not frustrate the both of us just now. Could you put Rosie on the line for a minute? I need to speak to her before I let her talk to Brother Michael, who's been bending his elbow all the evening long."

"Really," I say, a little surprised. Michael is generally not much of a drinker. "Don't tell me there's no marijuana to be had in all of New York City?

"Oh, it's here for the asking," Gabe says. "But Michael started in on a bottle of Seagram's right after the sun went down and he hasn't let up. He's like a crazy man, he misses Rosie so much. After she told him that since Sherman was acting so much nicer and she was going to let him come to Cait's party, he's got it into his head that they're getting back together."

"I wouldn't worry about that just yet if I were him," I say. "And he didn't make it to the party. The snow got him, too. But Michael had better not let Rosie know he's jealous. She had enough of that from Sherman to last a lifetime. Maybe you should talk to her."

I call Rosie from my bedroom where she went to check on Molly and Helen, who are bunked down there for the night. I am taking the sofa for the evening. Cassie and Meaghan are in Cassie and Molly's room. No one in the apartment would have slept with the four girls in one bedroom. I hear low buzzes of conversation from both quarters. Rosie takes the phone into the kitchen as soon as she hears Gabe's voice.

When Caitlin whimpers, I go to her, take her from her crib and bring her back into the living room. I pull the rocking chair to the dining room window to watch the falling snow. Unable to remain asleep due to party excitement and an overabundance of chocolate cake, Caity doesn't want to be rocked and wiggles out of my arms and onto the floor. Rocking on her hands and knees, she moves toward Mickey Mouse. Reaching him, she pulls the big rodent to her and cuddles him.

"Ook," she says to no one in particular as Rosie comes back into the room.

"Hey, baby girl," she says to her daughter. "Let's you and me run away someplace where there's no men. We could have ourselves a good time, just you and me."

"I understand Michael's a wee bit besotted this evening," I say to her.

"Besotted, my hind foot," Rosie comments. "Drunk as a skunk is more like it. Just when I'd got used to him when he's mellowed out on pot, he switches poison."

"It's probably not permanent," I tell her. "When he's back in B'ham with you, he'll be back to his weed toking self."

"We'll see," Rosie says, not convinced. She removes her guitar from its case and strums it softly. Caitlin puts Mickey back down and crawls toward her mother, who is playing something I don't recognize. Maybe it's her own tune."

Chapter Sixteen

Through A Glass Darkly is touted with banners and media promos. The power-suits-and-heels crowd somewhat outbalances the jeans-and-t-shirt attendees. So many women are crowded into Meeting Room A in the Athena Villa Civic Center that Merlilee Snowden and I open the folding partition that divides the two rooms and hastily set up more chairs. The other library page and a Rec center worker help us. I look around for Charlotte and find her cornered in the hallway by Sherri and Terri. Perri-Young is barking orders to two maintenance workers on loan from City Hall for the duration of the conference. With opening remarks due to begin in twenty minutes, the least I can hope for is that everyone finds a seat and the p.a.. system doesn't fail.

"Perri had me and Daddy up at 6:30 this morning assembling folders," said Merilee, Handy's daughter, who is home from her Birmingham Southern dorm for the holidays. "I hate to take Perri's side against Aunt Eleanor, but this one looks like a winner."

"If luck holds," I say. "How about rescuing Charlotte from the Youngettes so she can finish her own setting up."

"Done," Merilee says as she sets up her last folding chair and moves off in Charlotte's direction.

In the next several minutes, the women fill the newly set up rows of chairs.

"I'll call upstairs and tell Cora we're full up if anyone else calls," I tell Perri-Young, who is directing the last few women inside. She nods as we close off the outside doors and set a sign in the hallway reading, "We apologize for the inconvenience. Due to regulations by the Fire Marshall, we cannot allow any one else to enter. Please plan to attend tomorrow s session: 'Eve and Mary in Modern Literature,' and the final seminar on Sunday afternoon 'Ruby Tuesday or Lady Madonna: the Female Icon in Popular Music.'" I step into a small office and use the telephone to buzz the circulation desk. When Cora picks up, I tell her the conference is full up for today.

"And just what is it that I'm supposed to say to these women up here fussing at me because they cannot get in?" Cora asks, heatedly. Definitely in Eleanor's camp, Cora has done her best to be uncooperative about the conference. I spend a few minutes removing the bees from her bonnet and then go across the hall to the meeting rooms.

The crowd is laughing as I enter and quietly take my place beside Perri at the Discussion Leader's table. Charlotte, clad in a black suit with matching hose and heels, winks in my direction. Like many of us, my former roomie and partner in crime, has developed her intellect and neglected her figure as the years have passed. None-the-less, she is as imposing as when she streaked fifty feet from one restroom to another back in '74. She already has the crowd following her bouncing ball.

"The underlying credo of advertising, and some would say of the mass media itself, is hyperbole. Without overstatement, they'd be out of business," Charlotte is saying. "From the 'Come Hither' Noxema Girl of years past to the moonstruck teenager tapping away on the Internet to her love she left five minutes earlier, the women shown in Advertising are about as natural as **Playboy** centerfolds. Let's take a quick glance as some familiar faces from the small screen's commercial breaks and then we'll talk about them."

Charlotte cuts the lights and we view a half hour pastiche of clips from forty plus years of television advertising—everyone from Josephine the

Plumber to the poor benighted soul of "Mother, please, I'd rather do it myself," When the screen goes blank, Charlotte flips the lights and passes out sheets of paper listing all fifty clips with space for our responses.

"I want visceral reactions to these larger-than-life ladies of the tube. Advertising doesn't aim at the intellect." We take a few minutes to jot down some thoughts as Charlotte moves about the room, glancing over shoulders and nodding or frowning.

"Feel free to shout out any thoughts," she says.

"I think a Prozac prescription would fix most of their problems," one woman says.

"Or it would at least seem that way for awhile," someone else chimes in.

"If all our troubles were as simple as waxy yellow build-up or yellow plaque on our pearly whites, what a wonderful world it would be," Charlotte comments. "Now, with this intelligent crowd, we can take the time to see some of these commercials for what they are: over magnification of difficulties—real or imagined—countered with a too-simple and all encompassing solution. But let us move on to imagine—in the John Lennon realm of imagining—a world where there is actual truth in advertising. What if, instead of an Ivory Soap dream baby who grows up to be Brooke Shields, we have this scenario instead."

For the next hour or so we look at commercials produced in a women's studies mass communications class. In a ten-minute segment, we see a mother and young daughter quietly go about their day, employing the use of various commercial products with brand names in plain sight. The bond between them is very evident as they move through an ordinary day. At bedtime, they stand together at the bathroom mirror, washing their faces with Ivory. The mother tucks the little girl in on sheets done in Ivory Snow.

"I find this quite affecting," Charlotte says. "But sponsors would never go for it. It calls for contemplation and cooperation. Not exactly buzzwords in the wonderful world of advertising."

When we break for lunch, Charlotte is engulfed with questions and offers for more speaking engagements. I wave, tap my watch and hold up ten fingers, letting her know I will rescue her in that many minutes. Farther down the hallway, I see Perri and the Youngettes basking in the triumph of yet another successful venture in this suburban desert of New Age Culture.

"Let's blame the whole thing on the apple," Charlotte says as she stands before us on this second day of *Through A Glass Darkly*, holding up a Golden Delicious apple. "This unholy mess that we call the human condition—this post-lapsarian distopia that our forefathers would have us believe is all Eve's fault—could just as easily be ascribed to the irresistible essence of the Golden Delicious." She tosses it in the air as she cruises the room, talking. "In light of the Twinkle Defense, I find entirely feasible to lay the whole Original Sin guilt trip on the forbidden fruit. That transference is probably as logical as what the Old Testament writers got away with for, yea, these many centuries."

Seeing nods of assent throughout the conference room, she continues, "Let us fast forward beyond a didactic tirade on the unfairness of the Creation myth. This initial version of 'who stole the cookie from the cookie jar'—aside from being the source of all misogyny—heralds the advent of Woman as temptress. I want to examine Eve in this light. Not as Earth Mother, but as the archetypal siren, the sensuous seductress with the heart of stone. Her manifestations are legion. If you will kindly consult your handout packet, we'll begin with everyone's favorite Zelda, Daisy Buchanan from *The Great Gatsby*."

"Isn't it true that Zelda was at least as gifted a writer as Scott, but he wouldn't allow her to pursue her writing?" someone asks.

"No, in all fairness, that isn't really so," Charlotte says to her. "Zelda very much wanted to do something artistic and do it very well, but the truth is that Zelda was schizophrenic. Her illness wasn't diagnosed until she was in her '30's, but her more honest biographers indicate that there was evidence of it from her childhood years. Some of her writing does show a cleverness and the seeds of a modest talent, but casting her in the role of a male oppressed genius would be a distortion of the facts. Scott, I truly believe, loved her to distraction, but could neither make her happy nor be happy when he was with her. So, she became his obsession. And to exercise, or perhaps exorcise, his monomania, he relegated her to myth—to the fictional world where he was god. I deliberately selected Daisy because of her portrayal by Mia Farrow in the '74 *Gatsby* extravaganza. Please be good enough to share some of your impressions of Daisy after that particular performance by the former inamorata of Old Blue Eyes himself, not to mention Andre Previn and Woody Allen."

"I never thought she was quite pretty enough," one older woman says. "Whenever I picture Daisy, she's drop dead gorgeous, like Michelle Pfeiffer or Sharon Stone."

"That's an interesting point," Charlotte says. "Many viewers and even critics observed the same thing. But I think this little girl, freckle faced Mia was chosen for just that reason. Very often the women who inspire such adoration are not classic beauties. Wallis Warfield Simpson, for example. Zelda herself, queen of the flappers that she was, was no Greta Garbo. No, these fatal flowers—so secure in their own, very subjective concept of their allure and power simply have 'It.' Now, never having had 'It,' I am at a personal loss to explain. Perhaps one of you women who either has 'It,' has had 'It,' or is in recovery from 'It,' can expound on the subject for us." Glancing quickly around the room, she focuses on Perri-Young, who grins in delight.

"It's control, honey. Pure and simple," Perri states. "Do it to them before they do it to you."

"Hmm," Charlotte says, not knowing how to respond politely. "I think that we can safely say that for all of Fitzgerald's gorgeous prose and sensitive characterization, Daisy was still Daisy—an adult child of materialism. She liked the idea of the newly rich, worshipful Gatsby from her youth, but in the end, Tom and his old money won out. Eve, or woman, is shown as the spoiler, the devourer. Myrtle Wilson and Gatsby die because of her. Eve, however, has many more faces. The Great White Master, Vladimir Nabokov, reveals her in a twelve-year-old child, Dolores 'Lolita' Hayes. I know all the arguments on this one—Old Humbert Humbert really wasn't a pedophile, perish the thought! Lolita is but the bodily symbol of Literature itself. But I've never bought this, for several reasons."

"Why would anyone make Literature feminine?" A woman from UAB's faculty asks. "To me, it has to be masculine. In the best of Literature, there's way too much ego on parade for anyone to refer to it as female."

"Amen to that," someone else says.

Charlotte nods and continues, "The final personification of Eve I would like to mention in this morning's session embodies the kinder, gentler side. She is Woman with a capital 'W' as well as a lower case one. She is both romantic and maternal. She is Eve and Mary, the new Eve. Molly Bloom is the bawdy Earth Mother, illicit lover of Blazes Boylan, wife to Leopold, who is Everyman."

"Oh, Charlotte, come on," the woman from UAB protests. "Good God, not *Ulysses*. If there's ever been a bigger pig in all of literature than Jimmyjoyce I'd love to find him."

"Possibly," Charlotte concedes, twisting a lock of her hair. Recognizing this as one of her stress gestures, I attempt to hide a smile. As students of English in the '70s, we were thoroughly versed in the critical thought of Eliot, Pound and their successors. To this very day, we share the closet with our predilection for the writings of a certain few of the prominent Dead White European Males—Joyce, Shakespeare, Yeats, Donne, Herrick, to name a few—whom our radical sisters wrote off long ago.

"But to give the Pig the benefit of the doubt," I interject. "Putting all that stream-of-conscious stuff aside, Joyce at least moved Molly beyond woman as object or as idol. I found Molly very real in all her earthiness.

Hold her up to the light of Joyce's contemporaries—Hemingway, for example. Compare her to any woman from a Hemingway novel and you can see her humanness."

After a few more minutes of debate, Charlotte reminds us it's time to break for lunch. "Eat hearty," she advises. "This afternoon, our quest leads us to Mary—woman as icon, woman as Virgin, woman on a pedestal. There's even a third face of Woman, but I'm saving that for the very end."

We leave the civic center in groups, heading for the parking lot, where we meet R. Andrew Swayne in the flesh, heading into the Civic Center complex.

He stops, dramatically covering his head as though under possible attack, and smirks, "My, my, this must be the Multitudes of Misandrists moving toward their mid-day meal."

"Good day to you, too, sir," I say to him. "I believe you just depleted your entire stockpile of alliteration in your opening sentence." Behind me, Charlotte takes her half-glasses from her purse, settles them on her face, and examines Andy cooly.

"Charlotte Johnston, Andy Swayne," I say in introduction. "Charlotte is the presenter of *Through A Glass Darkly*, Andy."

We chuckle as he reddens, struggling for something to say.

"Andy is one of the judges in the Junior Winter Solstice Maiden Competition," I tell Charlotte. "And actually a pretty decent librarian when he's not being clever."

"I'm impressed so far," Charlotte says.

"I do apologize," Andy says quietly, with as much dignity as he can summon. "Some of my staff are here today, I think. They were quite excited when they found out you were conducting the conference. I've read some of your articles in *The Georgia Review*. You had some lovely things to say about women in Seventeenth Century poetry. I quoted you in one of my classes."

"Oh, are you the Andy Swayne who teaches at Birmingham Southern?" Charlotte asks, relaxing a little. "I read your piece in *The Virginia Quarterly*, 'Gathering Rosebuds in Seventeenth Century Verse.' I appreciated what you had to say about women and flower imagery."

They converse in Academese for several minutes. Despite his incomplete dissertation, Andy teaches a couple of night classes at Birmingham Southern College and occasionally is published in literary journals. Charlotte is respected throughout the Southeast as a middle-of-the-road-feminist literary scholar.

"I am really pleased to have met you," Andy is saying. "I hate ending this conversation, but my nubile contestants await me inside. Good day to you, Miss E.D. Be sure to check your e-mail soon for an update." He waves over his shoulder as he goes into the Civic Center.

"Now there's an example of testosterone overload put to a fairly good use." Charlotte says as we climb into her Explorer and head for Red Lobster. "What's this about e-mail, Ellie Belle? Not nursing a case of the galloping hots for that silver-tongued devil, are you now?"

"Our relationship is strictly virtual and virtuous for that matter," I tell her. "We 'like' each other. Remember how you used to 'like' boys in the 5th grade and exchange notes? That's what we do, except it's online. He's fun to flirt with, but somewhat vacuous in certain key areas. Remember what Gertrude Stein or maybe Dorothy Parker said about California, 'there's no there there.'"

"Does he run the gamut of his emotional depth from A to B?" Charlotte laughs. "Well, how about that banjo picker who operates on alternating frequencies? Does he still make your heart go 'clang, clang, clang like a trolley?'"

"Ding, ding, ding goes my bell," I tell her. "But I'm not entirely sure that it isn't the same 'bell that tolls for thee.'" With that, we go into the restaurant to feast on seafood.

"When the only dead Beatle wrote 'Let it Be,' he spoke of Mother Mary coming to comfort him in times of trouble." Charlotte opens the afternoon session. "One does wonder if that was the way John saw Yoko, as the older, wiser woman he could both venerate and make love to. I think any similarity to the Blessed Virgin ends there, though. Mary, the second Woman, is an equally important feminine archetype. She is Eve's kinder, gentler successor, who instead of bringing sin into the world gave birth to the One who redeems us from that sin. No earthy temptress, but pristine saint, embodiment of all that is holy. Like the Good Woman of the Old Testament, her price is far above rubies. Both Eve and Mary manifest themselves in all literary genres, permeating the canon from the Dark Ages to the Age of Information. They are Snow White and Rose Red, Melanie and Scarlett, Amy and Beth. But I want us first to consider Mary in one of her more complex manifestations, as the title character in William Styron's *Sophie's Choice*."

"Sophie is Mary, Mother of Sorrows personified. Forced to choose which of her children would die at Nazi hands, she ultimately loses them both. A kind of displaced person in the Post War United States, she channels her maternalism into a doomed relationship with the charming, but mad Nathan and into a friendship with Stingo, the Southern gent narrator. And it is through Stingo's worshipful eyes that we have a window into Sophie's sorrow steeped existence. Her fatal fiat, her 'yes,' to Nathan's mandate to die with him is the antithesis of Mary's Magnificat, her acquiescence to God that she bear His Son. But Sophie is obedient and that's the operative word here. It is what separates her from her willful predecessor, Eve. Comments, objections, observations?"

"Sophie is beautiful, and she is also sexual," someone points out. "How can she be a Mary figure if she is those things?"

"Her beauty is neither her tool, nor her weapon," Charlotte answers. "And it ultimately gives her no lasting pleasure. The same may be said of her sexuality. She is Tragedy epitomized. Meryl Streep masterfully interprets her in this light in the film, which I hope everyone has seen. Her suicide is the only internally consistent ending for a life like that."

"In addition to being the Mother of Christ, is Sophie also Christ?" The woman from UAB asks. "And if she is, who is she sacrificing for?"

"Maybe it's atonement," someone else says. "For the deaths of her children."

"To me she is more like a character in a Greek tragedy," another woman says. 'Or maybe one of Thomas Hardy's heroines. She sees her fate and is irresistibly drawn to it."

"Let us leave Sophie and move on the third and final Big Mama of the literary cosmos," Charlotte interrupts, looking at her watch. "Eve and Mary have another sister. Some might call her the pick of the lot. In Jewish folklore "Lilith was Adam's madam before Eve. She also has a co-history as female demon and devourer of young children. God created her from the same dust he used to fashion Adam. Lovely Lilith has a human shape, angel's wings and a definite mind of her own. Main dude of the universe that he was, Adam proceeded to put Lilith in what he believed to be her rightful place, just under his thumb. Ms. Lilith, however, had a slightly higher elevation in mind—right by her mate's side. She reasonably pointed out to him that they were made with the same dust, so they should be equal. Adam disagreed and Lilith split. When Adam complained to the Almighty about his mate's desertion, God sent a band of angels in hot pursuit. When Lilith refused to go back, the angels threatened to drown her. To save herself, Lilith had to promise to spare all children whose nurseries contained amulets with images of three angels. Then God gave up and made Eve. Lilith has spent her eternity roaming the earth, flying at the head of 480 hosts of destroying angels and evil spirits, wailing her hatred of man and threatening vengeance on Adam for causing the whole mess. Superstitious Jews in ages past hung coins with images of protecting angels in the rooms of all newborns as an amulet against Lilith. These coins had a label: Lilith be gone, or Lila abi, which some feel the English word lullaby is a corrupted form of. I don't know. I guess it could be."

Charlotte stops for a sip of water and continues, "Feminist lore, however has afforded kinder treatment to its First Sister for Equality. One of her best literary manifestations in modern times is from the pen of John Fowles, fairest of the fair among white male contemporary writers. Sarah Woodruff, *The French Lieutenant's Woman*, was yet another big screen triumph for Meryl Streep. Intelligent, beautiful, independent, self-ostracizing in a beneficial way, Sarah unwittingly turned Charles 'Stuffed-Shirt' Smithson every which way but loose."

"Could Charles' attraction to Sarah be a case of wanting what you can't have?" I ask.

"I think so," Charlotte says. "Yeats expressed that best in a poem appropriately titled, 'The Fascination of What's Difficult.' I don't recall exact verses. Yeats is actually discoursing on playwriting, but I think he is also lamenting his unrequited love for Maud Gonne, another Lilith if ever there was one."

We go on to dissect Sarah, that antithesis of helpless Victorian femininity. Just before the mid-afternoon break, Charlotte leaves us with this: "Men say they want beauty, obedience and intelligence in women. Unable to find these embodied in one woman, they seek these characteristics wherever their libidos lead them. Writers are no different. They extend their quests to the written page so that a little control can be had."

Chapter Seventeen

In the darkened auditorium, I sit beside Sherman waiting for the contest to begin. To his left, Minnie Beth holds Caitlin in her lap. Molly is whispering to Ree Reese who is next to Fred. The three hundred seats are filled with anxious kith and kin of the forty contestants. Winter Solstice Maiden was crowned last evening. Tonight girls from twelve to fourteen compete for the junior title. The muted buzzing of the crowd stops as a blue spotlight brightens the stage.

"She walks in beauty like the night/Of cloudless climes and starry skies/And all that's best of dark and bright/Meet in her aspect and in her eyes." Andy Swayne's mellifluous voice recites Lord Byron's "She Walks in Beauty like the Night," as the blue spotlight expands to reveal a wintry scene on stage. I recognize the set from Athena Villa High School's production of *Camelot*—the cavorting in the snow scene. The backdrop is an expanse of puffy cottonballs embellished with a suspension of silvery icicles and snowflakes. Strolling in from right and left to Willie Nelson/Julio Iglesias' "To All the Girls I've Loved Before," the forty young lasses fill the stage. Bathed in the baby blue lights, the teeny bopper angels radiate expectant elation.

Rosie will remain backstage with Cassie, who is near the end of the talent competition. Molly is twisting in her seat, trying to see her sister. "There she is in the second row," she whispers loud enough for all around to hear. "I hope she minded Momma and didn't stuff those kleenex down her bra."

Two women in front of us stiffle their giggles as a tuxedo clad Handy Snowden enters from backstage and walks up to the mike set in the middle of the girls.

"If beauty is truly in the eye of the beholder," Handy says. "Then only the blind would fail to behold the beauty present tonight."

"Whoops, Perri-Young's probably having apoplexy," I whisper to Sherman. "She couldn't have heard his speech or she'd have had him say visually impaired."

The preliminary interviews took place this afternoon," Handy continues. "Tonight will feature the performances of these talented young ladies. After the final act, we will recess for an hour or so while the judges make their decisions. The Athena Villa Ensemble will entertain us at a reception in the Parthenon Room in the Rotunda during intermission. Let us now welcome our first contestant, Miss Heather Allman, who will provide us with a jazz dance interpretation of 'Chantilly Lace.'"

As the voice of the Big Bopper booms over the sound system, I glance down the aisle at Fred, who is smiling vacuously as he watches the shapely dancer. He absently pats Ree on the head. His thoughts, I am certain, drift to a cold night more than twenty years ago when Grace Ann charmed a similar crowd.

"I think if somebody in the row behind us set off a cannon, Fred wouldn't even jump," Sherman whispers to me. "He's about as aware of where he actually is and what's going on around him as a baby in church. On the ride down, he read us every newspaper article that's ever been printed that had Grace Ann's name in it. And not just the ones about the murders. The butter's done slipped off his noodles this time for sure."

We watch several more acts until Caitlin begins to squirm and fret in the warm auditorium. I take her from Minnie Beth's lap and Sherman follows me as I walk down a hallway into the rec center where there is a little nursery. Athena Villa mommies park their infants here while they exercise.

"Are Ree and Harley, Jr., still staying with the Reeses?" I ask Sherman as I set Caitlin down on the carpeted floor. She reaches into a tub of blocks and begins to remove them.

"Yeah, Fred didn't want them to at first, but my Momma talked to him about it. She said it wasn't fair for them to do without their momma and their daddy and for him to be gone all the time, too. They need some of their family. Fred gives the Reeses money every month and he's still paying for the kids to go to that Catholic school. I don't know why he does that. He used to be Methodist before he got hooked up with Brother Anson. Bud's family is Baptist. Ma 'Ree was from Louisiana, though, so she could've been Catholic."

"I don't know that religion is the major consideration," I tell him. "It's the quality of education. Your kids are getting a much better education than they would in public school."

"That's probably right as far as it goes," he says. "But I don't see that Cassie 's behaving a whole lot better."

He jerks at the knot in his tie as he watches Caitlin stack the blocks and knock them down again.

"Sherman, she's nearly 13," I tell him. "Be glad she doesn't have six holes in each ear and two in her nose and belly button."

"And I am that," he says. "But the stuff she tells me! God in heaven! Seventh grade girls slipping out in the middle of the night to meet boys. She says the only reason she doesn't is that ya'll are on the fourth floor and she'd break her leg."

"She might indeed break her leg," I say. "But she's pulling yours. Rosie and I both keep tabs on her, Sherman. She's in a lot of outside activities. She makes decent grades, B's and a C or two. She's not about to become a night roaming nymphette the minute we turn our backs."

"I talked to Momma about it. She said I need to encourage her more. That's one reason I pushed her to get involved in this thing here tonight after she told me about it. I know Rosie thinks it was just because she'd hate it, but it wasn't." He pauses a few minutes and hands Caitlin a toy she can't reach from the shelf above her.

"You're heading in the right direction," I tell him. "She likes the extra attention from you. I really don't think she's as boy crazy as she'd like you to believe."

"She may not be right now," Sherman says. "But I don't want her latching on to some no-count boy because I'm not around all the time and she needs a daddy."

"I find that unlikely," I say. "We need to go back to the contest. It's probably close to time for Cassie to be on stage."

He takes Caitlin from the floor and follows me back to the auditorium where Meaghan is completing a piece by Bach on her flute.

Cassie walks calmly onto the stage. Rosie sits on a low stool to the back and left of her daughter. She positions her guitar. The opening chords of "What Child is This?" resound as Cassie—arrayed in blue velvet and Grandma Minnie Beth's pearls—sings out clear and tender. There's hardly a sound in the auditorium.

"She may be better than Rosie was at her age," Sherman marvels as he listens raptly to his oldest daughter.

I decide not to remind him that he really didn't know Rosie very well at almost 13. As the blue light from the control tower radiates onto her royal blue velvet gown, Cassie is transformed to a near-mystical realm. Rosie plays soft and low as Cassie moves easily about the stage, continuing her song of praise to the Mother and Child. Not a sound is heard until she finishes. The applause is genuine and extensive. Tears roll from Fred's cheeks as he watches. Following four quick dance numbers, the stage darkens and the overhead lights come on, signaling intermission. None of us speak until we enter the Rotunda stairwell leading to the Parthenon Room.

"She's got her momma's face and talent, no mistake about that," Minnie Beth says. "Even little Caitlin was quiet while our Cassie sang.

That little girl just might have a career in front of her. See there, Sherman. I told you this thing would be good for her."

Sherman tells Minnie Beth that, indeed, she was right as we reach the second level of the Rotunda and enter the hallway. The others go into the reception as I linger a minute, waiting for Fred, who is a bit slower on the stairs. As he leaves the stairwell, he looks disoriented and bit teary-eyed.

"Fred, do you want to step outside a minute?" I ask him. The hallway is very hot. It is near freezing outside, but I feel the air might clear his head. We step into the back parking lot, just beyond the door.

"She was good, so very good," Fred says to me, slurring his words. "My Grace Ann knew how to sing, too. You remember that, don't you Ellott, honey? But she got away from us before her song was finished. Seems like to me that they never will find out who did that to my Grace Ann. It's been an awful long time, don't you think? They ought to have found something out by now." He begins to weep a little now.

"The sheriff's department needs help, Fred," I tell him. "You have to keep them up to date with what you're getting on the website." His e-mail has accumulated to such a degree that I am certain he never looks at it. Over the past few weeks since Zaia-Danda provided me with the password, I have personally added several tips to the murderx2 page. Most related to the black and yellow Skylark seen near the trailer on the morning of the murders. A message last week included a recent sighting of the car, on a back road in the acres of woods behind the trailer. Whenever I move any information to the info-page, I send an e-mail to the Caloosa County Sheriff's office, informing them of what I've done. Curiously, I've had no response.

"I'm just not any good at that computer stuff," Fred tells me, wiping his eyes. "Brother Anson was helping me out for awhile with it. He was going out with me at night, too, to see if we could find out the one that did it. I've decided that it wasn't Bud. I never did like the boy, but he loved my Grace Ann. Brother Anson's stopped helping me hunt the killer in the last week or so. Don't know what it is he's up to. Did you know he had a thing for my Grace Ann back when you all were teenagers? That was when they still called him Jimmy. But Grace Ann wouldn't give him the time of day. Old Sherman in there even tried to get next to her. I'm betting it was one of them old boyfriends of hers that killed Grace Ann and that Tanner. All them boys were so wild about my Grace Ann..."

I allow Fred to continue his tangent for a few minutes before I try to steer him back inside. We are both shivering in the cold night air. As we enter the Parthenon Room, Andy Swayne strolls over to us and brings me a cup of egg nog. Fred wanders over to join Sherman and Minnie Beth who are standing with the younger girls and Ree.

"This is certainly a charged atmosphere to put it mildly," he says. "One would think Miss Universe was being crowned." He sips from his glass punch cup as the Athena Villa Ensemble, a six piece orchestra, serenades us with 'White Christmas,'" in the overcrowded room.

"Beauty is a little more than skin deep when it moves into the pageant realm," I say.

"Evidently," he says. "I thought it was going to get physical before we ever reached a decision. Howell Rushton told Rainier Brown she had no business judging a beauty contest considering all the feminist propaganda she's always spouting. He suggested that only men were qualified to ascertain the quality of feminine beauty. Rainier's reply can hardly be repeated it was so vile. It took all of Eleanor's tact to calm them down. I had considered asking Rainier out but after witnessing the ferocity of her temper, I believe I'll let sleeping beauties lie."

"If you think Rainier's easy to rile, you should see Mamma," I tell him. "And wherever Rainier is, Mamma is sure to follow."

"Well, then, as the man said, 'include me out,'" Andy says. "What brings you here tonight, Miss E.D.? I thought I'd be about as likely to find you at one of these events as a whore in a convent." He lifts his cup in a mock toast.

"I'll overlook your language," I say, a little surprised. Andy is usually quite euphemistic in public. "I realize it's out of character, but my roommate's daughter is a contestant. She was near the end. The one in blue who sang 'What Child is This?'"

Andy is about to tell me something when Handy Snowden's voice comes over the sound system, inviting us back to the auditorium. We all file out. When we are seated, Handy steps up to the microphone.

"Solomon himself may have been faced with a more difficult choice, but not by any great degree," he says. "My beloved sister, Eleanor Edge Snowden, who has served as guardian angel of this contest since its inception, will announce tonight's winners."

Diamonds dangling from her earlobes, Miss Eleanor is elegant in her black satin gown and fur wrap at center stage. "Who would have dreamed back in the early '60s when our little competition first began with ten girls in a meeting room at City Hall that it would ever be this splendid?" She pauses as Athena Villans vigorously applaud. "For some years now, we have been forced to decline many young ladies wishing to be part of our annual ritual. After much discussion, we agreed that forty entries is a truly fair cut-off point. Some few months ago, our mayor and council decided that in keeping with current political and legal considerations, we must no longer allow the contest to be titled Miss Merry Christmas and Junior Miss Merry Christmas. So, with our brave new name, Winter Solstice Maiden and Junior Winter Solstice Maiden, we now embark on our fourth decade of competition. Our judges worked so very hard to select our winner and runners-up that I feel it only just to allow them to each present a winner. First, I want to introduce a former competition winner and last year's Athena Villa business woman of the year, Ms. Rainier Brown."

Rainier, in black velvet and white sapphires, takes the microphone. "I present to you the second runner up for Junior Solstice Maiden, Miss Cassandra Lee Jackson, who so charmed us with 'What Child is This?' Cassandra, please join us on stage and greet your audience."

Walking quite steadily for a child in her first pair of high heels, Cassie enters from the left and goes forward to receive a dozen roses and an embrace from Rainier. Our little party of seven is up and cheering wildly. I am unable to restrain Sherman who sounds an unabashed two-fingered whistle. Even Ree, who seemed uninterested in it all, is clapping and cheering. Fred is crying unashamedly, as is Minnie Beth.

"Atta, girl," Sherman shouts out. "Way to go, Cassie Lee."

Rosie remains backstage, so we are unable to share our joy. The other runner-up is someone from a neighboring over-the-mountain community, whose hand Howell Rushton pumps so vigorously I fear it will fall off. Junior Winter Solstice Maiden is, not too surprisingly, Heather Allman, the premier hoofer extraordinaire. Apparently this "Chantilly Lace," enchantress evoked a response in Andy Swayne similar to that of the Big Bopper's for his own teenaged queen. "A giggle and a walk" will do it every time. Andy looked all of 15 when he crowned the little darling. Infatuation dripped from every syllable of his congratulatory speech.

When it is over, we stand in the freezing night air, loading suitcases into Sherman's Brand New Mustang, 1965. The older girls will stay with him until the morning of Christmas Eve when he will drive them back to the Magic City. I hold a sleeping Caitlin wrapped inside my coat. Cassie is fondling her roses and talking to Ree, who seems genuinely glad for her.

"Go for it, whatever it is," Ree tells her. "If my momma ever taught Harley, Jr., and me anything, it was that. This might not be my thing, but if it's yours, then give it all you've got. There are a lot of contests like this in Good River. You could stay at your dad's and enter some there. One of my friends at school does things like this all the time. I'll ask her."

"And I wanted to take our little beauty and all the rest of you lovely ladies to dinner, but it's so late now, perhaps another time," Fred is saying as he turns to his grand daughter. "Ree, honey, all you'd have to do is put in those contacts I bought for you and stop wearing those school ma'arm glasses and you'd win one of these things just as easy as little Cassie here."

"I appreciate your saying that, Granddad," Ree tells him. "But I'm not really interested. Aunt Ell," she turns to me. "I saw some poster in the hallway about a conference going on here about women in popular culture. If I read it right, the final session is tomorrow. Is there any way I could go to it?"

"Sure, honey," Rosie breaks in. She looks a little overwhelmed by Cassie's success and the response to it. "If it's all right with Fred, you can stay with us tonight and go to the conference with Ell and me tomorrow. We'll get you back to Milltown when Sherman brings the girls back." She turns to Fred, who nods vigorously. Fred, I think, does not know how to react to Ree and her intellectual interests.

Rosie then hugs Cassie for the millionth time. "I knew you were good enough, sweetie. I just didn't expect you to win."

'I didn't really win, Momma," Cassie reminds her. "But I don't care. I'm just so happy. Aren't you happy, Daddy?"

"You bet, kiddo," Sherman says, hugging her, too. He turns to his ex-wife. "She couldn't have done it without you, Rosie. Your playing brought out the best in her singing."

"Thank you," Rosie says, simply and puts her arm around Sherman, giving him a squeeze. "I'm glad you pushed for this, Sherman. It turned out for the best."

After a few more quick hugs and arrangements for dropping off and returning children, Rosie and Ree get into my Cherokee. I buckle the still sleeping Caitlin into her seat and climb in front of the wheel. As we head back over Red Mountain toward home, The Magic City's holiday lights sparkle like diamonds in the December sky.

Perhaps it is the ghost of guilt trips past who returns to haunt our reveries when we are absent from church on Sunday mornings. Our mommas and our preachers always warned us of the consequences of that sin of omission. Poets and songwriters, not often a churchgoing lot, expound from time to time on the moods evoked by churchless Sundays. In the Wallace Stevens poem, the woman at her leisure dreams of death, of plunging "downward into darkness on extended wings." A country singer walking off a hangover on the Lord's Day morning is isolated by the signs of conventional life around him in Kris Krisofferson's song. There is something in a Sunday.

On this Sunday, five days before Christmas, I sit alone in my kitchen, drinking chocolate laced coffee and thinking of Gabe. We talked long distance until the sun rose this morning about everything and nothing at all. Bud Reese and I had many conversations like this outside the Seers High School band room where the buses were parked. I would wait there with him while Grace Ann finished majorette practice. He talked about his plans for Grace Ann and himself when all of us finished high school. He talked of his momma's work at the little Baptist mission church in The Hollow. He rarely mentioned his father. And although he did not say so, I felt certain Grace Ann seldom focused all her attention on what Bud had to say. Ree, their daughter, has her momma's body, her daddy's features and one of the sharpest intellects I have seen in a fifteen-year-old.

She, Rosie and I sat up late last night after the beauty pageant, eating Chinese take-out and talking about life in Milltown. Things, it seems, are better for them now that she and Harley, Jr., are temporarily living away from Fred. When I asked whether she had heard from Bud, she answered that they had, indirectly. A card addressed to her and Harley, Jr., with no return address, postmarked somewhere in Tennessee, came in last week's mail. It was not signed and only contained a few sentences, which Ree repeated to us: "I'm in a good place. I've got work here. I feel close to your momma. I will send something to my momma and daddy's for your Christmas. Love." At Daddy John and Mama Mary's, Ree says she and Harley feel at home.

In a few hours we will return to the Civic Center for the final segment of *Through A Glass Darkly,* "Lady Madonna or Ruby Tuesday: the Female Icon in Popular Music." Last night after Rosie, exhausted from the contest, retired, Ree and I talked on. After reading the handouts from the previous sessions, she asked me whether I ever felt like a gender apart, being that I have no husband or children. She said she meant nothing disrespectful, and that she intends to live her life the same way, but is worried that the loneliness might be hard to deal with. And I told this earnest child the truth. Sometimes it is. But that for me, solitary peace has a higher priority than fractious togetherness. Ree nodded as though she knew what I meant.

Old album covers deck the meeting room walls as the group trickles in for the final conference session. Surrounding us, in no particular order are—"Mona Lisa," "Earth Angel," "Honky Tonk Women," "Blue Velvet," "Peggy Sue," "Runaround Sue," and "Hello, Mary Lou." Rosie, Ree and I settle at a front table. Looking a bit more, I realize that the album covers are fake. Not finding the right rock and roll woman on the original covers, Charlotte superimposed drawings of each over the original cover art. It is most likely that her eleven-year-old son, Terrence—who plans an art career—rendered pencil and watercolor sketches of our heroines du jour. Today Charlotte is attired in period boots, a ruffled shirt and an ankle length denim skirt I recognize from days gone by.

"Peace my children," she says to us, holding up two fingers in the universal sign of Viet Nam days. "For those of you who were a mere twinkle in your parents' eyes in the '60s and early '70s, this session may be a bit vexing since it centers on the music of that era. But bear with me, I have provided charts, lyrics and synopses of the multitudes of songs we plan to talk about." She begins to distribute the stapled handouts.

"Because relationships between the sexes override most other things in rock and roll and because a significant part of rock music is made by males about females, women—or more often girls—are allotted many more personae than those we discussed yesterday. One way of viewing women in literature is to see them as Eves, Marys or Lilliths. Not so in rock and roll. These women, though they could probably be viewed as offshoots of various archetypes, will be given more vernacular labels," she sips from a bottle of spring water and continues.

"First we look at Woman as Goddess. We've all met her. And maybe for one brief shining moment we've even been her. You've seen a few in the posters around us. And I'll name a few more 'Venus in Blue Jeans,' 'The Wonder of You,' 'My Eyes Adored You.' Can anyone else fill in the blanks?"

"I always wanted to be the woman in 'Special Angel,'" a woman in a hot pink windsuit says. "But my husband says I'm 'The Devil in Disguise.'"

"We'll get to her in a minute," Charlotte says when we stop laughing. "Any more women on a pedestal anyone would like to name?"

"'Pretty Woman,'" someone else says. "I like the way the Big O sang about her, but Julia Roberts didn't do a thing for me in that movie."

"'Ain't No Woman (Like the One I Got),'" a black woman says. "Me and my girlfriends used to play that for our boyfriends all the time in school. They told us when we got to be women to come back and see 'em."

"Next we look at the Goddess' evil twin, the She Devil. Now She Devil has two faces: She Devil as desirable, yet wicked temptress DWT—and CCB, Cruel Castrating Bitch. DWT we find in 'Poor Side of Town,' 'Devil in Disguise,' 'Too Proud to Beg,' 'I Got a Woman (Mean as She Can Be),' 'Tutti Frutti,' and 'Lawdy Miss Clawdy.' Now Ms. CCB, her name is legion, honey. Tell you what, I'll do my contenders for the top ten and the rest of you pick it up from there. Let's kick this bad puppy and put her to rest. 'Cathy's Clown,' 'His Latest Flame,' 'Are You Lonesome Tonight?' 'Crying Time,' 'Crying,' 'Crazy Arms,' 'Crazy,' and 'Your Cheatin' Heart.'"

"'Runaround Sue,'" someone says.

"'There Goes My Baby,'" I offer.

"Going, going, gone," Charlotte says. "Now a few more rockin' icons before we break for a few minutes. Later we'll divide into groups and talk about all these ladies of good and ill repute. I want to assess how we see each of them, how we feel the songwriters see them, and finally, if we could or would change the song and still have it be good music."

"Let us consider the Seduction Song and its poetic origins. If 'It's Now or Never,' had been written three hundred years ago, would it have been 'Come Live with Me and Be My Love?'" She pauses for our comments and seeing some of us look baffled, she says, "Okay, skip that one. Was Gary Puckett the Andrew Marvell of his era?" When there is still no comment, she moves on.

"Last of all, I will leave you with these Dead Saint Songs: 'Patches,' 'Honey,' and, God love her,'Teen Angel.' 'Are you somewhere up above/are you still my own true love.' And finally, with apologies and deference to David Allan Coe, the 'I've-Done-Her-Wrong-And-Now-She's-Gone-And-I'm-Alone' songs: 'Working My Way Back to You, Babe,' and 'Take Good Care of My Baby.' And that, baby, is all she wrote," Charlotte takes a little bow and heads for the door. The rest of us stand, stretch, and move toward the drink machines.

"Ell, wait a minute," Zaia-Danda is running down the hallway toward Rosie, Ree and me. She, too, looks very retro-Sixties in bellbottoms and tie-dyed sweat-shirt. "I came in late and sat in the back. I just got through with a gardening workshop in Gulf Shores last night. I had to drive like a maniac to get here. Joe saw your announcement on the 'Net and called me this morning. Believe it or not, I take these clothes with me wherever I go. They're my only relics from 1969. They're holey in more ways than one. But anyway, I can name every top forty hit from '60 to '73 by listening to the first eight bars, so I just had to come to this."

"I'm glad to see you," I say, giving her a hug. "This is Rosie Jackson, my roommate, and this," I say, gesturing toward the long-legged teenager with dark shoulder length hair and rimless glasses, "is Ma 'Ree Beaulieux Reese."

"Oh, my God, you're Ree," Zaia-Danda says in delight. "Bud is so proud of you, honey. He couldn't stop talking about you and your brother. One reason I came here today was to let Ell know I heard from your daddy last week."

"Are you the gardener lady?" Ree asks. "Daddy talked a lot about you before he took off. Where is he? I want to see Daddy." Suddenly, she is a little girl again with a trembling lip.

"He's living in a commune in East Tennessee somewhere," Zaia-Danda tells her. "He used a cell phone to call me on my cell phone, so the call wouldn't be traced. He works on the cars of the people who live there. They even let him do his Elvis act from time to time. He's doing about as good as he can."

"Why can't he come home?" Ree is crying now and I gather her in my arms. "Granddad even says he doesn't think Daddy was the one who killed Momma and Tanner any more. Why can't the police find out who did it? Harley and I need Daddy."

The three of us take Ree into an empty office inside the Rotunda and sit down with her. Zaia-Danda says, gently. "Ree, honey, your Daddy's not altogether in his right mind yet. Your Momma's taking up with another man and then her getting killed like she did have almost driven him insane. I tried to tell him Fred's changed his mind and that the police only want to talk to him to see if he knows anything, but he won't listen to me. And, partly thanks to me, he's got some misguided ideas about reincarnation and meeting your Momma in another life. He may well do that, but he thinks it's going to take place right now if he can just make the right connection with her spirit."

"I don't understand any of that," Ree says. "I just know we need him. Harley and I are happy at Daddy John's and Momma Mary's, but

Granddad isn't going to let us stay there much longer. He told me that on the way down last night."

"Ree, honey, does Fred treat you all right?" Rosie asks her. "If he doesn't there are things you can do about that."

"Granddad isn't home enough to treat us bad or good," Ree tells her. "Harley and I spend all our time with the housekeeper, Mrs. Dawber, who hates being there. I think she hates us, too. Granddaddy says he's got to stay on the road until he finds whoever killed Momma and Tanner. But I don't know how much longer we can stand it there with just her." Ree sniffs and wipes her eyes.

"Maybe your Daddy can get himself together again, and you can live with him," Zaia-Danda says. "When I talk to him again, I'm going to tell him everything you've said. He needs to know this."

We return to the meeting room and Charlotte assigns Ree and me to the same small discussion group. Our first topic is the frequent use of the words "daddy" and "baby" in contemporary music.

"It's just trickle down patriarchy," the woman from UAB says. "Big Daddy, Big Man. Little Baby minds Big Daddy."

We toss that around for awhile and close out our gab session by naming our very favorite song title from that particular genre.

"That's easy," Ree says, firmly. "The Only Daddy That'll Walk the Line.'"

Chapter Eighteen

All is eggnog, fruitcake and goodwill on the day before Christmas Eve at Athena Villa Public. Our halls are decked and our demeanor jolly as we shut down normal operations and spread a feast for our patrons. Emmeleine and I have been here since 7:00, mixing punch and baking hors d'oeuvres. Ree is in back, arranging cookies and other confectionery delights on a tray. Merilee Snowden is helping Dottie Dunwald with her Mrs. Santa costume. Dottie—our appropriately named children's librarian—dresses seasonally for every holiday story time for the younger children. Throughout the year, she appears as various matronly characters from children's literature—Mother Goose, The Queen of Hearts, Old Mother Hubbard, and so forth. Her best has been as the Thanksgiving Turkey, feathers, wattle neck and all. Dottie and her husband, Dougie, who sells real estate in the same office that formerly employed Perri-Young, are long term Athena Villans. Transplanted Yankees who came and stayed in the early '60s, they have raised two daughters and made our little 'burb their home. Joseph, our annual Santa, is busy padding his costume with whatever he can locate. Even Cora Moon has the holiday spirit today. Under the circulation desk, she is hiding a cache of tiny wrapped packages for her special patrons. Emmeleine and I suspect they are Bible verse bookmarks from the Baptist Bookstore. Both of us hope they don't catch Perri-Young's eye when she drops in.

"Am I too early?" Eleanor Edge pokes her head through the doors. "I was hoping to arrive soon enough to help you with the egg nog. I love you dearly, Emmeleine, but your egg nog leaves something to be desired."

"We saved it for you," I tell her as Emmeleine pretends to be offended. Their friendship would probably withstand a knock-down-drag-out in the front parking lot. "Did you bring your cheese straws?"

"I have a huge tray of things in my back seat. Is there someone who could bring them in?"

"I'll get them, Aunt Ell," Ree offers.

"Eleanor, this is the daughter of some old friends of mine," I tell her. "Ma 'Ree Reese. This is Miss Snowden, honey."

"I do believe I saw you at the beauty competition the other night, Ma 'Ree," Eleanor says to her. "I remarked to Handy, my brother, who is the mayor, what a lovely girl you are. You might want to consider entering our contest next year."

"I'll certainly keep it in mind," Ree tells her with a straight face. I wink at her as she goes to Miss Eleanor's Lexus parked in front of the building.

Within the next half-hour or so, we finish our preparations and declare our house open. Perri, Terri and Sherri come in together, all seasonally attired in white and silver. After a surreptitious inspection of the premises to see whether we have imposed our religion on the innocent public, Perri fills a generous plate with fruit, hors d'oeuvres and cookies and heads in my direction.

"I wanted to let you know what a delight your friend Charlotte is," Perri-Young says to me. "Simply everyone wants to ask her back next summer, if we can get another grant. The support for the conference was just marvelous. Why, hello, Eleanor, I didn't see you standing there." She turns to her sister-in-law, who has just joined us near the Christmas tree. "Congratulations on the success of the Winter Solstice competition! I was so sorry I was unable to attend. I do hope Handy conveyed my apologies to you. I contracted one of my migraine headaches while we were straightening up from the women's conference and was practically prostrate the whole evening."

Eleanor, undoubtedly seeing this for the white lie that it is, is nevertheless gracious in return. "Yes, he did, Perri. And I do think our change of title actually boosted the number of entries this year. People were so intrigued by the new name, we had to turn away numerous young ladies. Fortunately, Ellott's roommate's daughter, Cassandra registered just in time and was one of our runners-up. Such a gorgeous young girl! And what a singer! Her momma may have to watch out in a few years."

I slip away as the two previously dueling in-laws kiss and make up. Merilee comes over to me as I sit down at my desk to finish my plate. "I didn't notice hell freezing over," she remarks. "Are Step-Mamma and Aunt Eleanor actually talking politely? And just when I had saucers of milk all ready and waiting."

"It's the Ghost of Christmas Pleasant," I tell her. "Enemies often declare Yuletide truces. Give it until about January 2. If it stays that long, then maybe there's hope of it lasting. Could you do me a terrific favor? Would you involve Ree with the children's storytime and little party? I'd ask Dottie, but I think it would have more effect if it came from you. She's a bit at loose ends and needs to keep busy. This is her first Christmas without her mother."

"Do you think she'd wear an elf costume?" Merliee asks. "One of the people who was supposed to help out didn't show, so I'm the lone elf right now."

"I think she might," I say to her and she approaches Ree, who is serving a plate for one of the city council members. I gaze out the window onto the dead landscape of the playing fields and jogging trails, quietly sipping my egg nog.

"Do you have a cup of kindness for a tired traveler?" I look up to see Gabe standing in front of my desk, wearing jeans, a faded leather jacket, an exhausted face and a big smile.

"I think we can arrange something," I say, barely able to contain my joy as I stand up and squeeze his arm. "Come over to the buffet table with me." I lead him by the hand to a linen draped study table near the Circulation Desk, where Eleanor and Emmeleine are serving.

"Ladies," I say, giving Gabe a cup of egg nog. "This is my friend, Gabriel Pace. Gabe, Emmeleine Riley, our director, and Eleanor Edge Snowden, sister to our mayor and Queen of Athena Villa."

After Gabe is duly examined and found satisfactory, I walk him to the stacks room and close the door. My face crushes against his jacket in a sturdy-armed embrace. His aroma—old leather, Old Spice, and old sweat—goes deep inside me. Unlike President Clinton, I do inhale.

White lights twinkle in the trees of Caldwell Park on Christmas Eve. Rosie, the older girls, their special friends, Michael, Gabe and I await the rest of our caroling party on the sidewalk surrounding the park. Mabel June is babysitting Caitlin back at the apartment. The temperature sign above a nearby bank reads 16 degrees. The four girls stamp their feet to keep warm. I see Charlie, Curtis, and a bundled-to-the-teeth Maithel heading our way.

"Joyeux Noel, you all," Charlie says. "I got on long johns and three undershirts and I'm still cold."

"This is sure some wild ass idea to come out in this kind of weather," Curtis complains. He is thin, cold-natured and his teeth chatter as he speaks. "How come the four of you don't look all that cold?" He indicates Michael and Rosie and Gabe and me.

"They got their love to keep them warm," Maithel says. Her voice is so muffled by layers of scarves that it's hard to understand her.

"Which way are we heading first?" Charlie asks, calmly. "Did somebody bring a guitar?"

"I brought my old harmonica," Gabe says. "We figured everybody's fingers would be too cold to play a stringed instrument."

"Let's head 'em up and move 'em out, then," Curtis says. "There's a bottle of Cutty Sark back at the house that's calling my name."

"Momma, there's a man sitting in one of the swings down there all by himself," Cassie says as we head up the sidewalk. "Can we see if he wants to come with us?"

"I don't think so, sweetie," Rosie says, glancing uneasily at a man in an old Army jacket and ragged jeans, drifting aimlessly in the plastic swing. "I'm sure he's got other things to do on Christmas Eve."

"I bet he doesn't, Momma, or he'd be doing them," Cassie replies and motions to Meaghan. The two girls head down the hill into the park. "Hey, mister," she calls to him.

"I'll go with them," Gabe says and runs to catch up. I can hear Cassie talking to the man, but I can't make out the words. Then Gabe is speaking. In a few minutes, the four of them come up the embankment and onto the sidewalk.

"This is Brother Joseph Mary," Cassie announces to us, catching her breath. "He's a monk, see, but he doesn't have a place to stay right now. The rest of his brothers went back home to North Carolina, but Brother Joseph Mary says his work is here in Birmingham."

Brother Joseph Mary extends his hand to Rosie. "Very glad to meet you. You have a nice daughter. She must recognize a lonely soul when she sees one." His hair and beard are curly and a little scraggly. He emits a faint, but inoffensive body odor.

"We're glad to have you," Michael steps in and extends his hand. "Michael Pace. Listen, not to interfere, but you look cold. I've got another coat in the car that would probably fit you. Do you want it?"

"I do, thank you," Brother Joseph Mary says, gratefully. "Actually I had one on earlier, but I gave it to a young boy riding his bicycle down by the projects on 24th Street. Then I walked over here to the swings to pray for awhile and forgot the time. This is one of my favorite spots to pray—sitting right here, swinging up to God."

His grayish blue eyes are watery and red-rimmed and seem focused on something beyond us. His hands tremble and he puts them inside his armpits until Michael brings him the coat. He nods his thanks and puts it on.

Gabe pulls out his harmonica and plays the opening bars of "Away in a Manger." We move as a group up Highland Avenue, past apartment houses and churches and on toward Five Points. We all sing. Brother Joseph Mary's baritone blends well with the group's sound.

Singing carol after carol, we walk steadily toward the fountain and reaching it, we stop to rest. Maithel and Curtis go to one of the open restaurants across the street to fetch coffee for the crowd. The night is cloudless and the temperature is dropping by the minute.

"What order do you belong to, Brother Joseph Mary?" I ask him as we wait. "My boss is Catholic and I've gone with her a few times to the monastery in Cullman."

"Oh, our order is a very small one," Brother Joseph Mary says. "Nothing like the Benedictines. We're not even officially recognized by the Church. But I have met the Bishop a few times and he seemed quite friendly. We call ourselves the Brothers of the Creche, honoring St. Francis' simplifying of the manger scene. You see, in the 13th century, when St. Francis lived, manger scenes had become very ornate, some would say even gaudy. Francis took them back to their original, humble settings—barns with real straw, live animals and a poorly dressed Holy Family. Our mission is to embody that spirit."

"And how do you go about that?" I ask, politely. This sounds a bit suspect to me and very unlike any religious orders I've encountered, Catholic or non. Rosie, Michael, Gabe and the girls are talking to another group of carolers who have stopped for a breather. There's a peaceable crowd of merrymakers congregated near the fountain. Many of the restaurants keep their doors open to accommodate the throng.

"We all work low wage jobs so we can free our minds to do the work of Jesus," Brother Joseph Mary explains. "If we have a trade, we practice that. But none of us hold white collar jobs, even if we have the education for them. We feel that would go against the teachings of St. Francis."

"Brother J," a young, well-dressed black man and woman come up to us. The man is holding out his hand to Brother Joseph Mary. "How you doin', man?"

Brother Joseph Mary's face breaks into a smile. "Josiah. I was thinking about you earlier today. How are things with you? Are you still living with your sister and going to school?"

"Sure am," the young man says. "This my sister here, Evangeline. She say she want to meet the man got me off rock. This him, Vangie, Brother J." The woman shakes Brother J's hand and they talk for several minutes. The young man offers his hand again and they talk for several minutes before he leaves with his sister.

"One success story," Brother J says with a smile. "They don't come very often. Addictions are hard to shake. And it's not always drugs or alcohol, is it?"

"No," I agree with him. "Sometimes it can be to a person or an idea."

"You're speaking of obsession now," Brother J says, sadly. "I'm not sure obsessives ever get over it. They center themselves on one person or concept and just won't let go. If you know someone in a situation like that, don't bet on it turning out well."

We stand there silently and in a few moments, our party returns to us. Maithel brings coffee and doughnuts. Molly runs up to us and hugs me first and then Brother J.

"Hey," she says. "It's Christmas Eve. Be happy."

"You're exactly right," Brother J laughs and pats her on the top of her hooded head. "Do you know what my favorite carol is?"

"'O Holy Night'?"

"No, 'Joy to the World,'" he says. "That's what the shepherds and the angels felt on the very first Christmas Eve. Will you play for us, Gabriel? Shouldn't you have a horn, like your namesake?"

"I played a trumpet in high school," Gabe says with a laugh. "Let's sing, folks." The other group of carolers and a contingent of bystanders join in. Business people, street people, students and professionals blend their voices to hail the birth of the Baby Son.

Some few hours later back at the apartment—with the children in bed and Brother J allowed temporary shelter in the warehouse behind Picker's Palace—Gabe and I lie in bed together, half dressed and half dozing. We are biding time until the kids are good and asleep and we can help Michael and Rosie distribute presents.

"Do you think Brother J's telling the whole truth and nothing but?" I ask him.

"Hard to say exactly," Gabe answers me. "He's got that broken veined drinker's nose and bloodshot eyes. I don't think his hands were shaking from just the cold. He may be stretching the facts a bit here and there, but he's honest enough to let stay in the warehouse. Hell, I wouldn't put the Unabomber on the streets on Christmas Eve."

"I wish you and Michael could go with us to Milltown," I say to him, snuggling into his arms.

"Lawzy mercy, Miss Scarlett," he says in his Prissy voice. "Amelia Gayle Pace would have a permanent case of the vapors if her two boys didn't return to the old maternal grandparent's homestead for Christmas." He switches accents to his best Savannah blue blood drawl. "Robillard Manor, our grandparent's last remnant of wealth and esteem, would collapse at its very foundations if such an event were to occur within the Pace family household. Sorry, babe, we have to make the quarterly pilgrimage back to ol' Savannay. There's no excuse except death."

"I don't think you really mind it that much," I say to him.

"I don't," Gabe admits, smiling. "Michael and I make out like bandits at Christmas. It's dull and slow paced, but all in all, it's not bad."

"You will be back by New Year's Eve, though?"

"Cross my beating heart," Gabe says. "I wonder how Brother Michael is faring. It was all I could do to talk him out of buying Rosie a diamond for Christmas."

"Good that you did," I say. "She's not even been divorced a whole year. I don't think she's ready for anything permanent again just yet."

"Same argument I used," Gabe says

"So, what did he get her?"

"Emerald earrings and a necklace to match," Gabe says. "And how about you, Fair One? Are you ready for that Golden Fleece of a present I finally located for you?" He reaches into the pocket of his coat lying on the floor beside him, extracting a package wrapped in white satiny paper and bound with a red velvet bow.

I open a first edition of *Final Harvest*, the first complete edition of Emily Dickinson's poems.

"Gabe, my God! Where did you find this?" I find myself unable to say very much.

"In some damn little hole-in-the-wall on a side street in New York that took me and Michael two hours to find," he says, pleased by my response. I kiss him long and hard without speaking.

"And this is yours," I say to him, minutes later as I reach into the drawer in my bedside table. "Mine's not quite as exclusive, but I believe you'll like it."

Gabe carefully unwraps a CD collection of the complete recordings of Flatt and Scruggs with the Foggy Mountain Boys.

"You do know how to make a man happy, Ellott Hailey Seers," Gabe says quietly, looking into my eyes. "Come lay down and love on me a little longer 'til we have to get up and play Mr. and Mrs. Santy." We turn out the lights and are just settling into the darkness when we hear Rosie and Michael call to us from the living room.

No Christmas lights or tinsel garland deck the porch of the Culp farmhouse. Inside the front room in the far corner where the coal stove once stood, there is a voluminous cedar tree trimmed in popcorn strands and dozens of crocheted ornaments that are stiffened with starch. Large colored glass balls with names and birthdays of Millie's four children, Miller, Millie herself, Rosie's children and Sam and Clettus are the only other decorations. The one with Sherman's name has been removed. Every year she can recall has been exactly like this one, Rosie told me on the drive up. Rosie's three brothers, who co-own a huge commercial farm in Tennessee near the Kentucky border, are snowed in and unable to come home. Millie sees them twice a year at most, when they can spare the time from their work. Two are older than Rosie and one is younger. None have ever married. They are kind, dispassionate men who have devoted their lives to the land.

It is late morning when we arrive and we sit down to a Christmas dinner of quail, dressing and a multitude of vegetables home grown and canned or frozen right here at the farm. And there is Millie's special ambrosia and coconut cake for dessert. Sam and Clettus join us for the meal. Sam's cough seems better. Millie wrote us that he is trying to stop smoking and when I see him chewing something I ask if it is Nicorette. He quickly lets me know that he is stopping the habit all on his own and is chewing Juicy Fruit to keep his mouth busy. Clettus tells me later that his father tried both the gum and the patch and found neither to his liking.

"I sure wish he would find something," Clettus says to me as Rosie and I are helping Millie clear the table so we can get ready to open gifts. "He gets up and rambles around the cabin half the night, he gets so agitated. And he's about to eat us out of house and home."

I did notice Sam going back for second, even third helpings at the dinner table.

Rosie and I pooled our money this year to buy Millie a microwave and I commission Clettus to bring it in from the Cherokee. Millie is busy watching Caitlin who is clinging to Rosie's hand and taking tiny steps. When Clettus sets the huge box in front of her, she looks at it and shakes her head.

"Rosalee, honey, I told you not to go all out for me, now. This looks like entirely too much." She slowly unwraps it and cannot speak for a few minutes when she determines what it is.

"I saw you looking at them in that catalog the last time we were here," Rosie says. "You can cook things quick and not have to drag out all those pots and pans. You'll have time to go to the Community Center and still come in to a good meal. Uncle Sam told me when we were here when Grace Ann died that you like to go there two or three times a week."

"Lots of the girls I grew up with in Milltown go there," Millie says, as she examines the inside of her new microwave. "Most of their husbands are dead and gone, too. I'll have to read this little book that come with it and learn how to use this gadget. I really do thank you girls. Molly, honey, look under the tree over there and get the presents I got for you all. You and Cassie can play Santy Claus."

Molly and Cassie deliver the gifts Millie made for each of us. Mine is a patchwork quilt to fit my queen sized bed. Each square has a different colored bow-tied ribbon stitched to it.

"It's a wedding quilt," Millie says with a laconic grin. "I seen how that Gabe looks at you, Ell. It's still not too late for you to tie the knot."

She crocheted slippers and matching afghans for Mollie and Cassie. For Caitlin she knitted a sweater and matching bonnet. She leaves us and goes to a back bedroom, returning with a long dress bag. "There wadn't no way to wrap this thing, Rosalee. Unzip it and go try it on. I'm not too sure about the length."

Rosie lifts a full-skirted antebellum style dress of deep green watered taffeta from the garment bag. Its flounces are edged in lighter green. There are slippers of the same material in the bottom of the bag.

"I even found a hoop you can wear with it if you want to. It's in yonder in the bedroom. I know you wore an outfit something like it to one of them festivals you all's string band played at," Millie tells her. "Run in there and put it on, girl. We want to see it."

A gift laden Sherman is coming in the front door as Rosie emerges from the bedroom. "Happy ho-ho," he says to rest of us and stops dead still as he catches sight of Rosie. There is such a look of naked longing and love on his face that it is difficult to witness. He recovers quickly and says, "I might be some early, but I couldn't wait any longer to give the girls their presents. Clettus, my man, could I have some help bringing the rest of this paraphernalia in from my car?"

The two of them make several trips until Millie's front room is crampacked with wrapped boxes. The older girls unwrap Caitlin's present for her. It is a giant rocking horse which Sherman and Clettus commence to put together.

"It's got the three most dreaded words in the English language on the box," Sherman laughs as Clettus brings in his toolbox. "Some assembly required. Remember that, Rosie? How we used to stay away from toys that…" He catches himself before he reveals Santa's identity to his middle daughter. "Anyhow, we'll get it fixed up, won't we, Clettus? Molly, that other big box is yours."

Molly whoops with pleasure as she opens *Medieval Microcosm*, a miniature 12th century village with characters with moving parts. Dragons, damsels, knights and blacksmiths are hastily pulled from their bags and placed in their proper settings. "Look, Daddy, the catapult really works. Me and Helen can have battles. This is the greatest."

"Yours is a little more practical," he tells Cassie as she opens three smaller boxes. One contains an elaborate tape player-recorder with an expensive microphone attachment. The next is a camcorder and attachments. The last is a VCR.

"I thought since you may be the next teenage singing sensation, you'd need something so you can see and hear yourself and learn from your mistakes. All of us need to do that now and then." He looks solemnly at Rosie.

"Momma Millie, could we hook this thing up to your tv set?" He asks his former mother-in-law. "I brought a cassette of the beauty contest Cassie won and I thought you might like to see it since you didn't get to come."

"Go right ahead, son," Millie tells him.

"Just a minute," I say to him as he begins to connect the wiring. The girls have temporarily abandoned their gifts to hold Caitlin up on the rocking horse. "Rosie and I got something for you, too. For those long nights at the Circle K store." He opens a set of video tapes of *WWF: Monday Night Raw*. Viewing professional wrestling is one of Sherman's favorite pass-times.

"Hot damn," he is clearly pleased. "I got the two of you a little remembrance from days past. Look at those other two packages under Miss Millie's tree."

Mine is duplicate of my high school class ring, which I lost fifteen years ago on a hiking trip. Miss Samantha Jane Seers' young face is set in its center. "How did anyone copy this so well?" I ask Sherman, giving him a hug. "Thanks, old boy."

Rosie is examining her gift, another replica. It is the sterling i.d. bracelet Sherman gave her our junior year with the same engraving: *SLJ + DRC Love can't fail.*

He and Rosie sit beside each other, quietly talking as the rest of us watch the tape. At one point, he takes her hand and holds it for a long time and she does not pull away. I fast-forward the tape to Cassie's performance. He and Rosie interrupt their intimate conversation and Sherman takes the remote from me. He zaps to the part where Cassie receives her winner's bouquet, freeze framing the young girl smiling so radiantly in her blue gown.

It's a different kind of Auld Lange Syne this New Year's Eve. Most often I am alone on that most noted of all evenings to party. Last year, Caitlin had colic and Rosie and I took turns rocking her. The four of us had planned an evening of revelry this year, but at the last minute Mabel

June, our designated babysitter, came down with the flu. We debated for a bit over possible replacements or alternative arrangements, but Rosie finally settled it by deciding to stay home. She claimed fatigue from work and the holidays, but the rest of us sense it is not exactly that. Since the return of the Pace brothers from their extended business trip, Rosie has begun some subtle, but unmistakable distancing from Michael. She did not seem overly pleased with his Christmas gift and has made excuses not to see him in the days between the year end holidays. More than once I have heard her talking long distance to Sherman late in the evening after Caitlin is in bed. The older girls remain at Minnie Beth's house with him until he brings them home on Sunday.

Intuitive—as are most musicians—Michael is playing out this difficult arrangement in very low key. After a day or so, he stopped calling so frantically. Bolstered by a significant intake of the substance that soothes him, he agrees to a quiet evening at the apartment with Rosie. His plans are to see in the New Year with her and then return home. Although I think she meant to be alone with Caitlin, Rosie consents to this and Gabe and I leave them to themselves.

We decide to cancel our reservations at the Merritt House. Instead, we run into Bruno 's at the last minute and buy steaks, potatoes, salad makings and a bottle of wine. Gabe grabs a cheese cake and we hurry through the line. They are closing their doors behind us as we head to Gabe's car. We drive to the Pace home, which I gleefully point out to him for the dozenth time, is within the city limits of Mountain Brook, the Magic City's most elite suburb, one of the wealthiest in the South.

"I am more than aware of that," he says, ignoring me as I pontificate on this. "We bought the house, not the location. Their taxes are enough to choke a horse. When Michael and I first moved here, we had a good time at the store telling our customers that we made genuine mountain music from our home in Mountain Brook."

Their abode lies within the Crestline Village area of what is called the Tiny Kingdom by some envious outsiders. White frame and one story with two bedrooms, two baths, kitchen, living room/dining room combo and sunroom. Not elaborate, but nice with a small back yard and detached garage. We combine our efforts for a satisfying meal and when we have loaded the dishwasher, Gabe shows me to the sunroom. I sit in a wicker rocking chair while he lowers the blinds and opens out the futon in the corner. He removes his shoes, lies down and pats the spot beside him.

"It's spider and fly time, O Queen of my heart," he says and tries to look menacingly seductive.

I am laughing so that by the time I am settled beside him, I find it hard to become serious. He reaches over to the table beside us and fills two wine glasses, handing me one. "To a night of peace and love," he says and I am laughing again.

"What do you want me to say, 'Candy's dandy, but liquor's quicker?'" He is beginning to sound a little vexed. "There aren't any good lines for this situation. They've all been said."

"Just give me a little time and a few glasses of wine and I'll be in the proper mood of the evening," I tell him. "It's been awhile, remember?"

"Why don't you talk to me about how it was with Bryan?" Gabe says to me. He begins to massage my shoulders. "Was it good between you?"

"It seemed to be at the time," I say, relaxing a bit. "Of course, both of us were totally inexperienced. Two introverts mating with one another."

With Gabe patiently leading me through, I open up to him about Bryan and me all those years ago in a tiny off-campus apartment at the U of A. My marriage of two months that ended with a brief parting in a cemetery and then death. As he removes my clothes, the vestiges of hurt and hesitation slip from me as well. His body, large and sturdy, so like my own, feels right against mine. Bryan was tall and slender and I could never position my body right against his angularity. As the evening ends, Gabe and I rock the time-honored cradle of love into the new year

Chapter Nineteen

In Low Country along the southeast Atlantic coast where Voo Doo is still practiced, long time residents paint the shutters of their houses "haint" blue to keep spirits away. Gabe, who grew up there, says that people are often more meticulous about this than in installing adequate locks or bars. In Milltown, Alabama, where fundamentalism prevails, it is not a custom. When White Cotton Mill closed its doors in the late '60s, its owners surrounded it with a chain link fence and barred the doors. This did not prevent young boys from scaling the fence, breaking out the windows and climbing inside. Some who did said they could still hear the sounds of the looms and shuttles in the empty rooms. A local news reporter interviewed the boys and then went on to write that the real ghosts were the mill workers left without jobs and the area businesses that gradually began to close when the mill ceased to operate. The mill plant was used to store cotton for some years, but it is now vacant. Milltown began to die on that April day more than a quarter of a century ago, but like a terminally ill patient with an indefinite life span projection, it has not passed on.

    Millie called Rosie and me last night to say that they are tearing down White Cotton Mill. On February 23, Ash Wednesday for liturgical calendar watchers, local politicians and ministers will join forces for a giant send-off before the old building implodes. In its place, the city of Good River will erect a new multi-complex with something for all. Milltown

Community Village will feature a spacious community center, a few shops, and a new library. Broadway, which is adjacent to the old mill, will be refurbished as an outdoor mall, replete with greenery and open air markets. The demolition/dedication day will be a big to-do for Millltown and Millie wants us to be present. Local musicians are being encouraged to bring their instruments for impromptu performances following the speeches and fanfare.

I am pondering last night's news from my usual thinker's post, my desk in the Library's Reference area.

Late January days often tend to cast "that certain slant of light that oppresses," as the good poet once wrote, and any bit of diversion can only help. As I turn to face a different direction, I watch a mom in a sweat suit jog-strolling her infant up one of the trails on civic center grounds. The babies I have observed who are subjected to this seem not to mind it, but I would think it would jar every newly emerging tooth from their little heads. With Caitlin now in the toddling stage, I expect our strolling activities will be somewhat curtailed. My musings segue to dream babies of my own and how I would tend to these perfect children when my telephone intercom buzzes.

"Ellott Seers." I always answer professionally at work, especially when I am uncertain who is buzzing me.

"Ell, I need to see you and Joseph in my office in about five minutes," Emmeleine says. "And bring your monthly planner." She hangs up without waiting for my reply. In the sixteen years I have worked for her, I have never known Emmeleine Riley to waste anything, words included.

I pass Joseph in the staff area, planner in hand, heading for Emmeleine's open door. We seat ourselves in her cozy office, awaiting her arrival. My attention centers on the Riley family portrait that hangs behind her desk. Posed underneath a blossoming magnolia in the Riley backyard, Emmeleine and Redmon, her late husband, each stand with a hand on the shoulder of one of their daughters, Mona and Maureen.

Redmon and Maureen are laughing and jaunty in their Easter finery. Emmeleine and Mona smile very slightly and are dressed similarly in suits of white linen. Although it was taken many years ago when the girls were still in their late teens, I feel it perfectly captures the essence of the Riley four.

Twenty years older than Emmeleine and deceased several years ago, the always smiling Redmon Riley was one of the architectural innovators of Athena Villa. Many of its Greek Revival structures are his creations. He met Emmeleine at the grand opening of City Hall, which he designed. A young, single and serious minded librarian working for the Birmingham City system and still living at home with her parents in Athena Villa, Emmeleine's heart was won on that very day.

She and Redmon soon married and in time produced the two girls. Mona, the older girl, dutifully attended the finishing school and Ivy League college her parents selected for her. Her business career took her first into middle management at the headquarters of a large cosmetics corporation and then into upper management for a subsidiary firm, Balmy Mist, a bath and beauty chain. Married in her late twenties to another company executive, the couple have two daughters, Kathleen, 8, and Karis, 6. Maureen, who is much like Redmon, college hopped from coast to coast throughout her late teens and early twenties, Settling finally, she completed a post-graduate degree in art history in her early thirties and immediately began work as a curator for the Atlanta Museum of Art. Maureen is happily unmarried and determined to remain so.

Emmeleine enters in an atypical rush and sits down behind her desk, folds her hands and smiles at us. "I'll just cut to the chase here," she says. "I spent most of yesterday and this morning making arrangements to be out of town the rest of this month, all of February and part of March. Mona and Malcolm's company is flying them to London for six weeks or so to open the Balmy Mist franchise there. Eleanor has agreed to accompany me to Boston to stay with Kathleen and Karis. Ellott, you are in charge until I come back. And, Joseph, you will assume responsibility when Ellott is not here. One of you will have to be here anytime the library's doors are open. I am sorry this is happening in two of our busiest months, but that's the way it is. I'll talk to Dottie and Cora. I've already spoken to Sha 'Neece. Ellott, you can speak with Merliee and Cross," she says, referring to our pages. "Questions?"

"Huhhh," I say, intelligently. The longest sabbatical Emmeleine has taken in the sixteen years I have worked for her has been three weeks, which occurred at a time when we had an assistant director. "Emmeleine, the two of us can't cover Reference and Circulation, we..."

"I'm way ahead of you," she says. 'I called Rainier Brown this morning and she says she can help out in Reference. It's about time she put that Bryn Mawr education and that library degree back to work. I am sure you can train her fairly easily, Ell."

"Most likely," I concede. "But what is Perri-Young going to say when she hears this? Won't she go running to Handy when she finds out someone was given a city position, temporary though it is, without going through the regular hiring procedures?"

"Actually, Eleanor said the same thing," Emmeleine tells us. "And she suggested that we have Perri and the Youngettes, as she calls them, help Cora out with Circulation at night and on the weekends, You know how cranky Cora gets when she has to work much at night or more than one weekend a month. I am happy to say that Perri, Terri and Sherri jumped on it with both feet. And they are even volunteering their time. Lord only knows, they can afford it. In addition, Sha 'Neece has agreed to work eight more hours above her twenty, just for this time. She can help you with Reference on Monday and Wednesday afternoons and evenings since her classes are Tuesday and Thursday this time. Rainier's schedule will be Tuesday, 2-9 and Thursday and Friday, 2-6. That would only leave you with no reference help on Thursday nights, but I've even taken care of that. I put in a call to Andrew Downtown, who said he would be more than happy to swing by and help you out on Thursdays, since Downtown closes at 6:00 then." She beams mischievously at me, awaiting my reaction.

"You'd better buy a truck load of chastity belts for all the high school girls if Andy Swayne's coming on board," I say to her, only half teasing. "He operates under watchful eyes Downtown, but here he'll be unbridled and unabashed."

'I think you take Andrew's banter far more seriously than it's intended," Emmeleine says. "In my day, men who talked about it all the time were the very ones who weren't getting any."

Joseph, who is turning all the colors of his Biblical namesake's coat, interrupts us. "How are we going to work the weekends?"

"You will both have to work every other weekend," she says. "Dottie will also work every other weekend as will Sha 'Neece. Dottie can help out with Reference, too. Perri and the Youngettes will work the desk and the pages can alternate weekends as they usually do. Won't that work all right?"

We agree that it probably will and wish Emmeleine a safe flight. She thanks us and says, with some misgivings, "It's been several, several years since I've practiced the gentle art of child rearing. Thank God, Eleanor agreed to go with me. If two sixty-something ladies of very considerable ability and courage can't handle two girls under ten, then something's very wrong. I'll call when we get to Mona's house." She dismisses us with a wave. "Tell Dottie and Cora I need to see them."

Joseph and I exchange grimaces and inform Dottie and Cora that they are wanted in Emmeleine's quarters. We agree to watch the desk while they chat. When they have gone in and closed the door, Joseph says, "I think I know how the Indians felt when they saw all those Pilgrims getting off the Mayflower. Do you realize we have to train three people who have never worked in a library? I know Rainier has, but it's been a long time. They're smart women and all that, but…"

"Joseph, Joseph, ye of little faith," I say to him. "All of these women are used to meeting the public and have college degrees. Rainier even has an MLS. I vote we get Perri and the Youngettes all in here together this afternoon, if possible, for a marathon training session with us and Cora. Cora's going to be a bigger problem than they are, really. You know how she is when anybody but her or Sha 'Neece works the desk for very long."

"What about Rainier?" Joseph asks innocently. "I wouldn't really mind helping train her."

"I'll see that you' re included in all instructional sessions," I tell him with a laugh. Joseph checks out one of Cora's favorite patrons, who inquires after her. His knee jerk reaction to Rainier is rather comforting. At least he's still human. Actually, Rainier Brown would have him for lunch on the half-shell without even breaking one of her pretty fingernails if he got on the wrong side of her. The only living being who can strike fear or respect in her overly endowed bosom is Mamma Brown, who calls the shots with the tip ends of her three pronged cane at home and, equally important, at monthly meetings of the Athena Villa Library board. A definite deciding factor in Emmeleine's decision to hire her, I am certain.

In a few minutes an excited Dottie and a red-faced, angry Cora Moon emerge from Emmeleine's office. If looks indeed did annihilate, I'd be drawing my last breath after the menacing glare Cora aims in my direction as she takes her place again at the Circulation Desk. She neither thanks us or acknowledges our presence as we move away.

Breathless as usual from her continual sinus problems and overly excitable personality, Dottie looks ready to burst. "My goodness," she says to us in a low voice as she walks back across to the Children's Section with us. "You would think Emmeleine was firing Cora instead of giving her more help. I think it'll be just such fun to do something besides work with the children. Not that I don't love them and all, but there are only so many ways to read 'Goodnight, Moon.' I haven't done any real reference work since library school. But I know you'll get me through it, Ellie. Now I can really repay you for all those times you helped me out with story hours and parties and things. Maybe we can start this afternoon. You can teach me all about the Internet We have it at home on Dougie's computer, but he never has time to show me anything." She smiles so daffily at me that all I can do is promise to do my best.

At two o'clock, long before the huddled masses from the schools start arriving, I suggest to Cora Moon that she go and straighten the closed magazine stacks while I instruct Perri, Terri and Sherri on front desk procedures and the computer system.

Clearly against the whole notion of "those women" working her front desk, Cora has plenty to say about this. "I need to be the one doing this, if it's got to be done," Cora says. "You hardly ever work the front desk any more. I am the circulation manager, not you or Joseph."

"No one is arguing that, Cora," I say to her. "But Emmeleine, who is the boss of us all, specifically asked that Joseph and I train all the people who will fill in while she's gone.

"Have it your own way, then," Cora says as she heads toward the stacks. "But don't come whining to me when Ms. Perri-Young or one of those other silly women start passing out the incense and crystals to our patrons. You might not can have the Baby and the Manger or Jesus on the cross, but I expect crystals and incense and moons don't violate anybody's civil rights." She marches off haughtily to the stacks as Perri, Terri and Sherri come through the door.

"Here we are, as promised," Perri-Young says and holds up a foot. "In our best running shoes and comfortable clothes. Emmeleine said we should dress to make the patrons feel at home."

"You look great," I tell them. "The main thing to remember is be polite and make sure everyone is served. The rules aren't hard to learn and neither is circulation procedure. Joseph will talk to you about library membership forms after I'm finished. None of this is difficult. If anyone tries to argue with you about a fine, then let them talk to Joseph or me. When we finish, I'm going to let Cora go over reserves with you."

The three women in their designer wind suits listen attentively to me and later to Joseph's instruction. I then decide to begin online searching lessons with Dottie Dunwald. As I approach her at the story castle in the children's area, I can hear her singing, "Where is Thumbkin," for perhaps the fifth time today to yet another group of toddlers from a daycare center. Anyone that patient is bound to be able to learn computer searching.

Around 4:30 that afternoon Sha 'Neece and I shift our sister act into high gear. The Reference Section is hopping and so are we. Many of the teeming teenagers are working on Black History Month assignments a bit ahead of time. The others are seniors seeking their ten sources for literature papers on 20th Century British writers—a must-do for those aspiring to graduation. Two study tables are loaded down with sources—Black History and literature books mixed with a selection of collective biographies. I adopt a field-of-dreams approach to massive assignments like these: put all the good sources out there and the students will come to them. I don't, however, extend that to spoon-feeding. I refuse to mark pages or locate answers. "Seek and ye shall find," is our maxim.

I hear Sha 'Neece saying, "No, no, not that one, darlin'. You're not gon' find Ben E. King in a book on Black politicians. Ben E., baby, not Martin Luther." And then, "Yes, look on that table right there, over on the left hand side. That's the one. Now, pick it up and open it."

"And you do the hokey pokey and you turn yourself around and that's what it's all about," I sing in a low voice as we pass each other.

"I'm saying," Sha 'Neece says. "How about you doing this one for awhile? I'll handle Mr. Yeats and Mr. Eliot and company."

"Fine by me," I say. "It's hard to keep being patient when the little darlings insist on my finding them ten sources on 'Ol' Possum's Book of Practical Cats.' They say so sweetly, 'I just looooved the play, Ms. Seers. There just has to be something else besides play reviews.' Uh huh, kid, then you find 'em."

"I see the cavalry coming to the rescue," Sha 'Neece says, indicating Joseph coming toward us.

"I'll take it for awhile," Joseph says. "Rainier's waiting over by the Circulation Desk for you. Don't keep her too long." He smiles expectantly at me as I move in Rainier's direction.

"You've seen this mob and you haven't turned tail and run," I say as I offer her my hand. "This must mean you're serious."

"Oh, absolutely," Rainier says as we shake hands. "The only book I ever get to spend any time with at work any more is the Multiple Listings. I can't wait. I'm sure it'll come back to me. Let's see, do I have it right? Is the Literature section where you find books on Picassio?" She grins, referring to one of my favorite Reference bloopers.

A persistent young man kept coming back to me on a very busy Sunday afternoon after I sent him twice to the Art History collection when he asked for books on Picassio. Finally he explained, "I need books about Picassio, you know, he wrote *The De Cameron*." Other favorites include annual requests for short epics and the video version of Beowulf.

"Why don't you observe awhile until the supper lull around 5:30 or so," I suggest to Rainier. "Then Sha 'Neece and I will show you a few of the sources we use the most. You've been in here enough to know how the catalog works. Do you have Internet access at home?"

"Oh sure," Rainier says. "I can surf the 'Net just fine. Sometimes I log into one of the university libraries and browse through *Electric Library* or *Humanities Index*. I still like to keep up with what's going on in literate America even if I do spend most of my working hours assessing square footage and resale values."

She seats herself quietly at my desk. As instructed, I hand Joseph a couple of our working assignments to go over with Rainier. He can barely contain himself as he leans over her delicate shoulders, explaining various aspects of term paper assignment terminology to her. Introverts usually make fine teachers in one-on-one situations.

I rush over to rescue Sha 'Neece from a jail-bait admirer who is hanging on her every utterance.

"Miss Robinson, there's a telephone call for you at the desk," I say and turn to the love-struck teenager as Sha 'Neece makes a grateful exit. "Is there a source I can help you find?"

"No ma'am, I'm finding everything all right," the boy says with a frown. I can understand his frustration. Sha 'Neece is one beautiful woman when she's not stressed out. She returns in a few minutes and we bring Rainier in to help. We work until almost 6:00 when the last student leaves.

"Why don't you take a supper break?" Joseph suggests. "And then Sha 'Neece can go when you get back."

"Let me go with you, Ell," Rainier says. "I showed houses all morning and I didn't ever get any lunch. I'll treat."

"I'm right behind you," I say as we head out the door toward her black Mercedes. Its leather interior is a deep wine color. "Where are we going?"

"Is Antonini's okay?" she asks. I nod and we're off to a small, luscious Italian restaurant near the Galleria.

When we arrive and I order my usual eggplant parmejan, Rainier orders and then takes a cell phone from her purse and begins punching a series of numbers.

"Mamma," she says. "I'm having dinner with Ellott. Yes, I'll tell her." She pauses to listen a few minutes. "If he calls again, tell him my answer is still the same. Okay, I will. Goodbye." She hangs up the phone and smiles, almost apologetically.

"Mamma says hello. She frets when I don't call. And if she frets too long, she starts in on the bottle. Mamma has a little problem in that area."

"Is that why she lives with you?" I ask before I think better of it. "Not that it's really any of my business, but inquiring minds and all of that."

"Oh, it's okay. I know our own little private version of 'Mama's Family' fans the gossip flames for all of Athena Villa. Mamma and I do what we do because that's what we've always done. Do you remember that lovely image Faulkner used about the Sartorises? That they were drawn to destructive behavior like a moth to a flame. Well, I sometimes think that's me. I can't resist Mamma's demands, no matter what they are. She can push my buttons the same way she could when I was 9 years old."

"Being married twice didn't change that?" I ask as we share an order of stuffed mushrooms.

"Good God, no," Rainier laughs. "Marriage hardly affected me at all and certainly not my relationship with Mamma."

"You sound as though you have little use for men," I say to her.

"That's true to some extent," She admits. "I guess men have their uses. But they're mostly like second rate gems, the closer you get, the more apparent the flaws. The best description of marriage I've ever heard is this: 'Marriage is a novel in which the hero dies in the first chapter.'"

The anchor team on the 10 o'clock news is sharing a private joke as I lie on my living room sofa, watching. A fortyish man and a somewhat younger woman, they have remained together longer than many married couples. I heard somewhere that she miscarried last year and is pregnant again and that he is divorcing his third wife. On screen though, they are all upbeat talk and endless cheer. Somehow, this is easier on the sensibilities than a similar display of happy demeanor from the early morning news crew. The post-sunrise hour is not a time for inane optimism. Given my 'druthers, I would select, say, Dan and Roseanne Connor to deliver the news at daybreak: snappy sarcasm with an inner core of concern.

"The girls and I were about ready to call the Athena Villa Police," Rosie says, emerging from the shower in a terrycloth robe with a towel swathed around her wet hair. "Cassie finally thought to listen to the phone message that said you were being held captive by homework crazed teen aliens. What happened to your usual Monday schedule?"

"Emmeleine is off to Boston for six weeks," I tell her. "And I'm the Head Cheese until she returns. Four new people are helping fill in and Joseph, Sha 'Neece and I had to get them oriented."

As I detail the fruitbasket turnover at my work establishment, I can sense Rosie is only partially attentive.

"So, how was life on the couch today?" I switch the conversation to her focal point these days: once a week family therapy sessions along with Sherman and the girls.

"Intense is the best word for it," Rosie says. "Cassie had her private half-hour first and then Dr. Knowles had all of us meet to talk about Cassie's concerns. She misses being away from Sherman and even Milltown a lot more than she ever lets on. Molly gets her turn to talk next week. God only knows what she'll say."

"Are you satisfied with the way it's going?" I ask her. Rosie and Sherman's Christmas holiday began a time of conciliation for my long time friends resulting in their agreement to enter family therapy. One of Rosie's customers recommended Dr. Kay Knowles, who is of the Albert Ellis school of Rational Emotive Therapy. It is, if I understand it correctly, an amalgam of stoicism, logic, common sense and acceptance of responsibility. Feelings are not the primary focus as is true in some types of therapy. It totally eschews the Inner Child. Rosie, who completed a couple of years at Good River Community College aeons ago, is not too cognizant of contemporary therapy trends. She had this to say about Inner Children: "Sherman doesn't have an inner child. His problem is the child on the outside that never left home."

"Oh, all of us are getting a lot out of it," Rosie says as she towels her hair. "That session last week with Sherman and me really cleared the air on a lot of our problems. She told us to read that book you're always talking about, *You Just Don't Understand: Men and Women in Conversation*. I picked up our copies at Books-A-Million this afternoon."

"I'll be interested to hear what Sherman thinks of Deborah Tannen's ideas," I say. Personally, I doubt that male/female conversational styles are something Sherman's given much thought to. "Does it seem like the Good Doctor is trying to steer you, ever so gently, toward reconciliation?"

"Not really, no," Rosie says. "She's letting us move at our own pace. She mainly is helping us look at areas of conflict and ways to approach them. She's really so low key that Sherman hasn't even complained too hard about having a woman therapist."

Rosie gets up to take the towel to the washer and returns in a few minutes with cups of hot tea. I take mine and sip it a few minutes before asking, "Any idea yet on how many more sessions you'll be doing?"

"This is our fourth and Dr. Knowles says at least four more before we and she can have some sense of whether we ought to even consider getting back together or just learn better how to live apart," Rosie tells me. "She gives us these worksheets to complete between sessions. The girls even get some. They are exercises to help us change crazy behavior. She doesn't put it that way exactly, but that's what they are."

"And does Sherman do his?" I ask her.

"Well, some of it, anyway," Rosie admits. "We don't discuss every section on all the pages, but he came up with some kind of answer for the ones we did talk about. I saw Dr. Knowles biting her lip to keep from saying anything about one of his responses. The situation was: 'When my wife fails to do what I asked her to, I feel…' The choices were (A) angry and frustrated (B) hurt (C) that she should be shown why she was wrong to do that, or (D) that maybe my request was inappropriate. Sherman chose (C) and was certain that was correct instead of his usual response which was (A). When Dr. Knowles suggested that he might consider (D), he looked at her like she had just landed from Mars." She closes her eyes and shakes her head.

"Molly and Cassie seem really glad to see Sherman more often," I say. "These weekly visits are good for them. Where did you all go to dinner?"

"The girls wanted to go to the Olive Garden," Rosie says. "So we went by the daycare center and got Caitlin first. Sherman's really getting much better with her, Ell. He fed her breadsticks and played with her the whole time we waited for our order. That's enough about us. I'm sorry I wasn't listening very well earlier. Tell me again about ya'll's new schedule. How are you going to be working?"

"Joseph is taking the mornings in Reference. I'll come in at 1:00 Monday through Thursday. Sha 'Neece will help me out some days and Rainier on others. And get this, Emmeleine asked Andy Swayne to help out on Thursday nights."

"Whoa, Nellie," Rosie says. "And what will Mr. Gabriel Pace have to say when he hears Mr. Personality's going to visit on a regular basis? He may be jealous, Ell. I'm sure you never let him read that e-mail Andy sent you after the beauty contest, now did you?"

"Hardly," I tell her.

Andy's e-mail message has had me mystified for some weeks and I've yet to reply to it. It was this "There is a pain—so utter—It swallows substance up/Then covers the abyss with trance—So Memory can step/Around-across-upon it/As one within a swoon/Goes safely—where an open eye/Would drop him bone by bone." It is, of course, Miss E.D. in one of her finest moments of wounded eloquence. But it is so uncharacteristic of the contained Mr. Swayne that I don't know how to reply to it.

"Don't even tell Gabe," Rosie advises. "He is Michael's brother and a man as well. I wish I hadn't told Michael half the things I did about Sherman and me. I don't know that it did either of us much good. It's easier right now, in a way, that I'm not seeing him. I didn't feel like there was any other way to do it while Sherman and I are in counseling. But..." She stops herself and shakes her head. "Enough on that. We both need to get to bed. Call me sometime tomorrow night and let me know how things are going at work." She hugs me and goes off to her room.

Stepping into the dining room, I part the curtains and stare into the night and the blackness of the dead trees in the floodlights on the back lawn. I make plans to visit the Brothers Pace at their work place tomorrow morning. I am picturing Gabe in his flannel jacket standing before me in the grove of hardwoods as the cordless pulses and I pick it up to hear his voice.

Chapter Twenty

All inner walls of Picker's Palace are torn away and an "Under Construction" sign hangs on the front door. Gabe and Michael direct Brother J, one of his brothers, and a crew of workmen inside the site. Drink cans and snack wrappers litter the floor and sawdust is thick in the air. Brother J notices me standing at the front and waves. Gabe looks up and comes in my direction.

"Hey, babe," he says with a hug. "Glad you decided to come and help us accommodate the chaos. Come meet Brother J's compadre. I've told you about him."

We step gingerly across loose boards, flooring and equipment to the far side of the store's showroom. Brother J touches a short, round man on the shoulder and he looks up and dusts his hands as he comes toward us. "Ellott Hailey Seers," he repeats my name. "Not a common Southern name, but definitely below the Mason Dixon Line. How did your parents choose your name?"

"It's from my father's side," I tell the man attired in old Army fatigues like Brother J. He is bearded, bespeckled and probably from the South Bronx. "My father and mother searched his family's cemetery until they found mutually agreeable combinations of names from the tombstones. When I was born a couple of months later, they chose Ellott Halley. I was almost Penelope June, so things could have been worse."

"I like your name," he says quickly. "It's distinctive. Names are quite important. You either become your name or your name becomes you. Take mine, for example. I didn't have to take a different name when I took my vows. My mother named me Anthony Jude Ruggerio and then died of an infection three days later. My dad and uncles raised me. Anthony and Jude are the patrons saints of lost articles and lost causes."

"He once said that with those names he had to either be a monk or a drunk," Brother J says, smiling. "And to tell the truth, he's been both."

"Enough of you," the other man says. "Call me Brother Tony, Ellott Hailey Seers. And Gabe here says you prefer Ell."

"That's what my mother called me when I was good," I say. "It was only Ellott Halley when she was unhappy with my behavior."

"I would bet you excellent money that wasn't very often," Brother Tony says. "Names have been the talk topic of choice here today. Michael and Gabriel are hiring Brother Joseph and myself when their business reopens to work the cafe. Meanwhile we've both worked construction in our time, so we'll help oversee the workmen. And being that everything will be different, the place has to have a different moniker. Want to hear some of the choices?"

"Sure," I say, not really listening as he reels off a few possibilities. Across the room, Gabe is drinking from a litre bottle of Mountain Dew as he talks to one of the workers. Every time I am with him lately, he has something to drink in his hand. Propped against an empty display shelf, Michael appears to have that mellow facade that translates to "fiddle players on the grass, alas." Grass, pot, weed, or chronic in current slang. The separation from Rosie has bonded him to his bong and on some days the fog is thicker than on others. The visibility level is fairly negligible today. His floaty smile and faraway eyes tell me he is in our company, but not of it. He nods a greeting to me.

"Hey, sweetheart," I say and hug his tall, lean body into mine. "It really is going to be okay, you know."

"Thanks for that thought, anyway," he says in a mumble. "What I'd welcome most right now is a visit from Dr. Kevorkian, if you want to know the truth. Does Rosie still talk about me, Ellie? Does she remember who I am?"

"Yes, honey, yes," I say gently and look to Gabe for advice. Michael is barely able to stand. Gabe rolls his eyes toward the door. "Sit down, Michael," I say and steer him toward a folding chair. I follow Gabe to the door. The monks join the workmen as they remove a section of flooring. Michael sits alone and watches them, trying to follow the movement in the room from eight miles high.

We step outside into the cold and Gabe and I huddle together. "God grant us mercy, Gabe. How could you let him get that stoned? He shouldn't be out walking around."

"I know that," Gabe says, passing a hand over his face, wearily. "Do you think you could drive him home? I've got to stay here awhile with the Brothers and the work crew."

"Sure," I say, kissing him on the cheek. "I'll see if I can bring him down a level or two. Does he go to sleep when he's stoned?"

"Eventually," Gabe says. "Feed him and get him to lay down. I'll call you in an hour or so and maybe later we can go to lunch. Thanks darlin'," He hugs me and goes back inside, returning in a few minutes, steering his younger brother toward my car.

"I think we ought to name the new store Wabash Cannonball," he says to Gabe as he pushes him into the passenger seat. "Don't let Brother J talk you into Orange Blossom Special. That's too much like California. Nobody wants California in the Bible Belt."

By the time we reach Crestline, Michael is asleep. I rouse him and with his arm draped across my shoulders, we walk slowly up the driveway.

"Unreal city under the fog of a winter dawn," Michael mutters, looking around us. I can feel the mini-blinds parting around us as the young wives observe yet another spectacle at the Pace household. What a tale to tell when hubby comes home.

The house is cold and dark and after I help Michael to the sofa, I flip a switch and bump up the thermostat. Taking a pillow and blanket from the hail closet, I cover him as he mumbles his thanks.

"You never answered me," he says as he closes his eyes. "Does Rosie even remember my name?"

"I answered you, Michael," I tell him, sitting down on the edge of the sofa. I stroke his tangled hair. "Rosie just needs some time, that's all. Just time."

"Hurry up, please it's time," Michael quotes bitterly. "Maybe T. S. Goddamn Eliot wrote this farce. My life is the fucking 'Wasteland' without Rosie."

"I'm glad to see your undergraduate studies are not going to waste," I say, dryly. "Rosie has to do this, Michael. For her sake and the kids'. It's not just to drive you nuts."

"I know that," he says, sitting up a little. "I also know I'm being a pain in the ass. To Gabe and to you. I'd say I'm sorry but I don't know that I am. Could you fix me something to eat, Ell? I promise to shut up and go to sleep if you will."

"Deal," I say and head for the kitchen. "Just keep this in mind: Rosie lived with Sherman for twenty years that were mostly unhappy. Eight weeks of therapy aren't likely to wipe that out."

Perri and the Youngettes have the Circulation Desk rocking and rolling on Cora's day off. Terri and Sherri stand at the checkout terminal, swiftly moving patrons along, not stopping to chit-chat as Cora often does. At the other terminal, Perri-Young is checking in stacks of books and tapes as she calls patrons to pick up their reserve books. Despite my initial reservations, they are doing an excellent job. Years of pounding real estate turf molded Perri-Young into an efficient business-woman. Perhaps this little stint of public service will soften her image among Athena Villans. Many residents of my fair daytime city consider Perri-Young our own Hilliary Clinton, radical feminism personified to our largely Republican populace.

"Does Cora have any reserves on *Dogwood and Desire?*" I ask Perri-Young as I pass the front desk. It is almost 5:00 on Thursday afternoon. Rainier and I have straightened the index tables and she is dealing with the last of the afternoon students. I go behind the Circ desk for paper to refill the printers by the search terminals.

Hanging up the telephone, Perri-Young checks Cora's written list of reserve books. Through extensive prompting and insistence on my part, Cora now finally enters the reserves online. But she still maintains a hard copy listing of each reserve, which is actually quite handy on occasion.

"I don't see anything," she says. "Just the order card for fifteen copies and a review taped to the back. It sounds like something Eleanor might read. Bodice ripper, right?"

"Right," I answer solemnly. Our little joke has probably run its course. Rainier almost told Cora the other day when she was clucking and sighing over a fictitious review of the non-extant book. One night a week or so ago, Sha 'Neece and I composed a glowing review of our little creation and taped it to the back of the order card. I plan next week to say its publication has been canceled. We decided the truth might stretch the limits of Cora's patience.

I see Rosie at the front doors, waiting to join me for supper. "Back in an hour," I tell Rainier as I head to the back for my coat. "Joseph's in the back if you need him." And only too delighted to offer assistance, I should have added. Gentlemanly as always, Joseph has maintained a professional attitude, but Rainier's presence has certainly brought him into the public service area much more frequently than usual.

"My showing's not until 6:30," Rainier says, passing a literature index to a waiting student. "Take your time."

"Where to?" Rosie asks me as we get into her newly acquired vehicle. Following the demise of her '72 Beetle last week, she made arrangements through Sherman to purchase a late model Ford Taurus one of his customers was selling.

"Let's do Mexican," I say as we head up the highway to Casa Consuela. Located in front of a chain motel of questionable repute, Casa Consuela is housed in an old Chinese restaurant with its former decor still intact. Its former owner doubled as a procurer of female flesh for motel dwellers. Athena Villa's Finest finally jailed the owner and the restaurant closed several years ago. It stood empty awhile until Consuela and Carlos Rodriguez bought it and set up business. Although they've done well, they have not invested their profits in redecorating. Locals refer to it as The Mexican Chinese Whorehouse Restaurant.

In a few moments with a basket of chips and a couple of beers before us, I ask Rosie about the girls. When she called earlier in the afternoon to suggest dinner, she merely told me she had some news from Milltown to impart.

"Sherman took them roller skating," she says, sipping her beer. "He took me to lunch and talked the whole hour about Fred and Ree and Harley. He said he felt like you ought to know it, too. I told him I could tell you when you get home. But he said he wanted to take the girls and Caitlin to Skate City. They've got that Baby Gym there, so she can play."

The image of Sherman Lee Jackson leading a toddling Caitlin through the tiny tot exercise equipment would certainly be a Kodak moment. "Where are Ree and Harley, Jr.? Did they go back to Fred's after the holidays?"

"Sherman says they did," Rosie tells me. The Latino waitress is setting generous plates before us and cautioning us of their heat. "But Fred never stayed home and they were left all the time with that Mrs. Dawber. The one Ree said reminded her of the woman in 'Throw Mama from the Train.' Anyway, Mrs. D, as Ree calls her, packed up and left on Saturday morning and Ree and Harley had to take a cab to school on Monday. They're only 15 and anyway, Fred keeps all the cars locked up.

They existed on take-out pizza for a few days, but then Ree decided to call John and Mary to come and pick them up."

"Does Fred know?"

"He does now. They got DHR involved. They had a social worker they know to accompany them when they picked up the kids. She recorded it as abandonment and left a note for Fred and a message on his answering machine, telling him where the kids are."

"When did all this happen?" I ask her, taking a bite of enchilada. "And when did Fred find out?"

"Just this week and Fred found out yesterday when he put in an appearance at home and found it empty," Rosie says. "Sherman says he's getting a lawyer. The Reeses already had one and had asked for custody. The hearing doesn't come up until March, but until then the kids get to stay on with the Reeses."

"Hmmm," I say and down the rest of my beer and request some coffee. "Who is the social worker? Maybe we could talk to her and find out what we ought to say to the Reeses' lawyer to help their case. If we testified about all the things Ree said to us when we saw her over Christmas and all the goofball stunts we've seen Fred pull these last few months, I don't see that there would be much question of the Reeses being granted custody, at least until Bud comes home."

"We know her," Rosie says, ordering another beer as the waitress brings my coffee. "She graduated with us. You remember Coley Frost?"

"I didn't know Coley was living in Milltown again," I say. "She's probably a good person to work with. I always liked her in high school."

"She and her mother moved into one of those old bosses' houses on Palace Walk just down from the Blacks," Rosie tells me. "Her other sisters and brothers married and moved away. Coley came back a few years ago after their father died. She was really helpful to me last winter when Sherman tried to withhold child support. She doesn't work in that department any more, but she advised me on what to do."

"I'll call her in the morning," I say, glancing at my watch. "I've got to get back to the crazy house. Are you okay to drive?"

"I only had two beers, Ell," she says defensively and then hesitates. "I don't know though. Maybe you should drive us back to the library and I'll just sit there awhile. It's like an involuntary response or something. I start thinking about Michael and I know he's just sitting there in the dark in that house of theirs, smoking joint after joint. I can't do that, so I have a beer or a candy bar or something. I wish the band was practicing and at least I'd get to see him. Maybe when Maithel and Charlie get back from Bermuda, we can get back into our routine."

As I drive the year-old Taurus back to the library, I consider telling her about Michael's anguished behavior earlier in the week. She is humming softly to herself as I turn into the parking lot and I can see the tears on her cheeks glisten in the streetlights.

It's nearing 7:00 when she leaves for home and a short time later, Andy Swayne comes in, sporting after-hours jeans and a sweatshirt embossed with Alfred E. Newman and "What? Me Worry?" As he slides smoothly into a chair beside my desk, I sense he is smiling a bit too tightly.

"What do the little dears have on their tiny little brains this evening?" He asks, blinking his eyes and massaging his temples. "You know I only agreed to do this so I could pinch a few minor behinds over there in the stacks."

"Uh, huh," I say, recognizing his bluff "Humbert-Humbert, eat your dust."

"Swayne's the name, debauchery's the game," he mumbles as he gets up to assist a group of students with the Internet. We work steadily until 9:00 and he remains with me until the computers are shut down and the lights are out.

"Let us go then, you and I," he recites as I lock the doors and we walk to our cars. "When the evening is spread out against the sky,"

"Is there something in the water supply?" I ask as we pause beside his Honda Civic. "Everyone seems to be dredging up Ol' Possum this week."

"The Prophet of Moroseness speaks to us all," he says. "How about a cup-a-java with a tired old man?"

"You're hardly old," I say to him, hesitating, thinking of Gabe waiting for my call when I get home. "Let me go back inside and make a quick call, then I can probably spare a half-hour or so."

"Use my car phone," he offers. "I'll even wait here in the cold until you're through."

Opening the passenger door for me and locating the phone, he stands outside as I punch in Gabe's number. Gabe answers quickly and is silent a few seconds after I explain what I'm doing.

"Okay," he says, finally. "I do trust you, Ellott Hailey, but show him my picture and mention that I can get very physical when I need to."

"Yes, sir," I say, laughing. "I'll call you by 10:30 at the latest. Bye now."

Andy drives us to a Waffle House, a sure sign he's off center. Generally he's so cuisine conscious that I find it difficult to dine with him. We take a table by the window and order two coffees, my second of the evening. Sleep won't come the whole night through sure enough.

"When you didn't answer my e-mail, I decided you might not want to get involved," he says. "But then when Emmeleine called me into service, I decided to lay my troubles at your empathetic doorstep. A fair exchange for two hours a week of excellent reference assistance."

"I didn't know how to respond to your e-mail," I tell him. "It was so, shall we say, up close and personal that I was a bit baffled."

"Not my usual song and dance, was it?" he admits. "I am in real pain, Ellott. Marion and Andy, Jr., are moving to Washington state in a month. She got a job teaching art in a private school up there. The teacher left at mid-term and it's too good for her to pass up."

Andy is as equally devoted to his young son as he is to his quest for the perfect woman.

"I am truly sorry," I say and squeeze the top of his hand. "Is there any chance it might not come through?"

"No, it's definite," he says, sighing and taking a sip of coffee. "I can see Andy in the summers and over Christmas break and as frequently as we can manage through the school year."

"Could you maybe move closer to them?" I ask.

"No, I sort of owe my soul to the company store, workwise," he says. "I've been there too long."

"I know it hurts," I tell him.

"Life sucks and then you die," he says with a hint of a rueful smile. He shakes his head and says, a little more lightly. "I take it that the earlier phone call was to your newly acquired Significant Other?" He smiles as I blush.

"Am I the topic du jour among my colleagues?" I ask. "I didn't realize it was that widely known."

"As the grapevine twines," he answers. "Anyway, if you care about this guy, do what you can to make it work out."

"Is that what you wish you had done?" I say as we get up and head for the door.

"If wishes were fishes," he says, opening the door.

"Well, the witty Swayne is alive and well someplace in there," I say. "Not to be pat, but you will feel better about this in time."

"Oh, I'll deal with it," he says as we drive back to the library parking lot to my Cherokee. "But it's as though the fallout from divorce just never ends. It's like what Joyce said about history, 'It's the nightmare from which I am trying to awake.' And you do know, of course, when it will end?"

"Of course," I answer, picking up his allusive beat. "'When human voices wake us and we drown.'"

On the morning of Abe Lincoln's birthday, Coley Frost and I stop our week-long round of phone tag. At home until early afternoon when

I am due at work, I stand at the dining room window, holding the cordless and relate to her Ree's conversations with Rosie and me over the holidays.

"Did she ever tell you that Mr. Hardaman physically harmed them in any way?" Coley asks me.

"No, just that he was rarely there and always left them with Mrs. Dawber who spent most of her time watching tv or talking on the phone. And that all she ever fixed for them to eat were tv dinners. Ree usually cooked or ordered pizza."

"In your opinion they are definitely better off with the Reeses?"

"Yes," I tell her. "John and Mary raised seven kids and Ree seems to love being there. I can't speak for Harley, Junior, but he is usually content to be wherever his sister is."

"Okay, then," Coley says. "I would like to talk to you some more before you see the Reeses' lawyer. I've got to be in court in about a half-hour though. When can we talk again?"

"I'll be in Milltown on Wednesday next week," I tell her. "How about sometime in the afternoon then?"

When we settle on a time, I hang up and continue staring into the leafless trees on the back lawn. I am half expecting a call from Gabe at the music store, which is coming along. The inner walls are now intact and the lunch counter is set to be installed today. Between Michael's overindulgence in his inebriant of choice and the renovation of Picker's Palace, Gabe is looking the worse for wear.

As the phone pulses, I answer, "Gabriel Pace's Do Right/All Night Woman here."

"Good morning, ma 'am," the voice at the other end drawls. "Is this the residence of Ellott Hailey Seers?"

"It is," I answer, a little embarrassed. "This is Ellott Seers."

"This is Sergeant Bob Tolson, Caloosa County Sheriff's Department," the man says. "Ma'am, we were told by Mary Jean Jones to contact you.

We have some questions about your knowledge of Fred Hardaman and the website he had put up to help us catch his daughter's killer."

"Ask away," I tell him. "I have edited the e-mail for the Timeofgrace site for a few months now, since Fred's not exactly been at himself. I have been very careful to include anything that looked like evidence on the murderx2 page. I sent you several e-mails telling you that, but no one responded. Is there something specific you need to know?"

"Our man that fools with the computer failed to tell me that," Sgt. Tolson says. "My apologies. But yes, what I need to know is, was there anything else about the black and yellow Skylark that might not have been included? Like what kind of wheels it had and maybe a tag number?"

"They were mag wheels I'm pretty certain," I tell him. "But I don't recall anything about the tag."

"We're fairly certain we know the owner of the car," he says. "We traced all the '68 Skylarks that that are on register and the only one with that color and those wheels belongs to Anson Gallworthy."

"Oh, my Lord. You can't suspect Brother Anson of being involved in this?"

"At this point we don't know. We have talked to him and he says that his car's been missing since before the murders. And it was put on report as stolen near the end of August. We have tried to reach Fred Hardaman since the car apparently belonged to him first, according to Mr. Gallworthy. But we've not been able to locate Mr. Hardaman. Did any of the e-mail indicate where the car might have been seen since the murders?"

"Nothing I've seen said that, but then I've not looked in a few days," I tell him. "Let me give you the password and you can look yourself."

"I'd appreciate that," Sgt. Tolson says. "Our computer whiz will get back to the station in just a little bit and he can have a look at it."

Before we hang up I say, "If I can help you with anything else, please let me know."

I walk to the bedroom and log on and bring up Timeofgrace. After looking at the e-mail, I then pull up the contents from the trashcan. A two line message that someone tried to get rid of reads "'68 Skylark in barn on County Road 16. Look in trunk."

I add this to murderx2 and quickly peruse the other discarded messages, which have little new to add and click away from the site to allow the Sheriff's Department to edit it. Then I spend awhile 'Net surfing to kill some time.

An hour or so later, the phone pulses again. "This had better be you, Gabriel Pace. I'm tired of embarrassing myself with the way I answer the telephone," I say.

"Miss Seers, this is Anson Gallworthy," the voice says. "I understand the Sheriff's Department here spoke with you a little while ago."

"Yes, they did, Brother Anson," I tell him. Have they found your car yet?"

"They did," he answers. "Just a few minutes ago. Exactly where that last message they found said it would be. And in the trunk they found a gun that's registered to Mr. Fred."

I am quiet for so long that Brother Anson finally inquires if I am still on the line. After I affirm this, he goes on, "I haven't laid eyes on Mr. Fred for over a week. He quit asking me to ride out in the middle of the night with him a few weeks back, but I've tried to keep a check on him at least once a week. But his car's not been in the driveway in several days and all I get is the answering machine when I try to call him."

Chapter Twenty-One

Down Yonder Music Store and Cafe Emporium opens its doors tomorrow morning. It dominates a third of the commercial block in the Lakeview area of Southside where the former Picker's Palace stood. The old storefront is replaced with a plank porch stoop, complemented with armchair rockers and a mourner's bench. A rough wood sign bearing its new name hangs from the facade. Neighboring businesses have generously accommodated the restructuring and enlargement. The man who runs the hot dog stand next door is bring over a white bag of food and containers of coffee as I arrive.

"Hidy, hidy," he says as I hold the door for him. "Just in time for lunch."

"Smells good," I say as I walk inside. With the construction complete, the new showroom expands across the front of the store. A lunch counter and two booths stand to the back and right with a kitchen behind them. Two classrooms, a storeroom and a practice room for the band occupy the former warehouse. Michael, Gabe, Brother J and Brother Tony are positioning fixtures and instruments in various areas of the showroom.

"Lift that barge, tote that bale," I say loudly and Gabe looks up.

He smiles but his hands are trembling and he blinks as though he can barely see me or the hot dog man. "My favorite lady and lunch. Perfect time to take a break."

Gabe looks more exhausted and ill than I have seen him in these past few weeks. Many times I have tried to get him to acknowledge it and he refuses. He has accused me of hovering, so I try not to nag. The hot dog man lays the bag of food on the new cafe counter. Gabe pays the man and he leaves. Brother J goes to the open kitchen area and takes several soft drinks from the refrigerator. Michael, who seems to have recovered from reefer madness, arranges various types of guitars on a new display stand. Brother Tony joins us in the restaurant area.

"What's your prognosis, Ellott H?" He asks me. "Are music lovers city-wide clamoring to storm the doors tomorrow morning?"

"If they have any taste at all," I tell him. "What's the plan for feeding hungry customers?"

"Brother J and I are doing short orders here at the grill," he says, indicating the shiny new grill. A range top, oven, deep fryer and microwave sit to the left of it. "And Gabe and Michael have worked out another plan for more substantial food."

"I didn't tell you about that yet," Gabe says, looking up from the booth where he is sitting. Sweat is beaded on his unusually pale face. His pulse beats beneath the skin at his temple. "I talked to Mabel June about doing some carry-in cooking for us to serve at lunch. We just got a contract worked out." He drinks from his bottle of Moutain Dew and stands up, immediately grasping the edge of the table. Sweat is pouring from his face and his entire body is shaking.

"Gabe, what is it?" I shout at him. Michael stops what he is doing and hurries over. Brother J and Brother Tony stop their conversation.

Gabe's eyes wall up and he passes out, his head banging the table's edge as he falls. I rush over to him as Brother J dials 911.

Brother Tony squeezes in beside Michael and me, probing Gabe's eyelids and checking his pulse. "Used to be a paramedic," he mutters. "Unless I'm way off base, it's a diabetic reaction. I've seen the signs for awhile now. Gabe didn't want to listen to me."

Men in white are coming through the doors. After briefly examining Gabe, they lift him onto a stretcher. "Which hospital?" One of them asks.

"UAB," Michael answers. They take Gabe to the waiting ambulance and the four of us follow, heading for my car.

"Where are my damn keys?" I say, rummaging in my purse.

"Right here. You laid them on the counter when you came in," Brother Tony says, gently, holding them up. "Let me drive, Ellott H. You and Michael sit in the back and hang on tight, now. Gabe's going to be okay."

As we drive the several blocks to University Hospital, Michael says, "If I hadn't been so caught up in my own misery, I'd have seen this for what it is. One of Dad's brothers is diabetic. I ought to know the signs."

"I was certain something was wrong." I speak slowly and formally, doing my best to keep control. "I even told Gabe that, but he said he was just tired from all the work in getting the store ready to reopen. I didn't realize it was this severe." My late mother told me that ladies do not exhibit strong emotions in public and they never, ever cry. I try to maintain that as Brother Tony finds a spot in the parking deck and we make our way to the hospital's emergency room.

I begin to shiver in the icy cold waiting room. Brother J puts his coat around me as Michael takes my hand and holds it in both of his.

Hospital waiting rooms often evoke startlingly personal confidences from their occupants. Stark and uncomfortable furnishings mix with dread or tense expectations and people begin to reveal things to strangers they would be loathe to share with their own friends. In the ICU waiting room Michael and I sit with legs propped and coffee cups in hand. The woman next to us is recounting the details of her son's accident.

"Little Tom, he's our baby boy, just 19. He's been a-working for Pitt Construction here at the University since he graduated high school. They always seem to be a-puttin' up new buildings or taking down old ones around this school. He figured it'd be steady work. Anyhow, they was tearin' out a wall in a old building down the street yonder and it collapsed against Little Tom. Just pure-D COL-lapsed." She stresses the first syllable of collapsed. "They said both his leg bones just crumbled up like a cookie."

"Was it only his legs that were broken?" I ask her.

"Yes, ma 'am," she answers. "That's what they told me. He's got some internal bleedin' they got to get stopped and then they can get them legs set and get him in a room. I been knowin' this was going to happen. Been knowin' it for days. Big Tom, that's my husband, said I was just worry-wartin'. Seems like to me that after twenty six years and four children he ought to listen to me when I say I know somethin'."

"Are you psychic?" Michael asks her.

"I don't like that word," the woman says, frowning. "It sounds too much like them people that got goofed up running around on dope back in the '60s. I have a gift God gave me to see what's going to happen to people I care about. It started coming to me when I first married Big Tom. Two nights after we was married his daddy shot his momma to death in their front bedroom. I told Big Tom there was somethin' awful goin' on at his house and sure enough, two hours later we found it out. The Clawson men just cain't listen to nothin' common sensical from a woman. They always got to be in the right. That's why Old Man Clawson did Louella in. They was arguin' about plantin' the garden. All she said to him was that plantin' the garden on Good Friday'll bring a good crop. He didn't do nothin' but pick up that shotgun and blow her head off for spitin' his word. He always planted on the last day of March." She continues her tale of life with the Clawson clan, hailing from Argo, Alabama. Michael and I listen to this little country woman with the weather beaten face and heart full of caring and endurance. More than a quarter of a century with a mule-headed man, raising his four sons and withstanding his tom-fool ideas has not quaffed the love-light in her little brown eyes.

The ICU itinerary is ten minute visits every four hours. Gabe was still comatose when we saw him at 1:00, but his doctor told us that when his blood sugar stabilizes a bit more, he would regain consciousness. Hours ago I called Joseph at the library to arrange for a substitute for the evening. Michael and I lose ourselves in the Annette Clawson life story again and when the nurse calls us at 5:00 to tell us we can see Gabe again, we are surprised at how quickly the time has passed.

Inside the curtained-off unit, Gabe lies white and still with two iv's feeding into his arms. The left side of his face is bruised from hitting the table. As I take his left hand, his eyes blink and he tries to smile. "Like W.C. Fields said…" he whispers in a voice so soft we have to bend down to hear him.

"On the whole, I'd rather be in Philadelphia," Michael finishes for him. "Hey, man, you didn't have to do all this. A simple 'I think I need to go to the hospital,' would have sufficed."

"He wanted to go out with a bang, not a whimper," I say and kiss his hand. "I am so very glad you're back. I'm here, Gabe. I'm here."

"I know," he says, and closing his eyes again, he sleeps.

We find his doctor in the hallway and stop him. He tells us that Gabe will be moved to a room later this evening and that he has insulin dependent diabetes mellitus. He talks with us for some time, recommending books to read and warning us of symptoms to be aware of. As he and Michael go over a list of suggested foods and beverages, I step to the hallway windows facing the overpass. A black orderly is pushing an old man in a wheelchair toward the parking deck. Tied to the chair and floating above him is a mylar balloon. I can't read all of the words, but one of them is "hope."

"Yes, as far as I know he'll be there by 7:00. He's not so bad to work with, Joseph. And he's really good with that assignment on Chaucer that's ongoing with the middle school kids." It is the third day of Gabe's hospital stay. I am listening on the phone a few minutes to Joseph's good-natured grousing over the coming evening with Andy Swayne. Then I say goodbye.

Gabe has finished most of his plate and is pushing the tray aside.

"What time did you say ya'll are leaving for Milltown in the morning?" He asks me. He is getting antsy. The tubes are removed from his arms and he is sitting on ready-to-go.

"Rosie and I are taking the girls to school and Caitlin to daycare and then we're hitting the road," I say.

"And you said they are staying with Mabel June until ya'll get back?" This is the second or third time he has asked this. I recognize it as a ploy to keep me talking about things other than his diabetes. Whenever I bring it up, he changes the subject. He has been outwardly cooperative with the medical staff and dieticians, but I detect a glimmer of rebellion on the periphery.

"Did you ever find out if your insurance will cover this?" I ask him.

"Michael was on the phone with them for over two hours yesterday," he says. "When he hung up, he said it sounded like everything would be taken care of. Some of the nurses were telling me that there's all kinds of cheap ways to get diabetic supplies. I'm not going to worry about it. It'll work out."

Reclining, he takes the tv remote connected to the nurse call button and light switch and locates the evening news. It would seem as though the medical discussion is closed.

"...Caloosa County Sheriff's deputies have what they think is a major break in the six month old double murders. Fingerprints on the gun in the trunk of the black and yellow '68 Skylark have now been identified as belonging to Fred Hardaman, father of one of the victims. A ballistics report earlier revealed that the bullets in the gun matched those used in the murders. Hardaman, a Caloosa County businessman, has been absent from his home for several days. Anyone knowing his whereabouts..."

Gabe raises the head of his bed a little and we watch as the blonde reporter interviews Sgt. Bob Tolson. "We have a few ideas on where Mr. Fred might be," he says in answer to her question. "I'm confident we'll find him before long. Mr. Fred's got a lot of explaining to do." Sgt. Tolson went on to extrapolate on Fred's setting up the website in an outward attempt to help them and then concealing key evidence.

"When did all this come about?" Gabe asks me. "I guess it pretty much explains Old Fred's wild-ass behavior. Did you ever, at any time, think it might be him?"

"I first started to wonder when all that information about the Skylark started showing up in the e-mail and never made it the murderx2 page," I say. "But somehow I couldn't make myself believe it was Fred. God, Gabe, he worshiped Grace Ann, especially when we were little."

"Maybe that was the whole trouble," Gabe says. "Doesn't seem like to me you can put another person in that glorified a state, especially your own child. Everybody's human."

"I just hope they find him soon, before something else happens."

"Should make tomorrow's mill razing right lively," he says. "With an at-large murderer lurking around." He looks at me fondly. "And before you ask me again, no, I do not want you to stay here with me. Go with Rosie. Miss Millie doesn't ask much from ya'll and this seems to be important to her. I'll be at home by tomorrow night and you can give me a full account."

"It does mean a lot to her," I admit. "But Rosie nor I can figure out why. Rosie says she always talked about how much she hated working in the Cloth Room for all those years. But now that they're tearing down the Mill, it's like a family member's dying."

"I think it's got something to do with loss," Gabe says. "Like when you have a bad tooth pulled and you can still feel the hollow space it left in your gum. When something stood there as long as White Cotton Mill, it's a shock to have it gone."

The rain will not fall and the damp hangs like held breath over Milltown. As we exit the freeway, heading for Minnie Beth's house Rosie remembers we need to pick up Sherman at the Circle K out in the county. Fifteen minutes later, we find him reading off an order list to a couple of route men stocking the shelves. When he finishes and makes certain the counter girl has his beeper number, we climb back into my Cherokee and ride to his momma's house for breakfast.

"Nobody's actually found Fred yet," Sherman informs us. "But there's been about as many sightings of him as there was of ol' Bud right after the murders."

He unfolds a copy of *The Good River Journal* and reads the headline, "Local Businessman Sought in September Murders." The article begins, "Double murder in a double wide culminated in multiple tragedy in Caloosa County today. Evidence in the August shotgun slayings of Grace Ann Hardaman and Tanner Hope points to the father of one of the victims, area business man Fred Hardaman." It includes several statements by Sgt. Tolson and other members of the Sheriffs Department about finding the gun in the trunk of the Skylark. A quote from Anson Gallworthy concludes the front page story, "Brother Fred loved that girl more than life itself. It's got to be something maybe accidental or something gone bad wrong in his head if he is the one responsible. I hope people take that into consideration."

"People around here's been flapping their gums more over ol' Fred's disappearance than they did over the murders," Sherman comments. "When it first come out a couple of days ago that the car belonged to Brother Anson and the gun in the trunk belonged to Fred and that nobody could find him, the telephones haven't stopped ringing. Everybody that's come in the store or by the shop's had something to say about it. There was some speculating at first that Brother Anson was in on it with Fred, but that mostly come from people that don't like the Temple of the Almighty. I think it was all Fred's doing myself, even if I can't understand why."

"We might not ever find that out," Rosie says. "What does your momma have to say about it?"

"Don't even bring it up," Sherman says as I am parking the Cherokee in Minnie Beth's driveway. "She's so tore up by it she can't even sleep. She's got right fond of Fred in these last few months."

"Look what the cat drug in," Sherman announces as we go in the back door into Minnie Beth's kitchen. Eggs, sausage, pancakes, cheese grits and biscuits with a pitcher of milk gravy are warming on the stove top.

"I'm proud to have some company," Minnie Beth says a little too cheerfully as she pours tall glasses of orange juice. Her hair is freshly permed and she wears a new navy blue dress with tiny pinstripes. The dark circles around her eyes are not quite covered by her makeup.

"Me and Sherman's nearly always got a refrigerator full of leftovers," she says to us as we begin to fill our plates. "After this long, it looks like I'd learn how to cook for one or two, but I declare I can't seem to do it to save my life. Are you girls ready for all the big doins' today? I hear they're even bringing Ol' Arkansas Pate from the nursing home to read the Bible and say a few words."

Longtime Weave Room boss at White Cotton Mill, Arkansas Pate was the bad boy of Milltown in his day until Anson Gallworthy's daddy brought him to the Lord. Arkansas followed the straight and narrow from then on. Whenever one of his workers would get out of line, Arkansas would take him to his office and read him a scripture passage, usually from Proverbs, relevant to the nature of the offense. Then he would make the worker sit down and memorize the passage before he went back to work. Residing in Milltown Nursing Home these past ten years has not dulled him. Apparently, he holds Bible study in the smoking room every Sunday afternoon.

"Momma and Sam ought to be here in a few minutes," Rosie says after swallowing a mouthful of biscuit and gravy. "She said Sam bought him a pair of new overalls just for today."

"Way back yonder, me and Samuel Culp used to go together some," Minnie Beth tells us. "That was a long time before Ludie Mae Jones started twisting herself all around him."

To hear Millie tell it, Ludie Mae, Sam's long-absent wife, led him a merry chase in the short time they were together. Miss Ginny, Ludie Mae's momma, ran the company store for the Mill and Ludie Mae helped her after school. One winter when the sawmill closed and Sam was working at the Cotton Mill, Ludie Mae noticed him drinking coffee one afternoon at the store after his shift ended.

"Hey, there, Sam-u-well," she drawled out his name when her momma went to the storeroom for a dip of snuff. "That sure is one pitiful cup of coffee for a fine man like you. Let me get you a bigger one and add some sugar to it."

After that Sam began to take her to Saturday night dances in the dancehall above the store. And by summertime, right after she graduated high school, Ludie Mae was carrying Sam's child. Miss Ginny threatened to have Sam—in his middle twenties—jailed if he didn't do the right thing by Ludie Mae. I imagine she was secretly relieved that it was Sam who accepted paternal responsibility. Ludie Mae ran with more men in her 17 years than Miss Ginny could keep up with.

They wed, but life in the little cabin behind Miller and Millie's farmhouse was not for Ludie Mae. She pestered Sam into moving into Milltown where they occupied the lower floor of an old house near the town square. Sam spent the summer fetching her lemonade and ice cream when he was not working at the Mill. The older man who lived in the apartment above them had a wandering wife who left him for weeks at a time. In her absence the man would play Ernest Tubbs' 'Walking the Floor over You," for hours at a time on his record player.

Shortly after Clettus was born, Ludie Mae got the runarounds her own self. She would leave her baby with anybody who would watch him and go to meet her old friends at Confederate Cove. One day she didn't come back, so Sam eventually returned to his cabin in the country where Millie could help him out with Clettus. Rosie thought for the longest time that Clettus' momma was dead until Millie finally told her what happened. Ludie Mae returned only once for Clettus' high school graduation. He refused to talk to her and no one has seen her since.

Minnie Beth's front doorbell rings and in a minute Millie comes in wearing a new dress similar to Minnie Beth's. "They say great minds think alike," Minnie Beth laughs as she gives Millie a hug. "Ain't it nice to see our boy and girl together here in my kitchen again?" She asks, looking over at Sherman and Rosie who are finishing their pancakes.

"I can't remember when I've seen a finer sight," Millie says. "Is it all right if I ride with you all? Soon as Sam and Clettus and me pulled into the driveway, he remembered something he was supposed to bring and him and Clettus went to get it. You know him and Clettus both put in time at that Mill. I reckon nearly anybody around here past 45 or 50's done the same."

"When did Clettus work in the Mill?" Rosie wants to know as she gets up from the table. She begins stacking her and Sherman's dishes and flatware and takes them to the sink to rinse them. Probably as involuntary a response as breathing after living twenty years with a man.

"Right after you first moved in with Vancene to go to school in town," Millie says. "He finished up high school at Caloosa County and got hisself a job in the Weave Room. Worked there right up 'til they closed it down. Then he come back to the farm and ain't hardly left since then."

Rosie and I clean up Minnie Beth's table and load the dishwasher while she finishes her hair and puts on her earbobs. "Country women don't wear earrings," she once told us. Fifty-five years away from the farm have not taken the country out of that old girl.

We head for Milltown Square with Sherman escorting Millie and Minnie Beth in the Mustang. He suggests we take two cars in case he needs to get back to the shop. Rosie and I follow in the Cherokee. Milltown is done up to beat the band for the day's festivities. Banners on every building proclaim, "Milltown's Coming Back," or "Red Creek's Gonna Rise Again." The old bandstand is decked in balloons and streamers. Across the street flags flap in the breeze above the Post Office and Library. Beyond the bandstand, the gates of the Mill swing wide. Its front doors are no longer barred. Millie tells us that one of the early afternoon ceremonies will take place inside the old Spinning Room.

Sam and Clettus are walking toward us as we park the cars behind the library to cross the street. Clettus is pushing a huge box on a dolly toward the bandstand. "It's the old Mill bell," Clettus says. "Arkansas Pate had it stored at his boy's house all these years. His boy couldn't come today, so he called up Daddy and asked if we could go get it. Arkansas and some of the other bosses took it down and hid it before the owners knew what was going on. You remember this old thang, don't you, Aunt Millie?"

"Yes, sir, I can say I do," Millie says. "I loved the sound of it at 3:00 when it was time to go home. But I surely did hate hearing it at 7:00 the next morning. I sure never thought Ol' Silver was still somewhere around."

"It's a survivor, just like the rest of us," Sam comments as he pulls a package of Nicarette from the pocket of his overalls. "Rosie, girl, you didn't forget that guitar, did you? Me and Clettus and Junior and Jimmy's lined up to play right after the speeches."

"It's in Ell's car, Uncle Sam," Rosie says. "We never did get to practice that one song though. I've run through it some, but we ought to do it together once or twice."

"Soon as Junior and Jimmy gets here, we'll slip off and do just that," Sam promises.

Just past 9:30 groups of elderly men and women flanked by their children and grandchildren converge on Milltown square. With the temperature hovering in the low 70s, the rain still has not come. Warm, sunless days like this in winter often mean tornado weather, but the light wind that continues to blow takes away that fear. People begin to seat themselves in the folding chairs lined up around the bandstand. I spot Brother Anson looking over-anxious and uncomfortable in a too-tight blue suit.

"Miss Ellott," he nods at me. "This is one of those times when we must close our eyes to the circumstances around us and trust in Jesus. I am praying every minute that Mr. Fred will turn himself in to the sheriff. I cannot yet conceive how or why…" He stops then, unable to go on and moves toward a crowd of people from the Temple who are calling him over.

"Let's get those chairs out of the back of your car," Rosie says as she and Sherman come up behind me. "We should save the ones they've already got set up for the millworkers." Sherman volunteers to do this and brings back three of the lawnchairs Rosie and I keep in the back of the Cherokee for music festivals. We place them at the edge of the crowd.

The dead grass on the square overflows with the life-and-blood of Milltown. Several generations seat themselves in the chairs and wait for the festivities to begin. Children run and play around the bandstand, stopping only at their parents' or grandparents' warning. Wheelchairs and walkers, canes and crutches bolster former millhands who have come to say goodbye to the old house of labor.

At 10:00 the microphone squeals and pops as old Mr. Black, Lainie's father, welcomes the crowd. "I can't think of a thing to say but, 'welcome friends and neighbors,'" he begins. "For many years we spent more time with each other in that old building back yonder than we did with our own families. And when they shut it down, it was like the landlord foreclosing on the mortgage. They took our home from us. We still see each other—on the streets or at church or in the grocery store, but it's not ever been the same. It's been more than 25 years, but don't it seem like yesterday?" He pauses to look out at the crowd and sees heads nod in assent.

"As much as some of us might have hated all the hard work and long hours at the time, White Cotton Mill kept food on our tables and a roof over our heads. And it's not anything but right and proper that we put this old building to rest with some dignity. I'm going to call on one of our own to help us do that very thing. Arkansas, old feller, come on up here and talk to your good friends." He smiles fondly at the ancient bald man in the front row of wheelchairs. A younger man wheels him up the bandstand ramp to the microphone.

"The Lord giveth and Lord taketh away. Blessed is the name of the Lord," Arkansas recites. "A lot of ya'll's faces is familiar, but the names are stuck somewhere in this old bald head of mine. God was good to Milltown for more than 70 years while the mill was up and running. And the Good Lord only knows how many times me and some of you went head to head over some little trifle in the Weave Room. But the Good Book got us through those struggles. Why, I can remember when…" And he begins to relive a mess of memories, long forgotten by or perhaps unknown to much of the crowd. But we listen respectfully to him and several other old men join him on the bandstand to eulogize White Cotton Mill. At the end of the speeches, two men transport the old bell front and center.

"Mr. Pate and his boy's kept it for us all these years," Mr. Black says. "And when Milltown Community Center's complete, it's going up on the very top to ring in the good times again."

The crowd applauds and then many of us move inside the gates and into the building itself. The old Spinning Room is clean-swept and welcoming. Rosie goes with her uncle and cousin and Junior and Jimmy to practice for their performance. Other local musicians mount the bandstand to entertain those who choose not to listen to Brother Anson's talk inside the Mill. A small podium sits in the middle of the high-ceilinged room. Beside it is an ancient spindle from the earliest days of White Cotton Mill operations. Brother Anson greets us as he would his congregation as we assemble.

"Good morning to you," he greets us. "Look around you, good and hard now. In the short time it takes you to do that, this building will collapse on itself and return to the dust. Just like each and every one of us at the end of our time here on earth. 'Dust thou art and to dust thou shalt return.' But before the men set off the explosives that they will pack in holes you already see drilled here into the very walls and foundations of White Cotton Mill, we want to look back on its importance in our lives. Most of us know the general history of White Mill: that John Henry White and his brother, Franklin, built the mill in 1894. And it eventually grew to employ over 3,000 before a union-management dispute shut it down in the late '60s."

"Many today have shared the stories of their work lives in their years here. I never worked here myself, but my Daddy, Deacon Gallworthy, spent 36 years in this very room, feeding cotton into the machines to make the thread. He labored here through the week so he could preach the gospel at Milltown Assembly of God on Sunday mornings. And me and my brother, Robert, had a hard time understanding why our Daddy couldn't just be the preacher. Why he had to have two jobs. And then he explained it to us, and I'll never forget it. He said the Mill was our bread from heaven—that it filled us up and gave us the material things we needed in order to obtain the true Bread of Life, Christ Jesus. Now, that could have just been Daddy's way of saying the church couldn't afford to pay its preacher a fulltime salary, I don't know."

"But I was remembering that statement the other day and it brought to mind the Book of John, chapter 6. And here, Jesus is speaking to the crowds at Capernaum about the bread from heaven. And they're thinking he means to give them physical bread. But Jesus is talking about himself here. He is telling them if they just believe in him, they'll have everything they need. Jesus says to them, 'I am the living bread that came down from heaven; whoever eats this bread will live forever. The Bread of God is that which comes down from heaven and gives life to the world. Everyone who sees the Son and believes in him may have eternal life. And I shall raise him up on the last day,'" Brother Anson repeats, "'And I shall raise him up on the last day.'"

Everyone is attentive and children are quiet in their parents' laps as Brother Anson continues, "In the morning, White Cotton Mill will stand no more. This is the last day. In the rubble and ruin, as the dust from the bricks and the mortar rises up to the sky, a part of our souls will rise with it. But, remember, the words of the Master, 'This is the will of the One who sent me, that I should not lose anything of what he gave me, but that I should raise it up on the last day.'" Brother Anson says. "Let us give thanks to God for the blessing he gave us all those years of our lives that we spent here at the Mill. Let us remember them with love. Amen."

So many people crowd around him when the "Amen," resounds, that I am unable to speak with him again about Fred. I step back outside and rejoin the crowd around the bandstand. A performance by the Seers High Confederettes is ending as Rosie, Sam and Clettus climb onto the bandstand. They tune their instruments as Junior and Jimmy slip in beside them. Rosie's clear soprano rises like a flock of starlings into the overcast sky.

> "At the east end of town
> at the foot of the hill,
> there's a chimney so tall
> that says Aragon Mill,"

> "But there's no smoke at all
> coming out of the stacks,
> for the mill has shut down
> and it ain't coming back..."

"And the only tune I hear
is the sound of the wind
as it rolls through the town
weave and spin, weave and spin."

"Now I'm too old to work
and I'm too young to die,
and I can't find no work
for my old man and I."

"And there's no hope at all
in the narrow empty streets
for the looms have shut down
it's so quiet I can't sleep."

"And the only tune I hear
is the sound of the wind
as it rolls through the town
weave and spin, weave and spin."

Chapter Twenty-two

Rain falls lightly on our bare heads as we walk the streets of Broadway and on to the Confederate Cove. Sherman gallantly opens the double glass doors for Rosie and me. We step inside to a full house of memories and old friends. Many of the same faces we saw here on the day of Grace Ann's funeral are present today. Buck and Olive Ann have added a wall of photographs taken during our years at Seers High. We stop to admire them and wave a greeting to Buck who is working the grill.

"Me and Olive Ann call that the Rogue's Gallery," Buck says with a laugh, indicating the snapshot collection.

Bud's sister Mary Joyce gets up and pads over to us. "I reckon you all have heard the news about Mr. Fred." She does not pose this as a question. "I've done told everybody I know that it didn't come as no surprise to me. That old man and the girl never did see eye to eye after her momma died. He must have been crazy drunk to kill her though. Underneath all that anger, why, he loved her more than God." She seems not to expect a response and wanders back to her seat.

More of our friends and classmates join us at the Rogue's Gallery. As we stand there, finding ourselves in the faded photographs of our youth, we talk of Bud and Grace Ann and Fred. The sounds from the implosion just blocks away are evident, but no one comments on this as we examine each picture from our past. It's as though we are trying to call back something very real but not clearly defined.

"That one's from our junior year," someone says, indicating a full bus parked outside the school. It is plastered over with "Best Band in Dixie" posters from a competition for marching bands held each year in New Orleans. "Remember how Dr. Lear talked Mr. Fred into to giving us the rest of the money to get there? All we lacked was $300 and he just opened up the cash register there at The Smart Shoppe and handed over the money."

"Lord, will you look at that one?" Sherman laughs. "It's me and Bud in the Womanless Weddin in our senior year. Didn't I make a pretty bride, Rosie?"

"Your wedding dress is prettier than mine was," Rosie agrees. "I remember Minnie Beth doing up that wig at the House of Beauty and what a good time she had fitting it on you." Several minutes pass as we continue our little walk down memory lane.

"And there's Grace Ann as homecoming queen," someone else points out. "Mr. Fred ordered that dress all the way from Paris, France. I remember it clear as day. I was working at the Smart Shoppe after school and me and him spent the better part of an afternoon looking through catalog after catalog. We looked at dresses until we were blue in the face until we found that one. When Grace Ann come by after school and he showed it to her, she actually agreed with him for once that it was the one. I though it was the prettiest thing I ever saw in my whole life. The neckline…"

Brother Anson bursts through the door just then, out of breath as he hurries over to us. "Police have got Mr. Fred," he says as soon as he can breathe again. "Caught him stumbling around at the Mill site just a little after the explosives went off. Miss Ellott, he's asking for you. Will you come with me?"

"Of course," I say and follow him into the street. Many of our classmates standing at the Rogue's Gallery join us as we run the three blocks to the Mill site.

Shattered as the debris from the implosion that lies in pieces around him, Fred Hardaman stands with head bowed, talking quietly with two policemen and Sgt. Tolson.

"You must be Ms. Seers," Sgt. Tolson says. "Mr. Fred here wants to make a statement to us, but he asked if you could be here when he did it. Could you come over here by him while I turn on the tape recorder?"

Stepping around the glass shards and rubble, I move to Fred's side and gently place my hand on his arm. His old blue eyes are filmed over with defeat as he struggles to focus on my face. "Ell," he begins in a hoarse voice. "I never went there that morning to kill my Grace Ann. All I ever wanted was to get that Tanner boy to leave. Grace Ann belonged with Ree and Harley, Jr, not that Northern boy that laughed in my face when I told him to get on home. I held the shotgun in his face, but he grabbed onto it. We started fighting over it and it went off and hit Grace Ann in the face. And that Tanner ran over to her. I wanted him to just get away from her, so I fired off a shot at him. I must have hit him, and I just kept on shooting until that shotgun was empty.

"A little bit after I quit, I heard something outside and looked out. It was that motorcycle of Bud's coming up the drive to the trailer. I took the gun and hid in the closet when he come to the door. I reckon he come in, too, but he didn't stay but a minute and he was off again. When he was good and gone, I threw stuff around in the room and took some of their things and hid 'em in the woods. I went there in that car of Brother Anson's and hid it in the woods before I went to the trailer. I knew I might have to get rough with that Tanner and I didn't want nobody knowing it was me there. When I left I drove it off and hid it in that barn where I reckon they found it. I kept that car all them years, letting Grace Ann think it was sold. I kept saying to myself that if she'd ever behave long enough, I'd let her have it back. But she never did and

I finally sold it to Brother Anson, not all that long ago." He stops talking and looks up into my face.

"You'll be wanting to know why I stayed on Grace Ann so hard all these years. She was my daddy made over. My daddy, Freeman Hardaman, who never hit a lick at a snake if he could get somebody else to do it for him. He led me and my momma all over Alabama and Mississippi for fifteen years, taking no-count jobs and chasing after women. He was a charmer, Freeman was. My poor little momma, not any bigger than Ma 'Ree ever was, loved him to his death. When he'd leave us for days or weeks at a time to go run with some ol' gal, she'd get herself a job and I'd go to work with her. I hid whenever the bosses come in. We lived right here in this town from the time I was 6 years old until I was 9. And my momma—my momma was named Grace. She worked at this very mill most of them three years.

When Freeman come a-trucklin' back with his tail tucked between his legs, we moved off to Mississippi. It didn't get no better. We moved seventeen times from then until I was 15. Freeman died when I was 15. Some man shot him dead while Freeman was climbing in to his window. My momma had an insurance policy on him and we took that money and bought a grocery store. Me and momma run that store until she died when I was 23. I started building my businesses from there. I bought me a clothing store first and then an antique shop and just kept goin'. Ma 'Ree nor Grace Ann never knew anything about my family. I was too ashamed to tell them about my daddy. We named Grace Ann after my momma, but she had my daddy's heart and soul. I started seeing that more after Ma 'Ree died. I thought I could get it out of her, though. But I never did. Never did."

Sgt. Tolson leads Fred to a waiting car and they drive away. We stand silent in the wake of the implosion and the words that fell from Fred Hardaman's mouth.

"I'd say he's just a pitiful old man that's done hisself more harm than he done to my brother, but that wouldn't exactly remedy the situation, would it?" Mary Joyce comments. "And not one word of regret over blaming this thing on Bud, not the first one."

"I think we need to spend some time in prayer," Brother Anson says, quietly. "For Mr. Fred's soul and for the safe return of your brother, Miss Reese. And for ourselves, that we can find a way to heal the hurts this thing has brought to everyone involved."

And so we do. Some bow their heads and others kneel in the ruins around us. Brother Anson begins and each of us add a sentence, asking understanding and mercy for all.

With the dedication still a couple of hours away, Rosie, Sherman and I stroll the streets of Broadway. Besides the Confederate Cove, only one business remains from our youthful days—Milltown News and Novelties, the small newsstand next to the vacant Elmore's that my father used to manage. A doorway behind its counters leads to a pool hall, the true source of its financial survival. It is a haven for Milltown men who want to escape their wives and children. The only telephone is up front in the newsstand. Alton Brown, the owner, will only summon pool hall occupants for the direst of emergencies. We go inside to find him behind the counter, sorting comic books.

"Hi-do," he says. "Folks can't find what you need, you let me know." He repeats the same words he said to us over twenty-five years ago when we would wander in to check out Veronica and Betty's latest goings-on or to perhaps find the classic comic book version of *Great Expectations*. We stay a few minutes without finding anything to purchase. Alton does not look up from his sorting as we leave.

Back on the streets, we talk of Fred's deception.

"He's always had it in for Bud," Sherman contends. "This was just a prime opportunity for him to do him in. He never liked anybody Grace Ann went with. Bud least of all."

"I don't think that's entirely true, Sherman," Rosie says. "I think he just panicked after he calmed down some and realized what he had done. He was just too ashamed to face the truth and tried to think of some way to hide it."

"I don't mean to eavesdrop, but I believe your former wife has a point, Sherman," Brother Anson, who has been walking quietly behind us, says. "While it is true that he had no regard for Bud, he did admit toward the end that Bud was probably a better father to the twins than Grace Ann was a mother. It hurt me to hear that, but after some of the things he told me, I believe it to be the truth."

"Fred told me once that you were interested in Grace Ann, back when we were all teenagers," I say to him as he joins us in our stroll. "Is that why you continued to help Fred look for her killer?"

"That's part of it," Brother Anson admits. "I got over my feelings for Grace Ann some years ago, but when she came back to Milltown, we started talking again. I went to see her a few times. This was before Tanner Hope joined her. I actually bought the old Skylark from Fred to surprise her with, but Tanner showed up before I could give it to her. I never told Mr. Fred any of this. When he found out about Tanner and then about the baby, he nearly broke down then. He had no idea I was seeing her some."

"Didn't Fred send you to talk to Grace Ann and Tanner about, um, the error of their ways?" I ask him. "That must have been very difficult for you."

"It was," Brother Anson admits. "But Jesus never said it would be easy, did He? Maybe He was trying to show me my selfishness or whatever it was that made me try to initiate a friendship with Grace Ann. That wasn't anything but old pride rearing its head. If-she-didn't-want-me-then, she-might-now kind-of-a-thing. The only thing I tried to say to Grace Ann and Tanner was that they should do what was right for the child. I believe they meant to do that."

"All I can say is, that from everything I observed about Fred after the murders, he must have had a complete breakdown and dissociated himself from the whole thing. Maybe he was really able to convince himself Bud did do it for awhile."

We continue our walk, giving our regards to the Old Broadway that will be gone after today, replaced by an outdoor walking mall. When we decide we are hungry, we stop to go back inside the Confederate Cove and ask Brother Anson to join us. He politely declines, saying he is needed back at the dedication site. We go through the doors to find Mary Joyce, Mr. and Mrs. Reese, Ree and Harley, Jr. seated at a table with Coley Frost.

Ree is white-faced, but composed and calls out, "Aunt Ell, come and sit with us. Ms. Frost has something she wants to ask you about my daddy."

Sherman and Rosie go to a booth in the back corner as I sit down beside Coley at the Reeses table. John Reese wears a clean white shirt and old blue jeans. He holds a protective arm around Ree's shoulders. Harley, Jr., who is small and looks like Fred, is fidgeting with a GameBoy. Recognized early on as suffering from ADHD, he constantly occupies his hand whenever he sits for any length of time "Much obliged to you for joining us," Mary Reese says, pleasantly. Her white hair is pinned neatly in a bun at the nape of her neck. "Ma 'Ree here's been telling us what all you and your friend with the New Agers has been doing to keep in touch with Bud. And she told us all about that thang on the Internet, too. I don't know that I understand it all, but I'm grateful to you just the same."

"I never thought Bud could hurt Grace Ann in any way," I say to all the Reeses. "It just took some time for all the facts to come out."

"Is it possible to get in touch with Bud?" Coley asks. "He's the one who should have custody of his children, if he's capable of it."

"Mary Jean Jones is the one he calls every so often," I tell them. "But I haven't heard anything from her since we saw her at the women's conference at my library right before Christmas. I've tried to call her a few times and haven't found her at home. She was supposed to let Bud know about Fred's trying to get the twins back to his house."

"Ree told me this and I contacted Miss Jones," Coley tells us. "Apparently, she talked to Bud once since then and he promised to think about trying to come home. She says she has no number to reach him."

We discuss ways to bring Bud back. "I think somebody ought to drive up to Tennessee and bring him back," Mary Joyce says. "When he finds out it was Mr. Fred that did this, he'll just go to pieces."

Ree, who has had very little to say until now, looks at her aunt and says, quietly, "It wasn't really Granddad who did that, Aunt Mary Joyce. No more than it was Daddy acting like Elvis all this time."

"That's the best way to look at it," Coley tells her. "But we can't go up to Tennessee to bring him home if we don't know where he is. Harley, you've been awfully quiet. Tell us what you think would be the best way to get your dad to come home."

Looking up from the tiny video screen, the small teenager with Fred's eyes, says, "Is that what ya'll are talking about? Dad sent me his beeper number. It's on a piece of tape inside the case for this GameBoy here. He sent it to me for Christmas. He wrote in his card for me to tell Ree about the beeper number, but I forgot. You're not mad at me, are you, Ree?" He looks at his twin anxiously.

"No, Har, I'm not mad," Ree tells him. "Could we go someplace and call him? Granddad gave me a cell phone for Christmas. It's at Grandpa John's house. We'd have to use a cell phone to leave a message or Daddy wouldn't call back. He probably still thinks the police want him."

Coley agrees to accompany Ree to get the cell phone and place the call. They exit the double glass doors, but in a minute Ree runs back in and hugs me.

"We're going to be all right," she says, as much for herself as for me. "I don't usually ask other people to pray, because I think prayer is a private thing, but would you maybe say a little one that we'll get Daddy back home?"

"All of us will," I tell her, indicating the restaurant full of Bud's old friends. She squeezes my hand and leaves again.

I sip my coffee and look around for Sherman and Rosie, who are no longer occupying their old booth in the rear. "Did you see where Sherman and Rosie went?" I ask Buck, who is still at work at the grill.

Olive Ann, now at the soda fountain with him, is building sundaes and banana splits. She answers for him. "Rosie left out the back about ten or fifteen minutes ago. I think Sherman stepped into the restroom."

In a few minutes he emerges, smelling of cigarette smoke. Having quit the foul habit some years ago, Sherman only returns to it when under major stress.

"What gives?" I ask him as he falls heavily into the booth where he sat with Rosie.

"Not a damn thing," he answers shortly. "Except eight weeks of family therapy down the toilet."

"What makes you say that?" I ask him. "The girls seem in a lot better spirits. Cassie's even got so she lets Molly have her whole time in the bathroom without banging on the door. And she's stopped giving Rosie hell about every little thing that goes wrong. Seems to me like things are looking up."

"So you would think," he says. "So did I until about twenty minutes ago. All those sessions with that therapist woman. Us having to talk about every little thing that happened in the twenty years we were married and the four years before that that we went together. I thought all that was moving us closer together, her and me. But it turns out I was wrong."

"What exactly were you wrong about?" I ask him.

"About me and Rosie and the girls getting back together again," he says. "About us getting married again. I come out and just asked her, a little while ago. And she said no. Not 'hell no,' but no just the same. What's all this been for if it wasn't for that?"

"Is that the reason you agreed to go with them to therapy?" I ask him.

"Well, yeah. Why else would I go through all that shit?"

I can sense Sherman Lee is in no mood for anything but appeasement, so I suggest that while we are waiting for the afternoon groundbreaking ceremonies to begin at the old Mill site, we should take a little drive to visit Miss Samantha.

"Let's do it," he says, ready for some distraction. As Sherman drives the Mustang to downtown Good River, he points out new buildings going up and the old businesses of our youth that have once again changed types and owners. Downtown is sparsely populated on this early Friday afternoon and we are able to park near the statue at the foot of the river bridge.

"You know, it's right amazing that she's still standing after all these years," Sherman remarks as we stand on the grass and gaze upward underneath Miss Samantha 's outstretched arm. "They put her up, when? In the 1920's, wasn't it? Remember that time somebody from Good River High broke her finger off? When I was a little kid and they used to talk to us about angels watching over us in Sunday school, I pictured them looking like Miss Samantha."

"I think she does look out for us," I say. "Who knows where we'd be if she didn't?"

"True enough," he said. "I want to stand here a little bit longer, Ellie May. Then I'll drop you back at the Mill site. I'm not feeling too festive just now, so I think I'll go on back to the shop. If you see my momma or Miss Millie, don't tell them nothing about what went on with Rosie and me. Just say I had to get back to work, that they beeped me or something."

I hug him and he hugs me briefly before I cross the street and get back into his car. I watch him a few moments—a paunchy, proud, middle aged man trying hard not to confront his own pain. Removing something from his coat pocket, he steps up on the base of the statue's pedestal. Steadying himself, he places a tiny Rebel flag between the parted fingers of Miss Samantha's left hand. Then he drives me back to the Mill site.

With an hour to kill before the last round of ceremonies, I take the Cherokee to my old street back in Milltown. Some people I never met own the house on Western Avenue where I lived until I went away to school. No one is home when I knock on the door. I walk around to the back yard where the old sweetgum tree still grows, tall and strong. I climbed this tree often, but only as far as the fifth limb to placate my mother. Neighborhood boys, Sherman included, braved their way to the very tip top and shouted down ebullient messages about the view from way up there. I loved the tree in summer when it was full and green. I could take a book, settle onto the fifth limb and read away the afternoon. I hid there once from someone's pesky little sister who was always after me to play Barbie dolls with her. Before I leave my old back yard, I gather a handful of dry brown sweetgum balls and put them in the pocket of my sweater.

The movers and the shakers of the proposed Milltown Community Center are yammering away when I arrive at the old Mill site. Knee deep in ruins, they hype the new creation to come. I find Rosie at the edge of the crowd beside the old Mill gate. Placing an arm around her shoulders, I slip up beside her.

"Sherman went to counsel awhile with Miss Samantha," I tell her. "And after he dropped me back here, he was going back to the shop.

"That's probably for the best," Rosie says with a sigh. "Where has my head been for the last eight weeks? Why did I ever think Sherman Lee Jackson might be interested in building family relationships? All he wanted was his sweet little Rosie back at his beck and call. Well, that girl is gone and she ain't a-coming back."

"Did he really surprise you with the proposal?" I ask her as Seers High School band plays a patriotic medley–"The Star Spangled Banner," "The Battle Hymn of the Republic," and a quick snatch of 'Dixie." I am unsure how they get away with that one. Good thing Perri-Young doesn't visit Milltown.

"I'll say he did," Rosie answers, cupping her hand to my ear so I can hear her over the music. "We were laughing and cutting up with George and Dee Ann. You remember them? They were two years ahead of us. And after they left, Sherman was saying how good they looked and how well their kids turned out. Then he says,'the girls can turn out that good if you and me get back together.' And just flat out asks me to marry him. I couldn't say anything for a few minutes. Finally I told him it just couldn't be. The therapy sessions have helped us all deal with our situation a little better, but they've also pointed out a lot of our basic differences that caused the trouble to begin with. He didn't say one more word. He just gave me that old familiar glare, like I was Molly caught with my hand in the cookie jar, and stomped off to the restroom."

"He'll come to terms with it after awhile," I say. "Give him a little time. Sherman's got to have awhile to sulk."

We hush then and listen to Good River's mayor, a Milltown boy himself, outline the construction schedule for Milltown Community Village and Walking Mall. "And the new library will honor the finest librarian this state has ever known, Miss Vancene Collins Frazier. If you're like me, you never would have made it out of Seers High without Miss Vancene's help. I spent many hours at that library across the street with her helping me with my homework." He holds up a blueprint for the new community center complex. "The Vancene Collins Frazier Memorial Library will sit to the right of the community center complex. And the old library will be taken in by the new post office. In April, when we break ground for the new Frazier Memorial Library, we are planning to have a little celebration and fund raiser. So, you good people, save up your nickels and dimes so we can do Miss Vancene proud." He steps down to a round of applause.

"I hope Momma's somewhere around here," Rosie says, craning her neck. "This will tickle her to death."

"Rose," says a voice behind us. We turn to see Michael in ragged jeans and a sweatshirt. He wears a stubbly beard and a determined look. "I can't stay away from you any more. Will you talk to me?"

Rosie, gently smiling, reaches out her hand to him. "I will," she says. They walk from the crowd, cross the street and seat themselves on the Post Office steps. In the dim light of late afternoon, I see them talking earnestly, gesturing intently as they move closer together. After a few minutes they leave, moving down the Broadway streets to Michael's car.

When the speeches end and the symbolic shovel of dirt is spread, I meet Millie and Minnie Beth as I am returning to my car.

"Where did Sherman and Rosie get off to?" Millie wants to know. This reminds me that I need to offer them a ride. "I was going to have you all out to the house for supper before you drove back to Birmingham."

"Sherman had to get back to the garage," I tell her. "And Rosie had some other things to take care of." I am not about to spill the beans.

"Well, all right then," Millie says, clearly disappointed. "I can find Sam and ride back home with him. You're welcome to come, Ell. You know you're my girl as much as Rosie is."

"I know that," I say and hug the little woman with Rosie's hair and eyes. "I've got to get back, too. I'm playing hooky today and I need to get back and check on the folks at my library."

On the short drive back to Minnie Beth's place, she and I chat about the events of the day. Minnie Beth has little to say, sensing perhaps that her baby boy's best laid plans might have gone haywire. As we say our goodbyes, I promise to return for the fundraiser. In a few minutes, I am turning left onto the freeway, heading home to Gabe.

Early evening dining in the Pace household, Gabe and I share a modest and bland meal I prepared in the Pace kitchen. Gabe eats his skinless, boneless chicken breast without too much complaint. Actually, the King of Cholesterol is not doing too badly on the new regimen. He keeps assuring me he is following doctor's orders, so I try not to press him for details. I plunge into a graphic account of the day's many happenings. Gabe eats quietly, interrupting with questions and comments.

"You think Old Fred's going to survive jail?" he asks.

"I honestly don't know," I say. "I have never in my life seen a more ravaged face or a more broken spirit than Fred Hardaman's was today. I just hope that now Ree and Harley Jr., can get their daddy back again."

"Me, too," Gabe says. "What time did Michael get there? I nearly told you last night that he was planning to show up, but I was afraid you'd tell Rosie."

"About 3:30 or 4:00," I tell him. "And thanks for your vote of confidence, dear. I have been known to keep a secret or two every once in a while. All my friends in high school and college gave me plenty of practice with that."

"Oh, do excuse me, dahlin'," Gabe breaks into his Savannah Blue Blood accent. "I had truly forgotten that the Dear Abby of Milltown is always discreet."

"Hmm," I say, pretending not to be mollified.

Gabe grins and pulls me toward him in an embrace. "How about Abby joining me in my chambers for a little R and R? Maybe even the Big R if we're up to it."

Still walking a bit unsteadily from the recent trauma, Gabe holds tight to me as we go to his room. We get into bed fully clothed and hold each other for a long time. We talk softly together as evening moves into night. Gabe begins to stroke my hair and our conversation lulls. Our touch is light and affectionate, our breathing slow and regular. And before much time passes, we sleep.

Chapter Twenty-three

On the margin of the Caloosa River, we celebrate the April day. It is the afternoon of Vancene Collins Frazier Day in our county and the fund raiser is going strong. Pink dogwood and azaleas in bloom brighten the river banks. Smoke rises from barbecue pits, wafting the smell of burgers and chops through the crowd. Seated in the Special Guest's lawn chair in the front and center of the crowd, Mildred Mae Frazier Culp looks serenely about at all the folks and their children and grandchildren who have gathered to honor her only sister. She waves toward our table and Michael, Rosie, Gabe and I wave back. Local bands have entertained us, clowns have amused us and politicians have bored us for several hours now. As it nears 4:00, the designated supper hour, Rosie and I get up to help spread tablecloths and bring out the many dozen covered dishes from picnic baskets and coolers.

"Is there enough here Gabe can eat?" Rosie asks me as we take the foil from dishes of baked beans and potato salad.

"I brought something for him," I tell her. Due to a business boom since the store was revamped and the restaurant opened, Gabe has worked himself senseless. His blood sugar levels are ricocheting like crazy—a condition that probably worries me more than him. Feeling more than a little like Aunt Bee, I do what I can to see that his diet coincides with doctor's orders. "He and Michael are really putting in the hours since the weather turned warm."

"Michael says they have more music students than they can handle," Rosie says. "And the Down Yonder Cafe is cram packed every day at lunch. Mabel June's talking seriously of quitting the dry cleaners all together and investing her savings so she can work full time at the cafe."

"I've not heard that," I say as we finish filling one food table and move to another. "Our boys may be moving into the big time." We glance fondly over at the Brothers Pace, who are escorting Millie over to her picnic table where several of her old friends from White Cotton Mill days are seated.

Following the day's groundbreaking and fund raiser for the new library, we will journey back to the Culp farm for the Miller Culp Memorial String Band Festival this evening. Sam and Clettus are putting the finishing touches on the dance floor this very afternoon. Wildwood Flower will perform at 8:00.

Cassie, flanked by Meaghan, comes through the woods. Molly and little Helen, who is leading Caitlin by the hand, soon follow. "They want us to go boat riding," Cassie tells Rosie importantly, gesturing at two boys waiting for them near the water's edge. The girl looks so much like Rosie did at 13 that I want to take her hand and caution her of things to come.

"Well, can we?" Cassie asks.

"Who are 'they'?" Rosie wants to know. "Can I meet them?"

"Oh, Momma," Cassie says in exasperation. "Just a couple of guys. John David's got a license to drive the boat. He's 14. It's his dad's. You know him. He's somebody you went to school with. Donald Wheeler." Cassie indicates a gangly boy in cutoffs standing at the ramp beside a small speedboat. Another boy is bringing life jackets and placing them on the seats.

"We won't stay long," Meaghan joins in. "Just down the river and back a few times.

"Be careful," Rosie says as they jump and hug each other. "Keep the life jackets on and don't stand up in the boat."

The girls are already down at the dock. The two boys buckle life jackets onto them and give them a hand down into the boat.

"They'll be fine," I reassure Rosie as the boat starts up and moves off at a moderate speed. Molly, Helen and Caitlin wait for our attention. They hold treasures from their walk in the woods—wildflowers, various rocks and a tiny frog in a jar

"Me and Helen and Caity just want to look at him for awhile," Molly tells her mother, holding up the captured frog. "He makes Caity laugh when he jumps."

"You and Helen take Cait and get all your hands washed," Rosie tells them. She places the jarred frog under the picnic table. "Then go over to where Michael and Gabe are sitting. We're about to eat in a few minutes."

"Why don't I take Cait and change her," I say to Rosie. The active Little One's blue romper is a smudged and wrinkled mess. I extend my finger to her as Molly and Helen head in the other direction, talking their own private language, which I have learned is part traditional sign language and part symbols known only to them. Toddlers always amuse me with their tiptoe walking. It's as though when treading on unfamiliar ground if they tiptoe across it, nothing bad will happen. "Ell-ee," Caitlin says and looks up at me, grinning happily as she tiptoes through the clover. When we reach the Cherokee, I pull a yellow romper with tiny flowers that Gabe purchased for her from the diaper bag. With Cait dry and clean again, I lift her from the back seat and down to the ground. I take the insulated bag with Gabe's lunch and then lock and slam the doors. As we reach the edge of the campsite, Caitlin says "Dadd-ee," and points ahead of us. Sherman and a Sweet Young Thing (SYT) are emerging from the Brand New Mustang, 1965. "Dad-dee," Caitlin repeats and releases my finger to run toward him on her tiptoes.

"It's Caity Rose," Sherman says to SYT, who, as if on cue, begins to exclaim over Sherman's offspring.

"You are the cutest little girl I think I ever saw," SYT says as she tosses her blonde hair from her eyes for a better look. "Are all your girls this cute, Sherm? They must get their good looks from their daddy."

Sherman, nearly to the blushing stage, smiles almost defiantly at me as he introduces us. "Susan Tompson, this is my former wife's roommate, Ellott Seers," he says as he lifts Caitlin up above his head and makes her squeal. "Ell and I have known each other all our lives," he adds as Susan extends a manicured hand to me.

"Oh, are you the librarian?" Susan asks sunnily. "I used to love going to the library when I was little. I don't think I've ever been back since then though."

"Really," I say as I check out the deeply tanned, shapely legs on the young woman before me. Glowing white and even teeth sparkle from a cosmetically enhanced face that might even put Tammy Faye Baker to shame. Young Susan Tompson has definitely been present and attending at all her Merle Norman classes. "What do you do, Susan?"

"I'm a make-up artist at Fashion Photos in the Mall," Susan tells me, referring to Good River's newest photography studio, which renders its subjects as remarkably better looking than they are in its finished products. "I live down the highway from Sherm's service station. He just did the most wonderful repair job on my little Honda." Her smile at him is a pale specter of Grace Ann's—that you-are-the-only-thing-in-the-universe-worth-a-damn smile that could cause blind men to see.

"Where are Cassie and Molly?" Sherman asks me as he sets Caitlin back on the ground.

"Cassie and Meaghan are boat. riding with Donald Wheeler's son and his friend," I say, expecting an explosion.

"Oh," Sherman says, not seeming upset. "Ol' Don brings his family over here a lot to fish and water ski. They live out close to the station. He stops by a lot to get gas for the boat. What about Molly? Is that little Helen girl with her? I think I must scare that kid to death. She never says a word when I'm around."

"Sherman," I say to him, patiently. "The child is deaf. And although she can speak, she uses sign language most of the time."

"Oh, good," Sherman says. "I thought it was me. Tell the girls I'll see them later tonight at Momma's. I reckon they'll all spend the night."

"Even Caitlin," I tell him. "Rosie thinks she's big enough now."

"Hear that Caity Rose," he says and smacks a big kiss on her cheek. "You get to go with the big girls this time. Grandmomma Minnie Beth's been looking forward to you all coming for a week. It'll be just like when my sisters were younger and they had spend the night parties." He puts his baby daughter back on the ground and pats her on the head before he goes off in the other direction with Susan. "Be a good girl, Cait. Daddy will see you tonight."

"Well, Miss Caity. Looks like your Daddy's found you a new big sister," I say to the little girl as we make our way back to the picnic area. Actually, to be fair, Susan is probably only eight or nine years younger than Michael, who hovers just past the 3-0 mark.

Our table is full to overflowing with food and folks as I place Caitlin in Michael's lap and slide in beside Gabe. "Your lunch, dear," I say, handing him the bag.

"Thank you for your trouble but not the contents," he says in disgust as he looks at the bags of raw vegetables and sandwiches of fat free bread and meat. "Did I tell you that I have the Afterlife all figured out? St. Peter admits all diabetics to heaven, unconditionally. We've already had our fill of hell with a lifetime of rabbit food."

"I see," I say and am relieved to see he is smiling as he says this.

Michael is sneaking bites of pork chop and barbecue to Caitlin while Rosie's back is turned. These items are not generally on her menu. Apparently, Rosie has spotted Sherman and SYT (surely her middle name must be Yvonne) at a table near the river's edge. As she turns back with a bemused look, she notices Michael's activity and thumps his hand.

"Sherman Lee must have been shopping uptown recently," she says lightly as she sits down to her meal.

"Caity and I met them in the parking lot," I tell her. 'She really is past jail bait age but she probably doesn't look like it from here."

"From here she looks like a dead ringer for your friend Grace Ann, if all those pictures in your old annuals do her justice," Gabe comments as he cranes his neck in their direction.

"Bottle blonde," Michael says, dismissively after a quick glance. He squeezes Rosie's hand contentedly. He has maintained an uninterrupted state of near bliss since late February when he and Rosie reunited. Rosie seems equally satisfied. She and the girls continue their weekly therapy sessions sans Sherman. She now allots large portions of her week exclusively for herself and the girls. Her encounters with Michael are a great deal more discreet, confined to times when the girls are away from the apartment or to Michael and Gabe's abode in Crestline.

Our fellow fund-raising picnickers settle into a happy, bloated stupor as the afternoon drifts by us. Hardly anyone notices three latecomers quietly entering the picnic grounds. A famished Cassie and Meaghan join us at the table and it is Cassie who says, "Hey, Momma, there's Ree and Harley, Jr., with their daddy."

Many of the crowd get up to welcome a pale and solemn Bud Reese. Clad in the white shirt and faded jeans of his teen years, Bud shakes hands all around and waves to us from a circle of friends. Rosie and I hurry over to him.

"Hey, old boy," I say, grasping him to me in a smother hug. "I can't tell you how glad we are that you're back. When did you get here?"

"I been at Momma and Daddy's since Thursday night," he says with a hint of his old smile coming in to play. "Ree and Harley talked me into coming here today. They thought some folks might want to see me," he adds with a genuine smile this time.

"They were right on the money," Rosie says, squeezing between us to give him a hug of her own.

"Daddy had to be in the hospital," Harley, Jr., says in his matter of fact way. "But they said it was okay for him to come home again now that he knows who he is again."

"I guess you could say that Elvis has left the building," Bud says, looking a little ashamed. "I don't know where all that came from, but I hope it's gone to stay."

"If you're thinking about coming back to work anytime soon, I can sure use a good man at the garage," Sherman says as he enters the circle and grasps Bud's hand. SYT stands at the periphery, looking as out of place as she probably feels in this crowd of mostly middle aged, mostly blue-collar baby boomers. She nervously twists her blonde locks through her artificial fingernails as she waits for Sherman.

"I'll give that serious thought, buddy," Bud says to his former employer as he continues to shake his hand. "My brothers give Daddy about all the help he can use in his little shop behind the house. Now that I got the twins back, I got to have some way to bring in the dough." They discuss practical considerations for a few minutes before Sherman rejoins SYT.

Rosie and I invite Bud and the twins to our table. Michael and Gabe make room. Molly and Helen join a game of badminton set up on the side lawn. Cassie and Meaghan finish eating and return to the dock with the other teenagers, who sit in a clump around a boom box going full blast. They ask Harley, Jr., and Ree to join them. They look to their father who waves them on.

"Hey, man," Gabe says as he shakes Bud's hand. "We met one other time, but I'm not sure you remember it."

"After the funeral, wasn't it?" Bud asks as he sits down. "I don't remember much from that day but a bunch of faces and the road in front of me. I probably rode two or three hundred miles that day. I doubt I was making much sense."

"I'm glad things turned out better for you," Michael says. "I know you're happy to be back with your kids."

"You got that right," Bud says. "All the time I was acting like the King come back to life, the only thing I wanted to do was get back to Harley and Ree. If Fred hadn't sicced the cops on me I might could've got past Grace Ann dying a little quicker."

"I imagine ol' Fred's regretting that now," Gabe remarks as he offers Bud a plate of barbecue and beans. "He may have bought himself a little time, but he nearly wrecked what was left of your family in doing it."

"Fred never thought I had a right to my family," Bud remarks. "From the time Grace Ann and I said, 'I do,' til the day I went off to Atmore, he was right there between us."

"I tried my best to get Grace Ann to move off somewhere with me. I could've stayed in the Army after 'Nam, but she couldn't let go no more than he could. They latched on to each other after Miss Ma 'Ree died and you couldn't pull them apart with a crowbar."

I fill Bud in on Fred since his incarceration two months ago. At first he shut down completely, refusing to eat or talk. Then he ate everything in sight and talked the ears off anybody in hearing range. Then I tell him of Fred's ramblings about Grace Ann and his father on the day of his arrest. Bud listens and begins to nod.

"So that's what it was. That's not really as bad as what I thought. For a long time, I had the idea there might have been something, well, physical that went on at some time or another between Fred and Grace Ann."

The same notion had occurred to me, but I was never able to express it to Grace Ann.

"You and Fred had yourselves set on the same person," Rosie says as she pours Bud another styrofoam cup of tea. "And you got in each other's way."

Bud is about to reply to this when Ree calls from the boat dock, "Daddy, they're saying something on the radio about Granddad." She listens for a moment and continues, "He broke out of the county jail early this afternoon and they've got the whole County Sheriff's Department out looking for him."

Chapter Twenty-four

"There's a better home a-waitin'
in the sky, Lord,
in the sky."

Michael's tenor resounds in the midnight air. The other pickers and singers join him in a repeat of the chorus of that universal finale for music of rural persuasion. Wildwood Flower, The New Squirrel Hollow Puddle Jumpers and the other gospel and string bands crowd the stage and invite the audience to join in. Most of us comply. Several feet behind me I hear Millie's rusty soprano. As I turn in surprise, she smiles uncertainly as the music ends.

"I come to tell the boys that I set the rollaway beds up in the cabin," she says, moving toward me through the noisy crowd. Rosie and the rest of the band hear her and look up.

"Momma," Rosie says in delight and steps off the platform to hug her mother's neck. "I'm so glad you came. How long've you been standing there."

"About an hour," Millie tells her. "I wanted to tell you and Ell and the boys and Sam, and Clettus if they're interested, that I'm serving a country breakfast at 11:00 tomorrow morning. That ought to give a bunch of night owl musicians time for their beauty sleep."

"We'll be there," Gabe tells her. "I may have to lock Ell in the closet so I can eat some of it. I doubt that biscuits and sawmill gravy are anywhere on my doctor's list of food choices." He puts his arm around me to show he appreciates my concern.

"A few bites if you eat carrots and celery the rest of the day," I tell him sweetly.

Sam, Clettus and a crew of helpers are cleaning up and closing down. They wave us away when we try to help. Michael, Rosie, Gabe and I escort Millie through the woods back to the farmhouse. Charlie and Curtis head to their van for the drive back to Birmingham.

"Make Sam and Clettus shut the living room door or their snorin'll blow you clean out of the cabin," Millie advises Gabe and Michael as she bids us goodnight.

"She used to hold Daddy's nose when he snored," Rosie says as she and I and the menfolk perch on Millie's front steps. "But he got her back. Not too long before he got sick, he borrowed my tape recorder and made a tape of her snoring and played it back to her. She got mad at first, but then she thought it was funny."

"Your Momma's a good lady," Michael says, kissing Rosie on top of her head. "She's not too subtle about reminding us of proper sleeping arrangements for unmarried couples though, is she?"

"There'll be no fornicating if Mildred Frazier Culp has anything to say about it," Rosie says, laughing as she pulls Michael's mouth to hers. Following their kiss, she says, "There's always tomorrow, Love of my Life. Sherman's bringing the girls back to Birmingham late tomorrow night. They've got something going on that lasts through most of Sunday night."

"Good things come to he who waits," Michael says and heads off through the woods to the cabin. Rosie goes up on the porch and sits down on the swing.

"The same code of conduct applies to us, O Anxious One," I say to Gabe, who is fondling my breast as he kisses my neck.

"And she's not even your Momma," Gabe says, pretending to be very sad. We walk entwined to the wood's edge.

"Are we still on for the picnic in the cemetery?" I ask him. "I think Millie'll let us take some flowers from her garden." Gabe and I plan a small outing to Cedarwood Cemetery to visit my parents' and Grace Ann's graves.

"Leaving on time to arrive by 2:00, I believe," he says. "See you at the breakfast table," he says and touches my hair as he moves off into the darkness. Sam's outdoor light shines a dim path.

When I return to the Culp front porch, Rosie is still swinging and humming to herself. "Want to sit here awhile with me?" She asks. "I'm not the least bit sleepy."

Truthfully, I could climb into the big feather bed in Millie's back bedroom and sleep until midweek, but instead I select a rocker on the dark front porch. "Tell me the coolest thing you know," I say, echoing one of Grace Ann's most repeated phrases from high school days.

"Hmmm," she muses for a minute. "I guess that would have to be that I conditionally accepted Michael's proposal earlier today."

"Rosie, oh my God! Are you sure?"

"Chill, as Cassie would say," Rosie tells me quietly. "You need to hear the conditions: that we wait six months or so to make it public, that Cassie and Molly have to be okay with it, and that all of us go to counseling before we make it legal."

"That sounds terribly romantic," I tease her. "Did you shake hands on it?"

"And you'd do it altogether differently, Ms. Sensible Soul?" She shoots back.

"Most likely not," I concede. "Well, future congratulations, then."

"Thank you," Rosie says. "It's important that the girls feel right about it. They've really started feeling like the apartment is home to them and I don't want to wreck that. Cassie wasn't even too bent out of shape when she figured out Sherman and I won't be getting back together. She just said, 'At least I can stay at the same school and we won't have to move away from Aunt Ell.' She's a lot happier than she was for awhile."

"Well, you know the girls like Michael," I say. "Just make sure you time it right."

"God, I wonder what would have happened if Fred hadn't killed Grace Ann and Tanner and the baby and they had gotten married like they were planning? Ree and Harley, Jr., would probably have to babysit alot while Grace Ann and Tanner did their thing."

"Tanner did seem as hypnotized by Grace Ann as Bud ever was, I agree. That ability to totally enrapture a man is certainly beyond my comprehension. There wasn't anything anybody male wouldn't do for Grace Ann up until the time she died."

"Tell me about it," Rosie says. She is quiet for a few minutes and then says, "Did you know that one time she and Sherman did the, uh, horizontal hop, as Michael sometimes calls it? It was the summer right after we graduated." She pushes the porch swing with one foot and waits for my reaction.

"Not for certain," I tell her. "Fred said something one time about Sherman trying to go with Grace Ann, but I wasn't sure he was telling the truth. How did you find out about it?"

"Sherman told me himself, right in the middle of an argument. It was back about a year or so after Bud got sent to Atmore. Grace Ann had already taken off for the Wild West by that time. Sherman was stomping mad at me about something, I can't remember what, and he threw that in my face. At first he made it seem like a really big deal, but later when he apologized for it, he said it only happened once. And that they were both ashamed of it. It was when I was off with Daddy and Uncle Sam, singing and playing with whoever would let us. Bud was already in Basic and getting ready to go to Viet Nam. It probably happened while neither one of them was paying much attention. Grace Ann always had to feel like everybody was wild about her. I doubt Sherman took much persuading. It was hard for me to feel the same about Grace Ann though, after I found that out. I know it was one thing that made me start thinking about leaving

Sherman, but then I got pregnant with Caitlin. I tried to forget about it, but I'm not sure I did."

"It was before you were married," I remind her. "Were ya'll even engaged then?"

"No, he didn't give me the ring until that September and then we got married the next spring. It's just that I thought I was his one and only. He was certainly mine until Michael."

"At least they saw their mistake and didn't make it worse," I say. "Two takers like Sherman and Grace Ann wouldn't have lasted a month. It might have suited Fred, though. He always thought a lot of Sherman."

"Where do you reckon Fred's gone off to?" Rosie asks as she continues to swing. "I turned on the radio a few minutes ago when you were still with Gabe, but they've not found him yet. I hope they get him back quick before something else happens. Ree and Harley, Jr., have had enough upset."

We talk more of the Reeses and the Hardamans. Rosie feels like Bud and the twins should move away from Milltown and start over again. I feel like their only chance as a family is here where it all started and where it has to carry on. We end the long night as Rosie recounts her encounter with SYT.

"I didn't plan to get out of the car at Minnie Beth's when we dropped the girls off," she says. "But they wanted me to come in with them, so Michael waited in the car. Susan was sitting in Sherman's lap at Minnie Beth's kitchen table, feeding him peach ice cream. He about dumped her in the floor trying to get up from the table when he saw me and the girls. She was still wearing those short shorts that rode halfway up her butt and hung down below her navel. When he introduced us, I thought she was going to shake my arm off. Then she started in on how adorable the girls are. I think she thought Helen and Meaghan are ours, too. Sherman was still straightening that out when I left. But at least she's polite and seems kind of sweet. Peggy Ann Prewitt wouldn't give me or the girls the time of day when she was living at our old house with Sherman. Things may be looking up for old Sherman Lee."

Cedarwood Cemetery is green and blooming in the April sunshine. On a tiny hilltop in a deep valley of south DeKalb County, the small country graveyard is old, but well tended. Its church once served as a focal point for Cedarwood community activities. Some years ago, the old white clapboard Cedarwood Community Church was moved a few hundred feet up the road to be preserved as a historic site. The new brick and red frame building that replaced it opens its doors to any churchgoers without a building. Its back quarters are home to the local chapter of the Masons. When Gabe and I arrive shortly after 2:00, we park in a grove of twisted cedars where the hill crests. There is no one around as we get out of the car and walk down the graveled path leading to the dirt road in front of the cemetery.

"I want to show you the old church," I say to Gabe as we head up the road. "My father's people grew up around here. A preacher from that church baptized my grandmother in the creek that runs behind the cemetery."

"I've heard tales of creek baptisms," Gabe says as he takes my hand in his. "Dad's from North Georgia. As in hill country, shades of 'Deliverance,' North Georgia. He never wanted to go back, but he talked about it a lot. He was actually baptized in a creek like that. One of those communal things where everybody wears white. There's a picture of it that hangs in the dining room at their house."

A few cars zoom by us, heading for the two lane blacktop nearby that leads to Cross Roads Drag Race Strip. On quiet afternoons here, you can hear the roaring engines and squealing fans. There's a special section of Cedarwood Cemetery allotted to victims of the many fatal accidents at Cross Roads.

The church sits at the edge of a huge field where cotton once grew. Its owner now raises soybeans and is said to be one of the few farmers in this part of the county to make a decent profit when harvest time ends. A glass encased sign at the church's entrance reads, "Cedarwood Community Church, established 1871 by Rev. Fuller T. Goode and the Cedarwood Community." Its door is unlocked and we step inside. Rows of polished oak pews gleam in the light shining through the stained glass windows. The altar, pulpit, baptismal pool and tiny choir loft are roped off.

As I settle into the front row, I say, "Empty churches are still holy places. Can you feel the love and the reverence that must have settled into this little church?"

"I think I can," Gabe answers. "Do people get married here any more? Or is it no longer for public use?"

"I couldn't say," I tell him. "Why, are you thinking of it for Michael and Rosie in the near distant future?"

"No, Miss Ellott, ma'am, I had it more in mind for you and yours truly at some duly appointed hour." He smiles and turns my face toward his, gazing deep into my astonished eyes.

"Not yet, darlin', but later when I've got this diabetes bear back in the cage. I have to see how that's going to play out. I don't want you to get stuck with a blind man or one with missing appendages."

"Blindness might be an asset if my body continues its outwardly mobile trend," I say in a haze of pleasant delirium. Me, married?

"I would say that just makes more of you for me to love, but instead I'll quote you a line from old Ed. Sir Edmund Spenser, that is. Noted suck-up to Good Queen Bess the First. '...for the soul the body form doth take, for soul is form and doth the body make.' You've got so much soul, babe, that your body is just trying to accommodate it all." He winks and gives me a hug across my shoulders.

"Why, you Silver Tongued Person of the Demonic Persuasion," I say returning his embrace. "I may paste that on top of my scales."

"I recommend it," he says. "But what's your answer to my meandering declaration of undying love?"

"You know it's yes," I say. "I expect there's world enough and time for two middle-aged baby boomers to get things right before the knot is tied." We spend some time in the little church talking about our plans.

The cross on the altar catches a light ray from the open doors as we leave the church. At my urging, we journey down the road, past farmhouses and planted fields to the little country store at the road's end. We buy cartons of milk and some fruit to supplement our picnic. The ice filled soft drink box still occupies a back corner of the store. Its interior has altered little from all those years ago when my father and I would rush in on Sunday afternoon while Mother waited in the car for her Grape Ne-Hi.

Returning to Cedarwood Cemetery, we spread our blankets underneath a spreading magnolia. As I open the basket and spread our picnic before us, I hear a low moaning from the other side of the graveyard.

"I can't hear anything," Gabe says when I mention it to him. After years of various instruments, fretted and non, blasting his eardrums to dust, I am surprised he can hear at all. It's fortunate diabetes does not affect the auditory senses.

"When our marriage made in Purgatory does come to pass..." Gabe begins after a chomp of celery.

"Why made in purgatory?"

"According to Brother J and Brother Tony, Purgatory's a good place, a place of purification. It's where most people end up for a time before they get to the perfect place, Heaven. So, it seems to me that the union of a late thirty-something bachelor with some androgynous traits and a fortyish spinster librarian who was married for ten minutes twenty years ago is probably not perfection, but close enough."

"Okay then, proceed."

"What I want to say, is there anything we should do about the patter of little feet? Although any life emanating from the two of us who sport double digit shoe sizes wouldn't have small feet for long."

"Gabe, honey," I say, flattered but laughing a little. "My biological clock is due to strike 13 any time now. I don't know that a first baby's advisable for a woman past 40."

"Oh, deary me, and Amelia Gayle Pace has been waiting for grandchildren since Michael and I got out of college," he laments, sighing overly dramatically.

"She'll have three ready made ones when Michael and Rosie tie the knot," I tell him. "Although from what I understand, that won't be anytime real soon."

"She'll have to make do then," Gabe says. "I feel like those kids are part mine anyway. Especially Molly and Caitlin. Cassie is fast approaching that hateful teeny bopper stage that turned me against women for yea, these many years."

"Did some mean teen queen break your tender heart?" I ask him as I pass him some of the fat-and-sugar-free cake I packed for us.

"Any number of them," Gabe answers. "That's really when I started thinking I must be gay. Until you, I never was around a woman I could be comfortable with romantically. But, truth be told, I wasn't intimate with that many men. Ian and a few others. Really."

"It's not as though I'm asking you, 'How Many Arms Have Held You?'" I say firmly. "As the lyricist wrote, 'I really don't want to know.'"

"You're not worried that the DC might become AC again?"

"No, that's not really a concern," I answer truthfully. "Your use of moldy euphemisms is more troubling than that."

"Why, exactly?"

"Because, Gabriel Pace, we fit. And I hesitate to use invoke this overused phrase, we're soul-mates."

"Why, lawsy me, Miss Scarlett, I do believe you're right," Gabe says, leaning over to kiss me and smear my mouth with sugar free icing.

We spend the remainder of the afternoon weeding and planting flowers on my parents' graves. As the sun grows lower in the April sky, we then seek out headstones for rubbings from the upper left-hand side of Cedarwood Cemetery. One Civil War soldier's grave proves particularly difficult, but we keep at it until we get an imprint of the unusual military symbols etched into the granite. It sits on the farthest edge of the graveyard and when we head hand in hand back toward the Cherokee, the sun is nearly set.

"Stop, Ell," Gabe says, suddenly. "There's something in the grass over there at one of the graves."

"God, Gabe, it looks like somebody," I say as I squint at the form on the ground near Grace Ann's grave.

Pushing me firmly back, Gabe runs ahead to check it out. "Jesus, Mary and Joseph," he yells. "I think it's Fred Hardaman, darlin', and he's not moving."

Gabe is kneeling beside Fred by the time I reach them. He lies face up, sprawled across Grace Ann's grave. Blood from two bullet wounds permeates the front of his prison coveralls. He does not draw a breath. He clutches a pistol in his right hand. Gabe says that he cannot feel a pulse, but that one of us should go down the road to the little store and call 911.

"I'll go, babe," he says. "Unless it bothers you to stay here with him." He is already moving quickly toward the car, looking back anxiously at me.

"I'll be all right," I say to him and begin to cry. "Fred finally caught up with himself and what he did and it was just too much for him."

Hours must have passed since he fired the bullets into his chest wall. Gabe or I would have heard the shots. His mouth gapes wide and slack. And in death, his eyes are open, staring into eternity. Fred Hardaman did not end his life with ease or dignity, reflecting, perhaps, his last year on earth. I sit down in the dirt beside him to wait for the paramedics to come.

It is not long before Gabe is back beside me, holding me against him. In due time, the small cemetery is covered over in police cars and ambulances. Sergeant Bob Tolson steps from his car.

"I've been expecting this," he says. "But I just didn't know where it would happen. We even searched up here earlier this morning, but Fred must have been somewhere else, biding his time. When did you all get here?"

"Around 2:00," Gabe answers, keeping his arms around me. "How was it he got out in the first place?"

"That's not been determined yet," Sgt. Tolson says. "I can't get anybody to tell me the truth, but we'll find out. Did ya'll not see Fred until just now?"

"I reckon he must have hid himself pretty well. We didn't come across him 'til right before I called," Gabe says. "We thought we were up here by ourselves all afternoon. When we were eating lunch, Ell said she thought she heard something coming from the other side of the cemetery, but I didn't hear it and then we didn't hear anything else. Poor old man. I guess he had to finish it out."

"We've had men watching his house and Grace Ann's trailer and his places of business," Bob tells us. "It's hard to see how he got this far on foot, but like I said, we checked it out earlier today. You say ya'll been up here the whole afternoon?"

"We have," I say, emerging from Gabe's protective embrace. "But we walked down the road for a good long while and then when we came back, we stayed over here on this side. But back over there on the right side, there's an old closed up outhouse near the edge of the woods. That's where I thought I heard the noise coming from."

"You all want to walk over there with me?" Bob asks us.

Police, Sheriff's deputies and state troopers swarm the graveyard with flashlights and equipment. Two medical examiners continue to work over Fred's body. At Bob's urging, Gabe and I show him the way to the outhouse. This is probably his polite effort to get us out of harm's way. In the light of Bob's high beam lantern, we see drops of blood that speckle the gravel behind the church. We move down the slope to the cinder block outhouses. The boarding has been prized away from the front of the left building.

"Looks like where he was, all right," Bob says. "Let's go back so I can get somebody else over here. If you can stand it awhile longer, I've got a few more things I need to ask you." We follow him back to his patrol car. Men are lifting Fred onto a gurney. They secure his body inside the ambulance and drive away.

It is fully dark as we sit under the dome light in Sgt. Tolson's back seat. As he records our account of the afternoon, I watch the other policemen and deputies pack up and move on. Soon only the three of us are left. His voice drones placidly through endless questions. Gabe provides most of the answers. All I can think of is Fred lying there and hope that his blood did not spill on the ground where Grace Ann and her baby are at rest.

Chapter Twenty-Five

My mother was scared silly of the ocean. Any body of water deeper than mid-calf made her more than uneasy. I was almost nine before she allowed me to participate in swimming lessons at Milltown Community Pool. For six weeks of the next three summers, she sat on a poolside bench nervously clutching her purse while I perfected the jellyfish and the butterfly stroke.

Her hydrophobia precluded family vacations to Panama City or Gulf Shores. Once, however, when I was four after my father's insistence that his only offspring should at least see the ocean, we set out for Myrtle Beach, South Carolina. An outbreak of the polio virus in that area rerouted us to the Great Smokies. And for the remainder of my childhood, any of our infrequent family excursions were to the mountains of the Volunteer State.

Because it was forbidden territory, for a time in my teens I obsessed over the sand and surf. Miss Vancene shared my mother's view on seaside ventures. Fred's many business concerns did not allow him large periods of leisure time. So, Grace Ann, Rosie and I listened to stacks of Beach Boy recordings and faithfully attended double features of "Beach Blanket Bingo," and "How to Stuff a Wild Bikini."

In the summers after we were legally allowed to drive, Grace Ann, Rosie and I would pack the black and yellow Skylark and burn the highway toward Lake Rhea, a longtime teen hangout in the lower reaches of

Caloosa County. Its owners regularly sanded the banks and kept the water reasonably sanitary. They also stuffed the indoor jukebox with Top 40's from various years, blaring its contents to an appreciative audience of swimmers and sunbathers. Surrounded by acres of woods and picnic grounds, Lake Rhea also sported an indoor dance hall—a part of the long concrete building that ran the length of the lake—where fledgling Rock-and-Roll bands rattled the rafters on Saturday nights. The Milltown Threesome spent many a pleasant Saturday in that spot, long since closed and made into a landfill site. Toasting ourselves to a light pink by day, we applied coats of Noxema when evening came and slipped into our clothes without too much pain to listen to the discordant Battles of the Bands. Rosie and I sat on the low benches that lined the walls while Grace Ann danced with carefully chosen partners until she grew tired of it and we left for home.

When even these distractions did not entirely satisfy our longing for the beach, we would walk several blocks to the viaduct beneath I-59. We knew the hours when fleets of truckers passed through. If you shut your eyes, the echoes from the rush of the diesel engines sounded like the ebb and flow of ocean waves.

In our senior year, we were allowed to accompany our class to PC—Panama City. We resided in Peek's Motel for three days and tripped the light fantastic on the Miracle Strip—an array of amusement park rides and souvenir shops—when not basking in the bright white sand and water green with seaweed. Overexposure to the sand and sea fricasseed my lily-white skin on the first day out. I spent the second day dip coated in sunburn ointment, miserable and shivering inside our tiny room with the window unit air conditioner. I ventured back outside on the final day, swathed in terry cloth to sit under the giant beach umbrellas and watch my classmates.

Perhaps because of that, I have not made a return visit to the Sea, the Beautiful Sea. My University years proved too busy with the allure of intellectual pursuit. My friends at that time scorned the beach as too middle class, preferring backpacking jaunts to state parks and primitive camping in the woods. Adult working life at Athena Villa Public Library does afford me a few weeks a year, but I tend to fill them with short trips to other interesting places within driving distance.

Several weeks ago Mabel June decided definitely to quit Paradise Dry Cleaning and Laundry, invest her savings and retirement, and hitch her star to the Down Yonder Music Store and Cafe Emporium. Her last day will be in mid-June and Rosie claimed the first two weeks for R and R before assuming the proffered manager's position. I arranged my time off to coincide and we began a lengthy discussion on where to make our retreat. Cassie and Molly, who have only twice experienced the wonders of the ocean, begged for a return trip. We settled finally on Gulf Shores, reserving an ocean front cabin at the Low Tide Family Resort. Early on this first Saturday of June, we pack the Cherokee for our imminent departure.

"I told Molly what you said about taking so much stuff, but she didn't pay me any attention," Cassie informs me as she hands me her own three bags.

"Imagine that," I say as I stand in the parking lot in front of the apartment building, rearranging bundles in the back of the car. "You girls need to make sure Caitlin's sunscreen is where we can all find it. I want us all to be conscious of keeping every inch of her covered in it. You girls need to wear some, too."

"I already have some tan," Cassie says. "Me and Meaghan's been laying out by the pool at their condo for a long time."

"It's different at the beach, though," I say, but she does not hear me as she runs up the steps and back inside to hurry her sister.

Rosie emerges with Caitlin's playpen, which will serve as a travel bed. "Are we really taking that cell phone Gabe and Michael got for us? I thought after all the tacky comments you've made about 'idiot drivers blabbing away while tires screech around them,' that you would hide it in the closet or something."

"They have the number," I tell her. "And they plan to call us once or twice on the way if we don't report in. But you've got to talk while I'm driving. I do draw the line there."

"That seems a little over cautious on their part, but I'm not complaining," she says. "Are we about ready? I told Michael we'd be at the store by 9:00."

Down Yonder is hosting a barbeque cook-off and fiddler's contest on this sunny day in June. Hailed as "all male, good music, and good eatin'," the day-long event is the talk of Southside. Its oddity seems to appeal. The multicultural, gender-blending Southside of the Magic City that I have called home for most of the past two decades scoots over and makes room for anything different. The seemingly redneck nature of the day's event gives it a campy allure. Gabe and Michael's good business reputation is a dead giveaway that nothing too culturally insensitive will occur.

A gathering of men—old, young, Black, white, Latino and Asian—spent Friday night grilling meat on the pits behind the store. Other competitors will bring in their delectables for the taste testing which begins at 11:00. After the ribbons are awarded for the best all around BBQ and everyone is full as the tick on the proverbial hound dog, the fiddling will commence. Even Sam and Clettus are due to drop by.

"Does everybody have everything she needs or wants for the next two weeks?" I ask, ready to slam the back of the car shut.

Rosie and Cassie answer in the affirmative. Molly then emerges, carrying a beach-ready Caitlin, attired in swim suit, terry cloth beach coat with matching hat, tiny sandals and a pair of Molly's sunglasses.

"Caty beach," she announces proudly as Rosie buckles her into the carseat. Over the past few weeks, the girls have read her endless Chubby Books with beach related themes. "Bye-bye," she waves to the apartment complex as I pull out of the parking space.

"I wish Meaghan could go with us," Cassie says to her mother with a pout. "Her mother said she could."

"For the last time, Cassandra Lee, no," Rosie tells her. "This is my vacation, too, and I'm not going to spend it being responsible for someone else's child. You can survive for two weeks with just the five of us. I'm sure there will be other kids your age at the Low Tide. It is a family motel."

"Oh, right. They'll probably be six and under. Nobody 13 goes by herself with her family on vacation. Maybe Molly will have a good time."

"I am not six and under," Molly informs her. "I was seven three weeks ago. And, so what if there's nobody your age or even my age there. We're going to the beach, Cassie. The beach! We haven't been since I was four. Stop being a whiny butt." She glances at Rosie, who frowns at her word choice. "Grandmomma Minnie Beth says it," she tells her. "She said it to Daddy the last time we stayed at her house."

"Daddy says she's letting her tongue slip now that she's getting older," Cassie confides. "She calls Susan Miss Hot-to-Trot when she wears short shorts. And Grandmomma says Daddy needs to wake up and smell the coffee. That women Susan's age only date men Daddy's age so they can get them to buy them things. She says..."

"Never mind, Cassie," Rosie tells her. "I'm sure if Minnie Beth wanted that repeated, she'd have told me herself. That's your Daddy's and Susan's business, not mine or yours. Or Minnie Beth's for that matter."

"Why doesn't Daddy just get his own apartment?" Molly asks, sensibly. "Then he and Grandmomma wouldn't have to get mad at each other."

We consider this as Cassie turns her attention to the stack of CD's on the floor in front of her, pops one in her DiscMan and shuts us out as she slips the earphones into place. Molly and Caitlin are playing with the Barnyard See N' Say, Caitlin being partial to the mooing of the cow.

The Down Yonder parking lot is full up and I do not find a parking space until halfway down the block. We enter to find tasting stations with warming plates set up throughout the music store and restaurant area. Mabel June waves to us from her post in the kitchen as she stirs a pot of sauce. Beside her, Brother J chips fragrant meat away from the bone and places it on a platter.

"Welcome to Hillbilly Heaven," Brother Tony says as he comes in from the alley. "Barbecued pig and Country Music. And that's what I like about the South." He is wearing a checked shirt and bib overalls for the occasion.

"Where are your white socks?" I ask him. "You can't be a genuine Son of the South without 'em."

He lifts his pants leg to show me he has complied.

"The Beach Bunnies have arrived," Gabe says to Michael as they come in the back door. "Any last words for the fans at home before you hit the road for the Redneck Riviera."

"Only a word of caution to one of the home folks in particular who needs to take care of himself and stay out of the barbecue and beer," I say, walking across the room to his side.

"I'll see to that little item," Mabel June says from the kitchen. "I've done caught him trying to sample my sauce, but I don't expect he'll be trying that again anytime soon." She smiles with triumphant satisfaction in Gabe's direction. "Am I right?"

"Yes, ma'am, Boss Lady! I has learned my lesson," Gabe shakes his hands and rolls his eyes in mock terror.

"What did she do?" I ask him as we walk through the store. Men with plates of barbecue and sauce are setting up their stations. Michael is fixing a plate of samples for Rosie and the girls.

"Cracked my knuckles with that wooden spoon she's stirring with," Gabe says. "I thought for a minute she'd broken a finger. I only wanted a taste."

"Her intentions are good," I say. "And you know you wouldn't stop with a taste. Where is that barbecued chicken with the sugar free sauce we fixed last night?"

"I've got it in the refrigerator," he assures me. "I'll be all right, darlin', except for missing you. Today we'll be too busy for me to have food cravings. If everybody who's called about this thing shows up, we'll be tastin' and fiddlin' til sometime next week."

"Should be great for business," I say as I signal to Rosie and the girls to head back for the car. "We need to head 'em up and move 'em out, dear Man of Mine. Give the Old Lady a proper goodbye'"

Gabe plants a deep soul kiss on me and Michael is clinging to Rosie across the room. "Goodness," I say. "You two act like we're going off for six months."

"Goodness has nothing to do with it," Gabe quips. "It's a little more carnal than that."

"Hmmm," I smile at him, tracing my finger over his face. "Save it up, Sweetie. A little deprivation is good for the soul."

The Pace Brothers accompany us down the street to the tightly packed Cherokee. Michael lifts Caitlin high and swings her around. She squeals with pleasure. "Caty, bye-bye. Beach," she tells him as he fastens her into the carseat. "Bye-bye, Mi-kee."

Michael is so pleased that he kisses the top of her head. "She said my name, Rose. When did she start doing that?"

"Just this week," Rosie tells him. "Her vocabulary's expanding again. For awhile, all she would say is a word or two or worse just point and grunt at what she wanted. Cassie and Molly were letting her get by with it and doing whatever she wanted, but I stopped all that and made her tell us what she wants."

"Now she can say lots of words, can't you, Caty?" Molly says to her sister as she climbs across her and buckles herself into the back seat. "Who's that?" She asks, pointing to Gabe.

"Ga-ee," the baby says, solemnly. "Big man."

We all laugh at this. Rosie and I kiss our men good-bye a final time and get into the front seat. On the other side of Caitlin in the back seat, Cassie reattaches the DiscMan to her ears. Everyone waves until we round the corner.

"Think they'll bring out the topless dancers once we're on the road good?" Rosie asks a little while later as we head into Shelby County.

"They'll probably save that for tonight, after all the beer and BBQ are gone," I say.

We ride in comfortable silence for several miles, past the elite suburbs of Shelby County and into the rural area. Our trip is not a hurried one. I chose the two-lane route down Highway 31 deliberately to ease us into a relaxed vacation state of mind.

"What was it you were saying last night about Zaia-Danda?" Rosie asks me. "You said something while we were helping the boys get all that meat on the grill, but I wasn't sure I caught it all."

"She came by the library for a few minutes yesterday," I tell her. "She and her brother Joe and that whole group that was living in the house across from the high school are packing up and moving to Gainesville, Florida. Joe hooked up with some people on the Internet who want to give them financial backing in exchange for part interest in their business. New Age activities are pretty heavy down that way."

"Did Bud ever find out exactly how much Zaia-Danda helped him when he was on the run?" Rosie asks me.

"She didn't say," I tell her. "I don't think Bud's been by to see them since he got back. He's been pretty busy getting to know his kids again. And he's been helping John out a little with his shop. I called Ree last week to see if she wanted to come to the programs we're having at the library at the end of the month. Charlotte's coming back for another seminar. Ree told me about her Daddy's activities."

"Sherman said he's not had any luck getting Bud to come back to work for him," Rosie says. "Bud doesn't have to be in any particular hurry, I don't guess. At least Fred's dying did that much for the twins and him."

Fred's will left all of his money, real estate holdings, stocks and businesses to Bud, Ree and Harley, Jr. They plan to sell the house in Milltown and buy a tract of land in the Hollow near the Reeses. Fred's lawyers are still working out the details, negotiating the sale of his many business concerns and seeing that his investments are secured. Ree, Harley, Jr., and Bud are well provided for.

"I can't forget what Ree said at Fred's funeral," Rosie says. "That's probably the best thing anybody could ever say about Fred Hardaman."

Eight months after his daughter and her unborn baby were buried, they laid Fred Hardaman in the grave beside them. As he was put to rest between Grace Ann and Ma 'Ree, genuine mourners and nosy spectators packed the hillside at Cedarwood Cemetery. Brother Anson spoke a few words but left the body of funeral for testimonials by Fred's survivors.

Only Ree chose to step to the podium. She said in a soft voice that carried across the brightly blooming graveyard, "Fred Hardaman was my Granddad. He was not a bad man. When Harley and I wanted anything, all we had to do was mention it to Granddad and he would get it for us. He let us live in his house and cared for us when our Momma and Daddy weren't there. He loved us. He loved our Momma, but it made him angry when she wouldn't do what he wanted her to. His anger got bigger than his love and that's what killed him. I want everybody here to remember Granddad as the man who dressed up like Santa Claus and gave out candy canes and new quarters at Christmas time. And who gave enough money for many years for the Seers High School Band to make out of town trips. Think about those things when you think of Fred Hardaman."

Many tears were shed at Grace Ann's graveside all those months ago, but few were shed for her father. A silence of regret and relief pervaded his funeral rites. Only a modest offering of flowers topped the newly dug grave. Milltown, I think, is still too stunned by it all. Forgiveness is yet to be born.

"Bud didn't have a word to say that day," Rosie says as I stop the car at the only light for the last several miles. "But he never let go of Ree's hand until she stood up to talk about her granddaddy."

"Minnie Beth's been taking flowers to his grave," she continues. "Sherman told me that. I expect they're the only ones he'll get besides Ree and Harley, Jr.'s."

"Do you think Sherman and Minnie Beth are headed for a major blow-up?" I ask her. In the back, Molly is curled against the door, asleep. Caitlin nods in her carseat. Beneath the DiscMan, Cassie's eyes are closed as she nods in time to the music.

"Could be," Rosie answers. "Like Molly said, Sherman needs to get his own place. He's too old to be living with his Momma again."

"That can work all right," I say. "Joseph and his sisters never seem to have much trouble, but then they've never known anything different. Did I mention Joseph's reaction when he overheard me talking to Emmeleine about Gabe and me."

"No," Rosie says. "Did he offer to furnish the trousseau? He's the most generous man I've ever seen."

"I don't believe he'll be doing that," I say. "He actually seemed somewhat hurt and a little jealous. I did some fast-talking and told him he'll always be my 'work husband', so to speak, and that seemed to help a little. We've never been anything but friends, so I guess I'm a little puzzled by his response."

"He probably daydreams about you a lot," Rosie says. "What did Emmeleine think about you and Gabe?"

"Oh, Emmeleine's really a romantic at heart," I tell her. "I've even caught her reading some of the better written romance writers, like Georgette Heyer, from time to time. She predicts a happy ending for one and all. The day I was telling her all this was right after Eleanor and Perri-Young staged one of their famous public duels and she needed a little diversion."

"Oh, tell me, tell me," Rosie says in delight. "What was it about this time? What New Age event does Perri-Young want to bring to Athena Villa for the summer?"

"Their fight's not over philosophy this time," I tell her. "It's moved to the homefront. Merilee, Handy's daughter, wants to spend the summer back-packing in Europe. Perri-Young wants her to take two more courses so she can graduate on time next spring. Eleanor accused Perri of just wanting to get Merilee out of Handy's house. And Handy's doing his usual back-off bugaloo. Merilee's ignoring all of them and packing her bags."

"Sounds a lot like Sherman and Minnie Beth's situation," Rosie says. "People mixing in where they've got no business. Wonder how we manage to avoid that, living like we do?"

"Probably because we're both so busy taking care of our own lives, there's not time to intrude," I say. "Besides that, we're family—you and I and the girls."

"We are that," Rosie agrees. "A lot more so, in some ways, than when Sherman and the girls and I were together." She touches my shoulder, allowing her hand to remain there in companionable affection as we watch the Cherokee lap the miles past Thorsby and Verbena.

"Beach, Mommy?" Caitlin wakes from her nap to inquire.

"No, baby, not yet," Rosie tells her.

"Caty beach," she insists loudly, squirming in her car seat.

"Yes, Caty beach," I assure her. "But not right now. Later on."

Molly stirs then and finds a book to read to her little sister. Cassie reaches into the cooler for drinks.

As we near Montgomery, Molly says to her mother, "Momma, is this where we drove for so long that time hunting that cemetery, when Daddy got so mad at you?"

"Yes, honey, it is," Rosie tells her and turns to me. "One time, two years or so ago, Sherman had to come down here to buy some automobile parts for the garage from some man who was going out of business. The girls and I came with him. Before we left I asked him if we could drive out to the cemetery where Hank Williams is buried. And we got lost. We drove for two hours and we never got there. Sherman would not stop and ask for directions if his life depended on it. I haven't seen Hank's grave since I was a teenager and Daddy and Uncle Sam took me there. It's incredible. Nearly as fancy as Elvis's."

"We'll go by there on the way back through," I promise her. The girls are clamoring for lunch and I look for a place to stop.

The sad and untimely deaths of two white working class Southern male musicians is hardly the ideal focus for this pleasant day in June. But Hank Williams and the King once won me a victory luncheon at the Highlands Bar and Grill. A few years after Elvis died, Andy Swayne and I coordinated a seminar on Southern culture for the county-wide library system. Funded by the state humanities foundation, it encompassed all aspects of life in Dixie—from magnolias to moon pies. A number of well-known scholars, local and regional, were in the lineup. The music scholar, however—a prissy little man from the University in Huntsville whom Andy engaged—refused to give more than a passing reference to Country Music. He chose instead to devote most of his part of the seminar to Dixieland Jazz and to the works by such popular composers as Johnny Mercer and Stephen Collins Foster. He totally ignored the quite influential Rockabilly movement that is a main Rock-and-Roll precursor if ever there was one.

At the time I was no great proponent of the rural music tradition and its many offshoots, but I was appalled at the man's deliberate omission, attributing it to class snobbery. Andy's defense of him—strictly for the sake of the kind of rhetorical gymnastics he excels at—was the lack, at that time, of a body of written scholarship on that kind of music. I countered that if the man had been truly interested in a well-rounded program, he'd have made the effort to find some. Andy then bet me that I couldn't produce a single piece of scholarly material to back up my claim and that if I did, he would treat me to lunch at a restaurant of my choosing.

An extensive search of various Humanities Index volumes resulted in my locating an article in a fairly well-known music history journal, which was titled, "The Hillbilly Cat and the Hillbilly Shakespeare: Elvis and Hank on the Highway to Heaven." It pointed out similarities in the youths of Hank and Elvis—poverty, strong mothers, the influence of blues and other forms of black music. "Poor Southern white boys with restless feet and a song in their hearts, King Hiram 'Hank' Williams and Elvis Aron Presley took hold of popular music and swung it around like a dead cat, until, miraculously, they brought it back to life," the article began. I read that line several times to Andy as I savored every mouthful of Shrimp Tempura. I even ordered dessert so I could enjoy his concession just awhile longer.

"Did I mention that Andy Swayne stopped by the library last week, too?" I ask Rosie as we pull into a Shoney's Restaurant on the far side of Montgomery.

"No, but I want to hear," she says as we herd the girls inside and wait for the hostess to seat us.

"Caty ice cream," Caitlin tells the waitress a few minutes later from her high chair.

"I will certainly bring you some ice cream, Little Doll," the older woman cooes at her. "But I bet Momma would like for you to have some mashed potatoes and chicken to start off with. They get a kid's meal free if they're under six," she says to Rosie.

The rest of us order and I continue my tale about Andy. "His wife is letting Andy Jr., stay the whole summer with his dad. And Andy's coaching his little league team. They came in late one afternoon and were dressed out for the game."

"So, how's his love life?" Rosie asks as the waitress sets our meals before us.

"You know, he didn't even mention it," I say. "He and his son were too anxious to tell me about the other players and which would have the best game and so on. I pretended to know what they were talking about, but you know how sports challenged I am. Andy looked the best I've seen him in quite some time. A lot less full of himself and his preoccupations."

"Sherman can actually be that way sometimes now when he's been with the girls for long stretches at a time," Rosie says and sips her tea. "This Susan thing will probably run its course. And if it doesn't, that's all right, too."

When dinner is eaten and we are back on the road again, all three girls nod off before we reach Butler County, Hank's home turf. In my college years, country music experienced one of its ubiquitous surges in the mainstream musical forefront. My dorm mates and I would listen to old 45's and LP's of Old Hank and his Drifting Cowboys. Half the musical universe has probably recorded a Hank Williams number, but there's always something so very intimate that emerges when an artist records his own music. The high-pitched wailing of that skinny white boy can soak the soul. But in film clips of his performances, he lacks the high-voltage stage presence of the King. Then he's just a common stock country boy, paler than pale, filling up the audience with his pain.

From Montgomery to Mobile, Spanish moss hangs like Christmas garland from the tall trees. The landscape stops rising. Little towns in the lower realm of the Heart of Dixie have an individuality not always present in those in North Alabama. The requisite railroad tracks that divide uptown from down are not always there. The humidity, however, is enough to wilt silk roses. I turn the air on full blast as we ride.

"At Fred's funeral," Rosie interjects. "Didn't it sort of surprise you that Brother Anson's sermon was so short and sweet. That's the least I've ever heard him say."

"Maybe the Spirit was leading him to hush his mouth," I say. "I believe the good Reverend has been a bit chastened by the events of the past few months. I think he was blown away by Fred's duplicity, especially him taking Brother Anson's car to get to Grace Ann on the day of the murders. He's probably a little ashamed of himself for getting interested in Grace Ann again. Fred was such a big contributor to the Temple of the Almighty that I think Brother Anson was willing to overlook a multitude of sins until the big one hit him square in the face. Maybe the next time he meets somebody with Fred's assets, he'll be a little more skeptical. As Bob Dylan says, 'money doesn't talk, it swears.'"

"I don't know that I've ever heard Brother Tony or Brother J schmoozin up to somebody for their money," Rosie says. "Michael says that when they're not at Down Yonder, they're usually over at the 24th Street projects working with some of the kids there. They finally found themselves a better place to stay. Michael and Gabe found them an apartment close to the store. They know how lucky they are to have those two."

"Mabel June's got Brother J a little cowed," I say. "But Brother Tony holds his own with her. Big Bad Mamas from the South don't phase somebody from the streets of New York. Gabe said Tony told her the other day that if she didn't cut her sass, he'd sprinkle some holy water on her. That shut her up for about fifteen minutes."

"She's just trying to see how far she can go with them," Rosie says with a laugh. "She told me she feels a little awkward around monks, like she can't joke with them the same way she did with the men that come in the dry cleaners. Lordy me, I am going to miss that woman. Her leaving will mean more money for me since I'll be the manager, but it won't be the same."

"Are your hours going to be any longer?" I ask her. Caitlin awakes and has to be assured that the beach is not yet in front of us. She smiles and goes back to sleep.

"Some," Rosie answers. "But the money is worth it. It's not likely that Wildwood Flower is going to produce enough income for me to quit working. Paradise has good benefits and there's even some kind of college savings incentive plan where they match your contributions."

"And what does Momma Millie has to say about her only daughter moving up in the world," I ask her. "Have you told her yet?"

"I did. And she was truly proud. I think she never really thought I would make it without Sherman or some other man to help me along.

But she's finding out for herself now that it's not really all that bad, living without a husband. Lonely sometimes, but better than being miserable."

The last time we stayed overnight on the Culp farm, Millie showed us the garden she and Sam planted on Good Friday with its neat even rows of corn and beans and other produce. "It ain't no different than what I done all them years you and the boys was growing up," she said to Rosie. "But it just feels more like it's mine."

"The one thing that has made her the happiest I've seen her in a long time was the new library dedication," Rosie says. "Momma never felt like she was very smart, her quitting school like she did to go to work at White Cotton Mill when she was 14. But all those big wigs treating her like royalty since she's the closest living relative to Aunt Vancene, well, that did her a lot of good. She's even taken out a library card and started reading some. She's not ever had much time for that until now. And you won't believe what she's reading, Perry Mason novels. She used to love that show on television. She didn't even know there were books."

"That's not too big a surprise," I say. "I'd have pegged Millie for a mystery reader. I sure can't picture her with a Harlequin Romance."

We both laugh at this. "I hope she'll spend a lot of time at the new community center and the Broadway marketplace when they open," Rosie says. "Some of her happiest times while she was working at the Mill were when she could go shopping on Broadway. She'd get her hair done and go to the movies. And I think she even hung out at the Chili Parlour, but she won't own up to it."

The Chili Parlour, a roadhouse cafe where some of the rougher crowd from the Mill spent time, closed when I was in my teens. Its legendary fistfights and love encounters linger in the stories old millhands pass through their families. Many a scene of blood and heartbreak took place inside its walls. A commemorative block is to be set in the sidewalk where it stood when the new walking mall is completed.

"You know who would have loved what they're doing with the old Mill and Broadway?" I ask Rosie.

"Grace Ann," she answers immediately. "She had us walking to Broadway every day, even when Fred was out of town and she didn't have to report in to him. She spent the whole afternoon with me at RexAll Drugs one time when you were helping Aunt Vancene at the library. She sat me down at the make-up counter and did my whole face from those testers they used to keep out on the counters. When she finished I thought I looked like a movie star. Now that's the Grace Ann I miss most."

When the big snow fell in the early winter of '67, felling trees onto power lines and blacking out Milltown, Rosie Grace Ann and I kept our night time vigil before the fireplace in the Hardaman's living room. In the early morning hours, the only sounds from the outside were the snapping of more tree limbs and the hard sleet pelting the ground. Rosie finally tired of the hours of indoor frolic and drifted to sleep, rolled into a mass of blankets on the thick carpet. Grace Ann and I sat wrapped in robes and comforters, poking intermittently at the fire, talking softly through the long night.

"My momma loved the snow," Grace Ann said. "If she could be here when we wake up tomorrow, she would be right out there with us, rolling snowballs and making snow ice cream."

It had been some time since Grace Ann talked of Ma 'Ree and I said something like, "Your mother always wanted to make sure everybody was happy having a good time," to encourage her to talk more.

"She did that all my life," Grace Ann said. "For me and for Daddy. If either of us was unhappy about anything, she fixed it, or tried to. And most of the time when she was sick, before it got really bad at the end, she smiled and acted like things weren't that awful. And now, when Daddy and I get into it and I feel like leaving this house forever, I just slow down and think about Momma and then I get past whatever it was. For a long time after she died, I felt like this wasn't my home any more. But now if I close my eyes, I can see Momma hurrying home from The Smart Shoppe and hanging up her coat to go fix supper. Then it's our house again and I don't want to leave."

Decades later when my own parents died within months of each other, I sold our home on Western Avenue. And I felt frayed and rootless. Years have passed and until very recently that feeling did not alter. Standing in the crowds at the razing of the Mill and the beginning of Milltown's rebirth from its ruins, I looked around at the older women in the crowd. Rural or rural once removed, they came to work at White Cotton Mill when their family farms failed or when they just needed to supplement their incomes. Simple women, like my mother or Millie or Minnie Beth. Women to whom Martha White, not Martha Stewart, is the queen of domestic culture. If my mother had lived she would have been uplifted by the revival of Milltown. And as the politicians and former workers praised its once and future glory, I felt the beginning of a fragile reattachment to my hometown. Home isn't only where you are. It is also that place in your past where you first felt love and security.

Before I entered school, my mother would take me on her lap and read to me from Little Golden Books which she purchased every week at Kroger's Grocery Store. One of my favorites was by Margaret Wise Brown with Garth Williams illustrations. Titled—if memory serves—*The Very Best Home for Me*, it chronicled the lives of several little animal protagonists, who shared a home in the woods. Being animals of various species and preferences, they did not get along well. Each decided to find a new place to live. Many of the particulars are hazy now, but its jist was that domestic harmony is hard to come by. I think of that often in our own blended household as we struggle to maintain our own delicate balance.

The cell phone shrills and Rosie and I both jump, guiltily.

"We forgot to call," she says and I grab the phone and cradle it against my shoulder. "Rosie and Ell's answering service," I say. "Our train of thought left the station and we forgot to call. At the sound of the tone, press one if you accept their humble apology."

"Damn, woman, you had me worried to pieces," Gabe says, anxiously. "I called a couple of times. It must have been when you stopped for gas or were having lunch or something. We've got wall to wall fiddlers here. I had to come outside to use the phone in the alley. Michael's inside keeping them from tearing the place apart. I was about ready to call the highway patrol. You…"

"I love you, truly. Truly, dear," I sing, very off-key.

"All right, all right," he laughs. "Are you actually driving while you're talking?"

"Yes, believe it or not," I say. "We're almost there. I can smell the salt in the air."

"Then call me tonight when you're on the beach and let me hear the ocean roar," he says. "I've got to get back. Michael sends love and cusses to Rosie for not calling. He'll touch base tonight."

"Are we in deep doo-doo?" Rosie asks as I put the phone back in its case. "I totally forgot about calling."

"Me, too," I say. "They weren't very pleased, but it'll pass."

"They do love us, after all," she says.

"Do you doubt that?" I ask her.

"Not really. I think it will last. But do you want to know something, Ellott Hailey Seers?"

"What's that, Dixie Rosalee Culp Jackson?"

"If it doesn't, I'll be very sad and hurt, but somehow that wouldn't be as bad as it would if you and I were never able to see each other again."

Smiling, I squeeze her hand and we continue the last leg of our journey to the sea.

We settle in at the Low Tide Family Resort as the afternoon begins to fade. The girls suit up and beg us to do the same so they can get to the beach. Even with the waning sunlight, we coat ourselves and them in high level sunblock. The beach behind Low Tide is brimming with folks of all ages and with just enough teenagers—who are playing a game of volleyball—to bring a smile to Cassie's face. Molly and Caitlin seat themselves on the beach with sand buckets and shovels and commence digging. With her modest swimsuit adjusted a little lower than it was intended, Cassie walks to the water's edge. She tosses a ball into the waves and lets it wash back to her. A tall young man with golden hair and skin notices and asks her to join them in the volleyball game. They play on the beach while the sun drops in the sky.

With just enough light left that Rosie couldn't say no, Cassie begs her mother to allow her to swim to the sandbar with some of the other kids. After low tide, big shells wash up on its surface. Rosie consents and we join a family group vigil at the shoreline, watching the young swimmers. I take Caitlin in my arms and snuggle her chubby body in a beach towel against me. The little girl gets very anxious lately whenever any of us leave, even briefly. Rosie says she cries and clings to her at daycare in the mornings when they say goodbye. Although she does not cry when her sisters do their very frequent leave takings, she mentions them often in their absence. Rosie and I always reassure her of their eventual return. I lift her up now and point to her big sister's head bobbing in the waves.

"Cassie bye-bye. Caty here," she says, pointing to herself.

"She's coming back," I tell her. "In just a little while."

"Not right now, later on," Caitlin says happily and smiles into the setting sun.

CPSIA information can be obtained at www.ICGtesting.com
Printed in the USA
LVOW040523130312

272814LV00003B/19/A